Heaven Official's Blessing

TIAN GUAN CI FU

6

Heaven Official's Blessing

TIAN GUAN CI FU

6

WRITTEN BY
Mo Xiang Tong Xiu

TRANSLATED BY
Suika & Pengie (EDITOR)

COVER & COLOR
ILLUSTRATIONS BY
**日出的小太陽
(tai3_3)**

INTERIOR ILLUSTRATIONS BY
ZeldaCW

Seven Seas Entertainment

HEAVEN OFFICIAL'S BLESSING: TIAN GUAN CI FU VOL. 6

Published originally under the title of 《天官賜福》
(Heaven Official's Blessing)
Author ©墨香铜臭(Mo Xiang Tong Xiu)
English edition rights under license granted by 北京晋江原创网络科技有限公司
(Beijing Jinjiang Original Network Technology Co., Ltd.)
English edition copyright © 2023 Seven Seas Entertainment, LLC
Arranged through JS Agency Co., Ltd
All rights reserved

《天官賜福》 (Heaven Official's Blessing) Volume 6
All rights reserved
Cover & Color Illustrations by 日出的小太陽 (tai3_3)
Illustrations granted under license granted by 2021 Reve Books Co., Ltd (Pinsin Publishing)
US English translation copyright © 2023 Seven Seas Entertainment, LLC
US English edition arranged through JS Agency Co., Ltd

Interior Illustrations by ZeldaCW

Seven Seas press and purchase enquiries can be sent to Marketing Manager Lianne Sentar
at press@gomanga.com. Information regarding the distribution and purchase of digital
editions is available from Digital Manager CK Russell at digital@gomanga.com.

Follow Seven Seas Entertainment online at
sevenseasentertainment.com.

TRANSLATION: Suika
EDITOR: Pengie
ADAPTATION: Lexy Lee
INTERIOR DESIGN: Clay Gardner
INTERIOR LAYOUT: Karis Page
PROOFREADER: Meg van Huygen, Alex Singer
COPY EDITOR: Jade Gardner
BRAND MANAGER: Lissa Pattillo
PREPRESS TECHNICIAN: Melanie Ujimori, Jules Valera
EDITOR-IN-CHIEF: Julie Davis
ASSOCIATE PUBLISHER: Adam Arnold
PUBLISHER: Jason DeAngelis

ISBN: 978-1-63858-551-0
Printed in Canada
First Printing: May 2023
10 9 8 7 6 5 4 3 2 1

CONTENTS

Contents based on the Pinsin Publishing print edition originally released 2021

HUA CHENG'S BREATH was warm, but his words made Xie Lian's blood run cold.

Could there really be someone hiding in the grand hall?

A thought flashed through Xie Lian's mind, and he quickly returned Hua Cheng's embrace.

He wasn't hugging him because he was afraid, of course. If there truly was someone hiding in the temple whom they hadn't noticed, then they must be a formidable character—and if that person sensed anything off, they might be forced to make a move. It would arouse suspicion if Hua Cheng was the only one hugging him and being so intimate. If the embrace was mutual, it might appear more natural.

Xie Lian began to inconspicuously analyze their surroundings. "Where do you think they're hiding?" he whispered.

There was only one entrance to the grand hall, which was the huge door they'd come through. The hall itself was completely empty; the whole room could be taken in at a glance, and there wasn't even a table or a chest that would provide a spot for someone to hide. Aside from the two of them, there were only the empty stone shells of the temple's attendants.

"The shells," Xie Lian and Hua Cheng whispered in unison.

Those stone people were hollow inside, which meant they could serve as a hiding spot. A human couldn't get inside, but a ghost certainly could!

When Xie Lian was sure they were both in agreement, he started to speak, but then he inadvertently looked up—and his pupils shrank. There was someone standing six meters behind Hua Cheng.

This person seemed to have been a young man of higher status. These statues each documented a Wuyong citizen's death, so most were curled into balls or hugging their heads and wailing—this statue was one of the very few that was standing.

But what made Xie Lian notice him wasn't his pose—it was his face.

Although the stone person's face was barely distinguishable, Xie Lian could still make out some details. The left side was smiling, and the right side was crying!

"It's that one!" Xie Lian blurted.

He drew his sword and struck just as Hua Cheng called out, "Gege?"

The stone person shattered, and broken fragments of the shell scattered across the floor. Although there was nothing inside, Xie Lian didn't dare drop his guard, and he began turning over every single shard until Hua Cheng caught his hand.

"Gege! What did you see just now?"

Xie Lian gathered a few fragments to show him. "San Lang, that stone person...his face...it was White No-Face's mask."

Hua Cheng's expression changed slightly, but still he said, "Wait a moment."

He gathered and pieced together the shards. When the face was reconstructed, the two fell silent.

Xie Lian had clearly seen a half-crying, half-smiling ghost face. But the face that Hua Cheng had reconstructed had indistinct features, no different from the other stone statues.

Was it a hallucination? Had he been bewitched by an illusion spell?

Sitting around wouldn't get them answers, so they searched the hall, smashing every stone person to ash as they went. But after giving it some thought, they realized that it was more important to deal with the others who were surely rushing to the summit at that moment. They decided not to stick around waiting for Pei Ming to return and left the temple to scale the mountain.

The mountain seemed to have a peculiar gravity—they tried, but the silver butterflies couldn't carry them, and flying on swords was a nonstarter. They could only climb on foot. The higher they hiked, the steeper the path became and the colder the air grew. The snow was sparse at first, but it became thicker as they ascended until it could swallow almost half a boot. They were up to their knees in it after four hours of climbing, and their trek was becoming more and more arduous.

Xie Lian didn't feel cold since they had been hiking nonstop. He was instead covered in a thin sheen of sweat, and his red cheeks gave a shock of color to his powdery white face. He wiped away the sweat and looked back, about to speak to Hua Cheng—but suddenly, his step caught nothing, and he dropped half a meter!

His body had sunk into the heavy snow. Thankfully, Hua Cheng had been following him closely and pulled him up quite easily, like he'd been prepared for it.

"Gege, be careful."

Xie Lian stood next to him and looked back at where he'd stumbled. A large section of snow had caved in, revealing a deep, dark hole that led to somewhere unknown. If Xie Lian hadn't grabbed hold of the edge in time, or if Hua Cheng had moved too slowly, he would've fallen in for sure.

"There are many holes like that in this area. I still remember their general locations, so just stay close to me," Hua Cheng stated. "Take your time and it'll be fine; gege was walking too quickly."

As it turned out, the mountain's body was quite weak. There were holes everywhere beneath the snow, large and small—but how many and how deep was unknown. But as they climbed, it seemed Hua Cheng really did remember where all of them were.

Xie Lian puffed a breath. "All right. Let's stick closer together," he suggested. "In any event, we can't yell or make loud noises on a snowy mountain like this, so it wouldn't be easy to call for help if anything happened..."

He stopped when they heard angry roars coming from up ahead. *"Are you done?!"*

"..."

Which good brother dared to yell like that on such a steep and perilous snowy mountain?!

Xie Lian was dumbfounded as he looked toward the source of the noise. Amidst the snow-covered landscape, he saw two little black dots engaged in a fight, their weapons clinking and clanking. One of them held a longbow and was shooting arrows nonstop. The other held a zhanmadao[1] and swung with the vigor of a tiger; they struck down every single arrow. Both the blade and the arrows had a sheen of spiritual light, and both parties were shouting curses at each other.

"I already said I didn't kill that little bastard; I'm looking for them too!" the man wielding the blade yelled.

It was Nan Feng and Fu Yao!

Without even trying to guess why they had come here too, Xie Lian very nearly let out a shout of "Shut up!" However, he caught himself

---

1   A zhanmadao is a single-bladed, two-handed saber meant to be wielded against cavalry.

in time and swallowed it before he added to the noise. If he started roaring the same way they were, and the three of them all began screaming at each other, could the snow on the mountain really remain still?

Hua Cheng hugged his arms and cocked an eyebrow. "Don't they know that they'll cause an avalanche if they yell like that?"

"They...can't be that foolish?!" Xie Lian said. "Maybe they do know. But that's just the way they are—they forget everything else when they're angry!"

Nan Feng and Fu Yao were both furious and cursed at each other as they fought, but they were too far away from Xie Lian—he couldn't tell what they were fighting over from their broken, muffled phrases, and for their part, they completely failed to notice that anyone else had arrived.

Xie Lian wanted to rush over and pull them apart, but there was no way he could make it there in time to stop them with the heavy snow dragging down his pace and the deep holes lurking beneath. He only managed to run two steps before he stumbled over another hole, and he came to a stop.

"We can't just let them keep fighting like this! We have to stop them!"

As soon as he said so, a silver butterfly darted past like an arrow. Xie Lian was startled but relaxed a moment later.

Good idea! If neither of them could make it in time, why not just use a wraith butterfly to fly over and transmit communication?

As expected, the silver butterfly's speed was miraculously fast—it made it over to the brawling duo after only three more shouts. But before Xie Lian could try to speak through it, he saw Hua Cheng's expression turn cold.

Xie Lian noticed something was amiss. "What's wrong?"

The smile on Hua Cheng's lips had disappeared completely, replaced by a look that was as frigid as the snowy mountain upon which they stood.

"San Lang, what's going on?" Xie Lian pressed.

Hua Cheng's lips twitched, but he didn't manage to answer before Xie Lian suddenly felt an inexplicable wave of panic. His head shot up to look at the top of the mountain, and his eyes widened.

Giant chunks of the snowy white bluffs were trembling. And then they collapsed.

Even engrossed in their heated fight, Nan Feng and Fu Yao also sensed that soundless pressure. Both looked up, and they finally realized what was about to happen.

The snowy mass was like an enormous embankment that stretched for a thousand miles. And when in the next second it broke, it carried a snow tsunami along with it. It rumbled, rolled, and pushed down toward them!

They had caused an avalanche!

Xie Lian grabbed Hua Cheng's hand, turned, and ran. But after dashing a few steps, he remembered that the other two were much closer to the avalanche's charge. He stopped abruptly, looking back. Sure enough, they had ceased their aggression to flee together. Fu Yao didn't get very far before stumbling into a hole and sinking down more than halfway; he was buried up to his chest in snow. Although Nan Feng ran faster than him, he hesitated for a moment and looked back, seeming like he wanted to save him. But the wave of snow was already bearing down!

Xie Lian released Ruoye the moment before they were swallowed. The white silk bandage instantly stretched far into the distance, lassoed Fu Yao and Nan Feng with sharp precision, and yanked them up.

"Gege! Leave them—don't bother!" Hua Cheng said darkly.

Xie Lian held Ruoye tightly, dragging the two as he ran. "I can't! They might end up buried for a hundred years if this goes wrong!"

"Too late!" Hua Cheng said, his voice dire.

"What?!" Xie Lian cried.

He looked up, and the enveloping shadow bearing down overhead came crashing in.

Nan Feng and Fu Yao had stalled Xie Lian after all. The thick, icy wave of snow surged relentlessly and swallowed him whole, separating him from Hua Cheng. The force knocked Xie Lian everywhere, and he tumbled along with the coursing snow—although he somehow managed to keep struggling, there was just too much snow and the force was too powerful. Xie Lian was buried again and again, suffocating over and over each time his head went under.

In the end, Xie Lian couldn't hang on. With a final shout of *"San Lang!"* he was devoured by the icy snow current.

An unknown amount of time passed before the snowy mountain finally calmed.

A long moment later, somewhere in the field, a pile of snow shifted a few times before a hand burst out from underneath!

The hand felt around randomly, then an arm poked out. Then a shoulder and then, finally, a head. Face covered in chunks of snow, he took a deep breath the instant he broke free, then let loose a flurry of coughing. Soon after and with some difficulty, the man crawled his way out, shaking his head as he sat down on the snow.

It was Xie Lian.

Digging himself out from beneath that heavy layer of snow was not unlike his prior experience digging himself free of a grave. Xie Lian's face and hands were chapped red from frostbite and essentially numb, but he only bothered to rub his face a few times and huff some hot breaths on his hands before looking up with a lost expression.

There was not a trace of that captivating red in the sprawling blanket of white.

And Xie Lian couldn't even call out for him—it would be all over if he caused another avalanche. He could only rise to his feet and wander aimlessly, all alone in that snowy world.

He called out in a small voice as he walked. "San Lang? San Lang? Nan Feng? Fu Yao?"

It was strange. Although he was walking the same path they had been hiking before, the air seemed so much colder than when he and Hua Cheng had been together. Ruoye was also gone from his hand. Xie Lian was puzzled, as Ruoye shouldn't have slipped off—it would still wrap itself around him even if he let go of it, so what happened?

He knew something was wrong but couldn't put his finger on what, so he continued to wander in confusion.

Suddenly, someone emerged from within the billowing snow ahead. His white robes and black hair flapped in the wind, and he kept his head down as he slowly approached.

Xie Lian was delighted at the sight of this traveler and pushed forward. "My friend! You..."

But just as he spoke, the man looked up. He was wearing a chilling white mask, half of it smiling, the other half crying.

Xie Lian screamed at the sight of it as though he'd been stabbed. His eyes flew open at the sound of his own scream, and he shot upright. He panted harshly for several moments before his shaken mind could process that he wasn't standing on the snowy mountain at all—he was lying in a dark, shadowy place.

So it had been a dream.

No wonder something had felt off. Xie Lian exhaled a long breath as he relaxed, wiping away the cold sweat on his forehead. After feeling around for a bit, he determined that there was flat stone beneath him, covered with a blanket of grass. Fangxin hung from his waist and Ruoye was wrapped snugly around his arm. Xie Lian steadied himself and ignited a palm torch to illuminate the room. He sat up immediately and called out.

"San Lang? Are you there?"

The moment the flames brightened the room, Xie Lian discovered that there was a person standing right next to him in the darkness, soundless and silent.

This was no small shock, and Xie Lian was awash in cold sweat as his hand flew to Fangxin. There was no way he wouldn't have noticed someone lurking so close by!

However, the cold sweat dissipated when he looked closer. It wasn't a living person but rather a stone statue—and not one of the many stone statues of the victims of the volcano's eruption. This was clearly a man-made sculpture.

Palm torch in hand, Xie Lian scanned the room and was soon certain of where he found himself.

The place where he lay was a cavern for cultivation. He had once gone into seclusion to cultivate in a place like this, so he was familiar with this type of chamber. It meant that the sculpture inside the cavern was not a regular statue but a divine icon for worship.

The divine statue had been erected in a cavern with an arched ceiling. Its figure was long and slender, its bearing was natural and relaxed, and its pose was graceful. Its right hand rested on the hilt of the sword at its waist. It had been sculpted with sublime skill; even the flowing lines and folds of its robes were exquisite.

However, there was something peculiar about it—the face of this divine figure was covered by a light veil.

The veil was light as flowing smoke. While it was quite strange to see a divine statue with its face obscured like this, it wasn't ugly. Instead, it added a mysterious sort of beauty. Xie Lian had never seen a divine statue like this, displayed with its face covered. He unconsciously reached out to pull the veil off but was interrupted by a voice from behind.

"Gege."

Xie Lian's head whipped around. A figure in red had appeared at the entrance of the cavern without him realizing. It was Hua Cheng. The mysterious face of that divine statue instantly went to the back of Xie Lian's mind, and he rushed over to him.

"San Lang! Thank goodness, I was wondering where you were. Are you all right? Are you hurt? That avalanche was so sudden."

Hua Cheng entered the room. "I'm fine. How's gege?"

"I'm always fine," Xie Lian said. "What is this place?"

Once he left the cavern, it became clear that this place was far more expansive than expected—the corridor he found himself in seemed quite long, and who knew where it led?

Xie Lian had long ago gotten used to Hua Cheng having the answers to everything, yet this time he replied, "I don't know. Most likely under the snowy mountain."

Xie Lian was amazed. "And I'd thought it was a shelter San Lang had found. I can't believe even you don't know where we are."

Well, this was a first. Hua Cheng had memorized the location of every ditch on the mountain path, but he wasn't familiar with this

place. The cave network clearly wasn't small—had he really never stumbled upon it before?

Xie Lian couldn't help but find it a bit strange, but he didn't press the matter and instead raised his palm torch higher. "How did we get here?"

Hua Cheng summoned a few silver butterflies and let them flutter about to shine their faint light. "Maybe we stepped wrong and fell into a ditch," he replied evenly.

That was the only logical explanation, as the alternative was that someone had intentionally put them here. Xie Lian couldn't help but recall the dream he'd just had, and a slight shiver went down his spine.

Remembering something else, he asked, "We're here, so where are Nan Feng and Fu Yao?"

At the mention of those two, a trace of hostility flashed across Hua Cheng's face. "Probably buried in the snow. Who cares? They're heavenly officials; this won't kill them," he replied unsympathetically.

Xie Lian didn't know whether to laugh or cry. "Even if they can't die, it still won't feel great to be buried for decades if no one helps dig them out. Maybe they fell in here too, so let's search for them. By the way, San Lang, what did you hear them say when your silver butterfly flew over?"

Hua Cheng snorted. "Just some meaningless argument. As if it could have been anything pleasant."

Xie Lian doubted it was that simple, otherwise he couldn't explain Hua Cheng's sudden change of expression when the wraith butterfly overheard the fight. Even now, Hua Cheng's eye was extremely unkind as he snorted. But if he wasn't going to tell, then Xie Lian wasn't going to pry.

The two continued down the cave's long corridor. After walking for a while, they discovered this stone tunnel beneath the snow was much more complex than they had initially thought—there wasn't just one path straight through but many forks that branched off into various other caverns, large and small.

And every one of those caverns held a divine statue. Some of the figures were teenagers, others were young men. The statues were all in unique poses: in lazy repose, leaning as though intoxicated, sitting poised, dancing with a sword... The clothing was also ever-changing: magnificent ceremonial robes, plain clothes, rags, half-naked, and more. The level of skill differed between sculptures as well—some of the work was rough and unrefined, while some was so extraordinarily exquisite and detailed it was astonishing. They probably hadn't all been sculpted by the same person, but the sheer number of them and the wealth of varieties made this a spectacular sight.

Xie Lian admired them as they walked, and he couldn't help but exclaim in awe, "This is a Cave of Ten Thousand Gods! I wonder who chose to build one in this place. They must have been an incredibly devout believer."

However, all the divine statues shared the same peculiarity: their faces were covered by light veils. Some of the veils were large enough to cover the statue's whole body, revealing only the hem of its robes or its feet. Xie Lian really was quite curious and wanted to pull the veil from a divine statue to see its face, but Hua Cheng spoke up behind him.

"Gege, I suggest you don't."

Xie Lian looked back. "Why not? Doesn't San Lang think these statues are odd?"

Hua Cheng approached him with hands clasped behind and explained. "It's precisely because they're odd that it's best that you don't uncover them. If someone covered their faces, they must have had a reason. Spiritual energy gathers in the head, and we can't be certain how the spiritual energy these strange statues have gathered would react if a veil is removed." He paused for a moment, then continued.

"Gege, weren't you searching for your two servants? Since we haven't found them yet, it'd be better not to touch these statues. Best to avoid any unexpected complications."

While his explanation sounded slightly far-fetched, it made logical sense. It wouldn't be a laughing matter if removing a veil awakened something within these statues. Xie Lian wasn't prone to touching what he shouldn't. He thought it over and, in the end, dropped his hand.

"I was only curious which deity these sculptures depict. That's all."

There was something else strange—Hua Cheng was not the kind of person who feared unexpected complications; if they saw what the veil covered, so be it. Xie Lian hadn't expected him to use that as the reason not to touch them.

"This is the Kingdom of Wuyong, so they're probably the Crown Prince of Wuyong," Hua Cheng said dismissively. "Nothing notable."

Xie Lian countered, "I don't think so."

"Oh? What do you mean?" Hua Cheng asked.

Xie Lian gazed at him. "Judging by the murals we saw along the way, the clothing worn by the Crown Prince of Wuyong and the Wuyong people was particularly bright in color. As the country existed two millennia ago, the prevailing style of dress was ancient and coarse—and a little wild. The clothing on these divine statues is quite different, though. I don't think these statues have anything to do with the Crown Prince of Wuyong; in fact, the sculptor might not have been from Wuyong at all."

Hua Cheng smiled brightly at him. "Is that right? Gege really has an eye for detail."

Xie Lian also smiled. "Ah, no. It's simply that the style of these statues—the sculpting work, the clothing design, and the way details such as the flow of dress are handled—all looks like something from a later period. And it's one I'm more familiar with too...the style of Xianle."

Hua Cheng quirked his eyebrows. "It seems gege is also deeply gifted in this topic."

"Nah, it's nothing. You'd naturally gain a bit of knowledge after seeing a lot of something, and that includes divine statues," Xie Lian said.

Although he couldn't quite put his finger on it, his instincts told him that there was something *off* with Hua Cheng since he'd awoken. It was only now that he finally realized what was amiss.

There was a subtle sort of nervousness about him.

However, Xie Lian still didn't pry. He said instead, "Since San Lang thinks it's best to not inspect them, let's stay cautious."

Hua Cheng gave a light nod, and the pair continued onward. Soon they came to another fork in the road, and Hua Cheng headed left without hesitation. Xie Lian paused and didn't follow.

Hua Cheng looked back. "What is it?"

"San Lang's never been in this cave before, right?" Xie Lian asked.

"Of course not."

"Then why are you so sure that we should go left?"

"Not sure, necessarily," Hua Cheng said. "I'm just choosing blindly."

"Since you've never been here before, how can you charge forward blindly? Shouldn't we consider which way to go more carefully?"

Hua Cheng smiled. "We should go blindly precisely because I've never been here before. No matter how cautious we are, we know nothing about this place's layout, so we might as well boldly bet on our luck. And my luck has always been better."

Although that certainly made sense, Hua Cheng had always let Xie Lian choose the way when they went out; it wasn't often that he took the initiative and led. Xie Lian nodded.

They were just about to enter the tunnel on the left when Xie Lian hastily spoke up. "Wait! San Lang, do you hear that?"

"What?"

"To the right," Xie Lian said. "There are voices."

Hua Cheng's expression changed subtly, and after listening intently for a while, he said, "Gege, I think you're mistaken. There's nothing there."

"There is!" Xie Lian insisted. "Listen closely. It's a man's voice!"

Hua Cheng tried listening again and frowned. "I really don't hear anything."

Xie Lian was taken aback. *Am I hallucinating again?* he wondered.

"Your Highness, there's something fishy about this; there might be tricks afoot," Hua Cheng said. "I suggest we talk after we get out."

Xie Lian hesitated for a moment, but in the end, he still declared, "No! It might be Nan Feng and Fu Yao. I must go take a look!"

Then he dashed off down the path while Hua Cheng called after him.

"Gege! Don't run off!"

But whoever had been shouting must have fallen into an extremely dangerous situation that allowed no delays, and Xie Lian didn't dare to be careless. He continued to rush down the righthand path. The farther he went down the tunnel, the clearer he could hear a man's angry roars.

Xie Lian was delighted. *It really is Nan Feng and Fu Yao!*

Xie Lian didn't know how long he'd spent hurrying through the winding tunnel, but he finally found the source of the voices in a giant cave. There were no divine statues in this cavern but instead a deep pit—and that pit was precisely where Nan Feng and Fu Yao's screaming was coming from. It looked like they were both trapped at the bottom, unable to climb up. But they were still yelling passionately at each other, so their lives likely weren't in danger at the moment.

It was too dark in the depths of the pit to see anything clearly. Xie Lian cupped his hands around his mouth and shouted from above.

"Hey—! What happened to you guys?"

When the two in the pit heard someone up above, they instantly stopped arguing.

Fu Yao's reply came first. "Your Highness? Is that you?! Hurry and pull us up!"

Nan Feng, on the other hand, didn't speak. Xie Lian was puzzled.

"You guys can't climb up on your own? The pit isn't *that* deep. What's happening down there?"

Perhaps it was because he'd been fighting the entire way, but Fu Yao was full of fire. "If we could climb up on our own, we would've done it already, duh! Can't you see for yourself, Your Highness?"

Xie Lian squinted. "Well, I can't see much right now. Do you still have spiritual power? Can you light a palm torch so I can see what the situation is down there? If you can't, I'll throw a fireball down…"

But before he could finish his sentence, the two at the bottom yelled in unison, *"Don't!"* Their voices rang with alarm and terror.

"Do *not* light any fires!" Fu Yao yelled.

If he couldn't light a fire, he'd have to find another way to illuminate the place. Xie Lian's first reaction was to look behind him.

"San Lang…"

However, there was no one there—Hua Cheng hadn't followed him. Xie Lian was surprised; at first he felt slightly uneasy, then confused. There was surely no way Hua Cheng could've lost his way, right...?

Hua Cheng had been acting quite strangely ever since they entered the Cave of Ten Thousand Gods, but Xie Lian couldn't quite put his finger on why. He looked to his left and right, then discovered a tiny silver butterfly resting on his shoulder. He touched it tentatively.

"Hello...?"

The wraith butterfly fluttered at his touch but didn't fly away— it seemed to want to show him its wings. Over the course of their journey, Hua Cheng had told Xie Lian that his silver butterflies fell into various categories. Xie Lian didn't know which category this one belonged to or what its duties were, but it could at least shine some light regardless of its purpose.

Thus he asked, "Can you go down and take a look for me?"

Sure enough, the silver butterfly fluttered its wings and flew into the pit. Xie Lian called out his thanks and waited until it reached the bottom. Once the soft silver light illuminated the situation below, Xie Lian couldn't help but widen his eyes.

The bottom of the dark pit was covered by an eerie field of white. The entire hole was blanketed with a thick bed of silk!

Nan Feng and Fu Yao had been tied up in that silk so thoroughly that they'd been bundled into two cocoons, like two little flies stuck in a spider's web. Their faces were battered black and blue, and their heads were covered in blood, but they might've done that to each other during their earlier fight. Xie Lian couldn't help but give himself a pat on the back for his caution; the entire pit might've been set ablaze had he thrown down a torch.

"What's going on?" Xie Lian asked. "Is that a spider's web? Could this be an arachnid spirit's lair?"

"Who knows?!" Fu Yao yelled, desperate to escape. "We can't break free anyway!"

Nan Feng, on the other hand, bore an unreadable expression. At first, he had looked like he also wanted to call for help, but he'd sullenly swallowed his words when he'd seen that Xie Lian was the one who'd come.

"Don't come down yet—the spider silk is really tough," Nan Feng said instead. "It'll be hard to break free once it grabs you."

"I won't come down," Xie Lian said.

After deliberating for a moment, Xie Lian tied one end of Ruoye to the hilt of Fangxin, planning to lower the sword to just see if it'd work. But Ruoye had only crept down halfway before the web discovered it. Tendrils of silk shot upward with violent intent at this interloper. Ruoye coiled away in terror, but it was too late—the webbing snagged the bandage, wrapped around it, and yanked it down, pulling Xie Lian in as well.

Xie Lian had never imagined that this web would be so strong and cunning!

The moment Xie Lian fell into the pit, the white tendrils of silk charged forward and trussed him up. The rest of the silk tendrils crawled along to further secure the "cocoons" that trapped Nan Feng and Fu Yao.

Fu Yao was absolutely furious. "How come you fell in too? Now look at us—three stupid fools! Let's all just die here together!"

"What are you griping about?" Nan Feng shot back. "This only happened because he was trying to save us!"

Xie Lian, on the other hand, was tumbling about and laughing. "Ha ha ha, ha ha ha, ha ha ha ha..."

Nan Feng and Fu Yao looked at him, dumbfounded.

"Did you hit your head on the way down? Have you lost your mind?" Fu Yao asked.

Tears rolled from the corners of Xie Lian's eyes, and he said with much difficulty, "N-no, ha ha ha... What's with this web...? Why is it...so ticklish?! I can't... Ha ha ha ha..."

The silk bed had caught him gently when he fell, and the tendrils that had bound him seemed to touch him with care and love. They brushed softly against Xie Lian's body while they worked, as if they were tickling him.

Xie Lian curled into a ball, fighting back with tenacity. "No, don't, wait! Stop! Stop! I give! Stop!"

Only then did the white silk tendrils bind his hands behind his back and stop their ticklish dance. Nan Feng and Fu Yao stared at him.

A moment later, Fu Yao said grumpily, "How come it was so rough when it tied us up but so lenient with him? It hasn't even covered his face."

Xie Lian finally caught his breath. "Aren't...aren't your faces uncovered too?"

Fu Yao rolled his eyes. "They *were* covered. We had to use our teeth to tear holes after we woke up. We couldn't have shouted otherwise."

Xie Lian tried struggling a bit, but the silk webbing was tough and unyielding; plus, his ribs faintly hurt from laughing too hard. For now, he was out of commission. He decided to relax a bit, lying down flat.

"So how did you two end up here?"

"Don't know," Fu Yao replied. "When the avalanche hit, snow came crashing down on us. When we woke up, we were already here."

"No, no, no," Xie Lian said. "I mean, why did you come to Mount Tonglu?"

Fu Yao was furious the instant the topic was raised. "I was pursuing that ghost woman Lan Chang and the fetus spirit! Who knows why *he's* here!"

"Me?! I'm here to chase after that mother and child too..." Nan Feng answered.

"Then why didn't you go after them?" Fu Yao spat. "Why did you hit me?! I... My general already said that he had nothing to do with the fetus spirit. He didn't kill either of them! His goodwill was taken for ill; there's honestly no point in trying to be a good person!"

Xie Lian mediated out of habit. "All right, all right, stop, I understand the situation now. Stop fighting, stop arguing. You're the ones who caused that avalanche, so can you just give it a rest? Let's think of a way out together."

However, Nan Feng was incensed. "Does your general really not realize how he usually acts? He has no right to complain if people are suspicious of him!"

Fu Yao glared. "What did you say?! I dare you to say that again!"

Nan Feng glared even harder. "I do dare, and I *will* say it again! You never had goodwill for anyone! You just want to show benevolence to people you can't stand so you can secretly feel all smug about it later. You're after your own satisfaction, and you love to watch everyone else make fools of themselves. Don't give me that 'goodwill taken for ill' garbage, and don't you dare think that you're a good person! Genuinely good people aren't like you—you've never been one!"

Veins popped on Fu Yao's forehead, and his lips began to twitch. "You've made all that up! It's pure nonsense!"

"You know best whether it's nonsense—as if I don't know you!" Nan Feng shouted.

Those veins now bulged all the way down Fu Yao's neck. "What right do you have to lecture me? Looking down on people from so high up—careful, you might fall and break a leg!"

"I'm better than you at everything!" Nan Feng yelled. "Do you think no one knows about that shitty stunt you pulled back then?!"

The mere mention of this mysterious incident seemed to inflame Fu Yao even more, his fire fueled by shame. "Yes, I admit I did it! But how much better are you than me, really? Acting like you're the model of loyalty—didn't you ditch the boss too when you got a wife? Didn't your wife and son suddenly become more important?! Everyone does things for themselves; everyone makes themselves top priority! Aren't you embarrassed to keep hanging that ancient shitty deed over my head?"

When he heard "wife" and "son," Nan Feng's outrage exploded. "You fucking... *You!* I...? You?"

Although neither could move, they were so intent on their argument that they didn't realize the way they addressed each other had slipped. They had dropped "your general" and "my general" in favor of "you" and "me," and in their fury they had completely failed to notice what this exposed. Only now did they realize their error.

Xie Lian had long since stopped talking. Nan Feng and Fu Yao both whipped their heads over to look in Xie Lian's direction and saw that he'd silently flipped on the silk bed, turning over and only showing them his back.

"Um...I saw nothing. Wait, I mean, I *heard* nothing."

" "
...

" "
...

Xie Lian faced the stone wall as he politely asked, "Are you two going to keep this up? I won't comment on anything else you were discussing, but, um...I do think that someone's wife and son should be most important. There's nothing wrong with that—it's basic human sentiment. But all this ancient history...let's not stew in it. Let's think of a way to escape—"

"You already knew?" Fu Yao cut him off.

Since it didn't seem he could get away with it any longer, Xie Lian could only concede. "Yeah..."

"When did you find out? *How* did you find out?" Fu Yao said in disbelief.

Xie Lian didn't have the heart to tell the truth. Instead he replied, "I forget exactly."

The real answer was that he'd known everything for a very, very long time. He'd already vaguely suspected it on Mount Yujun, and by the time they set foot in Banyue Pass, he'd confirmed it.

These "junior martial officials from the Middle Court"? They didn't actually exist. "Nan Feng" and "Fu Yao" were merely clones created by Feng Xin and Mu Qing!

Fu Yao seemed like he couldn't believe his real identity had been seen through so easily, and he began to relentlessly interrogate Xie Lian. "When? How? There must've been something that gave it away—what was the flaw?!"

"..."

Xie Lian really couldn't bear to tell him the truth. There weren't any secrets to give away because they had flaws all over them!

The three grew up together, after all—how could Xie Lian not recognize the way they behaved and spoke? From the sloppy fake names[2] to the completely unchanged personalities, it was too easy

---

2   The "Nan" / 南 of "Nan Feng" is the same character used in Feng Xin's heavenly title, Nan Yang, and the "Feng" / 风 is the same character used in Feng Xin's proper name. "Fu Yao" / 扶摇 literally means to "take off/take flight"; figuratively, it means "someone who climbs the ladder quickly" or "an ambitious person."

to guess. If he hadn't realized who was behind those two skins, he would've lived all these years for nothing.

There were always some things one couldn't say...and some things one couldn't do. For example, one couldn't easily roll their eyes or cuss when minding their behavior as a heavenly official. But they could be much freer and more relaxed while wearing a different identity. Thus, Xie Lian never felt the need to expose them.

Fu Yao—no, now he should be called Mu Qing—gritted his teeth and said coldly, "So...you've known who we are for a long time, but you never said anything. You quietly watched us put on an act. Am I correct?"

93
Cave of Ten Thousand Gods—Faces of the Ten Thousand Gods Revealed

SEEING THAT HE was taking the matter quite hard, Xie Lian decided to try to give some guidance.

"Actually, it's not that big of a deal..."

Mu Qing sneered. "I knew I was right! Was it fun? Did you enjoy watching me act? *Hmm?!*"

Now that they were being honest with each other, Mu Qing was *honestly* tearing him a new one. Nan Feng—or Feng Xin, rather—only looked awkward at first, but in the end he couldn't let Mu Qing's words slide without comment.

"What's with that tone?"

Mu Qing was pale-faced and thin-skinned, and his entire head turned bright red whenever his blood started rushing—making it impossible to hide that he was upset. He whipped his head around.

"What tone? Don't forget you're one of the jesters here too! I'm not as generous as you are, to have no complaints about being someone's entertainment for so long!"

"I wasn't trying to watch you guys make fools of yourselves," Xie Lian said.

"And stop thinking everyone is as narrow-minded as you are," Feng Xin added. "His Highness still tried to help you even when your shitty deeds landed you in Heaven's prison..."

"Ha! Oh, thank you *so* much. But I ended up in prison thanks to *your* son! What, you wanna fight for real?! You're not afraid to sire a son, but you *are* afraid to talk?!"

Feng Xin really wanted to knock him dead for raising the subject of his son. Unfortunately, all three of them were still rolled up tight by the silk webbing, so he couldn't move a muscle. Feng Xin and Mu Qing could only curse at each other, all manners and class gone.

Feng Xin's face was getting redder and redder from anger, and Xie Lian was afraid he'd blow his top soon and start cursing up a storm. So Xie Lian tried to wiggle a bit, managing to rock back and forth a few times and eventually roll to Mu Qing's side.

"Mu Qing, Mu Qing? Can you try turning around?"

Mu Qing stopped his yelling and took a breath. "What do you want?"

"Feng Xin is too far away—I can't roll over there. But since we know these webs can be torn by teeth, I want to try to break the bindings on your wrists," Xie Lian explained.

Mu Qing glared at him for a moment, then his expression swiftly cooled as he gazed upward like a dead fish looking at the sky. "No thanks."

"I really do want to help," Xie Lian said helplessly.

"Your Highness possesses a body of a thousand gold. I can't possibly trouble such greatness," Mu Qing said coldly.

Feng Xin cussed. "What the actual fuck?! Why are you being so sarcastic at a time like this?! Huh?! He's helping you, trying to save you, but you're acting like he owes you!"

Mu Qing's head shot up. "Who asked him to help? Xie Lian! Why do you always show up at times like these?!"

Xie Lian was a little bewildered, and he vaguely remembered that Mu Qing had asked him the same thing a long time ago. How did he answer him back then? He couldn't remember.

"Is there something wrong with showing up at times like these?" Mu Qing lay back down. "Doesn't matter. I don't need your help."

"Why?" Xie Lian questioned. "Everyone needs help sometimes just to get by."

"Don't bother with him anymore," Feng Xin said. "He's just a show-off. He thinks he'll lose face if he gets help from you."

Mu Qing and Feng Xin kept at each other's throats while the wraith butterfly leisurely danced around Xie Lian—it was unhurried and calm as it shimmered with faint silver light. It made Xie Lian remember something, so he interrupted their sniping.

"Stop arguing, you two. It'll be more of a joke if anyone else sees you like this. And someone will be along to help us soon."

"No one in Heaven or on Earth will heed a call from this hellish place, so who's gonna come save us?" Mu Qing said derisively. "Unless..."

A particular person came to mind before he finished, and he trailed off abruptly.

Feng Xin, however, asked directly. "Crimson Rain Sought Flower came with you?"

"You trust him that much?" Mu Qing asked doubtfully. "You sure he's gonna come?"

Xie Lian was confident. "He will come."

Hua Cheng had been behaving oddly for a while. Several times, he almost suspected the Hua Cheng next to him was fake. Nonetheless, his instincts told him that was impossible.

"Even if he wanted to, how would he find this cave?" Mu Qing added.

"Why don't we holler some more?" Feng Xin suggested. "The more people, the louder the noise."

"No need," Xie Lian said. "We only need to sit and wait. No, just lie down and wait. Because Hua Cheng and I are joined by a red string—"

Before he even finished his sentence, he could see Feng Xin and Mu Qing's faces twitching like worms had crawled into their ears.

"—What's with that look?" Xie Lian asked. "Don't misunderstand. I'm not talking about some frivolous notion about the 'red string of fate.' It's a spiritual device! Just a spiritual device."

Only then did they stop twitching.

"Oh, I see," Feng Xin replied.

Mu Qing was doubtful. "What kind of spiritual device? What does it do?"

"It's quite useful," Xie Lian said. "It's a red string tied on both our hands that invisibly connects the two of us, and one can use it to find the other. It will never break as long as one of us is still breathing—"

The others couldn't listen anymore and cut him off.

"How is that any different from a red string of fate?! It's exactly the same thing!"

Xie Lian was taken aback. "No, I don't think so... It's different!"

"And just *how* is it different? It's exactly the same thing, all right?!" Mu Qing exclaimed.

Xie Lian pondered the matter only to discover that it was true! The more he thought about it, the more he realized that the intent and function of this spiritual device really was quite similar to a red string of fate.

Just when he began to think he should drop this train of thought, a voice came from above.

"Gege? Are you down there?"

The moment he heard that voice, Xie Lian instantly felt himself relax. He looked up.

"San Lang! I'm down here!" Then he turned to the other two in the pit. "You see? I told you he'd come."

Feng Xin and Mu Qing both made complicated expressions when they saw how happy he looked. Hua Cheng didn't peek his head over the edge, but all of them could hear the helpless way he spoke.

"Gege, I said not to run off. Now what should we do?"

Xie Lian was confused by his tone, and his delight faltered. "Huh? Is this silk webbing that difficult to deal with? Can't Eming slash through it?"

"The silk isn't the difficult part..." he thought he heard Hua Cheng mutter faintly, but the words were so quiet he wasn't sure whether they were actually said.

A moment later, Hua Cheng quietly spoke. "Eming's not in a good state right now."

Xie Lian found this strange. Wasn't Eming perfectly fine and completely energetic just a little while ago? How could there be something wrong with it now?

Next to him, Mu Qing humphed. "No need to ask him anymore. How could the scimitar Eming be in a bad state? He's clearly looking for an excuse not to help."

"Don't say that," Xie Lian countered.

Xie Lian thought it was more likely that Eming was being disciplined and Hua Cheng wasn't allowing it out.

Suddenly, a black shadow flashed above, and a figure dressed in red landed soundlessly at Xie Lian's side. Hua Cheng leaned down to hold Xie Lian's hand.

"San Lang, why did you jump down too?" Xie Lian cried when he realized who it was. "Watch out for the spider silk!"

Sure enough, the white silk tendrils were flying at him in an attack, but Hua Cheng didn't even spare them a glance. He gave a casual wave, and hundreds of silver butterflies shielded his back, forming armor with their wings. They started ruthlessly fighting the silk tendrils.

Hua Cheng tore away the white silk that bound Xie Lian, then held him around the waist and shook out a red umbrella with his free hand.

"Let's go!"

The other two were dumbfounded when they saw that he had zero intention of saving them. "Did you forget something?"

Xie Lian hadn't yet spoken, but Hua Cheng looked back.

"Oh, that's right."

The heavily bound Fangxin flew straight into Hua Cheng's hand, and he passed the sword to Xie Lian.

"Gege, your sword."

"..."

That was what he forgot?!

Feng Xin and Mu Qing both cried, *"Hey!"*

Hua Cheng hugged Xie Lian closer and flung out his arm to open the red umbrella. "Gege, hold on tight to me!"

With that, the umbrella started flying upward, taking the pair along with it. Xie Lian hugged him tightly as instructed, and the other two began to scream again in earnest when they were about six meters off the ground. Xie Lian didn't know whether to laugh or cry.

"I haven't forgotten you!"

He sent Ruoye out from his wrist, which wrapped itself around the two giant cocoons a few times and began to drag them along behind the umbrella.

When they were halfway out of the pit, Feng Xin cried, "Wait! Wait! I left something behind!"

"What is it?" Xie Lian called back from above.

"A sword!" Feng Xin shouted. "It fell into the corner!"

Xie Lian looked down, and, sure enough, a sword's hilt was barely visible in all that white silk. He made Ruoye stretch out further to wrap the sword, and he pulled them all out together. Finally, all four made it back onto solid ground.

Ruoye threw the two thick cocoons to the ground and hurriedly wrapped itself back onto Xie Lian's wrist, trembling slightly. It almost seemed like it was terrified of the white silk webs, which were so much like itself but so aggressive and evil. Xie Lian soothed Ruoye while cutting the webbing on the cocoons with Fangxin. The moment Feng Xin and Mu Qing could move, they both leapt to their feet and ripped off the rest of the webbing. Xie Lian held out the sword Ruoye had helped bring along toward Feng Xin. Finally getting a good look at the blade, he stared at it in amazement.

"This is...Hongjing? Nan Feng, did your general repair that sword?"

It was an offhand comment, but the moment the words left his lips, he realized how bad it sounded. Feng Xin and Mu Qing were still in the forms of "Nan Feng" and "Fu Yao," and Xie Lian had forgotten that their identities had been exposed and was still sub-consciously going along with their act. Although he'd intended to be considerate, that consideration simply led to awkwardness. The two of them fell into a strange silence.

Feng Xin couldn't mask his expression—discomfort surfaced on his face. He transformed back to his true form and took the sword.

"Yes...it's fixed. There are plenty of ghosts on Mount Tonglu, after all. Flashing it around makes things easier."

Xie Lian took a peek at the one who shattered Hongjing, who was standing right beside him. He cleared his throat softly. "Sorry for the trouble."

After all, it wasn't easy to repair a sword that had been shattered to pieces.

Mu Qing also transformed back to his true form and brushed off the rest of the silk webbing on his sleeves. "It's good that it's fixed. So many of the nefarious creatures here are adept at disguise. If someone's not good at using their brain, using Hongjing is the only way they'll see through deception."

Feng Xin was pissed. "Who are you calling brainless so passive-aggressively? Did you think I wouldn't notice?"

And there they went again. Xie Lian shook his head and turned to Hua Cheng. "San Lang, I ran off too quickly before. Sorry for leaving you behind."

Hua Cheng tucked the umbrella away. "Don't worry. As long as gege doesn't run off like that again."

Xie Lian grinned, but just as he was about to speak, he saw that Mu Qing's glance at Hua Cheng had turned into a strange, pointed stare.

"Mu Qing? What is it?" Xie Lian asked.

Mu Qing immediately snapped out of it and gave him a look. "Nothing. I've just never seen Crimson Rain Sought Flower like this and found it curious, that's all."

Xie Lian couldn't fully believe his explanation. While this likely was the first time Mu Qing had seen Hua Cheng's true form, he'd certainly seen Hua Cheng in his youthful body, and the two skins weren't remarkably different. So why that look?

The four left the cave, but after only a few steps, Feng Xin asked in astonishment, "...What is this place?"

Mu Qing was also stunned. "What happened here?"

They had been trapped at the bottom of the silk webbing pit, so they hadn't had a chance to investigate the situation outside. They were astonished at the sight of innumerable unique divine statues filling cave after cave, and shocked to learn that there was such a mysterious place and such uncanny craftsmanship beneath this great snowy mountain.

"This is a Cave of Ten Thousand Gods," Xie Lian explained.

Mu Qing scanned their surroundings and mumbled, "Who knows how many years and how much blood and sweat it'd take to build something like this. This is honestly...honestly..."

He seemed at a loss for words to describe it. Xie Lian could understand his feelings. After all, a stone cave like this was meant for cultivation and worship of the divine; his parents had constructed caves like this for him. What heavenly official wouldn't be astounded by such a massive Cave of Ten Thousand Gods? If one of their own statues was worshipped in a place like this, it would be a huge boon to their divinity.

"What god is worshipped in this cave?" Feng Xin asked, confused. "Why are all the faces covered?"

"Naturally, it's to prevent future passersby like us from seeing," Xie Lian replied.

"Now that's strange," Mu Qing said. "They could've just smashed the statues' heads; why go through all this trouble? Thin veils like these won't stop anyone who really wants to see."

As he spoke, he walked over, intending to peel away the veil of the nearest divine statue. Xie Lian hadn't had the chance to stop him when there was a chilling flash. The tip of a silver blade loomed mere centimeters away from Mu Qing's fingers.

Murderous intent made the air between them grow tense.

"What are you doing?" Feng Xin asked in alarm.

Even with that blade so close, Mu Qing didn't seem scared at all. "Your scimitar looks just fine. Why'd you tell us that it's 'not in a good state'?"

Hua Cheng stood directly behind him and said lazily, "Didn't anyone teach you not to randomly put your hands on things in other people's territory?"

"It's not your territory, so whose justice are you upholding?" Mu Qing countered.

"I just don't want to cause unnecessary trouble," Hua Cheng said flatly. "This is Mount Tonglu, after all. Who knows what could happen if the veils are removed?"

"I can't believe there'd come a day when someone as arrogant as Crimson Rain Sought Flower would be afraid to cause unnecessary trouble," Mu Qing said.

He moved his hand downward to touch the statue's carved robe. The scimitar Eming followed and pointed at him once more.

"I'm only trying to touch the stone now, not remove the veil. Why is Crimson Rain Sought Flower stopping me again?" Mu Qing questioned.

Hua Cheng shot him a fake-looking smile. "I'm preventing you from causing problems."

Xie Lian put himself between the two. "Stop, stop. It's not like we *have* to see which god is being worshipped here. We shouldn't stay here too long anyway, so let's just go. Don't forget that we still have a mission to accomplish."

Hua Cheng stared at Mu Qing's hand. "Since that's what gege wants, have him put his hand away and I'll let it go."

"Mu Qing, back off, all right?" Xie Lian said.

Mu Qing glared at him. "Are you nuts? Why shouldn't *he* back off first? What if I back off and he doesn't?"

Between a heavenly official and a ghost, Feng Xin naturally chose to stand on the side of the heavenly official. "At most, we'll accept both sides standing down at the same time."

Hua Cheng showed no signs of doing so. "You wish."

Seeing that neither side would give in, Xie Lian rested a hand on Mu Qing's arm. "Mu Qing, drop it," he urged gently. "You're the one who started this, so you should be the one to let it go. All right? Can you think of it as giving me some face? I swear that if you back off, San Lang will keep his promise."

Although Mu Qing was clearly reluctant, he held the stalemate for another moment, then slowly dropped his hand. They all returned to the road. Finally, the tension relaxed, and Xie Lian sighed in relief.

They reached another fork in the road, and Xie Lian turned to Hua Cheng.

"Which way do you think we should go this time?"

Hua Cheng picked a path, seemingly at random. "This way."

Feng Xin and Mu Qing had been walking behind them and appeared to be at each other's throats again, but Mu Qing briefly paused their argument.

"How did you decide?" he asked. "Why this way?"

The two in front turned their heads to look at them.

"It was random."

Feng Xin frowned. "How can you pick randomly? Let's not go blindly—we might tumble into another pit."

Hua Cheng smiled. "Even if we fall into a pit, I have ways to pull His Highness out. You can follow us if you'd like, or you can head off on your own if you'd prefer. To be honest, I'd rather not have to rescue you again."

"You—!"

That was just the way Hua Cheng spoke—even if he had a smile on his face and his words were perfectly polite, it always sounded fake. The faker his smile, the more his tone enraged people, so much that Feng Xin nocked an arrow on his bow.

Xie Lian knew that he wouldn't actually shoot. "Sorry about this, Feng Xin. But considering our current situation, it really makes no difference which way we go."

Hua Cheng laughed heartily. "Ooh, I'm scared. Looks like I'd better stay far away from you."

He waggled his brows at Xie Lian and really did put some distance between them. Xie Lian knew he was just trying to leave the other two behind, and he smiled as he shook his head. He was about to follow Hua Cheng, but without warning Mu Qing reached out and pulled him to a stop. Xie Lian looked back, bewildered.

"Mu Qing? What is it?"

Mu Qing didn't answer. Instead, he simply shouted "Now!" Then he grabbed Xie Lian and dashed off down the other path.

Ahead, Hua Cheng had noticed that something was wrong, and he turned back to look. But Feng Xin had already punched the stone wall. Boulders rumbled and crashed down, blocking the road behind them. Mu Qing and Feng Xin rushed forward and slapped fifty or so talismans to the rocks in the span of a second. Hua Cheng was now separated from the three of them by the pile of boulders.

As it turned out, Feng Xin and Mu Qing hadn't been arguing when they were trailing behind them earlier—they had actually been discussing how to launch this sudden attack!

Xie Lian was dumbfounded. "What are you guys doing?"

He struggled free of Mu Qing's grip, wanting to check on Hua Cheng behind the wall of stone. However, Feng Xin tripped him, and he and Mu Qing each grabbed one of Xie Lian's arms and began to drag him off at a breakneck pace.

"Let's get away, quick! Those talismans won't last for long!" Feng Xin exclaimed.

"You have to ask what we're doing?! There's something odd about him—can't you tell?!" Mu Qing reprimanded.

"How is he odd?" Xie Lian questioned.

"You've really gone stupid! Odd is written all over him—you're the only one blind to it!" Mu Qing exclaimed.

"Stop talking and run!" Feng Xin roared. "Fuck, I think the wraith butterflies caught up!"

"Block the cave entrance!" Mu Qing barked.

Feng Xin continued to punch the walls as they ran, and many of the cave entrances were completely blocked by the giant rocks that tumbled down. The two dragged Xie Lian along as they fled through the endless, winding underground corridors, sending his head spinning from all the twists and turns.

"Stop! *Stop!*" Xie Lian shouted as they ran.

When they finally felt they'd gone far enough, Feng Xin and Mu Qing paused to catch their breaths.

Taking advantage of this break, Xie Lian said, "What I *meant* was, why did you two suddenly drag me away? Did you notice something?"

Feng Xin was supporting himself with his hands on his knees and panting harshly. "Let him...tell you...again."

Mu Qing straightened up and turned to Xie Lian. "It's so obvious! You didn't see it? That pearl! Do you remember that pearl?"

"What pearl?" Xie Lian asked.

Mu Qing said each word slowly and clearly. "The red coral pearl from the earrings of the God-Pleasing Martial Warrior costume— the one you wore for the Shangyuan Heavenly Ceremony. The earring you lost!"

Xie Lian thought for a long while, but he still couldn't remember. He looked confused as he tugged at his earlobe. "...Were those earrings red coral pearls? Did I lose one?"

The corners of Mu Qing's lips twitched, and he said furiously, "You two even wrongfully accused me of stealing that pearl! How could you forget something like this?"

"It's been eight hundred years—" Xie Lian began, but Feng Xin interrupted to rebuke Mu Qing.

"Stop making shit up! No one wronged you—*you're* the one who started making assumptions all on your own!"

Xie Lian waved. "Stop fighting, stop fighting. Why are you talking about that pearl out of nowhere?"

"Because it's been found!" Mu Qing exclaimed. "Did you see the red bead tied in Hua Cheng's hair?"

Xie Lian's eyes widened. "Are you saying..."

"I am!" Mu Qing stated with conviction.

"..."

So that was why Mu Qing had that weird look in his eyes when he looked at Hua Cheng earlier.

"Why would he have that red coral pearl? Are you sure you remember it correctly?" Xie Lian questioned.

Mu Qing cut him off. "I searched for that pearl nonstop for a whole year, and I've never stopped looking for it. I'm the only one who would *never* remember it wrong!"

Xie Lian crossed his arms and tucked them into his sleeves. He furrowed his brow in contemplation. "I still think you might be mistaken. There's no reason for him to have that pearl. Don't all high-quality red coral pearls look pretty much the same? Besides, San Lang has always liked collecting rare treasures. He's got antiques that are thousands of years old."

Mu Qing nodded. "Fine. Very well. You think I'm wrong? *Fine.* Then look at this."

He was standing right next to a divine statue, and as he finished speaking, he yanked the veil off its face.

"Why don't you take a look at *this*, then? Surely it can't be a mistake too!"

The moment the veil was lifted, Xie Lian's pupils shrank.

The divine statue's face wasn't deformed or frightening. It was the face of a young man who wore a gentle, kind expression—smiling and in high spirits. But when Xie Lian saw it, a chill raced down his spine and raised the hair on his neck.

How could it not be eerie? This face was nearly identical to Xie Lian's own!

Looking at this divine statue so closely was like staring into a mirror. Even that smile, previously kind, now seemed disturbing.

Xie Lian couldn't help but feel shaken by the sight of it. "This..."

"Are you still going to tell me I'm wrong?" Mu Qing said coldly.

With much effort, Xie Lian finally squeezed out, "...Why would one of my divine statues be here?"

"One?" Mu Qing replied. "Not just one. Look closely."

Then he yanked the veil from another divine statue—it too had a face that was undoubtedly Xie Lian's!

He pulled the veils from the faces of five or six more divine statues. They were all identical!

"This certainly is a Cave of Ten Thousand Gods," Mu Qing said. "But there's only one god worshipped here!"

Only Xie Lian!

He was surrounded by endless copies of his own face. It was like Xie Lian had fallen into a bizarre, hallucinatory dream. His mind spun for a good while before he abruptly realized something.

"Wait. Mu Qing. You didn't get a chance to see these statues' faces earlier, right? You were going to remove the veils, but he stopped you."

Mu Qing humphed. "I don't need to see the statues' faces to know that you're the subject."

"How would you know?" Xie Lian asked.

Mu Qing rolled all the silk veils into a ball and tossed them to the side, his veins popping slightly. "How would I know? Because all your clothes, accessories, and daily living needs were my responsibility back then. I washed for you, I mended for you—and every item in your wardrobe was unique. These statues are too detailed—everything is there, exactly the same, completely! When I saw those clothes, of course I knew whose face they would have!"

Xie Lian fell silent. He put a hand over his forehead and thought back on Hua Cheng's odd behavior along the way.

Next to him, Feng Xin said, "He wouldn't let us look at those statues, which proves he knows exactly what's weird about them. That whole excuse about how we all dropped in by accident after the avalanche was bullshit. He must know what this place is."

"Not just that. I bet he was the one who threw us into that pit of silk webbing," Mu Qing added. "He was serious about killing us."

"But...why are these statues like this?" Xie Lian wondered.

The statues had all been carved with such precision that they seemed nearly alive. The details were more than detailed, almost to the point of being frightening. It was clear to see just how closely the sculptor had observed their subject. Xie Lian didn't think even the work of Xianle's most renowned sculptors had reached this level of detail. It was as if the sculptor's mind was filled by Xie Lian and Xie Lian alone, as if his eyes saw nothing else.

The three of them were surrounded by countless statues that all bore the same face, and Feng Xin shuddered violently.

"Honestly, what the fuck. Too creepy... They're too fucking realistic."

And there were so *many*.

"I suspect these statues are components for some wicked spell. Let's destroy them," Mu Qing said.

He moved to shatter one with a chop of his hand. Xie Lian's mind was instantly pulled back to the present; he stopped him.

"Don't!" he cried.

Mu Qing looked at him. "Are you sure? The spell could be aimed at you."

Xie Lian pondered it, but in the end still said, "Let's not act recklessly. I think the chance that it's a wicked spell is very small."

"I think it's very large," Feng Xin said. "Honestly, what the fuck... Doesn't the sight of these things scare you?"

Mu Qing stared at Xie Lian, who stared at him right back. "And what are you basing that off of?"

"Nothing," Xie Lian said. "But these divine statues are quite nice and very meticulously sculpted. If we destroy them before we find out about them, we might regret it."

After a pause, he added, "San Lang...might have lied to me about something, but I truly don't think it's anything that would harm me."

Mu Qing couldn't believe his ears. "...Did he cast some spell on you to bewitch your mind? I think if he wrote 'suspicious' on his face, you'd suddenly forget how to read."

While they were talking, Feng Xin snapped to alertness, like he was about to face a dangerous foe. "Watch out!" he cried.

Xie Lian and Mu Qing both tensed and demanded, "What is it?"

"That spider silk is coming at us again!" Feng Xin exclaimed.

The palm torch illuminated the stone walls ahead; they were covered with large patches of dense white silk. The three cursed mentally, gearing themselves up for another clash. Yet unexpectedly, this white silk wasn't as aggressive as the silk in the pit; it neither moved nor attacked. It was acting like a gecko lounging on a wall.

After they had waited for a while, Xie Lian observed, "These silk nets don't seem alive."

"If they're not alive, then what are they for?" Feng Xin questioned.

Xie Lian had an answer in mind, which he confirmed when he went over to study it. "I think they're covering something."

All three of them stood before the stone wall. Xie Lian gave the white silk a tug and pulled off a large section. As expected, the strands were tough and difficult to tear down, but he could manage it with effort.

The veils had concealed the identity of those divine statues. So what was being hidden on these stone walls?

The other two joined him in tearing down the webs, each taking care of different areas. Soon, a section of the wall was revealed on Xie Lian's side.

"It's a mural!"

The webs had been hiding a giant painting. The entire surface of the wall was densely packed with lines, colors, and little people. The mural was divided into smaller pieces, each with a different style: some were coarse and wild, some elegant, some exquisite, some peculiar.

After studying it for a while, Xie Lian stated, "...He painted this."

"He?" Mu Qing echoed. "Hua Cheng? Are you sure?"

"Yes," Xie Lian said softly. "There are words on here, and he's the one who wrote them."

He pointed at a little blood-red person on the wall. Right next to it, there were a bunch of messy, twisted, indiscernible characters— it looked like they had been written in a state of delirium or scrawled to vent the author's feelings during a period of extreme suffering. Based on those characters, Xie Lian could guess that the little blood-red

person painted there was Hua Cheng himself, but for some unknown reason he had depicted himself as extremely ugly and disfigured.

Feng Xin glanced at it and couldn't help but comment, "That handwriting...it's so ugly I've gone blind. I bet even I write better than him."

Handwriting uglier than Feng Xin's was truly beyond saving. Xie Lian was dazzled; there was so much to see that he didn't even know where to start looking. Now that he'd confirmed this was Hua Cheng's work, it was like he had discovered a treasure trove. His fingertips began to tremble slightly.

Mu Qing seemed to have discovered something nearby and called out. "Your Highness, come quick! Come and see!"

Only then did Xie Lian snap out of it. "What is it?"

Feng Xin and Mu Qing were already rendered speechless and could only point at one of the images. This piece was considerably larger than the other ones depicted. Right at its center was a tall tower connected to a city wall. Below, a sea of people surrounded a magnificent stage. The lines were simple, yet they captured the scene perfectly with only a few strokes.

Mu Qing pointed at the center of the mural. "So...that...that was *him?*" he said with a trembling voice.

Xie Lian was also staring at that section.

This piece was mostly colorless; only two figures had been colored within it. There was a small figure at the bottom that had been painted pure white; it seemed to be glowing. The figure was looking toward the sky with hands outstretched. It was about to catch another little figure who was falling from the tower.

That little figure was bloody red.

"...Is that him? Was that *him?*" Mu Qing murmured. "The little kid who fell during the Shangyuan Heavenly Ceremonial Parade?

But how is that possible? I can't believe it. Crimson Rain Sought Flower...was *him*?!"

Feng Xin patted Xie Lian and Mu Qing madly and pointed to one side. "There's more in the back!"

Xie Lian walked over to the other mural and saw that it depicted a dilapidated little shrine. Upon the shrine's altar there was a divine statue, which also glowed faintly with white light. It held a sword in one hand, and in the other it offered a red umbrella downward. There was an ugly little blood-red figure at the bottom of the mural. It cupped a small flower in its hands, which it was offering to the statue.

Xie Lian felt a sudden headache coming on. His hand flew to clutch his throbbing temple, but he didn't look away.

The next mural depicted a battlefield. Large bands of soldiers were gearing up for war, and a little white figure floated in the sky overhead. It wielded a longsword in one hand and looked mighty and glorious. There was another little blood-red figure among the dense battalion below. Its head was raised to watch the one in the sky.

Xie Lian was absorbed in these paintings when Feng Xin's disbelieving voice rang out.

"That red one, it's all the same person, isn't it? It's all him?! They're all Hua Cheng?! Holy fuck... He's been following you all this time?!"

Mu Qing also looked incredulous. "He wasn't just following, he was *watching*. Watching very closely. Very, very closely. He was everywhere! Look, this is the main street, Buyou Forest—what's this? Beizi Hill? My god... Was he the one who carved all these divine statues?!"

Looking at the murals was giving Feng Xin chills. "My fucking god... Who the hell is he? He's had his eye on you since eight hundred years ago?! And he's still following you, even now? What the fuck?! This is terrifying! Is he bewitched? What the hell does he want? No normal devotee would go this far—so just what the hell does he want?!"

"There must be some plot...there must be!" Mu Qing exclaimed. "Let's keep looking. I'm sure we'll find a clue!"

Xie Lian was completely stricken. He stared at that little blood-red figure on the wall, unable to wrap his mind around it. It felt like countless memories were fighting to rush into his brain—he hadn't forgotten, but they'd never taken root. They were pouring in so fast that his breath could barely keep up anymore.

Just then, Xie Lian heard the other two yell, and he snapped out of it. "What is it now?" he asked.

Feng Xin and Mu Qing were both standing before a stone wall, and it looked like they had seen something outrageous. When they saw Xie Lian walk toward them, Feng Xin quickly turned around and stopped him, pushing him away.

"Holy fuck, *don't look!*"

"What?" Xie Lian was bewildered. "What was it? Why can't I look?"

Mu Qing's expression was dark. "Just...don't bother. There's nothing worth seeing here. Let's get out of here as soon as possible!"

The two of them each grabbed one of Xie Lian's arms and started to bolt once more. Xie Lian complained as he was dragged along.

"What are you doing? I wasn't done looking at the murals!"

"There's no need to look anymore! Things like that shouldn't be seen!" Feng Xin yelled angrily as he ran. "My fucking god! I've never witnessed anything like that in my fucking life. Nor anyone like *him*!"

Xie Lian was baffled. "What have you never witnessed? What's wrong with San Lang?"

"Why are you still calling him 'San Lang'? Stop it!" Mu Qing admonished. "You can't get away from him fast enough! Never go near him again—he's not normal! He's sick in the head! He's crazy!"

Xie Lian couldn't listen anymore. "Why are you two insulting him like this? None of us are all that normal, you know!"

"Stop asking!" Feng Xin cried. "You don't understand! He's not like us! He's crazy! He... Toward you, he... He..."

"'Toward me,' *what*?" Xie Lian demanded. "Please let me go. Let me go back and see for myself, all right?"

One wanted to go back, but the other two were pulling him forward. They were stuck in that stalemate until suddenly, a bone-chilling voice came from ahead of them.

"Didn't I say not to randomly put your hands on things in other people's territory?"

The three of them froze, then slowly turned to look.

Before them stood a man dressed in red. Hua Cheng was leaning against the stone wall, blocking their way with a smile.

"If you do, who knows what will happen?"

While his mouth was smiling, his eye held not a trace of mirth but was instead dark and muddied. He hugged one of his arms, while his other hand idly fiddled with something small.

It was the deep-red coral pearl tied to his thin braid. The coral's luminous red luster was as bright and dazzling as the red affinity knot on his pale finger.

Neither the hundreds of charmed talismans nor the heavy piles of boulders had stopped him!

Feng Xin and Mu Qing both reacted swiftly. Feng Xin shot a barrage of arrows as Mu Qing swung his saber to send an air-blade strike toward Hua Cheng, then grabbed Xie Lian and ran. Feng Xin employed his same old trick and struck wildly at the rock walls.

"What the fuck?!" he cried. "How did he find us so fast?!"

"How should I know?!" Mu Qing yelled back. "Wait—the red string! The red string! His finger is still tied with that red string!"

When it dawned on them, they both turned around to seize Xie Lian's hand—as if he would let them. Xie Lian clutched the red knot on his finger to protect it and exclaimed, "You can't!"

"Your Highness, he'll find us as long as you keep that red string tied to you," Feng Xin insisted. "If you don't want him to catch up, it has to be removed!"

Xie Lian still held on, guarding his finger. "I'm not afraid of him catching up. I...want to ask him about this face-to-face."

Mu Qing's eyes widened. "You still want to talk to him? I don't think you'll realize how dangerous he is until he's devoured you whole."

"But I already know he's dangerous," Xie Lian countered. "You guys won't tell me what that mural shows, and you won't let me go near him. You won't convince me of anything acting like this."

"He's a ghost king, and his behavior is abnormal. People would usually stay far away based on that alone! You shouldn't need to be convinced of anything!"

Xie Lian raised two fingers. "Two choices: either you let me go back and ask him to explain, or you let me go back to look at that mural."

Feng Xin and Mu Qing seemed to remember something terrifying. One's lips began to twitch, while the other's brow could not furrow any deeper. They both stood blocking him and yelled in unison, "We'll allow neither!"

Thus, Xie Lian rolled up his sleeves. "Well, since you both said no, let's solve this with our fists! Who's first? Or will you come at me together?"

Mu Qing turned to Feng Xin. "You first!"

Then he backed away to the side of the tunnel.

Feng Xin didn't seem confident that he could win against Xie Lian, but he was determined to give it his best shot to rescue this wayward youth. He gripped his bow.

"Very well! Your Highness, pardon my insolence!"

"Pard—"

Before Xie Lian could even return the opening courtesy, he felt something hot being stuck to his back. Someone behind him shouted, "Stay still! Don't talk!" and he was rendered as stiff as an iron board. And not just his body—he also couldn't move his mouth to speak!

Mu Qing darted out from behind Xie Lian. "Let's drag him away. That talisman will paralyze him temporarily, but it won't last long," he said to Feng Xin.

Feng Xin was slightly dumbfounded. "Why did you ambush him? Didn't we agree to go one-on-one?"

Xie Lian was shocked as well that Mu Qing would immediately go back on his word. He wouldn't have been deceived so easily had it not been for his wholehearted trust in both of his once-subordinates.

"Who has the time for you to go one-on-one right now?" Mu Qing said. "He's doing it on purpose; it's easy to see that he's dragging things out to give Hua Cheng time to catch up. Do you see the state he's in right now? Completely enchanted! No matter what you tell him, nothing will get through. Once they meet, Hua Cheng will probably only need to charm him with a few lies and he'll believe him, just like someone who's under a fox spirit's thrall."[3]

---

3   Fox spirits in Asian folktales are seducers who bewitch humans into falling helplessly in love with them.

Feng Xin considered this and decided that what Mu Qing said made some sense. "Your Highness," he sighed, "we didn't intend to deceive you, but his behavior toward you is really...unseemly. I can't even speak of it! Please, just come with us."

"Let's go," Mu Qing said.

Mu Qing's words weren't a suggestion or a plea—they were a command. He must have stuck a Command Talisman on Xie Lian's back, drawn in his own blood. A Command Talisman could ostensibly make its target obey the spellcaster's every whim, but in reality it could only realize simple commands like "do not speak," "walk," "stop," "run," and so on. More complicated commands were harder to execute, and the talisman couldn't confound the target's mind. Only powerful ghosts like the Brocade Immortal could manage such things.

The two hurried along with Xie Lian in tow again, but they were stopped by a pile of rubble blocking the way.

Feng Xin saw that their path had been cut off and wondered aloud, "Why are there rocks blocking the way? We can't go any farther."

"Weren't *you* the one who knocked them down? Why are you asking me?" Mu Qing said.

"You were the one leading the way, so you're the one who messed up. Why are we somewhere we've already been, anyway? Why would you circle back around?" Feng Xin questioned.

Mu Qing refused to be questioned. "What a joke. I don't know the roads here, so how could I possibly lead? Haven't we been running around randomly all this time?"

Sensing that they were about to get into another argument, Feng Xin waved it off.

"Never mind, it's not worth wasting my breath on you. Let's just dig through this!"

Hua Cheng was pursuing them from behind, so they could only go forward—retreat wasn't an option if they wanted to avoid running into him. Blocking roads was easy, but digging through that blockage was much harder. They made Xie Lian stand obediently in a corner while Feng Xin rained down random punches on the boulders, and Mu Qing, with bulging veins, swung his mighty zhanmadao to shatter the rocks. They cleared the path in no time; rubble rolled and dust clouded the air. But just as they were about to call Xie Lian over, they saw a red-clad figure standing in the now-open passage amidst clouds of settling dust.

Xie Lian's eyes instantly lit up. It was Hua Cheng!

The ghost king's gaze was cold. He stood silently with his hands clasped behind his back.

"Why won't you go away?!" Feng Xin blurted.

This man was the very definition of persistence. They had left him in the dust, so how had he managed to appear ahead of them? How long had he had been standing there, waiting in silence as they cleared away the obstacle blocking their way to deliver themselves right into his hands? He was frighteningly tenacious and sinister.

Feng Xin and Mu Qing quickly backed away, putting some distance between them. Hua Cheng didn't look at them. His gaze moved to the side of the tunnel, and he took a step in Xie Lian's direction. Feng Xin and Mu Qing realized why he was here and rushed to Xie Lian's side in a flash to guard him.

"Don't come any closer!" they both shouted at once.

Hua Cheng's expression turned extremely dark.

Normally, if someone dared to tell Crimson Rain Sought Flower to stay away, he wouldn't give a damn; he'd simply laugh and approach anyway. But at that moment he seemed genuinely wary, not daring to move recklessly. He paused in his step.

After a moment, he finally spoke. His words came slowly, and his tone was calm. "What do you two mean by this?"

Feng Xin, however, cut straight to the point. "You don't need to pretend anymore! We know this is your old lair. We've already seen what those divine statues are, and the murals too—we've seen everything!"

Hua Cheng wasn't directly facing them; he stood at an angle. The hands tucked behind his back seemed to jerk at Feng Xin's words, and two of his fingers curled stiffly inward.

"His Highness...saw it too?" he asked softly, inclining his head.

His voice was very, very quiet. While he still sounded unfazed, his voice was slightly cracked and obviously strange.

No! Xie Lian cried mentally.

The truth was that he hadn't seen much, but at that moment Xie Lian could neither move nor speak. He could only lean dutifully against the wall in the corner—which made it look like he was hiding behind the other two. It must've seemed like he was afraid to face Hua Cheng and refused to speak with him.

Feng Xin drew his bow. "That's right. We now understand your... intentions. With respect for your position as a ghost king—if you still know self-respect and conduct yourself with any dignity—we ask that you don't come near His Highness again."

Xie Lian's feelings were like a cottage on fire, black smoke roiling heavy and thick. Hua Cheng should've noticed that something was amiss, and Xie Lian could only hope that he would question him directly to find out what was wrong.

But Hua Cheng's current state seemed to render him unable to notice a thing.

"Don't go near him?" he said coldly. "What right do either of you have to say that to me?"

Not waiting for their response, Hua Cheng's eye flashed dangerously. "But you've reminded me that we have unfinished business to settle!"

The moment he finished speaking, countless shrieking silver butterflies shot forth toward them. In the face of such an attack, a spiritual shield was the only option. Feng Xin and Mu Qing cried in unison, "Shield!"

The butterfly deluge was blocked by the formless spiritual shield and shattered into shimmering silver light, which rapidly recrystallized into new silver butterflies and attacked once more. The onslaught was completely unstoppable—Feng Xin and Mu Qing gave ground slowly as they kept their shield up, and Hua Cheng steadily advanced step by step. The whirling winds raised by his spiritual aura stirred his raven hair, and it danced wildly with every gust. The mad fury and violence in his eye was on full display under the blinding light of the silver butterflies.

Defending alone wouldn't get them anywhere. Feng Xin and Mu Qing exchanged a look, silently agreeing to go on the attack. They maintained the spiritual shield as they charged forward; then, with weapons flashing, the three began to fight in the narrow stone corridor. Feng Xin battled the wraith butterflies while Mu Qing faced Hua Cheng. Hua Cheng flung out an arm, and the scimitar Eming appeared in his left hand, ready to strike!

This was the first time Xie Lian witnessed Eming fighting seriously. The scimitar was long, slender, and chillingly murderous, and it gleamed with threatening silver light—it was truly a wicked blade overflowing with evil!

The battle was truly thrilling to behold. Hua Cheng stood his ground even when fighting two against one, and Xie Lian watched unblinkingly with bated breath. With a flick of Eming's blade,

Mu Qing's zhanmadao was knocked off course and into the rocks. Although Mu Qing still had a grip on the hilt, the blade was stuck—he couldn't yank his weapon out. This only shocked Mu Qing for a moment, but Hua Cheng's fist was already swinging right into his jaw. The punch sent Mu Qing flying through the air, and he finally lost his grip on his saber's hilt.

Meanwhile, each arrow Feng Xin shot at the butterflies was snapped by their sharp wings. The sheer number of butterflies was ultimately too difficult to deal with!

At this point, both victory and defeat were a foregone conclusion. Countless white silk tendrils slithered from the corners of the corridor and wrapped Feng Xin and Mu Qing into giant cocoons once more. The more they struggled, the tighter their bindings became.

Mu Qing tore at the silk as he yelled. "I knew you were the one who threw us into that pit!"

"This isn't spider silk!" Feng Xin exclaimed. "This is…!"

It dawned on Xie Lian as well. It was butterfly silk!

Butterflies emerged from chrysalises, which they wove from their own silk. This strange white silk was completely of Hua Cheng's making, and it was probably linked to his aggressive wraith butterflies!

With the match decided, Hua Cheng sheathed his scimitar. "I threw you in to save you from disaster. Otherwise, you would've never had a chance to find this Cave of Ten Thousand Gods," he jeered. "And it was *your* yelling that caused the avalanche. Why don't you thank me for saving your puny little lives?"

Hua Cheng had probably planned to wait out the avalanche at first, getting Xie Lian out once the snowy mountain quieted down and leaving Feng Xin and Mu Qing behind. But unexpectedly, the pair had gnawed through the chrysalises and made enough noise that Xie Lian had discovered them, which led to all the trouble afterward. If not for all that, Xie Lian might have really just followed Hua Cheng straight out without looking at a single divine statue.

But the worst-case scenario had come to pass. Every secret had been torn out and exposed under the sun.

Despite the anxiety roiling under the surface, Xie Lian's body still sat obediently in place. Hua Cheng's gaze was growing colder and more intense as he stared condescendingly down at Mu Qing.

"It seems I'm the one with the real talent for sabers. Not you," he quietly stated.

Mu Qing's throat was bound by a few bands of white silk, and his face changed from blue to red and back as he was strangled. Blood leaked from the corners of his lips, and he choked out, "You! You...? I see, I get it..."

Feng Xin gritted out through his teeth, "What...do you...get?"

"I get...why this bastard...hates me so much now..." Mu Qing said. "He probably hates you...for the same reason!"

"Wh...why?" Feng Xin demanded through his coughs.

"Because he's insane!" Mu Qing said hatefully through his own coughing. "Have you forgotten what was in those murals? He was that...that young soldier His Highness wanted to promote after he returned from Beizi Hill. His Highness had said...his swordplay was good...and that he was well suited to the saber..."

"Why'd that make him hate you?" Feng Xin questioned.

Mu Qing didn't reply. *Bam!* Hua Cheng landed another punch on Mu Qing's face.

Hua Cheng gave a chilling smile and answered on Mu Qing's behalf. "Because he kicked me out of the army."

To think Mu Qing had done something like that!

Feng Xin was astonished. "What the fuck...?! Why'd you do that? How'd he piss you off?!"

Mu Qing's face was covered in blood. "I just made him go home— it's not like it's good to fight in a war! How could I have known he'd wind up being this crazy and holding grudges all this time—"

Hua Cheng cut him off with another punch, so forceful that Mu Qing's face almost contorted when it landed. *Bam!*

Hua Cheng smiled. "Did you think I couldn't guess why you kicked me out? Hmm?"

Mu Qing looked away, and Hua Cheng snickered.

"I guess it's clear which of us is actually useless trash, hm?"

"..."

Mu Qing spat out a mouthful of blood and grimaced like he'd been stabbed where it hurt. He replied, spitefully slowly, "Thank goodness I kicked you out. If we'd kept you in the army and let you get closer to His Highness, were you going to watch him all day with your mind full of unspeakable filth? Disgusting!"

Xie Lian's heart squeezed violently. Hua Cheng had his fist raised at first, but it froze in midair when Mu Qing spat the word "disgusting." Veins bulged on the back of his pale hand. The fingers clenched and loosened, loosened then clenched.

A long moment later, Hua Cheng said icily, "For now, I won't argue with you on that point. But tell me one thing, and tell me honestly: your argument before the avalanche—is that true?"

Mu Qing looked to Feng Xin with eyes wide; Feng Xin looked back, his own eyes round and bulging. Neither of them knew how to respond.

"My patience is limited," Hua Cheng said sharply. "Answer me on the count of three. One! *Two!*"

Such a rush for an answer!

An idea struck Mu Qing within his panic. "Your Highness, *run!*" he cried.

The moment the command was issued, the damn spell stuck to Xie Lian's back forced him to bolt. Hua Cheng swung around toward him, and two bands of white butterfly silk shot from the corners of the cave to bind Xie Lian. He fell to the ground before he'd even managed two steps.

To an observer, it looked like Xie Lian had been frozen in terror this whole time—or perhaps that he'd been struggling to accept the truth about Hua Cheng or had simply decided he didn't want to intervene in their fight. Now it looked like he'd finally decided to flee but had failed. The truth was, though, he had never even considered running away!

Xie Lian's hands and feet were tightly bound by the thick white silk. He lay sprawled on the ground with his black hair and white sleeves splayed out around him. His bamboo hat had rolled off to one side. Hua Cheng slowly turned to him, paused for a long moment, and then made his way to Xie Lian's side.

He'd only taken a few steps before Feng Xin could no longer hold back a desperate shout.

"Hua Cheng!"

Hua Cheng paused in his step and tilted his head.

"Let...let His Highness go!" Feng Xin forced out a plea. "He's suffered enough. Don't...to him..."

Hua Cheng didn't reply. He came to Xie Lian's side and, with one hand on his back and one hand under his knees, swept him into his arms.

Xie Lian lay against Hua Cheng's chest. Even though they were sealed in those giant white chrysalises, he could see Feng Xin and Mu Qing's expressions. Feng Xin looked like he was watching a lamb entering a tiger's mouth, as if Xie Lian was going to be ripped apart and devoured, and he started yelling. Mu Qing had started tearing at the white silk with his teeth again, but the awkward angle meant his struggles came to nothing.

Hua Cheng knew the pathways of this Cave of Ten Thousand Gods like the back of his hand. After many forks and turns, the two figures and their voices soon disappeared.

Carrying Xie Lian in his arms, Hua Cheng moved deeper into the darkness of the cave's innermost dens.

The only light around them came from the gently fluttering silver wraith butterflies. Xie Lian couldn't see the expression on Hua Cheng's face, but he could feel the tension in his body.

Hua Cheng had held him like this in the past, but it was obvious that something had changed—he wouldn't even touch Xie Lian's neck or hands directly. Xie Lian kept eyeing Hua Cheng's face, trying to blink hard enough that he'd notice, but Hua Cheng kept avoiding his gaze.

Hua Cheng took him into a chamber with a stone bed, where he quickly brought him and set him down. As he lay Xie Lian on the bed, he noticed something and checked Xie Lian's back.

"They cast a spell on you?"

Xie Lian was overjoyed. He'd finally discovered it!

Still, it had taken him incredibly long to notice that there was something off about Xie Lian, which just showed how badly Hua Cheng had been caught off guard. Xie Lian waited for him to remove the Command Talisman from his back, but Hua Cheng's hand paused before he touched the offending paper. In the end, Hua Cheng withdrew his hand and laid Xie Lian flat on the bed.

"Don't worry, Your Highness. I won't kill those two useless pieces of trash—for now," Hua Cheng said in a low voice, perhaps attempting to reassure Xie Lian. "Even though I'd really like to murder them."

There was a layer of thick, soft, fresh hay on the stone bed. It didn't jab Xie Lian at all as he lay there limply, but he was so anxious that his insides were smoking—he couldn't understand why Hua Cheng wouldn't release him from the spell. Just as he was trying desperately to struggle his way out of its control, Hua Cheng reach for the sash around Xie Lian's waist and begin to untie it.

In an unfortunate coincidence, that was the moment when the Command Talisman on Xie Lian's back started to fade; he kicked out hard with one leg as an *"Ah!"* escaped his lips. His spasm looked like nothing more than the jerk of a dying fish twitching in its last attempt at life and objecting with no real power. Still, Hua Cheng froze instantly and withdrew his hand.

"I won't!"

At that point, Hua Cheng seemed to decide that his tone was too harsh and that his actions might be scaring or repulsing Xie Lian. He backed away a few steps and softened his voice. His expression was cautious and resigned but otherwise unreadable.

"Your Highness, I won't do anything to you," he said in a low voice. "Don't...don't be scared."

Xie Lian finally understood.

Hua Cheng still wasn't sure what kind of response he would receive from Xie Lian upon releasing the spell, so he was refusing to hear it altogether.

Hua Cheng seemed to be holding back some sort of urge, and he once again assured him in a quiet tone that sounded like a vow, "Your Highness, trust me."

He'd said that exact phrase before, but this time, all his normal confidence was gone.

Xie Lian wanted to answer him but couldn't, and he didn't dare struggle anymore lest Hua Cheng's misunderstanding deepen. He could only lie there, flat and motionless, waiting patiently for the power of the Command Talisman to fade entirely.

Seeing that Xie Lian had stopped "resisting," Hua Cheng approached again, reached out, and gingerly finished untying Xie Lian's belt.

San Lang?! Xie Lian called out in his mind.

Xie Lian wholeheartedly believed that Hua Cheng would never take advantage of a helpless person, but this new development was completely unexpected—he couldn't help his eyes widening. Hua Cheng set about loosening Xie Lian's clothes, but he seemed to be avoiding touching Xie Lian's body, which slowed him down. It was a long while before Xie Lian's outer robes were removed and the inner robe followed. A wraith butterfly perched on the curve of Xie Lian's shoulder, and a warm, tingling feeling crawled over his skin.

It was only then that Xie Lian realized the state he was in—his skin was red and slightly swollen, even cracked in some areas. But when the silver butterfly perched on him, his injuries had started to heal.

This was frostbite he'd gotten from tumbling all over the frozen mountain, but Xie Lian hadn't noticed it since he was fairly used to pain at this point. If he had frostbite, then he had frostbite; even if he had noticed the injuries earlier, he probably would have left them to heal on their own. But Hua Cheng knew even better than Xie Lian himself where he was hurt, and he wouldn't let it go. He would address Xie Lian's injuries no matter what.

Xie Lian's thoughts were interrupted when Hua Cheng took his arm and raised it. There were even more patches of frostbite on his hands and feet, and many of the spots were bleeding due to all the frantic running and pulling he'd been subjected to recently. Xie Lian wasn't afraid of pain, but he *was* ticklish—and in spite of himself, fragmented memories from years past surfaced in his mind. The trembling, heated hands of a boy in a dark cave, random panicked touches, irregular breathing, and racing hearts...

At first, these memories were hazy and incredibly faint; Xie Lian had packed them away and tossed them into a corner of his mind long ago. But as the memories began to resurface, they had a surprisingly different taste, and it made Xie Lian want to hold his head and scream—especially with Hua Cheng right in front of him, doing very nearly the same things he'd done once upon a time. Xie Lian's face and mind were burning. He was afraid Hua Cheng would see his distress, but Hua Cheng didn't look at him at all; he fulfilled his promise completely and never crossed the line. He kept his head slightly turned away, averting his gaze from Xie Lian's half-exposed white shoulder.

Suddenly, a jeering voice rang out from behind Hua Cheng.

"Hua Cheng! You madman, what do you think you're doing to His Highness?! You're disgusting!"

Hua Cheng whipped his head toward the voice. Xie Lian looked past him to see who had reached the entrance of the cavern chamber.

The speaker was Mu Qing, with Feng Xin beside him. Despite being so recently wrapped in giant chrysalises, they had somehow broken free and found this place. Their faces had gone pale at the scene inside the cavern, and Xie Lian's face paled in turn.

What an awful sight!

Feng Xin pointed at Hua Cheng, then pointed at Xie Lian with his clothes peeled halfway off. It was a long moment before he could squeeze out, "You... You... Let him go right now!"

Hua Cheng quickly pulled Xie Lian's clothes back in place. "You useless trash dare hunt us down," he said coldly. "I think you're tired of living."

"Keep your filthy hands off him. Does the ugly toad want a taste of swan meat?"[4] Mu Qing sneered. "Never mind dreaming of it for eight hundred years—you can hope for a thousand more, but don't even *think* of touching a single one of His Highness's fingers!"

Xie Lian's heart dropped. But while the comments annoyed him, he could sense that something was amiss.

What was wrong with those two? They shouldn't have spewed such malicious words, even if Hua Cheng had beaten them to a pulp earlier—it was especially uncharacteristic of Mu Qing. It seemed like they were purposely trying to provoke Hua Cheng. But there was no reason for that; they knew they couldn't beat him, so what did they want? Moreover, their tone subtly pointed the spear in Xie Lian's direction. It was like they *wanted* to stir up confusion—as though they *wanted* Hua Cheng to do something to Xie Lian in a fit of anger.

Sure enough, darkness flashed over Hua Cheng's blanched face, and he threatened softly, "Since you both came seeking death—"

Xie Lian could see the naked murderous intent in his eyes, and horror filled him

"Don't!" he cried.

Too late. Hua Cheng unsheathed his scimitar, and Eming flashed cold.

Feng Xin and Mu Qing were both startled by the strike, and they reflexively looked down at themselves, but they saw no visible injuries on their bodies. Just a moment later, before they had the chance to breathe in relief or retaliate, the upper halves of their bodies split from their lower halves and fell to the floor with a thud.

Blood spurted and gushed, spilling over and flooding the ground.

---

4   癩蛤蟆想吃天鹅肉 / "A toad lusting for swan meat" is an idiom used to describe someone who lacks self-awareness and desires the impossible, especially an ugly person who romantically pursues someone significantly more attractive.

Xie Lian had never expected things to go like this. He lay limply on the stone bed, completely dumbstruck.

Hua Cheng had actually sliced Feng Xin and Mu Qing in half!

They weren't dead yet. They tumbled to the ground, one gritting his teeth, the other yelling furiously—it was a sight too tragic to witness. Hua Cheng's expression was frigid as he sheathed his scimitar. His face was dotted with only a few drops of blood, but the tinge of red complemented the aura of evil surrounding him and made him look even more striking.

Hua Cheng stood in the pool of blood for a moment, then turned to walk toward Xie Lian. Xie Lian stared with wide eyes at Hua Cheng's grim approach.

By the time Xie Lian snapped out of his stupor, Hua Cheng had already reached his side. He clutched one of Xie Lian's hands and pulled him up into an intense embrace.

"...How can I possibly let go?" he whispered.

Xie Lian couldn't speak, being held so tightly in his arms. And then Hua Cheng whispered something else in his ear. Xie Lian's heart was pounding so wildly he thought it might jump out of his chest...when he suddenly felt his body release.

The Command Talisman that Mu Qing stuck to his back had finally been released.

Even though Hua Cheng said he wouldn't let go, he still loosened his embrace just a little and let Xie Lian leave his hold once he released him from the Command Talisman. Xie Lian took a deep breath, then leapt to his feet and charged over to the pool of blood on the ground.

"Feng Xin? Mu Qing? Are you two all right?!"

Mu Qing's injuries were more severe; blood trickled from the corner of his mouth, and the light in his eyes had faded. But Feng Xin still had breath left, and he gripped Xie Lian's hand tightly.

"Your...Highness..."

Xie Lian clutched his hand in turn. "What? What do you want to say?"

Feng Xin swallowed a mouthful of blood and managed to grit out, "Watch out...for Hua Cheng... Don't go near him... He...he's a monster!"

It seemed that Feng Xin had used up all that remained of his strength to give Xie Lian that warning before he died. Unexpectedly, the expression on Xie Lian's face gradually calmed.

"Monster?" He let go of Feng Xin's hand and rose to his feet. "I wonder. Is he more of a monster than you two?"

That shocked Feng Xin. Without pausing for a response, Xie Lian drew Fangxin and pierced Feng Xin's heart, nailing him dead to the ground in a flash!

"Your Highness, you...!" Feng Xin sputtered in shock, but before he could finish, he stopped breathing.

Xie Lian withdrew Fangxin from Feng Xin's heart and shook it clean of blood before he retreated to Hua Cheng's side. He kept his sword pointed at the corpses on the ground all the while.

"Now that blood has been spilled, there's no need to keep talking through those skins."

"Ha ha ha..."

A jeering laugh echoed from the ground. Mu Qing's body had been sliced in half at the waist, but its head twisted around to show that it was the one laughing.

Its upper half was sprawled facedown, so even if it turned its head, its cheek should have still been pressed to the ground. But the corpse's head kept turning until it was fully backward and lifted it, laughing at Xie Lian all the while!

As suspected, these were not the real Feng Xin and Mu Qing but impostors from who-knew-where. The real Feng Xin and Mu Qing were still trapped in those giant white chrysalises trying to gnaw themselves free. That was what Hua Cheng had whispered when he released Xie Lian from the Command Talisman.

Their faces were pale not from shock or horror, but because they weren't human to begin with!

Xie Lian flashed his sword. "Feng Xin" and "Mu Qing" both smiled chillingly and replied in unison:

"As you wish."

They then melted into puddles of something that resembled thick blood. Hua Cheng moved to shield Xie Lian. The two bloody puddles flowed across the ground and merged into one, bubbling like they were boiling. Soon, the pool formed into the shape of a man. A chill spiked up Xie Lian's spine from waist to neck as he watched that indescribable mass contort itself and grow bit by bit.

Soon, "Feng Xin" and "Mu Qing" were completely gone. The person who had replaced them was a tall, slender young man dressed in white.

Judging by his size, the young man seemed to be about seventeen or eighteen years of age. He was wearing a mask, half of it crying, half of it smiling. While his face couldn't be seen, a youthful, crisp, bright voice came from behind the mask.

"How are you, Xie Lian?" he asked warmly.

Xie Lian's lips twitched unconsciously, and his mind went numb. Hua Cheng had been shielding him, but now the ghost king raised his blade and lunged at the man!

The white-clad man was dauntless in the face of Eming's wicked sharpness, and the blade missed him by mere millimeters as he sidestepped. In the span of a second, he flashed behind Hua Cheng. He reached for Xie Lian like he wanted to touch his face. Silver light streaked, and Hua Cheng blocked that hand, shielding Xie Lian once more.

Hua Cheng's voice was cold. "Keep your filthy hands off him."

He threw the warning right back at him! The white-clad man's right hand was severed by Eming's slash, and the limb fell to the ground.

But the man seemed like he'd barely noticed the injury. He simply shook out his expansive sleeve to briefly hide the severed limb, then shook the sleeve back again. A new hand had grown in the old one's place.

His fingers curled into claws, and he aimed directly for Hua Cheng's right eye!

It all happened in under a second. Hua Cheng dodged just as fast, but the attack still left two bloody scratches on his cheek.

For the first time, Hua Cheng faced an opponent he couldn't overtake in speed. His gaze turned sharp, and he changed tactics on the spot—he called forth millions of wraith butterflies, and they swarmed the man in a frenzy. The myriad butterflies wrapped the white-clad man inside a large, shimmering silver chrysalis, but that likely wouldn't last long. Hua Cheng was about to grab Xie Lian when the silver butterflies shrieked and exploded into sparkling powder!

Seeing the subtle change to Hua Cheng's expression as so many wraith butterflies were destroyed at once, Xie Lian knew that this wasn't good. The white-clad man had blown apart the wraith butterflies, and now he was hidden within the shimmering silver powder that choked the air. His newly grown hand struck out once more, aiming again for Hua Cheng's right eye!

This time, it was Xie Lian's turn. He pulled out Fangxin and slashed! His strike didn't just chop off the white-clad man's hand, nor his entire arm—it very nearly bisected him entirely.

Seizing the chance, Hua Cheng called out, "Your Highness, let's go!"
Xie Lian knew they shouldn't get entangled in this fight, and that they should quit while they were ahead. He retreated, and the two rushed out of the cavern together. They bolted down the dark tunnel, unhampered by any obstacles.

"It's *him*! He... He really didn't die!" Xie Lian exclaimed as he ran.

Hua Cheng led the way. He was faster and dashed easily, setting up butterfly formations and silk traps along the way to trip up any pursuers. "He might not be the original."

Xie Lian came to an abrupt stop and clutched his head. "No... I can feel it. He's the same! Not only is he still alive, but he's even stronger than before. Something let him be reborn... How else could he transform so easily into Feng Xin and Mu Qing? It's very difficult to impersonate heavenly officials—it should be nearly impossible to create fake skins of them!"

Hearing his tone go frantic, Hua Cheng also stopped and turned back. He took Xie Lian's hand and gripped it. "Don't be scared, Your Highness. He might not really be stronger. There's another possibility—he could be very familiar with Feng Xin and Mu Qing! That's why he could create fake skins of them. He must be someone all of you—"

Before he finished, Xie Lian's gaze fell to the hand that was clutching his own. Hua Cheng's words and expression both froze. He paled and withdrew his hand, tucked it behind his back, and turned to continue onward.

Xie Lian, however, didn't follow.

"San Lang," he called out.

Hua Cheng's body stiffened. He paused in his step but didn't look back. He only acknowledged, "Your Highness," in a carefully calm voice.

"A lot just happened, and everyone's a little flustered and confused," Xie Lian said from behind him.

"Mm," Hua Cheng answered.

"Everything is still kind of confusing, but I want to take the time to ask you a question," Xie Lian continued. "I hope you'll answer me honestly and seriously."

"...All right," Hua Cheng agreed.

"Who exactly is that 'noble, gracious special someone'?" Xie Lian asked solemnly.

Hua Cheng's finger—the one that was tied with the red affinity knot—subtly twitched a few times. He was silent for a while before he eventually answered, "If Your Highness already knows, then why ask?"

Xie Lian nodded. "I see. So I didn't misunderstand you. It really is true."

Hua Cheng didn't respond.

After a pause, Xie Lian asked, his tone flat, "Don't you want to know...how I feel about this?"

"..."

Hua Cheng inclined his head slightly—it was like he wanted to glance back but was too afraid to look Xie Lian in the eye. Only the two streaks of blood on his cheek could be seen.

"Your Highness, would you please...not tell me?"

His voice cracked as he asked.

"I'm sorry," Xie Lian said. "Something like this has to be made clear."

Hua Cheng didn't need to breathe, but he still sucked in a deep breath. Although his face was awfully pale, he still smiled and replied courteously, "That's true. It's for the best."

He was like a criminal on death row, waiting for his sentence. He closed his eye.

Yet his eye didn't remain closed for long—soon it snapped open once more as a pair of arms suddenly circled him from behind and caught him in a forceful embrace.

Xie Lian buried his face in Hua Cheng's back, but he didn't speak either. Though nothing was said, it was enough.

It was a long time before Xie Lian felt the man he was hugging turn around. Hua Cheng fervently returned the embrace, engulfing Xie Lian in his arms.

From above his head, Xie Lian heard Hua Cheng's staggering response. "Your Highness... You really will...be the death of me."

Just then, the sound of an explosion echoed through the deep recesses of the cave. A blinding white light flashed through the darkness, followed by a series of shrieks from the silver butterflies.

They both looked up, and their expressions changed. Xie Lian loosened his grip on Hua Cheng's sleeves.

"Let's talk later!" Xie Lian said.

And thus, the two continued on—except now they were running hand in hand.

Xie Lian's face was still hot, but he spoke with forced calm like nothing had happened. "San Lang, how did you discover that the Feng Xin and Mu Qing who approached us were dummies? Where are the real ones?"

Hua Cheng was in essentially the same state. "I left behind wraith butterflies to monitor the two useless pieces of trash. How could there be two *more* of them? Don't worry, Your Highness, they're fine. They won't die!"

"Then we have to release Feng Xin and Mu Qing from the chrysalises," Xie Lian said. "It'll be bad if he finds them while they have no way to fight back!"

"This way—follow me!" Hua Cheng answered.

The Cave of Ten Thousand Gods was indeed his territory. Even when they came to crossroads that branched into multiple different paths, he immediately and accurately knew which one to take. It wasn't long before they returned to the area where they'd left Feng Xin and Mu Qing. Even from a distance they could hear those two flinging accusations at each other and yelling.

"Why did you tell His Highness to run?! Now you've done it—he's been carried off!"

"What, should I have had him stand around to be butchered?!"

"Huh?! You just wanted him to distract Hua Cheng and lead him away! Am I wrong?!"

Xie Lian didn't know whether to laugh or cry. Both men in the giant white chrysalises on the wall were simultaneously gnawing at the silk and yelling at each other, and they were so surprised when they saw him return that they forgot to spit out the white silk dangling from their mouths.

"How did you escape?"

Xie Lian's bamboo hat was still on the ground where he dropped it, and he quickly picked it up and tied it around his neck. The heavy white silk released Feng Xin and Mu Qing before retreating into the shadows. The two of them tumbled to the ground, beaten black and blue. When they saw Hua Cheng emerge from behind Xie Lian, their faces twitched—they probably thought they were in for another round of beatings or that things would otherwise get rough again. However, when Feng Xin reached out to grab Xie Lian's arm and pull him back, Xie Lian grabbed hold of Hua Cheng first.

"Your Highness...?!" Feng Xin was flummoxed.

Hua Cheng was already starting to lead the way once more. "Gege, this way."

As if those two dared to follow him.

"Your Highness, why are you still with him?" Feng Xin questioned. "Didn't I tell you he's lost his mind?" Mu Qing said. "He's completely enchanted."

Xie Lian didn't bother to argue; he just gently but very firmly held on to Hua Cheng. "There's no time to explain now. Let's get out of here first—there's an enemy after us!"

With Xie Lian holding him like that, Hua Cheng's eye began to twinkle. A moment later, he smiled. "I suggest you both hold your tongues and follow. I'm in a good mood, so I won't fight you—for now."

Feng Xin and Mu Qing were left in complete disbelief by this display, complicated expressions plastered on their faces. They just couldn't comprehend why Xie Lian still walked so nonchalantly beside a terrifying devil who had stalked him for over eight hundred years with a mind full of unspeakable thoughts. It was like playing with fire and delighting in the burns.

Mu Qing was skeptical but eventually chose to focus on the other point. "You said there's an enemy here? This Cave of Ten Thousand Gods is *his* territory, so what kind of enemy could there possibly be? Did this enemy give him those scratches on his face? I doubt there are many out there who can injure Crimson Rain Sought Flower."

"It's White No-Face," Xie Lian replied.

At the sound of that name, Feng Xin and Mu Qing's faces both changed, and they followed Xie Lian without another word. They knew well that Xie Lian could joke or lie about anything except that one man. Xie Lian would never make light of him, nor would he ever mistake him.

Even though they'd just been fighting each other to the death in this Cave of Ten Thousand Gods, now they were fleeing like mad together.

"Just what is going on?!" Mu Qing demanded.

Xie Lian gave them an account of the white-clad man who had stolen their appearances, and they were both stunned.

"Disguised as us?! How is that possible!"

"It's true!" Xie Lian said. "Everything happened so fast, and I didn't get a good look, but it was absolutely you two at a glance!"

Feng Xin was dumbfounded. "But how can White No-Face still exist? Didn't the Emperor kill him?"

"I wouldn't be surprised if that thing can't be killed so easily," Mu Qing said. "Maybe it died at the time, but I'm sure it could revive itself given the right chance!"

That reminded Xie Lian of something, and he turned to Hua Cheng. "San Lang! Right after we made it into Mount Tonglu territory, you woke from your stasis with a start and urged us to hide from something. Did you sense him then?"

Hua Cheng gave a slight nod. "Yes."

"I knew it!" Xie Lian mumbled. "We chose the path to the west after that, but *he* was the one on the eastern path who'd killed thousands of ghosts. He's been reborn, but he's still a little weak—he needed to use the nefarious creatures coming to Mount Tonglu as a stepping stone... Now he's recovered and might be even stronger than before."

After all, he was the world's first Supreme Ghost King!

As they talked, Mu Qing noticed something amiss. "Your Highness, do you know where he's taking us? I don't think this is the way out."

It was Hua Cheng who replied. "Of course this isn't the way out, because there *is* no way out right now."

Feng Xin was astonished. "What? Isn't this cave your territory? You can't be lost!"

"Of course not…" Xie Lian replied in Hua Cheng's defense.

"White No-Face is blocking the path to the cave's exit," Hua Cheng explained. "If you think you can defeat him in your current state, then by all means don't follow me. I won't stop you. Go right ahead."

Feng Xin and Mu Qing were both from Xianle, of course—and just like Xie Lian, that creature had left an indelible shadow on their hearts. They didn't want to face him unless absolutely necessary.

Feng Xin gazed upward. "Can we punch through the top of the cave to get out?"

"The snowy mountain is above us. Do you want to start another avalanche?" Hua Cheng mocked.

Unfortunately, they had left the Earth Master Shovel with Yin Yu in case of emergency. Even if they did have it, none of them had studied how to use it, so they wouldn't be able to dig an escape route without making a racket and drawing attention.

"Then why are we running around aimlessly?"

"As long as we run around aimlessly, he'll chase us and we can lure him away from the exit," Xie Lian explained. "And then you two can use that chance to escape."

Mu Qing immediately caught the issue. "Wait… 'You two'? You mean you want to split up? One group is the bait to lead him away, while the other group escapes on their own?"

"Exactly!" Xie Lian said. "The Emperor must be informed that White No-Face has reappeared in the world. Once you both escape, find a way to notify the heavens—"

"Wait, wait!" Mu Qing cut him off. "You've already decided who's going to be bait and who's going to leave?"

Xie Lian shook his head. "I didn't decide. White No-Face did."

Mu Qing understood and didn't say another word—there was nothing they could do to choose who was pursued. Among their group, White No-Face would certainly be most interested in chasing Xie Lian!

"I will stay with you to face him," Feng Xin declared without hesitation.

In an emergency, Mu Qing had always been the one Xie Lian sent back to make a report, and Feng Xin had always stayed behind to assist him. It seemed that ancient history was about to repeat itself. But then Xie Lian glanced at Hua Cheng.

"Thanks! But there's no need. San Lang will stay with me."

"How can *he* be the one to stay? He..." Feng Xin blurted.

Hua Cheng's brow furrowed ominously, but Xie Lian only replied, "I trust him."

Although his voice was gentle, he was firm in his stance. Feng Xin was stunned in spite of himself.

"Your Highness..."

Xie Lian patted his shoulder. "You two go together. Mount Tonglu has closed its gates, so it's hard to say whether you'll even be able to get out to spread the word. Besides, don't you still need to search for...Lan Chang and the child?"

Feng Xin's face turned glum at this reminder.

A wraith butterfly emerged from the engravings on the vambrace around Hua Cheng's wrist. "Follow it," he said.

The two looked at Hua Cheng, then at Xie Lian.

In the end, Mu Qing said simply, "You two watch yourselves." With that, he turned and hurried after the silver butterfly down another tunnel. A moment later, Feng Xin followed.

The four thus parted at this fork in the road. As Xie Lian watched their retreating backs, another series of rumbling explosions echoed in the distance. The pair exchanged a look.

"He's here," Hua Cheng said darkly.

"Lead me," Xie Lian said.

The white-clad man had come after Xie Lian, as expected. To ensure he was kept at a safe distance, Hua Cheng set up wraith butterfly formations at various points in the caves to monitor the situation and slow their pursuer down. Every time an explosion went off and the wraith butterflies shrieked, Hua Cheng's expression grew grimmer and Xie Lian's heart ached. They wound around corner after corner until finally they reached a chamber.

Xie Lian couldn't help but sigh. "I can't believe it... So many silver butterflies have been lost."

While the wraith butterflies didn't have a good reputation in the Three Realms, Xie Lian saw them as nothing but sweet, adorable little spirits. He couldn't help but feel for them—they ceaselessly launched their suicidal attacks just to delay the enemy a few moments more.

But Hua Cheng only snorted. His gaze seemed to penetrate the thick rock walls, and he said, "Don't worry. If he kills one, I'll make ten more. Fast and furious as a storm, I will never back down. We'll see who's left standing in the end."

Xie Lian's heart skipped a beat for some reason, and he thought, *Oh no, this is bad.*

Although Hua Cheng had only displayed it subconsciously, Xie Lian really was quite weak to his aggressive, rebellious confidence.

Another moment passed, and Hua Cheng slowed his pace, seeming like he'd received some sort of signal. He turned to Xie Lian. "He's been led away. Those two are almost out."

"Great!" Xie Lian said. "Now we can take our time to come up with a strategy."

"Mm. There's no rush now," Hua Cheng said. "He's been left far behind. We can hide here for a while and think of a battle plan."

They both trailed off, and an awkward tension suddenly bloomed between them.

This wasn't the kind of awkwardness that stemmed from embarrassment; rather, they were both feeling strangely shy. With the creature hot on their trail and Feng Xin and Mu Qing with them, the feeling hadn't been nearly as obvious. But although Xie Lian had said, "Let's talk later," now that "later" had arrived and they'd caught their breaths, he had no idea what to say.

Xie Lian coughed lightly twice to clear his throat, then scratched his cheek with a finger. No matter what gesture he made, nothing felt quite right. He wanted to speak, but he worried that whatever he said would sound too abrupt, or too silly, or like he was trying too hard. In the end, he just hoped that Hua Cheng would say something first.

However, Hua Cheng's expression was just as strained. On the surface, he looked like he might have been seriously thinking through their battle plans, but it was hard to say whether that was true. The hands clenched behind his back were trembling slightly.

They walked past one particular divine statue. Most of the carvings in this Cave of Ten Thousand Gods were about the same size as the man himself, but this one was rougher in craftsmanship and it was shorter by half. When Xie Lian passed it, he casually peeled off the veil covering its head, and his eyes lit up.

"San Lang, did you carve this one too?"

Hua Cheng looked over and fell silent. It took him a moment to reply. "It was from my beginner years. Gege, stop looking at it."

That was clearly the truth—this divine statue was quite ugly indeed. Even though it was easy to tell that the sculptor had done his utmost to carve the perfect form he saw in his mind, his wish had been left unfulfilled due to the limits of his skill. While it wasn't cockeyed or crooked, the little figure was disproportionate in scale and smiled like it was mentally challenged.

Despite all that, the sculptor had still managed to include every single detail without fault. Xie Lian could easily tell that this was a God-Pleasing Crown Prince statue; its ears even had red dots for coral pearl earrings.

Xie Lian silently covered his mouth and turned away. He rubbed hard at his face in an attempt to seem natural.

Hua Cheng didn't know what to say, so he pleaded again as he tried to cover the statue with its veil. "Your Highness, please don't look at it anymore."

"Don't misunderstand! I think it's really cute!" Xie Lian hastily assured him.

But then he realized, wasn't *he* the one Hua Cheng had sculpted? If he called this thing cute, wasn't he basically calling *himself* cute? It'd be incredibly thick-skinned of him to lie so blatantly. Xie Lian couldn't help but laugh out loud. Seeing him like this, Hua Cheng bowed his head and lowered his lashes as he started to chuckle along with him.

As they both laughed, much of the nameless jittery air cleared away.

They continued onward and passed by another statue that was lounging on a stone bed. Its entire body was covered with a layer of thin, smoke-like white satin. Xie Lian was very curious and was just about to pull off the white veil over the divine statue's body when Hua Cheng unexpectedly seized his wrist.

"Your Highness!"

Ever since they entered this Cave of Ten Thousand Gods, Hua Cheng had mostly been calling him "Your Highness." Xie Lian looked at him, and while Hua Cheng let go of his wrist, he still seemed a bit uncomfortable.

"I already know it's a statue of me. I still can't look?" Xie Lian asked.

"If gege wants to look at statues, the best one I sculpted remains to be seen. I'll show you some other time. Don't look at any of the ones in this cave anymore," Hua Cheng said.

Xie Lian didn't understand. "Why? I think all the divine statues in this Cave of Ten Thousand Gods were carved really well. Really. It'd be a shame if I never got to see them. Which reminds me, those murals—"

"I'll go destroy them," Hua Cheng said promptly.

Seeing that he really planned to head off right now and do that, Xie Lian grabbed him hastily. "Don't, don't, don't! Why destroy them? Just because I saw them? Fine, fine, fine...I'll tell you the truth. I've only actually seen a few, like the one depicting the Shangyuan Heavenly Ceremonial Procession and the one of us in the army. I didn't see most of them because Feng Xin and Mu Qing wouldn't let me, so I have absolutely no idea what you painted. Don't destroy them!"

Only then did Hua Cheng turn to face him. "...Really?"

Xie Lian held on to him and replied with the utmost sincerity, "Really. If you don't want me to look, I won't."

Hua Cheng seemed to quietly sigh in relief, then he smiled. "They're no good anyway. If there's something you want to see, I'll just paint it for you on the spot."

This reaction made Xie Lian even more curious. But he didn't want to spur Hua Cheng into destroying those precious murals, so he could only push down his own desires.

After taking a few steps, Xie Lian suddenly frowned. "...Something's not right."

"What is it?" Hua Cheng asked.

Xie Lian turned to look at Hua Cheng. "White No-Face. Why would he come to Mount Tonglu?"

"Perhaps he hasn't fully regained his powers, and he wants to use the Kiln to be fully reborn into this world," Hua Cheng replied.

"If that's true...would it mean he's not currently a supreme?" Xie Lian wondered.

"That's...not entirely impossible," Hua Cheng said.

When White No-Face had dropped his disguise as Feng Xin and Mu Qing and attacked, his abrupt appearance had been both shocking and terrifying. Xie Lian's first reaction was to assume that their opponent couldn't be defeated, so he'd grabbed Hua Cheng and fled. But they hadn't actually fought him directly for long, so they couldn't precisely gauge White No-Face's current strength.

Was he putting on a front? Or was he stronger than he seemed? Nothing could be determined from a rushed exchange of blows that only lasted for a few seconds.

"I assumed he'd gotten stronger when I saw those two fake skins," Xie Lian muttered. "But maybe...he hasn't completely recovered. Maybe he's currently at his weakest. Otherwise, why would he come to Mount Tonglu? Maybe...I can give it a shot."

Give it a shot and try to take him down!

"Good. I'll go fight him," Hua Cheng immediately replied.

Xie Lian instantly snapped out of it and hastily said, "No, don't. Don't face him directly. My giving it a shot will be plenty!"

Supreme Ghost Kings would normally never face each other in combat so easily, as evidenced by the way Ship-Sinking Black Water and Crimson Rain Sought Flower had been able to coexist in peace. This was because ghost kings weren't like heavenly officials, whose profiles were well known to anyone who cared to keep track—from their strengths, to the parameters of their powers, to the size of their temples and number of worshippers. But ghost kings hid their true strength just as they hid their pasts. They possessed no knowledge of each other's abilities, and no one knew the potential consequences of a fight between two supremes. This encouraged them to maintain the balance at all costs.

"There's no need to worry," Hua Cheng said. "The victor hasn't been decided yet. Surely gege doesn't believe I would let you face him by yourself?"

Xie Lian shook his head. "...It's not that, San Lang. It's that we're not the same to him. He...won't kill me, I can swear it."

"Why?" Hua Cheng questioned.

After a moment of hesitation, Xie Lian chose not to explain. He only said, "You don't know how terrifying that creature is—"

Hua Cheng cut him off. "Your Highness, I *know*," he said grimly.

Only then did Xie Lian remember that Hua Cheng had also joined the Xianle army and personally experienced the Xianle battlefield. He'd seen the tragedy with his own eyes, the fields piled with corpses.

But Hua Cheng *didn't* know. He hadn't personally witnessed that horrific battle between Jun Wu and White No-Face. He had never crossed paths with White No-Face directly.

Having considered this, Xie Lian shook his head forcefully. "It's not that I don't trust you, it's just...I just...I don't want anything to happen to you."

Hua Cheng's eye twinkled at this. A moment later, he smiled. "Gege, don't worry. I'm already dead, so it won't be easy for me to die again. Besides, have you forgotten what I told you before? Unless he finds my ashes, he can't do anything to me."

Xie Lian had forgotten entirely that the ashes were a factor. He quickly said, "Wait! Everything else aside, San Lang, your... Have you stored your ashes somewhere safe?"

"A long time ago," Hua Cheng replied.

Xie Lian nodded, but a moment later he couldn't help but double check. "Are you sure they're properly hidden? That the hiding place is secure enough and won't be found?"

"To me, it's the safest place in the world," Hua Cheng answered leisurely.

Xie Lian didn't think there was anything absolute out there, however. "You're completely sure?" he pressed.

Hua Cheng smiled cheerfully. "If their hiding place is destroyed, then there's no need for me to exist either. Of course I'm sure."

Although Xie Lian was rather concerned about what "no need to exist" meant, they weren't in a safe place and there could be ears listening in. It wasn't the right time to probe this subject deeper, so he let it go. But it made Xie Lian want to ask Hua Cheng—just how had he died?

Xie Lian really wanted to know, but he didn't know how to ask. When mortals died, whether their souls could remain on the corporeal earth depended on their obsessions and attachments. In most cases, anguish and resentment were the strongest fixations. To become a Supreme Ghost King, one's obsession would have to be extraordinarily intense. So Xie Lian was afraid that Hua Cheng wouldn't be able to handle it if he asked about his death—it might cause him pain, like stabbing an old scar. And Xie Lian himself might not be able to bear the details either.

These past eight hundred years...how had Hua Cheng endured them?

A horrifying thought struck Xie Lian, and he was instantly awash in cold sweat. He quickly turned to Hua Cheng.

"San Lang!"

"What is it?" Hua Cheng answered.

Xie Lian's fingers twitched slightly. "I...I have another question I want to ask you."

"By all means," Hua Cheng replied.

Xie Lian stared at him. "Other than in Xianle, did you encounter me at another place or time at any point in the past eight hundred years?"

Hua Cheng slowly turned his head to look at him. "Regretfully... though I never gave up and did my utmost to find you, I did not."

Xie Lian pressed him. "Really?"

Hua Cheng looked him squarely in the eyes. "Really. Why does gege ask?"

Xie Lian sighed an imperceptible breath of relief and forced a smile. "Nothing. It's just... The way I passed my days in the earlier years wasn't the prettiest sight. I was a mess and very much a failure. I just wouldn't have wanted you to witness that."

Hua Cheng laughed. "How could that be?"

But Xie Lian didn't laugh at all. "It's not a joke. I really was quite the failure."

Hearing this, Hua Cheng withdrew his smile and turned solemn. "That's fine too. Your Highness, didn't you say so yourself?"

"Me?" Xie Lian was confused. "What did I say?"

"'To me, the one basking in infinite glory is you; the one fallen from grace is also you. What matters is *you*, not the state of you,'" Hua Cheng recited languidly as he gazed at Xie Lian. He blinked meaningfully, cocking an eyebrow. "I feel the same way."

Xie Lian was stunned speechless for a good moment, then he quickly slapped his hands over his face to cover it, feeling like his whole head was burning up. "D-did I say that?!"

"You did!" Hua Cheng insisted. "Gege, don't deny it."

Xie Lian used his arm to block his face. "I...I don't think so!"

"Gege, do you want to see the proof? I'll find it for you," Hua Cheng said.

Xie Lian's head shot up. "You... Did you... No way! San Lang, you... Have you been recording everything?!"

"I'm joking, joking."

"I honestly don't believe you..."

"Gege, trust me."

"I don't trust you anymore!"

The pair came to a fork in the road. Suddenly, a breeze blew in. Hua Cheng tilted his body to shield Xie Lian, raising an arm as if to protect him.

It wasn't a strong breeze and didn't call for anyone to block it, but Hua Cheng's action had come completely naturally. The wind passed, leaving strands of hair aflutter, tangled in the same way as Xie Lian's thoughts. Xie Lian noticed that Hua Cheng's expression and the contours of his face were cold when he wasn't looking his way. Beautiful in his nonchalance, Hua Cheng didn't even realize he'd moved without hesitation—as if protecting Xie Lian was innate to him.

"San Lang!" Xie Lian blurted again.

Hua Cheng tilted his head to look at him, and only then did he flash a smile. "What is it, Your Highness?"

Xie Lian felt that Hua Cheng probably didn't notice himself smiling. A clear and powerful voice in Xie Lian's heart told him that this man really saw him as a god.

Xie Lian's fingers clenched furtively. "Once we're out of Mount Tonglu, there's a lot I want to tell you."

Hua Cheng nodded lightly. "All right. I look forward to it."

"Have Feng Xin and Mu Qing escaped?" Xie Lian asked.

"They're already out," Hua Cheng replied.

"And White No-Face?" Xie Lian asked. "He didn't catch up to us, and he didn't go to stop them. Where is he now? How far is he from us?"

"He—" Hua Cheng's face changed before he could finish, and he lightly pressed two fingers against his right eyebrow. A moment later, he said, "...He disappeared."

"How could he disappear?" Xie Lian asked in shock.

Hua Cheng remained calm as he focused on searching. "He's just gone. Completely vanished."

This was impossible—not even a ghost could disappear into thin air while surrounded by wraith butterflies in this Cave of Ten Thousand Gods!

"Let me see?" Xie Lian blurted.

He gripped Hua Cheng's shoulders with his hands and went on tiptoe to touch their foreheads together. Hua Cheng rested a hand on Xie Lian's waist, then hesitated as if he was going to pull away. In the end, his hand stayed where it was and pulled Xie Lian even closer.

The scenes that Hua Cheng had seen moments earlier flashed before Xie Lian's eyes. The white-clad man strolled through a stone cavern. Countless wraith butterflies rushed him and wrapped him in a shimmering human-shaped chrysalis. In an instant, those butter-flies were engulfed in a crackling explosion of silver light, shattering them into a burst of sparkling glitter.

Once the silver light faded, the white-clad man was gone!

After that, Hua Cheng's right eye brought Xie Lian elsewhere in the caverns, sweeping through countless other tunnels. However, the white-clad figure was nowhere to be seen. Xie Lian was puzzled and pulled away slightly.

"Could he have left?"

Now that White No-Face had seen Xie Lian, he would stop at nothing to harass him. Others might not understand this, but Xie Lian knew it all too well.

"Maybe our earlier speculation was correct," Hua Cheng said. "His top priority is to use the Kiln to regain his supreme status, so he left ahead of us."

Hua Cheng's voice was right in Xie Lian's ear. He only came back to himself when he heard those words, and he realized that Hua Cheng's face was cupped in his hands. Xie Lian had pulled him down, making the taller man bend slightly at the waist. Xie Lian quickly let go.

"We have to stop him!" he cried.

Their mission was to prevent any candidates with the potential to become supremes from reaching Mount Tonglu. They'd run from the white-clad man earlier, but now that the situation was clear, they rushed through the countless divine statues in search of him. Before long, they reached the spot where he'd disappeared.

Other than some divine statues, there was not a single thing to be found. Silver shards of light covered the ground, and the little butter-flies that hadn't been completely destroyed by the shock wave were fluttering their broken wings. Xie Lian bent down; even if he didn't know whether it would help, he still wanted to cup them in his hands.

Just then, he heard Hua Cheng's voice from behind him. "...Gege, come over here by my side."

His voice was laced with suppressed anger, but the rage wasn't directed at Xie Lian.

Xie Lian looked up and saw that Hua Cheng's blazing gaze was trained on a divine statue ahead of them.

The statue was covered head to toe with a white veil, but the general shape of it could be made out. One section protruded sharply; it seemed to be pointing a sword.

A patch of caustic red at the sharp tip of the sword's point was spreading, staining, soaking the white silk veil.

There was blood on the sword!

Clearly there was something strange about this divine statue. Perhaps the original was no longer under the white silk and had been replaced with something else. Xie Lian leapt to his feet and stood at Hua Cheng's side, pointing the sword Fangxin at the strange form. Hua Cheng wore a dark expression. He gave a wave, and the white veil fell with the motion.

Xie Lian's pupils shrank.

It was a divine statue of Xie Lian beneath the white veil— a God-Pleasing Crown Prince statue. There was a sword in one hand, a flower in the other, and a smile on its face. But there were traces of blood on that smile.

The blood had come from the sword in its hand. A boy dangled there, pierced through. The boy had bandages covering his head and blood covering his body.

It was Lang Ying!

94

From the Sealed Kiln, One Supreme Shall Emerge

ANG YING'S HEAD had drooped to the side as though he'd lost consciousness. When Xie Lian saw it was him, he moved to save him without thinking—but he stopped dead in his tracks as his mind caught up with the situation. There was no one besides White No-Face here, so why would Lang Ying suddenly appear?

Seeing that the pure, holy statue of the God-Pleasing Crown Prince had been corrupted by dripping blood, Hua Cheng was obviously furious. His dark expression radiated rage, and the scimitar Eming exuded a chilling aura.

"Get the hell down," he said.

With that, "Lang Ying's" drooping head actually heeded and righted itself. He blinked open his eyes, then slowly pulled himself off the sword and dropped to the ground.

When White No-Face blew up the wave of silver butterflies that had surrounded him, he had used the distraction that the blinding silver light provided to hide himself under this divine statue's white veil, then he'd transformed. If he could disguise himself as Lang Ying, it meant he must've seen the boy somewhere before.

"Where's the real Lang Ying?" Xie Lian demanded.

"Your Highness, maybe there never was a 'real' Lang Ying," Hua Cheng said.

If "Lang Ying" had never existed to begin with and was only White No-Face in his weakened form, everything would be easy to explain. But when Xie Lian remembered the girl Xiao-Ying who had died on Mount Yujun, he wished that explanation made less sense than it did.

Xie Lian swiftly thought of another possibility. "Or perhaps...he devoured Lang Ying."

The "Lang Ying" before them was growing taller. His body stretched upward, and the bandages on his face unwrapped and dropped away to reveal the mask beneath. He lifted his head slightly when he heard Xie Lian's guess and seemed to smile.

"You guessed right."

So it was true.

After White No-Face was pulverized and dispersed by Jun Wu, all that was left of him was a wisp of a broken soul wandering the Mortal Realm. He drifted for who knows how long—and at some point in all that time, he met the ghost Lang Ying. He must've somehow coaxed or deceived Lang Ying into hosting him within his own body since his remnant soul might have been too weak to devour him outright. He had stayed glued to Lang Ying's body and gradually recovered, and the end result was standing before Xie Lian and Hua Cheng. Ghost-devouring ghost—White No-Face had bitten the hand that fed him, his host Lang Ying. Just as He Xuan had devoured the Reverend of Empty Words, Lang Ying had become White No-Face's slave.

It only took a few moments for "Lang Ying" to completely transform into White No-Face.

Hua Cheng eyed him. "Why would Lang Ying agree to lend you his spirit body?"

A request like that would be like a stranger asking a homeowner to open their doors and allow them to live there and eat their food. Lang Ying had survived as a ghost for hundreds of years—although he was timid and hesitant, he shouldn't have been so foolish.

"I can of course provide an answer to your question," White No-Face replied amiably. "But are you sure the one beside you wants to hear it?"

Hua Cheng looked at Xie Lian, whose expression was slightly strange. He surprisingly didn't notice the gaze sent his way.

"Surname Lang, Yong'an, and he suffers from Human Face Disease," White No-Face said. "Why did he agree to let me eat him? Can't you guess?"

Xie Lian's face instantly went pale. Veins popped on the backs of his hands, and he swung his sword with a shout of, *"Shut up!"*

White No-Face sidestepped and avoided the strike, but Xie Lian's attack sliced through the sword in the hands of his own divine statue. Now he'd done it—he'd left the God-Pleasing Crown Prince statue wielding a broken sword, making the statue itself a ruined artifact. Xie Lian snapped out of his frenzy like he'd been drenched by a bucket of cold water.

The wraith butterflies seemed outraged and swarmed over. White No-Face appeared completely unbothered and gave a toneless laugh as he covered his face with his sleeve. In an instant, he vanished into the darkness, leaving their conflict entirely.

Xie Lian stared at the broken stone sword on the ground. "I'm sorry—" he murmured to Hua Cheng automatically.

Hua Cheng cut him off. "Isn't it silly for Your Highness to apologize to me? He's gone. Now what?"

Xie Lian pulled himself together somewhat. "Did he flee? We can't let him enter the Kiln!"

The pair hurried out of the Cave of Ten Thousand Gods and back onto the snowy mountain. Right as they made it outside, they felt the earth quake and the mountain shake. Looking up, they saw even more waves of snow crashing down. This roaring avalanche was even larger than the one they had experienced before—it was as if something massive buried under the heavy snow was just waking up, and it was roaring and shaking off thousands of years of built-up snow.

"Can we still make it up there?!" Xie Lian cried.

Hua Cheng gripped his hand firmly. "We can if you follow me!"

They faced off against the crashing current of ice and snow. Their passage was grueling and perilous, and for every step forward they were forced three steps back, but they managed to avoid the most violent waves of snow and rubble and the countless pits as they blazed their trail up the mountain.

Finally, they reached the highest point. The volcano's peak was coated in an unfathomably thick layer of ice. Xie Lian thought he'd slip if he tried going even a bit faster, but Hua Cheng led him by the hand and moved forward with steady, fearless steps.

The pair came before the volcano's enormous mouth—a cavernous maw that seemed to snarl at the heavens. When Xie Lian peered into its depths, he saw nothing but complete darkness. Maybe it was his imagination, but he thought he saw a red light pulsing horribly in the deepest recesses. Sometimes it was there, sometimes not.

Xie Lian could feel himself starting to panic. He held his bamboo hat to his head to keep it from being torn away by the snowy winds. "Did he go in already?"

Hua Cheng glanced inside, and his expression turned grim. "Yes."

"How do you know?"

"The Kiln is closing."

That caught Xie Lian off guard. "What's going on? Why is it closing so soon? Don't there need to be at least a few ghosts inside before the slaughter can begin?"

"That's usually true," Hua Cheng said. "However, if the Kiln believes an entrant has an extremely high chance of breaking through, it will close upon their request." After a pause, he added, "That's what I did back then."

"So is he a supreme or not?" Xie Lian asked. "What will happen if a Supreme Ghost King enters the Kiln again?"

"The same thing that happens to an ascended heavenly official facing another Heavenly Tribulation."

In other words, his strength would increase exponentially! If they allowed White No-Face to pass this obstacle, the consequences were unimaginable—and once he emerged from the mountain, Xie Lian would surely be the first one he'd seek out.

After eyeing that infinite, bottomless abyss for a while, Xie Lian said slowly, "San Lang, I...I might need to go down there to resolve this."

"Then go. I'll come with you," Hua Cheng replied quietly.

Xie Lian gazed at him. Hua Cheng looked up and met his eyes. He cocked an eyebrow and smirked.

"All we're doing is heading inside to eliminate an eyesore, then breaking through the Kiln again. That's it. It's not like it's hard."

Seeing him so relaxed, Xie Lian's tensed emotions loosened a little as well, and he smiled.

A moment later, Hua Cheng said, "However, there is one thing."

Xie Lian made a curious noise and tilted his head. One of Hua Cheng's arms suddenly snaked around Xie Lian's waist and pulled him into his arms, and he lifted Xie Lian's chin gently with his hand. And then, Hua Cheng enveloped Xie Lian's lips with his own.

They kissed and embraced for a long time in the snowstorm before their lips slowly parted. Xie Lian was dazed for a good moment before he jolted out of his stupor. Flushed, he opened his eyes.

"Wh-what was that all of a sudden?!"

Although it wasn't the first time they'd done this, they had always used grand, dignified reasons to justify their actions—things like "lending spiritual powers," "transferring air," or "it was simply an accident." But now that certain things had been made clear, those excuses were exposed as falsehoods, and their actions were abruptly far more significant.

Xie Lian didn't know where to put his hands—should he cling to Hua Cheng's arms or push him away? Should he press Hua Cheng's head down or block his face?

Hua Cheng puffed a breath into his ear. "I'll lend Your Highness a bit of spiritual power in case of an emergency..." he whispered. "Won't you accept it?"

Xie Lian unconsciously gulped. "Th-this is 'a bit'?" he stuttered. "It seems like too much... I haven't...I haven't paid you back for all the times before..."

"It's not that much. And there's no rush," Hua Cheng said. "Take your time paying it back. The account will clear one day."

Xie Lian made a few vague noises of agreement and was just about to run away when Hua Cheng pulled him to a stop.

"Your Highness! Where are you going? You're running in the wrong direction," he pointed out.

Only then did Xie Lian realize that he was running back the way they'd come. He quickly turned back around, slipping on the ice in the process. He pulled his bamboo hat down.

"I...I wasn't... I-I'm just a little cold. Thought I'd jog around a bit to warm up..."

He put on the bamboo hat, then pushed it off to carry it on his back, then put it on again. Finally, he grabbed Hua Cheng's hand and held it tight. The pair stood side by side and looked into the immense abyss below.

Hua Cheng's voice was casual. "After this is resolved, I'll show gege my proudest achievement in sculpture."

"Okay," Xie Lian replied.

They jumped down together.

Gusts of wild wind whipped past his ears so fiercely that it felt like waves crashing into him. But even that force couldn't separate their hands—they held on to each other even harder.

Yet somehow, halfway down, Xie Lian's hand was empty.

His grip hadn't slipped, and Hua Cheng hadn't let go—the hand he'd been holding in his own had simply disappeared in an instant, leaving behind nothing but emptiness.

Xie Lian's heart lurched, and he shouted, "San Lang?!" He was falling so quickly that his cry was left dozens of meters above his head. It sounded unreal.

It was a long time before Xie Lian finally landed steadily on his feet. He immediately stood upright and called out again.

"San Lang?"

There was no answer. The hollow echo of the name told him of the immense size of the empty space where he was standing.

There was darkness all around except for above. Xie Lian looked up. He could see a snow-white sky above his head, but it was gradually shrinking. That had to be the Kiln's mouth closing.

But where was Hua Cheng?

Crackle, whoosh. Xie Lian lit a palm torch, hoping to illuminate his surroundings and see what things were like down here. But the darkness was immeasurably deep, and this little flame couldn't show him anything. The firelight itself seemed to be absorbed by the indifferent, dark void.

Xie Lian hadn't controlled his powers well in his haste, and the flames erupted a little too high, nearly burning his face. He quickly tossed the fire to the ground.

As it fell, the firelight just happened to illuminate the back of a faint white silhouette looming not far away.

Xie Lian was instantly on guard. "Who's there?!"

The white silhouette turned around and answered evenly, "You know who I am."

Although he answered, the muscles on the man's face did not move an inch. That was only natural, as he was wearing a half-crying, half-smiling mask.

"*San Lang!*" Xie Lian blurted.

Even though the sight of that face sent terror shivering through him, Xie Lian hadn't cried out due to fear but due to worry. Of course, there was still no answer, and the crying-smiling mask came another step closer.

"You're wasting your time yelling. The Kiln is sealed. It's only you and me here....no one else."

Xie Lian automatically looked up again. Earlier there had still been a small snowy-white sliver of sky, but that bit of light had been completely swallowed by the darkness around them. The Kiln had truly sealed itself.

Xie Lian had never expected things to turn out like this—trapped alone with White No-Face, just the two of them, locked inside the Kiln.

Just the two of them? Why was it the two of them?!

Xie Lian gripped Fangxin and pointed the sword at him. "What is going on here? Are you meddling again? Where is he? Where is he right now?"

White No-Face clamped the edge of the sword between two

fingers and flicked the blade with his other hand, making it ring clear and crisp. "He's gone."

Xie Lian watched this, and his eyes went cold. "Explain yourself clearly. What do you mean, 'gone'?"

"He doesn't want to follow you anymore. He left. He's dead. What do you think?" White No-Face said leisurely.

Xie Lian's heart dropped at first, but that was followed immediately by a violent rage, and he struck. "Stop your nonsense!"

White No-Face once again caught the blade effortlessly. "Fine, fine. I was indeed talking nonsense. Don't worry, I simply sent him outside the Kiln. Even if he wants to rush back in here, it's too late now."

Xie Lian was fine with Hua Cheng trapped outside as long as it meant he was okay. He quietly sighed a breath of relief.

"But it's probably for the best that he doesn't come in," White No-Face continued. "Even if he wouldn't agree right now, who knows if he'll still want to be with you when he sees what you'll become."

Xie Lian couldn't formulate a response. His patience fully gone, he swung his sword again, yelling, *"Shut up!"*

White No-Face easily dodged every single one of his strikes, and Xie Lian cried out in rage.

"I've had enough of you! What do you want? What *exactly* do you want?! How long are you going to keep clinging to me?! Why aren't you dead? Why did you come to the Kiln?!"

"Because of you!" White No-Face replied.

Xie Lian's movement faltered, and he huffed. "What do you mean?"

"You came here, so I did too," White No-Face answered languidly.

Xie Lian's expression twisted upon hearing that. But no matter how furious he was, how strong his murderous intent, it was as if

White No-Face could always predict his next strike and avoided each attack by mere millimeters. The more Xie Lian struck, the more he understood one cruel fact:

He couldn't win!

"That's right," White No-Face said, like he was reading his mind. "You can't win."

As soon as he spoke those words, a blade pierced Xie Lian's wrist. Excruciating pain spread throughout his body, and Xie Lian's grip on his sword faltered. In the next second, White No-Face grabbed him by the hair and yanked him backward, bashing him into the ground!

Xie Lian's ears were ringing, his nose and mouth were filled with the metallic taste of blood, and his head swam.

A little while later, Xie Lian felt a hand pull his head up from the shattered ground. A voice came from above.

"So sad, so pitiful."

Xie Lian choked out a mouthful of blood.

"Every time I meet Your Highness, you always look like this," White No-Face said. "Makes one ache. Makes one excited."

Xie Lian swallowed another mouthful of blood, refusing to cough it out. "...Don't be too smug," he croaked. "I might not be able to win against you, but...someone can. Even if you emerge from the Kiln, Jun Wu will just kill you again."

Besides, there was still Hua Cheng!

Yet White No-Face replied, "Who says I'm the one who will emerge from the Kiln?"

Xie Lian was shocked.

Not him? Who else could it be?

White No-Face lifted Xie Lian's face to look him in the eyes. "Your Highness, I think you might have misunderstood," he said amiably. "A supreme certainly will emerge from the Kiln, but it won't be me. It will be you."

"...What did you say?" Xie Lian stammered, shaken to the core. "I'm not..."

He understood before he even finished his sentence. His body broke out in a cold sweat.

"That's right. That's exactly it," White No-Face said. "Congratulations, you finally understand my real objective. Isn't this the 'Third Path' you love so much?"

Right now, the only beings inside the Kiln were one supreme ghost and one god. On the surface, there were only two paths to take: either White No-Face would kill him and break through the Kiln, or they could forget about leaving and remain trapped inside forever.

But there was a third path. If Xie Lian killed himself, became a ghost, and defeated White No-Face, then he could become a supreme and break through the Kiln!

Xie Lian struggled to snap out of his shock. "...What the hell do you want?! Don't even think about it! Why must you go this far— why would you force me to become a supreme? I'm not as crazy as you! Even if you want me to kill you, we both know that I *can't*! And if you feign defeat, the Kiln might not recognize me!"

But White No-Face replied, "Is that right? You can't defeat me? Don't be so sure."

As he spoke, he extended a hand. Thanks to the nearby firelight, Xie Lian could see that he was holding a mask—an exact duplicate of the one White No-Face wore.

"Do you remember this crying-smiling mask?" White No-Face asked. "It suits you well."

Xie Lian's eyes bulged. Terror crawled into his mind like a densely packed tide of insects.

"Take it away, take it away...*take it away!*" he forced out weakly.

White No-Face started to laugh. "It seems Your Highness's memory isn't very good. So why don't you let me help you remember, hmm?"

He had no chance to protest. The tragically pale crying-smiling mask melded with the infinite darkness as it was pressed heavily onto Xie Lian's face.

Heaven Official's Blessing

TIAN GUAN CI FU

ARC 4

White-Clothed Calamity

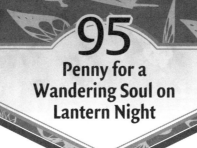

XIE LIAN JOLTED awake in horror.

Drenched in a cold sweat, he shot upright from where he'd been lying and buried his face in his hands.

He'd been jolted awake by a terrible nightmare. In it, his father and mother had committed suicide by hanging themselves with a white silk band. He had stared at their bodies with neither joy nor grief. He'd had no tears left to cry. Instead he woodenly prepared another white silk band for himself. Just as he stuck his head into the knot, he saw a white-clad man standing below him. The man was wearing a cry-smiling mask and was jeering at him. His heart jumped, the knot tightened, and crushing suffocation seized him.

And then, he woke up.

It was already daylight outside the window, and a voice came from the other side.

"Your Highness! Are you awake?"

"I'm awake!" Xie Lian answered offhandedly.

He violently panted for breath for a long while before he realized that he wasn't sitting on a bed, but a straw mat. Although it was layered with plenty of straw and was unusually soft, it still wasn't quite comfortable for him. Even now, he wasn't used to such crude, simple bedding.

The one who had called for him was Feng Xin. He had gone out early in the morning and had just returned with food, and now he was outside urging Xie Lian to take his meal. Xie Lian acknowledged him and crawled out of bed.

The sense of suffocation in his dream was too real, and Xie Lian's hand unconsciously went to his neck to touch it. He had only wanted to verify whether there really was a strangulation mark left there by a white silk noose—but unexpectedly, he did feel something.

Xie Lian was startled at first, and he pounced to grab a mirror that had been tossed nearby on the ground. When he looked at his reflection, he realized he had been touching the band of the black collar encircling his neck. He finally calmed himself and remembered everything.

It was the cursed shackle.

Xie Lian's fingers probed at it.

There weren't many privileges afforded to those banished from the heavens other than their now-mortal forms aging slower than a normal human's. However, Jun Wu had shown mercy when he made Xie Lian's cursed shackle and had added some accommodating clauses.

While the cursed shackle locked away Xie Lian's spiritual powers, it also sealed his age and his physical body—he could neither grow old nor die. Furthermore, Jun Wu had told him this: *"Everything in your previous life shall be forgiven if you manage to ascend again, and this shackle will be removed."*

But being forced to wear it was a bone-deep humiliation—it was hardly different from a brand seared onto a criminal's face. Xie Lian grabbed a white silk band from nearby and moved to pull it over his head. Yet the moment he raised his hand, he recalled the terrifying feeling of slow strangulation from his dream. He hesitated.

In the end, he still wrapped the white silk band thoroughly around his neck and the bottom half of his face before going out.

Feng Xin and Mu Qing were already waiting for him outside. Feng Xin had brought back steaming hot buns and Mu Qing was slowly munching on one. Feng Xin passed two over to Xie Lian, but Xie Lian lost his appetite when he saw how bland, dry, and crude they were. He shook his head, refusing them.

"Your Highness, you have to eat *something* in the mornings. We have to work, and it's not the kind that gets done sitting around," Feng Xin said.

Mu Qing didn't bother looking up. "Yeah. You can turn it down, but there's nothing else to eat. You can pass out again if you want, but you'll still have to eat this in the end."

Feng Xin glared at him. "Watch your tone."

Xie Lian had only lived as an ascended being for a few years, but he'd forgotten what it was like to need to eat. A few days ago, he had nearly fainted and had only realized afterward that he hadn't eaten anything for several days. This was the incident Mu Qing was referring to.

Xie Lian didn't want the two of them to start fighting so early in the morning, so he quickly changed the subject. "Let's go. We don't even know if we'll find any work today."

Not only had Xie Lian once been royalty, but he had also once possessed a celestial body that needed no sustenance—naturally, he'd never needed to worry about working for a living. But now... although he was still a crown prince, the Kingdom of Xianle was no more; although he was still a god, he had long been banished. Since he was essentially no different from a mortal at present, he needed to take care of all the normal matters of living. The trade of a cultivator was usually ghost-catching and performing religious services, but it wasn't as though there was a constant supply of nefarious creatures to be exorcized or rituals that needed to be performed every day. Most of the time, they needed to find other temporary work, such as helping transport goods here or performing manual labor there.

But even these odd jobs weren't always easy to get. There were far too many displaced, impoverished civilians right now, people who wouldn't even ask for a wage when they saw there was work—they'd be willing to labor in exchange for a bun or half a bowl of rice. They'd swarm the open positions, and Xie Lian and his coterie couldn't possibly compete. Even if they managed to grab something, after weighing the situation, Xie Lian might decide that someone else needed the work more.

Sure enough, they wandered for half the day and still they found nothing.

"Can't we find something more stable and respectable to do?" Mu Qing grumbled.

"Rubbish. If something like that existed, we would've found it a long time ago," Feng Xin said. "You need to show your face at any respectable job, and who doesn't recognize His Highness? How would any stable work remain that way if he was recognized?"

Mu Qing stopped talking, and Xie Lian wrapped the white bandage covering the lower half of the face tighter. Indeed, they would have to flee if anyone recognized who he was, or they'd risk being beaten and chased away. Even if they applied for work as armed escorts, what employer would be comfortable hiring someone with an unknown background who wouldn't show his face? They couldn't exactly take up work as hitmen either, so their choices were very limited.

Gods didn't need to worry about hunger, but mortals needed to eat. Xie Lian had never had to consider these matters when he was young, so this was the first time in decades that such a problem really seized him. Still, how could a god possibly understand the feelings of a starving devotee if they didn't even know how it felt? How could they possibly empathize? At this point, he could only try to think of this experience as a form of training.

A sudden cacophony of gongs and drums came from not far away, and a large crowd started to gather to see what was happening. The three followed along and went over to watch. A few clowns and martial artists were hollering with all their might—they were martial street buskers.

"If all else fails, why don't we go busk?" Mu Qing tried suggesting, not for the first time.

Xie Lian was considering the same thing, but Feng Xin spoke up before he could respond.

"Don't be silly," he said as he watched the buskers perform. "His Highness is highborn. How could he do something like that?"

Mu Qing rolled his eyes. "We've already carried bricks, so how is busking any different?"

"By carrying bricks, we feed ourselves using our own physical strength," Feng Xin said. "Busking is entertainment for the masses; we would be forced to act as fools purely for their amusement. Of course it's different!"

One of the clowns who was hopping around tripped and fell. The crowd roared with laughter as he pulled himself up and bent at the waist to bow, then picked up some scattered coins the crowd tossed to the ground. A deep discomfort surfaced in Xie Lian's mind at the sight, and he shook his head forcefully, striking out busking as a viable path of employment.

"Fine," Mu Qing replied, squinting at the display. "Then let's start pawning stuff."

"We've already pawned a lot of stuff," Feng Xin said. "Otherwise, we wouldn't have made it until now. Anything that's left can't be pawned."

At that instant, surprised shouts rippled across the crowd. Someone yelled, "The soldiers are here! The soldiers are here!"

With that, the crowd broke up. Soon, a band of soldiers strutted down the street with an impressive air, holding weapons in their hands and sporting shiny new armor. They were interrogating anyone who appeared suspicious. Xie Lian and his coterie hid in the crowd and overheard the conversation of the people nearby.

"Who are they after?"

"Don't worry, they're not here to arrest us. I heard they're trying to capture the Xianle royals who are still at large."

"Apparently someone saw suspicious characters around here, so the city has been really strict with their searches lately."

"Really?! My goodness, did they actually flee *here*?!"

Xie Lian and his companions exchanged looks.

"Let's hurry back and check on things," Xie Lian whispered.

The other two nodded. They silently left the crowd, splitting up. They only met up again after they'd walked a fair distance and confirmed they hadn't attracted any attention, and once reunited, they hurried away.

They ran until they reached a small mountain forest out in the middle of nowhere. Xie Lian could see a thick column of smoke coming from within the trees, and terror struck him. Could the Yong'an soldiers have already discovered this place and set fires to kill them off?

They rushed until they found a rundown little cottage hidden in the trees, left behind by some unknown hunter. The thick smoke was coming from inside that cottage.

"Mother!" Xie Lian blurted. "What's going on?! Are you there?"

A woman immediately emerged and greeted him happily. "My son? You've come?"

It was the queen. She was dressed in simple clothes and had grown quite thin—she looked fairly different from the noble lady she'd once been. Seeing that his mother was fine and that her face was full of delight, Xie Lian relaxed—but he quickly asked, "What's with the smoke?"

"It's nothing, really. I just wanted to do a little cooking today..." the queen replied, embarrassed.

Xie Lian didn't know whether to laugh or cry. "Don't! What cooking? Just eat the food Feng Xin and Mu Qing bring you every day. The smoke is too conspicuous; where there's smoke, there's people. You'll attract the Yong'an soldiers. We bumped into them in the city earlier. This city is tightening its security, so we'll need to move again."

Feng Xin and Mu Qing entered the cottage to extinguish the source of the smoke. The queen didn't dare to be negligent either, so she went to the back room of the cottage to talk to the king.

Feng Xin came back outside. "Your Highness, you aren't going inside to see His Majesty?" he whispered.

Xie Lian shook his head. "No."

The two of them, father and son...one the king of a fallen kingdom, and the other a banished god. It was hard to say which was the more pathetic, the more disgraced of the pair. If they were forced to sit down and face each other, they'd only glare at one another instead of having a heart-to-heart. Avoiding that confrontation entirely was for the best.

"Mother, why don't you start getting packed? We'll leave today," Xie Lian called out. "We'll come pick you up in the evening and head out."

The queen hurried outside again. "My son, you're leaving so soon? You haven't visited in days. Why leave so quickly?"

"I have to go train," Xie Lian said.

In truth, he was going to look for work—they couldn't possibly support this many people if he didn't.

"Have you eaten yet this morning?" the queen asked.

Xie Lian shook his head. The three of them were starving.

"That's terrible for your body," the queen said. "Fortunately, I just stewed a pot of congee. Come in and grab a bite."

Xie Lian wondered, *Why was there so much smoke if it was just a pot of congee? It looked like an entire palace was in flames...*

The queen turned to Feng Xin and Mu Qing. "You two children come eat with us too."

Feng Xin and Mu Qing hadn't at all expected to receive such treatment and tried to decline, but the queen was adamant. The two could only timidly sit down at the table, feeling rather surprised. In a good way.

But when the queen brought the pot over, their surprise soon turned to dread.

Even after they got back to the city, Mu Qing's stomach was still churning. "I thought...the congee, smelled like, bran water, but I hadn't imagined, it'd taste like, it too!" he said, stumbling over his words.

Feng Xin gritted his teeth. "Shut up! Don't force us to remember that stuff! The queen is...highborn, after all... Never cooked... This is already... *Ugh!*"

Mu Qing humphed. "Am I wrong? If you don't think it tasted like bran water, why don't you...go ask the queen to grant you another bowl?! *Ugh!*"

The two were heaving as they argued back and forth, and Xie Lian grabbed hold of both of them to pat their backs.

"Get ahold of yourselves! Look, up ahead...it seems there's some work available!"

As the three stumbled over, they could see a couple of little ringleaders shouting on the streets, looking for hired help. The pay was fairly decent, and there wasn't a limit on the number of hands needed; they would take anyone who came. The three of them quickly signed up and joined the large group of disheveled, bone-skinny paupers. They were led to a muddy, empty field. It seemed the landowner intended to build a new residence here, so the area needed to be overhauled—and filling in the grounds came first. The trio worked hard, and they were quickly covered in mud.

Feng Xin hauled earth as he hugged his stomach, his face green and his mouth cursing. "Fuck me...! I think that pot of stewed bran water turned into a spirit in my stomach!"

Xie Lian was carrying a basket full of dirt. He looked back and said in a hushed voice, "Can you hang in there? Or...do you want to sit down for a bit?"

Mu Qing turned to Xie Lian. "Why don't *you* go rest?"

"No. I can still hang on," Xie Lian replied.

Mu Qing rolled his eyes. "Don't be stubborn. I'm the one who has to wash your dirty clothes. I'd rather do your part of the work."

Not far in the distance, someone yelled, "Put your backs into it and don't talk! No slacking! You wanna get paid?"

Feng Xin was tenacious and continued to persevere, hauling twice as much mud as he had before. "It's not like this pays that well—why make so much fuss? Who do they think they are?"

After a grueling day of toil from noon to sunset, the work was finally done. The trio weren't completely physically exhausted, but their hearts were significantly more tired than their bodies—they had worked so hard for only a pittance and a bite to eat. When they were finally free, they lay down to rest on a part of the field that was slightly cleaner.

Just then, another rowdy, noisy group approached. Some men had arrived, their pace slow as they hauled a stone statue.

Xie Lian looked up slightly. "What statue is that?"

Mu Qing glanced at it as well. "Maybe a new divine statue to guard this place."

Xie Lian said nothing.

If this was the past, the one chosen to watch over a residence would have undoubtedly been one of his own crown prince statues. But now, he didn't know which god it'd be. It was most likely Jun Wu, or perhaps a newly ascended official.

Xie Lian did nothing for a long moment, but he just couldn't resist wanting to see who had replaced him. He forced himself to stand up and shuffled over to the crowd to take a look.

The stone statue's back was facing him, so he couldn't see the face clearly. However, it seemed to be kneeling. Now Xie Lian was even more curious—which heavenly official would have a kneeling statue? He circled all the way around to get a better look.

When he saw the statue's face, his entire mind went blank.

The divine statue's face was his own!

The kneeling statue was settled onto the ground, and someone rudely patted its head.

"Finally got done hauling this thing. This bastard's pretty heavy!"

"Why drag over a statue like this one? It's kinda ugly. Why not get one of the Heavenly Emperor? Isn't this what's-his-face..."

"It's *that* one, right? Didn't they say that praying to him brings bad luck now? You guys still dare to do it? And going out of your way to transport his statue all the way here..."

"Now, now. None of you get it. Worshipping a God of Misfortune would obviously bring bad luck, but this statue isn't for worshipping—it's for stepping on. If you step on a God of

Misfortune, doesn't that mean everlasting good fortune is guaranteed?"

Understanding dawned on the crowd. "That's so clever! Brilliant!"

Feng Xin and Mu Qing could sense something wrong, and they too fell silent when they saw it. Feng Xin was about to explode, but Mu Qing held him back, warning him with his eyes.

"The crown prince himself hasn't started anything, so what are you going to yell about?" he said under his breath.

Indeed, he was keeping quiet. Feng Xin wasn't sure whether Xie Lian had a reason to stay silent, so he didn't dare move recklessly and forced himself to swallow his angry words. However, his eyes were blazing like flames.

Finally, someone grumbled, "Isn't this rather...inappropriate? He was once a god—a crown prince."

"Oh, please. Xianle has fallen, so what's he crown prince of?"

"You're wrong. There's nothing inappropriate about stepping on a God of Misfortune," another man added. "In fact, he should thank us."

Xie Lian suddenly spoke up. "Oh? Why should he thank you?"

"Have you seen the thresholds of temples?" the man presumptuously began to explain. "They're trampled by thousands, hundreds of thousands. And does my lord know how many wealthy households fight to pay for a temple's threshold to act as their substitute? Every step on that threshold will absolve them of a sin, pay a spiritual debt, and earn a merit. This kneeling statue has the same function. If we step on its head or spit on it, aren't we collecting merits for the crown prince? He should thank us..."

Xie Lian couldn't listen anymore. His fist was already ready when that man said the word "thank," and he lunged.

The crowd instantly exploded in excitement.

"What are you doing?!"

"A fight!"

"Who's causing trouble?!"

Feng Xin had already been itching to beat people up, so he joined the brawl with a shout. As for Mu Qing, he wasn't sure whether he'd joined of his own volition or been pulled in, but in any case, all three of them started fighting. In the chaos of the brawl, the white bandage on Xie Lian's face was almost yanked off a number of times—however, it luckily didn't happen. The three of them were skilled in martial arts, but their opponents had the strength of numbers. They had an additional advantage in that Mu Qing held the other two back with warnings that killing mortals would only add to their crimes. The fight ended up being miserably restrained—though gratifying nonetheless—and in the end, the trio was chased off.

They walked alongside a river for a while, looking unkempt. Eventually, their steps slowed.

"We worked so hard all day, but in the end, we gained nothing. And all because of a fight!" Mu Qing complained angrily, his face black and blue.

Feng Xin wiped at the blood on his mouth. "How can you bring up money at a time like this?"

"It's precisely *because* it's a time like this that I need to bring up money!" Mu Qing countered. "'A time like this'? What time is it? A time when we're starving! Whether you want to admit it or not, we can't do anything without money! Couldn't you two have restrained yourselves a little?"

Xie Lian didn't speak.

"How could we? People made statues of him kneeling solely for the purpose of stepping on him!" Feng Xin said. "You're not the one whose face is being stepped on, so of course you can dismiss it."

"It's not the first time that something like this has happened since the war was lost," Mu Qing said. "And it surely won't be the last. If he can't get used to it soon, he might as well just die."

"Get used to it? Get used to what? Being humiliated by others? Mortals stepping on his face?" Feng Xin argued, clearly finding the idea offensive. "Why should he have to get used to something like that?"

"That's enough!" Xie Lian cried out in irritation. "Stop arguing. Is something this small worth fighting over?"

The two of them shut up at once.

After a pause, Xie Lian sighed. "Let's go and find a carriage to pick up Mother and Father. We're leaving the city tonight."

"All right," Feng Xin acknowledged.

Feng Xin and Xie Lian set off side by side, but they quickly noticed that Mu Qing didn't follow.

Xie Lian looked back, confused. "Mu Qing?"

After a moment of silence, Mu Qing said, "Your Highness, I want to talk to you about something."

"What is it?" Xie Lian asked.

"What's wrong now? I already said I won't argue with you anymore. What more do you want?" Feng Xin said impatiently.

"I want to leave," Mu Qing said simply.

"..."

Xie Lian already had a vague, bad feeling before Mu Qing even opened his mouth, but his breath still hitched when his companion actually said it.

Feng Xin thought he might have heard wrong. "What? What did you say?"

Mu Qing straightened his back. His obsidian eyes were unyielding, and his demeanor was calm. "Please permit me to leave."

"Leave?" Feng Xin exclaimed. "What will His Highness do if you leave? What about the king and queen?"

Mu Qing opened and closed his mouth a couple times, but in the end, he still said, "I'm sorry to ask this, but my hands are tied."

"No! You explain yourself right now! What the heck do you mean, 'your hands are tied'?" Feng Xin demanded.

"The king and queen are His Highness's parents, but I have my own mother to worry about," Mu Qing replied. "She also needs my care. I can't neglect my own mother for the sake of someone else, or someone else's parents. I pray Your Highness will understand that I cannot stay at your side."

Xie Lian felt faint and leaned against a nearby wall.

"Is that the real reason?" Feng Xin questioned coldly. "How come you've never mentioned it before?"

"It is one of my reasons," Mu Qing replied. "Another reason is that I feel we've become mired in this situation and have very different ideas on how to pull ourselves out. Pardon my honesty, but if we keep going like this, nothing will get better—even in a million years. And so, our paths have diverged."

Feng Xin was so angry he began to laugh. He nodded and turned to Xie Lian. "Your Highness, you hear that? Remember what I said back then? I said that he'd be the first to run off if you were ever banished. Didn't I tell you?"

Mu Qing seemed aggravated by his words. "Please stop trying to guilt trip me, thanks," he requested flatly. "I'm only speaking the truth. Everyone has their own outlook. No one was born to be the center of the world, the justice of the Mortal Realm. Perhaps *you* enjoy orbiting around another person, but others might not feel the same."

"Well, don't *you* have a load of sour, veiled excuses? I don't give a damn," Feng Xin said. "Is it so hard to admit you're an ungrateful traitor?"

"Enough!"

At the sound of Xie Lian's voice, the two of them stopped arguing. Xie Lian removed his hand from his forehead and turned to Mu Qing. He stared at him for a while before he spoke.

"I don't like forcing people."

Mu Qing's lips pursed, but he still stood tall.

"Go," Xie Lian said.

Mu Qing looked at him, not saying a word. Then he bowed deeply, turned around, and walked away.

Feng Xin stared at his retreating back without blinking as it disappeared into the night. "Your Highness, you really let him go, just like that?" Feng Xin said in disbelief.

Xie Lian sighed. "What else can I do? I just said I don't like forcing people."

"No... But...? That bastard!" Feng Xin exclaimed. "What's with him? He actually left?! He ran off?! What the fuck!"

Xie Lian crouched on the riverside, rubbing his forehead. "Never mind it. If his heart has already left us, what's the use in making him stay? Should I tie him up and force him to wash my clothes?"

Feng Xin didn't know what else to say either and crouched beside him. A moment later he spat angrily, "Goddammit. That bastard was happy to share the wealth but not the suffering. He ran away the moment things got tough. Does he remember nothing of your kindness?!"

"I'm the one who told him not to remember it," Xie Lian said. "So...you don't need to bring it up constantly."

"But he couldn't possibly forget it for real?!" Feng Xin refuted. "What the actual fuck! Don't you worry, Your Highness. I will never, ever leave you."

Xie Lian forced a small smile but said nothing. Feng Xin stood back up.

"Shall we go pick up the king and queen? I'll find a carriage—you just wait here."

Xie Lian nodded. "Thanks. Be careful."

Feng Xin acknowledged him and left. Xie Lian also rose to his feet and walked alongside the river for a while. His whole body still felt a little unsteady, like nothing was real.

Mu Qing's departure had truly shocked him to the core.

He never expected someone so close to him to leave just like that. Xie Lian had always believed in "forever"—friends would always be friends forever, with no betrayal, no deception, no breaking up. Perhaps there would come a time when they had to part, but it wouldn't be for a reason like "things got too horrible."

In all the stories he'd read, the hero and the beauty were a match made in heaven. They never parted and would remain true to each other forever and ever—and if they couldn't, it would be because they were forced apart by a tragic death and not because the hero preferred to eat meat while the beauty preferred fish, or because the hero scorned the beauty for spending too lavishly and the beauty scorned the hero for his bad habits.

It wasn't a pleasant feeling to lose your footing and plunge millions of miles, only to find yourself still in the Mortal Realm when you hit the ground.

As Xie Lian randomly wandered, he suddenly saw shimmering golden lights floating ahead. The sight snapped Xie Lian out of his haze. On closer inspection, he saw the lights were lanterns—lantern after lantern floated on the water, drifting with the river's current. There was a pair of children laughing and playing by the riverside.

"Ah, today is Zhongyuan," Xie Lian remembered.

There had been a grand service at the Royal Holy Temple for the Zhongyuan Festival every year; he'd always looked forward to it and would have never just forgotten. But now, it had completely slipped his mind. He shook his head and continued on his way.

Just then, a voice came from the road ahead. "Kids, kids, wanna buy one?"

The voice was extremely old and raspy, and it was laced with eerie ghost qi. Xie Lian instinctively knew something wasn't right. He looked over to see two children with lanterns in their hands stopped by the roadside. They were staring at something with curiosity—and fear.

Someone was seated in the darkness in front of them. He seemed to be an old man, unkempt and dressed in black robes that allowed him to blend in with the equally black night. With an unlit lantern in his hand, he beckoned the two children in a shady manner.

"My lanterns are very different from the ordinary lanterns you're holding, I tell ya. These are rare treasures; if you make a wish on them, it's guaranteed to come true."

The two small children seemed doubtful. "R-really?"

"Of course," the old man said. "Look."

The lantern in his hand was clearly not lit, but it glowed just then with an ominous red light. There were over a dozen other lanterns on the ground next to him, and they began to flicker haunting green. It was a terribly eerie sight.

The two small children were amazed, but Xie Lian knew exactly what he was looking at. Rare treasures? That was clearly phosphorescence from the souls of the dead!

A little ghost's soul must have been sealed into that lantern for it to glow with such a peculiar, ominous light. As for the old man, he had to be some sketchy scam cultivator who had captured those unlucky wandering spirits from somewhere and sealed them into the lanterns. The two children didn't know about those sorts of tricks and clapped in delight, wanting to buy the lanterns.

Xie Lian quickly rushed over. "Don't buy them. He's lying to you."

The old man glared. "What're you talking about, boy?!"

"These lanterns aren't treasures–they're wicked contraptions," Xie Lian stated plainly. "There are ghosts sealed inside them, and the spirits will cling to you if you bring one home to play with."

When the children heard that they were ghosts, they didn't dare linger. They ran away, wailing as they went.

The old man leapt to his feet, yelling angrily, "You dare ruin my business?!"

"How could you run such a business? Even adults who bought your wicked lanterns would fall into great misfortune—and you sell them to ignorant children? Vengeful ghosts could cling to them," Xie Lian lectured. "And wouldn't that be a great wrong? If you must sell such things, you should sell them in a specialized market."

"You make it sound so easy. Where would I even find a 'specialized market' to sell things like this?" the old man rebuked him. "Everyone just sets up shop randomly on the roadside!"

He gathered up his supremely ugly, poorly made lanterns, preparing to leave with a huff.

"Wait!" Xie Lian hastily called out.

"What? What do you want?" the old man said gruffly. "Are you going to buy?"

"Unbelievable! Do you actually plan to try to sell them somewhere else? Where did the ghosts in your lanterns come from?"

"I caught them on the barren battlefield. They're everywhere," the old man replied.

Then they were the wandering souls of deceased soldiers? Once he heard that, it was impossible for Xie Lian to leave the matter alone.

"Stop selling them. Today is Zhongyuan! It won't be a laughing matter if you stir something up. Besides, those are the heroic souls of warriors—how can you sell them like trinkets?" Xie Lian admonished solemnly.

"When people die, they become nothing but wisps. Who cares if they're heroic souls?" the old man said. "My own old bones are more important. We all gotta make a living, so what am I gonna do if you don't let me sell? Be homeless? If you're so passionate about this, why don't you buy them all, huh?"

"You..." In the end, Xie Lian admitted defeat. "Fine. I'll buy."

He reached into his pockets and scoured every corner, digging out a few pennies.

"Is this enough?"

The old man glanced at the money and exclaimed, "Of course not! How could that pittance be enough?!"

Xie Lian didn't know what over a dozen lanterns would normally cost; he'd never looked at the price when he purchased things in the past. However, his woeful situation was providing him a chance to learn how to bargain the hard way.

"Your lanterns aren't pretty or well made, and they're very unlucky. You might as well sell them to me for cheap."

"They're already priced this low, and you're offering less?" the old man argued. "I've never met anyone as broke as you—how embarrassing!"

Xie Lian could feel shame dig into his skin at those words.

"I'm a crown prince, I'm telling you. Never in my life has anyone called me broke."

He regretted his words as soon as he spoke them. However, the old man didn't take him seriously at all and laughed.

"If you're the crown prince, then I'm the good ol' Emperor!"

Xie Lian was relieved at his reaction but also felt a little awkward. Though at that point, what did he have to lose?

"Will you sell? This is all the money I've got," he said plainly.

After much haggling, they finally completed the transaction, and Xie Lian used that pathetically sad bit of money to buy over a dozen ghost lanterns. He brought the lanterns to the riverside. The old man ran off in a flash the moment he got the money, while Xie Lian sat down by the shore and began to untie each red knot wrapping the lanterns. He released all the little ghosts sealed inside and performed a simple service for them.

Haunting wisps of ghost fire floated from the lanterns. All of these souls were newly coalesced ghosts who had passed away very recently. They were bleary and unfocused, with no clear consciousnesses of their own, and were very feeble still—which was why the old man had captured them so easily. When they were released from the cramped lanterns, they all swarmed around Xie Lian, circling him affectionately and even nuzzling him every so often.

Xie Lian rose to his feet and urged softly, "Go on. Go."

Aided by the gentle push of Xie Lian's hand, the spirits rose higher and higher, floating toward the horizon and gradually dissipating. This was known as "spirits returning to the world"—they had moved on and were no more.

Xie Lian gazed at the starry sky for a long time before he heard a tiny voice calling out from behind him.

"Your Highness…"

Xie Lian blinked and turned to look for the source of the voice. Only then did he notice that one tiny ball of ghost fire had remained with him—it hadn't climbed into the sky, nor dissipated into embers.

This little ghost seemed stronger than the others. Not only did it possess its own consciousness, it could also speak.

Xie Lian walked over, bewildered. "Were you the one calling me just now? You...recognize me?"

The little ball of ghost fire became quite lively upon being noticed, jumping up and down. Judging by its voice, it seemed to be a young man like Xie Lian.

"Of course I recognize you!"

Xie Lian only felt more awkward when he remembered that he was covered in mud and looked so strange. He clenched his hand and pressed his fist against his lips. He really didn't want to admit to his identity and thought to instead tell the ghost fire that it was mistaken. A moment later, he schooled his expression.

"Why did you stay? Didn't I send you off? Did I miss a step, maybe?"

If he hadn't missed a step during the service, why would one of them still be there?

The nameless ghost floated before him, not too close, not too far. "No. You've done nothing wrong. I didn't want to leave, that's all," it answered.

"Do you have an unfulfilled wish or some attachment?" Xie Lian mused.

"Yes," the nameless ghost replied.

"Then why don't you tell me what it is?" Xie Lian asked. "If it's not too difficult, I'll do my best to help you."

Behind the nameless ghost, three thousand lanterns flowed

languidly through the night. The nameless ghost said, "I have a beloved who is still in this world."

After some silence, Xie Lian said, "I see. Is it your wife?"

"No, Your Highness. We were never married."

"Ah."

"In fact, I might not even be remembered," the nameless ghost said. "We never really talked."

You never really talked? Xie Lian thought. *Then how did this person become the "beloved" that tied your spirit to the world? What beauty they must possess.*

Humming for a moment, Xie Lian said, "So then, what is your wish?"

"I want to protect them," the nameless ghost answered.

Usually, such a spirit's wish would be something like *"I want to tell her I love her,"* or *"I want to spend some romantic time with her,"* or occasionally something more frightening like *"I want her to accompany me down below."* A wish to protect someone was quite rare, and Xie Lian was a little stunned.

"But you no longer belong to this world."

"What of it?" the nameless ghost replied.

"If you force your soul to remain, you won't be able to rest in peace," Xie Lian said.

The nameless ghost didn't seem to care. "I'm willing to never rest in peace."

This wandering wisp of a spirit was surprisingly stubborn. Such a willful spirit was typically extremely dangerous, but for some reason, Xie Lian didn't sense any murderous intent from it. So he wasn't concerned.

"If your beloved knew you couldn't rest in peace because of them, they might feel troubled and guilty," Xie Lian continued.

The nameless ghost hesitated for a moment but replied, "Then I just won't let them know why I haven't left."

"If you meet too often, they'll find out sooner or later," Xie Lian said.

"Then I won't let them know I'm protecting them either," the nameless ghost replied.

Something stirred within Xie Lian's heart. He could tell that this young man's love wasn't just talk.

The lanterns had contained wandering spirits that the old man had captured from the barren battlefield, so the one before him now must have been a young warrior.

"The war separated you from your beloved... I'm sorry I didn't win," Xie Lian said quietly.

However, the nameless ghost declared, "To die in battle for you is my greatest honor."

Xie Lian was stunned.

"To die in battle for the crown prince is the greatest honor for a Xianle soldier," was a slogan that some general from Xianle had taught the troops. They used it to hype them up for the fight, proclaiming that if they died, they would've died for a purpose, and in death they would pass on to the immortal realm. That was, of course, a lie. Yet even though this young soldier had passed away and his soul had been set adrift in the Mortal Realm, he still remembered the phrase so clearly—and said it with such solemnity and sincerity.

Xie Lian felt the rims of his eyes grow hot, and his vision went blurry.

"I'm sorry," he replied. "Forget me."

The nameless ghost's flickering flames flared brighter. "I won't forget. Your Highness, I am forever your most devoted believer."

Xie Lian forced down a sob. "...I've already lost all my believers. Believing in me won't do you any good; it might even bring disaster. Did you know? Even my friend has left me."

The nameless ghost declared as if swearing an oath, "I won't."

"You will," Xie Lian said.

The ghost was insistent. "Believe me, Your Highness."

"I don't," Xie Lian said.

He no longer believed in anyone, especially himself.

FLEEING BEFORE THE ENTIRE CITY was locked down for a thorough search, Xie Lian and company traveled through the night and arrived at another city. Xie Lian once again settled the king and queen in a safe hideout, then he and Feng Xin went out to earn money. However, those who couldn't earn much in one city wouldn't magically be luckier in a new one.

Like always, they worked a full day's labor for meager pay, but the once-inseparable trio were now suddenly missing one member, and the remaining two were having a hard time getting used to it. Mu Qing had always been responsible for looking after the money purse, and he had constantly kept track of their finances. Now that Mu Qing had left, Xie Lian had no choice but to keep the money on himself, as Feng Xin had admitted upfront that he might lose it by accident. Every time he counted that sad bit of money, he really couldn't believe it was all he'd earned after a hard day's labor. In his old life, he'd given alms to beggars that were more than this.

With Mu Qing gone, they had also lost the one who brought food to the king and queen, so Xie Lian had to personally deliver all sorts of daily necessities to their hiding place with the help of Feng Xin. The queen was very happy that she got to see her son so frequently, and when she was happy, she cooked. That day, she once again dragged Xie Lian and Feng Xin to the table to try her soup.

"You both need to fatten up! Look how thin you've become."

Feng Xin was streaming cold sweat, and he bounced back to his feet the moment his butt touched the bench. He waved both hands and assured her, "No, no, no, Your Majesty, your humble servant Feng Xin doesn't dare—I absolutely mustn't!"

"What's there to be afraid of, child?" the queen chided pleasantly. "Come, sit down."

How could Feng Xin tell her? He simply didn't dare, and the queen delivered the fruits of her labor after he forced himself to sit down. Xie Lian sat at the head of the table, and Feng Xin took a sharp breath before removing the pot cover. When the two of them saw what was in the pot, their expressions turned ghastly.

"This chicken...died a tragic death," Xie Lian said under his breath.

Feng Xin's lips trembled. "Your Highness, you didn't see right. There's no chicken in this."

Xie Lian was flummoxed. "...Then what's that thing floating in there that looks like a dead chicken?"

"I think it's thick soup...but the shape is a little off," Feng Xin replied.

The two spent a long time studying the pot's contents but still couldn't figure it out. The queen ladled a full bowl for Xie Lian, and Feng Xin hurried to serve himself. When the queen went to the back of the cottage to find the king, they instantly dumped the soup from their bowls and pretended to wipe their mouths, looking as if they had slurped it down in one gulp and enjoyed it so much that they couldn't get enough.

"I'm full, I'm full."

The queen was delighted at the sight. "Was it good?"

"It was, it was!" Xie Lian praised hollowly.

"If it's good, then have some more!" the queen said happily.

Xie Lian almost sputtered a mouthful of the soup he hadn't eaten and raised his handkerchief to pretend he was wiping at his lips.

The queen seemed to hesitate before she said, "My son, I want to ask you a question. Please don't blame your mom for being nosy."

Xie Lian stiffened and placed the handkerchief down. "What is it? Please ask."

The queen sat down next to him. "Where is that child, Mu Qing? Why hasn't he stopped by in the past few days?"

He knew it.

Xie Lian's heart squeezed tighter at the mention of Mu Qing. "Oh, I gave him some tasks to do, so he's set off elsewhere."

The queen seemed to breathe a sigh of relief and gave him a nod. "When will he be back?"

"He may need to be gone for a long time... He won't be back anytime soon," Xie Lian replied.

The queen seemed troubled by this news, and Xie Lian noticed. "Is something the matter?"

"Oh, it's nothing," the queen instantly replied.

Feng Xin had the sharper eye, and he spoke up. "Your Majesty, what's wrong with your hands?"

Hands?

Xie Lian looked and was shocked at the sight.

His mother's delicate, exquisitely maintained, upper-class hands looked awful. They were scraped and peeling at the knuckles, with faint traces of blood. Xie Lian stood up abruptly and grabbed her hands.

"What's going on?"

"It's nothing! I just washed some clothes and blankets, but I'm not very good at it," the queen quickly explained.

"Why are you doing the washing yourself?" Xie Lian blurted. "You could've..."

But he didn't know how to finish that sentence. Could've what? Could've had the palace attendants do the washing? Could've had Mu Qing do the washing? None of that was possible now.

Mu Qing had acted as their personal attendant on their never-ending road to escape, and his duties had included taking care of all personal necessities—including caring for the needs of Xie Lian, the king, and the queen. With him gone, there was no one to attend to all the mundane daily tasks.

No one to cook, no one to wash, no one to fold the blankets. The simple days of the past suddenly became difficult. Xie Lian could endure it, as there were far too many other things to worry about. But his mother had always lived a comfortable, luxurious life—when had she ever performed such crude labor? But how would it get done if the queen didn't handle that work herself?

After some silence, Xie Lian said, "Don't let this trouble you. I'll take care of the washing."

The queen smiled. "No need. You just take care of yourself. I've never done laundry nor cooked before, but I have nothing but free time every day, and doing the chores myself is quite fun. Especially since you both enjoyed the meal—that makes me quite happy."

The pot of soup had been stirred by his mother's battered hands, but they hadn't drunk a drop and poured it away on the sly. Xie Lian and Feng Xin exchanged a look, and both felt rather horrid.

Just then, the queen added, "Oh yes, there was another thing. Is there any way you can bring some medicine back tomorrow?"

Xie Lian's eyes widened slightly. "Medicine? What kind of medicine?"

The queen's face was troubled, and she sighed. "I'm not quite sure.

Why don't you go to the pharmacy and inquire about what kind of medicine should be taken when someone is coughing up blood?"

"Coughing up blood?!" Xie Lian was shocked. "Who's coughing up blood? You? Father? Why didn't you say something sooner?"

He had raised his voice, and the queen immediately hushed him. "Speak quietly!"

However, it was too late—an outraged voice came from the back of the cottage. "I told you not to run your mouth!"

It was the king. Now that he had already overheard them, the queen didn't worry about hushing anymore and called out toward the back room, "It won't do if this keeps up!"

Xie Lian walked straight into the back room and saw the king huddled on a bed of ragged blankets. He hadn't seen his father closely in a while, and observing now, he looked quite ill; his cheeks were sunken, and the ghastly gloom of the room made him appear even more sickly. He had no royal aura at all—he was nothing more than a defeated, scruffy old man.

Xie Lian didn't even need to check his pulse to know that he must have been ill for some time now and that it was serious. The suffocating, musty air of sickness permeated the entire room. Recalling that the queen had said one of his symptoms was "coughing up blood," he raised his voice in distress.

"What's going on here?!"

The king steeled his expression. "What's with that tone?"

The queen and Feng Xin entered the room as well.

"Who cares what tone I'm using?! Why didn't you say something sooner if you're sick?" Xie Lian admonished.

"Are you lecturing your king?" he angrily replied. "What your king does and does not say at any given time is not for you to dictate!"

He was still carrying on with that tough posturing, even now. Xie Lian was in disbelief.

"You're unbelievable! Are you still throwing your title's weight around at a time like this?"

The king was outraged. "Get the hell out! *Now!*"

The queen and Feng Xin immediately dragged Xie Lian out of the room, and the queen begged, "My son! Don't be like this. He's your father, and he's ill. Take a step back."

First on the run, and now there was an illness to manage—it was like adding ice to snow. Xie Lian buried his face in his hands.

"Mother! Why didn't either of you say anything sooner? If you had, the illness wouldn't have progressed to coughing up blood! Do you know how hard that is to cure?"

In their current situation, it was impossible!

The queen's reply was both dismayed and aggrieved. "We...we didn't know that it'd worsen like this."

"Yeah. Besides, we've been dodging Yong'an pursuit this entire way. There was no time to stop," Feng Xin added.

Xie Lian pulled his face from his hands. "I'll take him to a doctor in the city right now."

"No need!" the king shouted from within the room.

Xie Lian looked back and was just about to rebuke him with, *"I'm the one who makes the decisions right now,"* but Feng Xin responded first. "Your Highness, you'll be noticed for sure if you take His Majesty to a doctor in the city."

Xie Lian instantly froze.

The queen spoke up. "That's what we were afraid of, which is why we didn't say anything over the past few days. My son, why don't you just...think of a way to bring back some medicine?"

The king started coughing violently again, and the queen went into the back to look after him. Xie Lian was dazed for a good moment, then he turned and went into another room.

"Your Highness! What will you do?" Feng Xin called out.

Xie Lian didn't answer, just started rummaging through all the shelves and chests in the cottage.

"What are you looking for?" Feng Xin asked.

Xie Lian didn't respond. A moment later, he dug out something from the bottom of a chest—an ancient sword.

When he saw what Xie Lian had retrieved, Feng Xin asked, "What are you doing with Hongjing?"

Xie Lian was quiet for a long moment before he replied, "I'm going to pawn it."

"You can't!" Feng Xin cried in shock.

Xie Lian slammed the chest shut heavily. "I've already pawned so many swords. This is just one more."

By this point, he had pawned over half of his beloved sword collection to make enough money for the carriages and bribes at checkpoints they'd needed for their journey. And since they couldn't go inside the large, bustling pawn shops, they'd sometimes wind up blackmailed by shady merchants who had determined their identities, and they were forced to sell at a painful bargain.

"It's not the same!" Feng Xin exclaimed. "Don't you really like that sword? Otherwise, why wouldn't you have pawned it already instead of stuffing it in the bottom of a chest? And the Emperor gave it to you—it won't sound good if word gets out!"

"No matter how much I like it, it's still not as important as a life," Xie Lian said wearily. "Let's just go."

The two made their way to the city with the sword, both looking downtrodden. When they arrived at the pawn shop, Xie Lian stopped and glanced at Hongjing in his hand.

Feng Xin peered at him. "Why don't we forget about pawning it? Let's try...let's try to think of another way..."

Xie Lian shook his head. "It's too late. Besides, we don't know if there *is* any other way that will get us enough money."

No mortal would be a match for them if they stole, snatched, or employed other such trickery, and money would pour in much faster. But things were so difficult precisely because they had to uphold their moral compasses and adhere to the ethics of mortals, earning their money honestly.

Having made up his mind, Xie Lian said, "This has to be pawned. Once it's done, we'll go buy medicine."

Despite his words, his feet still didn't move.

Feng Xin knew he was reluctant to let go—this was Xie Lian's last sword. So he said, "Let's look around some more."

Suddenly, a clamor erupted on one end of the street; there was shouting and yelling, and someone cried out.

"Who's causing trouble?!"

"The audacity!"

"Catch him! Catch him!"

The two were both startled, and Xie Lian instantly ducked to the side of the road in alarm. "Who?!"

Feng Xin cautiously went over to check, returning only after he was sure of their safety. "It's nothing! Don't worry! It has nothing to do with us. It's not Yong'an soldiers or anyone else who's looking for us."

Only then did Xie Lian's tension ease. "What's going on?"

"I'm not sure," Feng Xin said. "It looks like a fight between some irate servants. Want to go see?"

"Let's go," Xie Lian said. "Hopefully it's not some local tyrant."

The two went over to watch. They saw two men brawling at the center of a crowd of onlookers, and the audience was cheering.

Feng Xin tapped the shoulder of a passerby who was enjoying the show. "Hey, buddy, what's going on here?"

The passerby chuckled. "You don't know? This is too exciting! The servant is beating the master!"

What an affair! Xie Lian was speechless. "How come? And why the cheering?"

"Of course we're going to cheer!" the passerby said. "That master is no good! His servant followed him since he was young and was very loyal, but the master only knew how to exploit him! He paid him badly and worked him to the bone, pushing him around all day. The servant couldn't take it anymore, and so you see, you see! Now they're fighting!"

Sure enough, the one throwing all the punches was cursing as he did, yelling accusations and declarations alike. *"I've had it with you for ages! Why don't you think about what you've really given me?! My family's so poor that we can barely eat, but you still lord over me, acting all high and mighty! From today onward, I ain't your dog no more!"* The master was hugging his head and screaming as he was beaten, all while the crowd cheered.

Their shouts made Xie Lian's heart lurch in waves, and chills shook his body. He unconsciously stole a glance at Feng Xin.

Feng Xin didn't notice his strange behavior at all, and when he heard those terrible deeds, he commented offhandedly, "I see, then that master really is no good. No wonder the servant is rebelling."

He didn't mean anything by it, but Xie Lian's heart dropped, and he gripped Hongjing tighter.

After much headache, Hongjing was pawned and the two finally had money. They immediately went to find a doctor and purchased dozens of different medicinal herbs to take back.

Medicinal herbs used to treat illnesses that made one cough up blood were expensive and needed to be bought in large quantities. It wasn't a matter of one or two doses over a couple of days, and they would need to keep a close watch on how his father responded to the treatment.

That evening, Feng Xin unwrapped a few packets of herbs and started boiling down the medicine outside the cottage, fanning wildly at the flames with a torn cattail leaf fan. As for Xie Lian, he was once again rummaging through the shelves and chests all over the house. After a while, he finally fumbled out a soft, shimmering golden belt.

Xie Lian originally had several golden belts, but they had met the same end as the swords—all pawned off aside from this last one. Xie Lian had wanted to keep it as a souvenir, but today he decided to use it for something else.

Feng Xin happened to look up at him just then. "Your Highness, what are you doing with that belt? You're not thinking of pawning it too, are you?"

Xie Lian walked over and handed the golden belt to him.

Feng Xin's eyes bulged with bewilderment. "What are you doing, giving this to me? Your Highness, did you accidentally lock your brain inside when you shut that chest just now?!"

Xie Lian was briefly speechless until he remembered that a gift of a golden belt had a special meaning in the Upper Court, and his expression instantly darkened. "You're overthinking it—I don't mean it *that* way at all. Just take it like it's ordinary gold!"

He shoved it on him, and Feng Xin glared back, shimmering golden belt draped around his shoulders.

"No. You still gotta tell me why you're stuffing me with gold out of nowhere."

"Just take it as long-overdue pay," Xie Lian said.

Feng Xin was confused. "No, but...what's with you all of a sudden? Why are you talking about pay at a time like this? You'd be better off pawning this to buy more medicine for His Majesty. Or it's fine if you don't pawn it—keep it for yourself. That belt is something only a heavenly official can own."

At the mention of medicine, Xie Lian looked back toward the cottage, where the king and queen were resting.

"I can think of other ways to get the medicine," he replied, "so just take it."

Xie Lian was determined to give, and Feng Xin couldn't understand why. Although he was confused, he also found it kind of funny for some reason. He shrugged, then picked up the ragged fan and continued to fan the flames to boil down the medicine solution.

"Fine then. I'll keep it for you for now. Whenever you want it back, just let me know."

Xie Lian shook his head. "I won't ask for it back. You can do with it as you will."

Their pockets were a little fuller after pawning Hongjing, and they finally managed to have a few good meals. Since the queen's skills were so shocking, Xie Lian stated that he would take over the chore of cooking and politely asked his mother to look after his father and *absolutely not* enter the kitchen. Xie Lian didn't have much experience, but it was as the saying went—even if he'd never eaten pig trotters, he'd seen pigs walk. His creations were mostly edible, so the party was saved from further dietary issues.

After he fought with the king that day, Xie Lian regretted what he'd said, but he couldn't swallow his pride. Instead, he silently did his utmost to care for him. A patient who was coughing up blood couldn't be allowed to suffer any cold, so he got more blankets and small heaters for him.

The Yong'an soldiers were cracking down hard in their attempts to catch the escaped Xianle royalty, and soon this city also heightened its security. They had finally settled in, but now they had to leave again.

Xie Lian had already lost count of how many cities he had passed while on the run with his parents in tow—and, to be honest, everything that he'd seen on the road was much more peaceful than he'd initially imagined. The only city that had met a tragic fate was the royal capital of Xianle; nowhere else seemed to have been affected that severely.

After all, the king, the crown prince, the royal capital, the nobility—all were extremely remote concepts to regular civilians. The change in ruler didn't seem like it made much difference, especially since the new king wasn't a tyrant and hadn't passed any particularly strict decrees after he ascended the throne. There were no further laments, and the matter was simply a new topic for lively after-dinner conversations.

"I worked this plot of land when the king was named Xie; I still work the same plot of land now that the king is named Lang!" Xie Lian heard someone say, and they weren't wrong. But strangely, everyone's feelings were oddly unified when it came to the storied crown prince who went from invincible to losing every battle—it was as though they'd suddenly become hardcore Xianle patriots whenever his name was mentioned. This puzzled him and also made him resentful.

However, he really didn't have much energy to worry about these things anymore. The money they had made from pawning Hongjing only lasted a few short months.

An illness that made one cough blood was already difficult to cure, and on top of that, the king was depressed. He needed a large amount of medication just to maintain passable health, and his condition would no doubt worsen considerably if the supply were cut off. Xie Lian had nothing left to pawn, and today, he thought and thought as they loitered on the streets before finally turning to Feng Xin.

"Why don't we...give it a try?"

Feng Xin peered at him. "I guess we could give it a try?"

It wasn't the first time the two had hesitantly suggested they "give it a try," but they hadn't ever actually done it before now. Besides, the king had once overheard them while they were discussing the topic and had flown into a rage and thrown a huge fit. He was adamant that Xie Lian was not to do anything so shameful for money, otherwise he would refuse to drink his medicine. In the end, they'd had to abandon the idea. But now that they were in dire straits, there was no need to spell it out; they understood each other. Xie Lian nodded and wrapped his white silk band tighter around his face.

"Your Highness, you don't have to do it. I can do it alone," Feng Xin said. "That way, it'll be fine even if the king asks!"

Then he inhaled deeply, held his breath for a moment, and bellowed at the pedestrians, "Dear folks on the street, don't miss out on this—"

The pedestrians jumped in surprise, and they all gathered around, chattering.

"What's with the yelling?!"

"What're you guys up to?"

"What've you got to show us?"

"I wanna see you shatter boulders on your chest!"

Feng Xin removed the bow from his back and began bald-faced bluffing. "My...my nickname is 'Wonder Archer'! I can shoot a bullseye from a hundred paces away. I will show off my embarrassing skill for everyone to see. If you enjoy the show, p-please grant me some coins!"

"Wonder Archer," "embarrassing skill"—those were phrases he had picked up from watching street performers. While they had kept saying they would never busk, they had long been observing how others did it without realizing.

"Stop wasting your breath! Just get on with it!" hollered the crowd.

"We've been waiting! Hurry up!"

Feng Xin nocked an arrow against his bow and pointed at an idle man in the crowd who was munching on fruit. "Will this uncle please step out! Place that apple on your head, and I will shoot it perfectly from three hundred paces away!"

The idler shrank his neck back and withdrew into the crowd. "I'm not doin' it!"

"I won't hit you, don't worry!" Feng Xin exclaimed. "If I shoot you by accident, I'll compensate you!"

"I'm no fool! If you shoot me by accident, it won't matter how much you pay me!" the idler yelled back. "Since you're out here to perform, don't you got your own equipment or somethin'? Shouldn't you be shooting at the one next to you?!"

The crowd all chimed in. "Yeah!"

"Let me," Xie Lian also said.

Someone from the crowd tossed over a fruit, and Xie Lian caught it, ready to balance it on his head. However, Feng Xin never planned to let Xie Lian get involved, so why would he allow this? In a moment of panic, he snatched the fruit and ate it in the blink of an eye, then changed the direction of his arrow to target a banner hanging high from a tall building.

"I'll shoot that!" he cried.

And he did. He was an extremely skilled archer, so of course he hit the target, and the audience cheered and laughed.

"Well, dang! You do got it!"

They laughed and chattered amongst themselves, and some really did toss a few coins. The small, round coins tumbled and rolled across the ground, and Feng Xin went over to gather them. Xie Lian silently crouched down to help. He felt a little depressed, like he'd lost something.

Feng Xin had once been the servant of the crown prince; even ministers had been compelled to be courteous and polite when they saw him, never mind the common folk. Some had even tried to curry his favor. Heeding the hollering ringleaders when they hauled rocks and earth had been depressing enough, and now they had to endure being watched like performing monkeys. Feng Xin's sharpshooting skill wasn't being used to kill enemies in battle but rather to entertain the masses. Just thinking of it made Xie Lian's stomach turn.

Suddenly, a woman's voice rang out sharply. "Who's shooting arrows in the streets?!"

Xie Lian's heart jumped to his throat. Everyone in the crowd pointed at Feng Xin.

"It's him!"

Feng Xin was confused, and the crowd parted as several women came stomping over, holding an arrow—the one he had shot earlier. The women surrounded him.

"You damned brat! Did you shoot this? What guts—randomly shooting off weapons in broad daylight! You destroyed the screen in our yard! Tell me, how are you gonna pay for it?!"

"Yeah, you've scared away so many of our patrons!"

As it turned out, Feng Xin's shot was so powerful that the arrow had flown all the way into someone's yard. Feng Xin didn't like interacting with women to begin with, and these ladies were caked with heavy makeup; the perfume of powder assaulted his nose and suffocated him. They probably came from a place of ill repute, and their accusations had him waving his hands and backing away.

Xie Lian hurried over to stand in front of him. "I'm sorry, I'm sorry. He didn't mean to. As for compensation, we'll think of something..."

The women's tempers flared, and they began to shove him. "And who are you?! You—"

The white bandage covering Xie Lian's face had slipped from all the pushing and pulling. When the women saw his face, their eyes lit up and their tones took a kittenish turn.

"Oh gosh, what a handsome little gege!"

Xie Lian was confused.

One of the women clapped once, her face blooming into a wide smile. "Very well, then! It's decided! You're together, right? We'll take *you* as payment!"

Xie Lian was even more confused.

Before he realized what had happened, the women had already dragged Xie Lian away to a rather lavish little establishment. When he looked up, he could see women on the upper balconies dressed like blossoming flowers and chirping like birds. Only then did Xie Lian realize he had been taken away by a bunch of brothel madams!

Goosebumps instantly raised on his skin. "Wait, I don't have money! I really don't have any money!"

The brothel madams cackled. "Of course you've got no money. That's why we're bringing you in to earn some!"

Xie Lian was flummoxed. "Sorry, but I'm a man!" he exclaimed.

"We know you're a man. We're not blind!" the brothel madams replied, annoyed.

Feng Xin finally broke through the sea of people surrounding him and rushed over, shouting, "Let go of His— Let go of him this instant!"

The two were in a horrid predicament and promptly bolted— they knew they were in the wrong, so they didn't dare fight back. The enraged brothel madams called over thirty hired goons, and the duo had to scurry all over the city to escape their pursuit. They had never been involved in a situation like this before and would never dare visit that area again.

All the same, the experience confirmed for them that busking was a viable way of earning money, so they found a new location and set up shop. They were fresh faces, so the locals were very interested, and Feng Xin was a strapping, honest-looking, rather handsome man. They managed to earn a small fortune in those first few days that paid for their food and medication for at least half a month— but good things don't last, and it took less than half a month for someone to come knocking.

That day, several beefy men came looking for them while Xie Lian and Feng Xin were packing up. Suspecting that they were Yong'an soldiers, Xie Lian was alarmed. Inside his sleeves, his fists were ready to strike.

"Who are you?" he demanded in a low voice.

The leader humphed. "You guys have been hanging around on our turf for days, but you don't know who we are?"

Xie Lian and Feng Xin were both puzzled.

Another man spoke up. "You've stolen so much of our business. Don't you think it's rude not to explain yourselves?"

The two of them finally understood what was going on—these were other local street performers. The street artists all belonged to a guild or gang, and those groups laid claim to turf. This new duo had shown up, taken all their customers, and stopped them from making any money, so of course the group came looking for trouble. But Xie Lian and Feng Xin weren't from the streets, so how could they possibly know this particular etiquette?

Who'd even want to steal your business if they weren't at the end of their rope? Xie Lian thought bitterly, but he still spoke courteously. "It's not really stealing, right? People watch what they want to watch. We weren't forcing anyone to gather for our...shooting performance."

As if these people would listen. "Not stealing?! No one's made any money the past few days—you've taken all the grub!" they exclaimed rudely.

Bang! The gang members jumped in surprise and saw that Feng Xin had slammed his fist into a nearby wall. There was a giant fist mark there, cracks crawling out from its center.

"Are you looking for trouble?" he asked coldly.

The gang of beefy men certainly *had* come there to start trouble and talk with their fists. But after witnessing Feng Xin's punch, they had no doubt that his fist was stronger than theirs, and instantly their fire was smothered by half. Still, they refused to let this go so easily. The leader was briefly stumped, but he quickly changed his tune.

"How about this: we'll do this by the book. Let's compete with our skills. The winner gets to stay, and the losers will pack up and leave, never to set up shop in this area again!"

Hearing that it'd be settled with a competition, Feng Xin laughed. Of course he did—how could mortals possibly compete with them? It was a sure win!

Xie Lian also breathed a sigh of relief. "That's exactly what I wanted. How do you want to do this?"

"We'll use our best busking trick!" the man proclaimed loudly. While he spoke, two other men brought over a few long, rectangular stone slabs of slate, which the man patted. "Shattering boulders on your chest! How about it? Do you dare?"

Seeing how smug he looked, it seemed this was indeed his specialty. Xie Lian crouched to touch the slate, then looked up.

"It won't be a problem for me, but will it really not be a problem for you?"

These stone slabs were the real deal.

The man laughed. "Judging by the shape you're in, you'd better just worry about yourself!"

Feng Xin crouched next to him. "Your Highness, let me?"

Xie Lian shook his head. "No. You've worked hard the past few days. Let me do it this time."

He wanted to make an effort too.

And so, both Xie Lian and the man lay down on the ground with slate slabs pressing down on their chests. Feng Xin was given a large hammer. He weighed it in his grip and was just about to smash it down when Xie Lian swiftly spoke up.

"Wait."

The others were delighted. "What, do you admit defeat? It's not too late to forfeit now—we'll let you go!"

"No. I want to add another slab," Xie Lian said.

The mob was shocked by this. "Are you crazy?!"

"Didn't you say it yourselves? This is a competition," Xie Lian explained lazily. "There's no difference in skill if we use one slate apiece, so how can we compare our abilities?"

The street performers looked doubtful; some thought he'd gone mad and others assumed he was bluffing. After much discussion, they stacked another stone slate on his chest.

After that, Xie Lian asked them to add *another*!

Now everyone was sure he'd lost his mind, and they added a third slate without further question. Thus, three heavy stone slates were stacked on Xie Lian's chest, a rather terrifying sight.

Under the scrutinizing gazes of the crowd, Feng Xin raised the large hammer and smashed it down without blinking. The three stone slates cracked into multiple clean pieces. Xie Lian crawled up from the ground amidst cheers, uninjured and fine. He calmly dusted off his robes while everyone watched with slackened jaws. The leader's face was pale, and his expression was dark.

Now he should know to back off, right? Xie Lian thought.

He had assumed the other party would concede and never come seeking trouble again. But that man's expression kept changing and changing, and suddenly, he gritted his teeth.

"Add two more to me too! No, add three more!"

"Bro, you can't!" the mob exclaimed. "This guy must be using some sort of evil spell, you don't have to go along with him!"

"Yeah, he must've faked it!"

"What the fuck?" Feng Xin exclaimed angrily. "You're the ones who lack skill, but you turn around and accuse us of cheating with evil spells?"

The leader said in a booming voice, "The stone slabs and the hammer belong to us! How could we not know about it if there was some evil spell in play? This brat does have some skill, but three slates is nothing! I can do four! As long as we win, they'll have to leave!"

"That's impossible! Give up!" Feng Xin said. "Don't throw your life away over this."

But the man was bullheaded and forced the others to stack four staggeringly heavy stone slates on his chest. "You just watch!"

Xie Lian could tell things were going awry. "Feng Xin, should we stop this? There's no way a mortal can manage four slates," he whispered.

"Let's watch, I guess? I'm sure he's not looking to die. After a couple smashes, he should know to back off," Feng Xin whispered back.

Xie Lian frowned slightly and nodded, deciding to wait and see. Sure enough, the man's face changed the moment the lackey who wielded the hammer gave a single apprehensive knock. The lackey immediately stopped, not daring to move again.

But the man yelled, "Harder! Did you forget to eat? Why is your smash so pathetic?"

The lackey didn't dare to be sloppy on the second go, and he used all his strength. *Bang!* With that loud sound, the man's face turned bright red like he was holding back a large mouthful of blood.

This didn't look good, and Xie Lian and Feng Xin quickly called out. "Wait! Don't force yourself!"

"Who's forcing himself?! This is my specialty!" the man yelled. "Just watch, I'll make you admit your defeat! Continue!"

With a distraught expression, the lackey smashed again. Now he'd done it—the man sputtered blood all over the ground, scaring the lackey into dropping the hammer.

The mob rushed up. "Let it go! Let it go, bro! If those two bastards want to cling to this place, then let them. Your life is more important!"

Veins popped on the man's forehead and blood foamed from his mouth. "I won't let this go! It's been days since we've had a bite to eat. It's our livelihoods gone if this keeps up! Continue! I refuse to believe I can't compete with that delicate-looking little brat! This is my specialty!"

Xie Lian couldn't watch anymore and spoke up. "That's enough. If that's how it is, then I concede defeat. Starting tomorrow, we won't come here anymore. Come on, Feng Xin!"

Then he turned to leave, and Feng Xin followed him. Behind them, the mob cheered.

"Your Highness, are we gonna give up this place just like that?"

They had finally found a way to earn money, but now they had to abandon it. Xie Lian sighed.

"There's no other way. He's already suffered massive internal injuries from just a few rounds—I fear he's nearly crippled. Someone was going to die if we kept the competition going, and we wouldn't have been able to stay if that happened either."

Feng Xin scratched his head and cursed. "Suicidal, honestly!"

"We're all trying to make a living," Xie Lian said simply.

Xie Lian felt rather guilty. Had he known that man would force himself to take on four slabs, he wouldn't have asked them to stack three—he would've just admitted defeat early. Although the man was boorish and reckless, he still had some respectable qualities.

"Besides, we don't *have* to busk here. That'd be putting all our eggs in one basket," Xie Lian said.

However, when they returned to their hiding place that night, the queen informed him with a face full of worry that the king's symptoms were worsening. He'd need a good, long rest and might not be able to endure any more moving. And that meant they couldn't leave the city for the time being.

Xie Lian rummaged through the shelves and chests again but couldn't find anything to pawn, so he sat next to the chest and spaced out. Feng Xin was boiling down medicine, humming as he did so. He hummed and hummed, sounding more and more off key, and while Xie Lian didn't care to pay attention at first, he eventually couldn't ignore it.

"What's with you? In a good mood?"

Feng Xin looked up. "Huh? No?"

Xie Lian didn't believe him. "Really?"

In the few days since they had started performing on the streets, Xie Lian had noticed Feng Xin acting a bit strange. Sometimes he'd grin like a fool for no reason, sometimes he'd suddenly seem troubled. Xie Lian and Feng Xin rarely left each other's sides when Mu Qing had been around, but after Mu Qing left, Feng Xin would sometimes have to deliver food for the king and the queen or run other errands. He'd be gone for a while on those days. Xie Lian assumed that Feng Xin must've stumbled upon something while he was out and about, but he didn't have the energy to concern himself with it any further.

Eyeing the medicine pot in front of Feng Xin, Xie Lian was quiet for a while before he asked, "Is that the last packet?"

Feng Xin flipped through the bundles on the ground. "It is. If we don't go tomorrow—" Upon remembering that the king was inside the cottage and they couldn't allow him to overhear, Feng Xin lowered his voice. "If we don't busk tomorrow, what'll we do?"

Xie Lian was silent for a long time. Then he abruptly stood up.

"Stay here and guard the cottage. I'll go out and think of something."

Feng Xin was doubtful. "Where are you going? What could you possibly come up with?"

Xie Lian left without looking back. "Don't worry about it. And don't follow me."

97
Blocking the Mountain Path, Crown Prince Fails at Robbery

XIE LIAN EXHORTED Feng Xin over and over to stay behind and guard the king and queen, then he left the small, rundown cottage. As he walked, he kept looking back, his heart racing. After walking a long way, when he was certain Feng Xin hadn't followed, he finally relaxed.

Steadying himself, Xie Lian continued onward for another dozen kilometers, stopping and going, before he finally found a place that seemed like an ideal location—a mountain road in the middle of nowhere.

Xie Lian scanned his surroundings. There was no one around. He covered his face with the white silk band, wrapping it tightly and securely before leaping into a tree and hiding himself in the branches. He held his breath and focused. The next step was to wait for travelers to pass by.

That's right—the "something" he'd come up with was stealing from the rich and giving to the poor.

In the past, Xie Lian had only heard of such chivalrous thieves from storytellers and books. He'd never stolen, never even considered it, since he'd always believed that no matter how it was prettied up and no matter how just the cause, robbery was robbery. Otherwise, considering Xie Lian's martial prowess, nothing would present an obstacle—never mind settling for scurrying across rooftops to pilfer small things, he could easily murder guards and clean out an entire treasury.

But now that they'd reached this point, there really was no other way. If he had to choose, he considered robbing people a tiny bit better than burglary, probably because the former was still somewhat out in the open. After much internal strife, Xie Lian ate his past self's words and decided to steal the wealth of others to relieve his own poverty.

This was the quickest way!

Xie Lian perched on the tree. The moon was hiding, the wind bellowing, and it was deserted all around him, empty of all things living. And yet his heart hammered wildly in his chest.

Even facing the most ferocious beasts, Xie Lian had never been this nervous. His hand trembled as he dug out a cold, hard bun.

If you could still be picky about food, you weren't genuinely hungry. When Xie Lian finally understood this, he'd quickly become accustomed to the taste of old steamed buns.

Winter was fast approaching, and the nights were extremely cold. Xie Lian munched on the cold bun and puffed out mouthfuls of white breath. Since he didn't want to be seen, he hadn't even considered finding a place where there'd be more people—he'd chosen a remote area on purpose. He waited a full four hours before a traveler approached, strolling down the mountain road.

Xie Lian perked up and stuffed down the rest of the bun in a few bites, training his eyes on the traveler who was slowly approaching. And then he saw that it was an old man.

He was such an old, old man, but his dress was rather vibrant, so he was likely somewhat wealthy. Still, Xie Lian of course wouldn't even consider him as a target. He couldn't tell if he was disappointed or relieved, but either way, he resolutely decided to ignore the old man and let him go. He went back to waiting for someone to pass.

Two hours later, Xie Lian's feet were going numb from crouching, and the lower half of his body was practically frozen. A second person finally appeared. When he saw that the figure was also walking slowly, he wondered, *Could it be another elderly person?*

When they finally got closer, Xie Lian discovered that this wasn't someone old or infirm but instead a healthy looking man. He looked humble and good-natured and wore a smile on his face. The reason he was walking so slowly was because he was carrying a heavy bag of rice.

Xie Lian's palms were sweating, and he wondered, *Do I...attack?*

After a moment of hesitation, he gave up on this target as well. The man's clothes were patched and the straw shoes on his feet were so worn they exposed his toes—he was obviously from a poor household. He must've been so happy because he finally had a bag of rice to fill his stomach. Perhaps his family had starved for many days, and perhaps that bag of rice had been bought after selling the only ox of the household. Wouldn't he fall into despair if he was robbed?

Xie Lian's mind spun all sorts of scenarios. After a while, he wondered if maybe he should've just taken half of the bag of rice, but by then the man was long gone. Xie Lian resolutely decided that he wouldn't dwell on it anymore and continued waiting for the next one.

He perched in the tree like that and waited helplessly for hours, from the dark of night to daybreak. Over a dozen passersby had traveled along that mountain road, yet every time Xie Lian was about to attack, there were always all sorts of reasons why it wouldn't be right to follow through, and he let them pass. Over and over he thought to himself, *Forget it! I should just go back!* No bandit would ever behave like him; it'd be a miracle if his efforts were actually fruitful. But then he remembered that there would be no more food or medicine if he went back empty-handed and forced himself to keep waiting.

After almost half a day, one last traveler appeared far in the distance on the mountain road.

He was a middle-aged man, decked out in fine clothing—which meant he was either wealthy or noble. He had a fiendish face and a greasy, slippery air that made him look obnoxious. At a glance, he didn't look like anyone good.

But one mustn't judge a book by its cover. Xie Lian couldn't help but think, *What if this man only looks fiendish, but he's actually a good person? Even if he's rich, does that warrant a robbery?*

As he was waging his internal struggle, a growling noise from his stomach startled him from his stupor, and Xie Lian sighed inwardly. *Never mind, I can't dither any longer. You're it!*

Making up his mind, he leapt down from the tree and shouted, "Stand still!"

At the sight of a masked man cutting off his path down the road, the man cried out in alarm. "Who are you? Sneaking around here with your face hidden... What do you want?!"

"G-give...give..." Xie Lian forced out.

There was a hurdle in his mind, and he stammered a couple of times before finally squeezing out, "Give me all your money!"

The man's mouth opened wide, and he screamed and leapt three feet in the air. "Somebody! Help! Thief!"

And then he turned and ran. More than his escape, Xie Lian was worried that his cries would alert others. The mountain road was barren and desolate and there was little chance that anyone would come to help—not to mention that it would be easy to hide even in the unlikely event someone showed up. But he had a guilty conscience, after all.

"Stop! Stop yelling!" Xie Lian called after him.

As if the man would listen to him. He fled into the woods, and soon there was a horrific yelp.

Xie Lian was afraid the man had been attacked by beasts in the woods, and he cried, "Wait! Watch out—"

But when he caught up with him, his face went pale with shock when he saw what he'd stumbled across.

There was a group of people gathered in the woods, and they were all staring at him. When Xie Lian looked closer, he noticed that something was off—these weren't people at all; the middle-aged man couldn't see them and was still in a panic. Moreover, there were some faces in the group that Xie Lian found familiar.

Of course they were familiar—he had seen a number of them in the Heavenly Capital. Some were from the Upper Court, some from the Lower Court, but they were all heavenly officials!

The man had cried out because he'd tripped and fell. He gripped a large bundle of protection charms while chanting to himself, "My god, my god! Come save me! Come save me, now!"

And the gods that he was calling really had come, just as he asked.

Countless heavenly officials stared at Xie Lian intently, freezing him on the spot with their gazes. When the man saw that the strange, masked robber was frozen in place, he quickly crawled to his feet and ran off. Xie Lian couldn't move a single step to give chase. His entire body was stiff and drenched in cold sweat, and his mind was filled with horror.

Yes, horror.

Xie Lian could only pray that the white silk band was wrapped around his face tightly enough that the junior heavenly officials he'd been acquainted with in the past wouldn't recognize him. However, things never went as one hoped.

One of the heavenly officials looked him up and down, then commented in surprise, "...Isn't that...Your Royal Highness?"

Xie Lian was speechless.

Another heavenly official seemed even more shocked. "Ah, it really is! Why is Your Highness here? And dressed like that?"

Xie Lian's heart sank deeper and deeper; it was going to sink to the very bottom of the earth.

"That man was screaming 'help,' 'robbery,' 'thief.' Was a thief chasing him? And was that thief...Your Highness?!"

"My heavens! Your Highness... You would actually do something like this?!"

Their comments nearly made Xie Lian faint on the spot. He didn't know how much time had passed when he finally croaked out, "I..."

He wanted to say *something*, but his words were stuck in his throat and wouldn't come out. The heavenly officials' expressions were mixed. A moment later, one of them patted him on the shoulder.

"It's fine. Don't worry, Your Highness. We understand."

The pats weren't hard at all, but Xie Lian almost lost his balance from them. He tried again to speak. "I—"

The heavenly official laughed out loud. "You're only doing this because you've got it really hard. It's understandable. Don't you worry, we won't tell anyone."

That was exactly why it was so hard for him to say a word. And once the other party brought it up first, Xie Lian had no idea what more he could say.

A long moment later, Xie Lian mumbled, "...All right, thank you. Then I'm...I'm going to head back now. Heading back."

He wasn't sure how he left either. When he finally came back to himself again, he was standing on another empty mountain road. The cold winter night's breeze had snapped him out of it.

Only then did Xie Lian finally realize the full horror of what had just happened.

He was Xie Lian, the Crown Prince of Xianle—and now a thief?! How had it come to this?!

Xie Lian was filled with regret. He must've been utterly mad to consider robbery, and now things had spiraled out of control. Why was he so unlucky that he'd get caught red-handed even though he hadn't even done anything?!

He had never encountered anything like this in his former life, so he was at a complete loss as to what he should do. He was burning up from head to toe, his mind completely muddled, and he hid his face in his hands. If only time could flow backward—he was even willing to sacrifice his bountiful health and cultivation in exchange for that alone.

As he wandered, lost in the depths of his distress, he suddenly caught a glimpse of a blurry white silhouette in the corner of his eye.

Startled, Xie Lian's head shot up. "Who goes there?!"

The figure had vanished the instant he looked. Cold sweat drenched him once more. Although he hadn't seen the man's face, Xie Lian could've sworn he had been wearing a mask!

Yet there was no trace of anyone when he scanned his surroundings, and Xie Lian couldn't help but suspect that the figure he had seen was nothing but a hallucination born from his panic. Whether that was true or not, he didn't dare to stay there any longer and hurried down the mountain.

By the time Xie Lian returned, Feng Xin had been waiting for him for nearly the entire day. The moment he saw him he exclaimed,

"Your Highness, where did you run off to? What idea did you come up with?"

Xie Lian didn't dare tell him; he couldn't tell anyone, especially Feng Xin. He couldn't even imagine what Feng Xin—who believed so faithfully in Xie Lian's utmost virtue—would think if he found out. He could only hope that the incident would be forever buried in his heart and rotted in his stomach.

Thus, Xie Lian replied ambiguously. "Nothing."

Feng Xin was dumbfounded. "Huh? Then why were you gone for so long?"

Xie Lian's mind was numb. "Don't ask again. I didn't do anything."

Feng Xin found this incredibly strange, but no matter how he questioned, Xie Lian refused to answer. As a servant, it wasn't his place to push, so he could only ask in a whisper, "Do we still go busk tomorrow?"

"I'm not going out anymore," Xie Lian replied.

His mind had been thrown into complete chaos, and his head was filled with impossible worries. What if he bumped into that middle-aged man? What if he was wanted all over the city?

Feng Xin noticed that he looked off. "Are you tired? Then why don't you stay in, Your Highness? I'll go myself. You just focus on training."

He didn't know that Xie Lian also couldn't bring himself to train and cultivate.

Xie Lian had been focused on cultivation at first because that was the only chance they had to return to the Upper Court. But now he was terrified of the prospect of returning there—even though those junior officials had said they wouldn't tell anyone, would they really? Had the affair already reached the ears of everyone in the Upper Court?

When he considered that possibility, Xie Lian couldn't breathe. There was no way he could endure being tainted by such a stain, pointed at by the Upper and Lower Courts alike—even by the whole Mortal Realm!

Heavily exhausted, Xie Lian passed out, but his slumber was unsettled. He tossed back and forth, assailed by unknown nightmares. By the time he startled awake and looked outside the window, the skies were already dark.

Feng Xin wasn't around—he must've gone out to busk on his own and hadn't yet returned. From the room next to him, he heard the king and queen speaking in hushed voices, and a few quiet coughs.

Xie Lian lay on the floor. Now that he was awake, he couldn't help but keep thinking about how his parents would react if word of the incident really got around and they found out. How shocked would they be? The king might stomp his feet in outrage, sputtering blood as he yelled that he was the shame of Xianle. The queen wouldn't yell at him, but she would certainly be extremely anguished by her beloved child and the embarrassment he had brought them.

As his mind dwelled on this, Xie Lian began to have trouble breathing again. He needed to find somewhere where he could be alone and calm himself, so he rolled off the straw mat and dashed outside. He ran blindly for dozens of kilometers with the frigid winds blowing at his face.

He didn't dare stop anywhere near other people—he always felt like they were staring at him and judging him for how unsightly he looked. He ran until he came upon a graveyard without a single soul present, and his midnight flight finally came to a stop.

That night was colder than the night before, and only after he arrived here did Xie Lian notice that his cheeks and hands were practically frozen stiff. His whole body was shivering, though that wasn't just from the cold—it was also from terror. Xie Lian hugged his arms unconsciously and puffed out a few mouthfuls of hot air. As his eyes swept across the graveyard, he spotted two jugs of liquor that had been offered at a tombstone.

It seemed the owner of this tombstone used to be a lover of drink, so others brought them liquor when they came to sweep their grave. Xie Lian crouched at the tombstone. He had never drunk alcohol before, but he had heard people say that it could warm the body and help one forget. After a moment's hesitation, he abruptly reached for a jug, yanked out the stopper, and started pouring the contents down his throat.

This was a large jug of cheap liquor, nothing fancy, and the taste was pungent and strong. Xie Lian chugged a few large mouthfuls and choked on it, breaking into coughs—however, he did seem to feel a bit warmer. Xie Lian wiped at his cheeks and sat on the ground hugging the jug, then continued to chug the liquor in large mouthfuls.

In his daze, he thought he saw a small ball of haunting ghost fire come flying over from nowhere. It circled around him, twirling about and looking quite anxious. Xie Lian was focused entirely on drinking and didn't react at all. The ball of ghost fire appeared to be trying to get closer to him with all its might, but it was nothing but hollow flames—it passed right through his body every time it came near, forever unable to actually touch him.

One jug down and Xie Lian was already tipsy and groggy, his eyelids slack with drink. When he saw the ghost fire darting here and there, he found it rather pitiful but also rather funny. He couldn't help but sputter a laugh as he rested his arm on the edge of the liquor jug.

"What are you doing?" Xie Lian asked.

The ball of ghost fire instantly froze in midair.

"**I**S THIS YOUR GRAVE? Am I drinking your liquor?" Xie Lian asked.

He was a drunken mess and couldn't hear clearly if the ghost fire said anything in reply. He just assumed the owner of the grave was upset and trying to chase him away.

"I get it. I'll go," he grumbled.

Xie Lian crawled upright, still hugging the jug in his arms, then took a few swaying, wobbly steps. He didn't get very far before he lost his footing and fell all over himself with a *thud*.

As it turned out, there was a giant pit in the graveyard. It was probably dug to prepare for an upcoming burial, but the deceased hadn't been buried yet, and Xie Lian went tumbling in instead.

Xie Lian's forehead had smacked the outer edge of the pit when he fell. It hurt, and it only made the spinning of his head worse. He sat there feeling woozy for a while before struggling to get up. His hands were muddy and bloody, covered in scrapes and cuts.

He held out his hands and looked at them without really registering anything, then tried to climb out of the pit. However, he had just downed an entire jug of liquor—his limbs were limp, and he couldn't exert any power. Every time he tried to climb out, he just went slipping back down. Xie Lian slumped back to the bottom of the pit and glared at the dismal, overcast night sky for a while, growing very angry.

This pit wasn't even that deep. Why couldn't he climb out of it no matter how hard he tried?

The more he thought about it, the angrier he became, and he started mumbling despite himself.

"...What the fuck."

Xie Lian had never cursed before; this was the very first time such language had come out of his mouth. It was very curious—the stifling tension in his chest seemed to disperse instantly the moment he swore. Like a child who had just had his first taste of sweets, Xie Lian clung to the side walls of the burial pit and used all his strength to yell at a deafening volume.

"God *fucking* dammit!" He slapped at the ground and yelled, "Is anyone there? Is there anyone who can help pull me out?!"

Of course there wasn't anyone. There was only a small ball of haunting ghost fire, blazing unceasingly as it flitted about. After Xie Lian fell into the pit, the ball of ghost fire rushed over, seeming to want to pull him up—but it would never be able to touch him.

Xie Lian didn't bother with the ghost fire at all, just continued his angry rant. "Someone might as well just come and bury me!"

Cursing was one thing, but he still had to try to get out. *Crssh, crssh.* Xie Lian finally climbed out on his own, but the struggle had left him incredibly unkempt, and he lay on the ground huffing and panting laboriously. It took some time before he was able to turn onto his side to curl up, hugging himself.

"So cold," Xie Lian whispered.

His voice was tiny, scared that someone would overhear. But the ghost fire did hear, and it came flying. It pressed itself against his body, its flames immediately burning much brighter than they had before. It was burning itself up with all it had.

Still, a ghost fire was cold. No matter how close it pressed, no matter whether it burned itself out, it still couldn't bring even a sliver of warmth to the living.

In his daze, Xie Lian thought he could hear a tiny voice.

The voice seemed so close and yet so far, like it was coming from a waking dream. It cried in despair, "Oh God, please wait for me, just wait for me... Please give me a little more time... Let me... Let me..."

...God? Is it calling for me? Xie Lian wondered to himself.

But even if it was praying to him, it would be pointless.

He was already powerless as a god, and he was even less capable now that he wasn't.

"Your Highness...? Your Highness? Your Highness!"

It was Feng Xin's shoving that woke Xie Lian up.

Xie Lian blinked his eyes open laboriously and found himself lying in a narrow alleyway. Feng Xin's face was hanging above him. He let out a breath of relief when he noticed Xie Lian was awake, but a moment later his relief was replaced with traces of anger.

"Your Highness! What's going on with you, running off on your own for two days without a word?! If you don't come back soon, I won't be able to keep hiding it from Their Majesties!"

Xie Lian slowly sat up. "Two days?"

When he spoke, he found that his throat was dry and his voice hoarse. His temples throbbed, and his head ached like it was going to split. He sort of remembered what had happened, but not really.

Feng Xin crouched by his side. "That's right! Two days! Where exactly did you go?! Why were you running around like a madman?"

Had he been drunk for two days? Why wasn't he in some wild graveyard... Why was he lying here? Feng Xin's tone made Xie Lian shiver with foreboding.

"What did I do?"

"You were possessed!" Feng Xin said gruffly. "Smashing stalls all over the place, beating people up. You even tried to confront some patrolling Yong'an soldiers! And I don't know what else you did before that!"

When Xie Lian heard he had even gone after Yong'an soldiers, he was shocked. "I confronted the soldiers? Then...what happened to them?"

"Luckily, I found you and stopped you," Feng Xin replied. "And since you look like *this*, they assumed you were just some crazy drunkard. They yelled at you but didn't bother doing anything else, otherwise you'd be dead for sure. What happened to you? Why does it look like you were drinking?"

Xie Lian looked down at himself and found that he was filthy, covered from head to toe with mud and grime. He scratched his head, and his hair was as messy as that of a criminal being dragged to his execution. He certainly did resemble a crazy drunkard who slept on the streets all day.

Xie Lian was briefly silent before he crawled to his feet and replied vaguely, "Yeah...I drank a bit."

Feng Xin couldn't wrap his head around this. "Huh? How could you drink? And how much did you drink to be drunk for two days?"

Seeing Feng Xin's look of disbelief irritated Xie Lian for no good reason, and he walked on ahead. "I already said I didn't drink that much—just a bit. No big deal. Why can't I drink?"

Feng Xin hadn't expected him to answer like this and was stunned for a moment, then chased after him. "What do you mean, 'no big deal'? Has Your Highness forgotten? Drinking breaks the precepts—you can't break them! Otherwise, how can you cultivate? You have to ascend again."

"…"

Xie Lian quickened his pace the moment he heard "cultivate" and "ascend." He didn't want to listen anymore.

"Your Highness!" Feng Xin called out. He caught up again, and after a moment's hesitation, he tried, "Did something happen? Won't you tell me?"

Hearing Feng Xin question him so cautiously, Xie Lian opened and closed his mouth, wanting to speak but unable to. He might break down if he didn't tell someone soon, but he also wasn't sure how Feng Xin would react if he told him.

He didn't dare make that gamble.

Seeing him distracted, Feng Xin added, "Honestly, it's not like you killed or robbed someone, so what is it that Your Highness can't tell me?"

"It's not like you killed or robbed someone"—those words threatened to suffocate him. Before, he might have wavered on the matter; he might have tried to tell the truth and trust his luck. But all such hopes were thoroughly shattered in that moment.

Xie Lian dipped his head and turned to keep walking. "It's nothing... It's just... I'm really tired. You..." he replied hazily. He was just about to make up an excuse when he noticed something on Feng Xin's cheek and stopped in his tracks. "What happened to your face?"

Feng Xin felt his cheek, and his muscles tensed when he seemed to prod somewhere that hurt. There was a gash on his face, and one of his arms had been wrapped carefully with neatly layered bandages.

Someone else had clearly taken care of them for him, but Xie Lian was primarily concerned about the injuries underneath the dressings.

"How did you get hurt?"

No mortal could easily harm someone with Feng Xin's skill—and it was his shooting arm that had been injured, no less. But Feng Xin didn't seem to care. "Oh, it's nothing. Just some thugs trying to wreck my business, that's all."

Xie Lian was shocked and bewildered. "Was it the street performers from the other day?"

"Yeah, them," Feng Xin replied.

"Why did they crash your show?" Xie Lian questioned, but then he understood. "Was it because you still went to busk after we admitted defeat that day, so they came to chase you out?"

That was pretty much the whole story. A sudden rage exploded in Xie Lian's chest.

"Don't go there anymore!" Xie Lian's voice was hard.

However, Feng Xin brushed him off. "Who cares about them?! I'll perform there whether they like it or not. You're the one who admitted defeat, not me, so it doesn't count as going back on my word. I'm gonna set up shop there and busk no matter what happens. Other than sneaking around and crashing the show, what can they do to me? I wasn't prepared this time, but next time I will be. If it comes to fist fights, I'm not scared of them!"

The abrupt hostility that had rushed to Xie Lian's head instantly dissipated as he listened, replaced by guilt. Feng Xin had been steadfast while Xie Lian was out wallowing in his own misery. How could he possibly face his loyal servant, this man who still hadn't abandoned him despite everything?

Xie Lian sighed. "I'm sorry, Feng Xin."

Feng Xin was taken aback, then waved hard. "Why is Your Highness apologizing to me? What rubbish."

"You were out earning money all by yourself for the past couple days. I'm sorry for the trouble," Xie Lian said.

"As long as you focus on your cultivation and ascend again soon, it'll be worth it!" Feng Xin replied.

There was the word "ascend" again. Xie Lian nodded heavily.

The king and queen believed Feng Xin's lies and thought Xie Lian had spent the past few days training. When they saw him return, the queen happily cooked a meal as always. Xie Lian didn't have the heart to make Feng Xin suffer, so he took his bowl and helped him eat the food. He didn't sleep that night.

The next day, Feng Xin rose bright and early and headed out while Xie Lian remained behind to cultivate. Although he'd pulled himself together by that point and regathered his energy by a millionfold, he still couldn't focus.

The only way to rise above the rest was to study and train diligently—that was just common sense. But was there even one in a million who had the ability to study and train to the extremely high level required? By the same logic, Xie Lian could tell himself to clear his mind a million times, but it wasn't so easily achieved by just saying it.

His cultivation progress remained at a standstill for a dozen consecutive days. Xie Lian wasn't accomplishing anything, and he couldn't help feeling anxious—especially since every night, Feng Xin dragged his exhausted body back home, and he and the queen asked after Xie Lian's progress. The pressure he felt was indescribably immense.

He didn't dare tell them the truth, so he could only vaguely answer that yes, he was making progress, which made Feng Xin and the queen both very happy. Still, he knew this couldn't last forever. After two months, Xie Lian finally couldn't let it go on any longer.

One evening when Feng Xin had returned very late, he and Xie Lian sat at the table together eating the previous day's leftovers. As they ate, Xie Lian suddenly turned to him.

"I'm afraid I'll have to leave for a while."

Feng Xin was taken aback, but he didn't stop stuffing his face with rice. "Huh? Leave? Where are you going?"

"I'm going to search for a quiet land filled with spiritual energy where I can cultivate in seclusion," Xie Lian said slowly.

A cultivation spot with abundant spiritual energy gave the cultivator significant benefits.

At first, Xie Lian hadn't wanted to leave his parents and attendants behind, so he'd never left them to pursue seclusion. But now he'd changed his mind.

Feng Xin didn't overthink it. "Great! Your Highness, you should've done this a long time ago! Cultivation is most effective in quiet seclusion, after all!"

Xie Lian nodded, paused, and then said, "I'll have to trouble you to look after Father and Mother while I'm gone."

Feng Xin was about to respond, but he hesitated. Although it was only for a moment, Xie Lian knew him very well—how could he miss that flash of uncertainty?

"If you must go, then go," the king bellowed from the back room. "This king doesn't need anyone to look after him."

Feng Xin and Xie Lian lowered their bowls and chopsticks and looked toward the back room. It seemed the king wasn't asleep yet and had overheard their exchange, then barged in on their conversation.

Xie Lian shook his head and whispered, "Acting tough again."

Feng Xin smiled. "Don't worry, Your Highness. Of course I'll look after them."

Well, that answer was completely straightforward. Still, Xie Lian didn't forget how Feng Xin had seemed to hesitate for a moment before answering—like he had some other conflicting concern.

But when he thought about it, perhaps he was mistaken. Feng Xin didn't know anyone outside their group and had no other attachments, so what other concerns could he have? Xie Lian stopped dwelling on it and moved on to planning what needed to be done before his departure.

The next day, Xie Lian packed a simple satchel and bid a temporary farewell to his parents and Feng Xin.

He walked on foot for dozens of kilometers, eating and sleeping in the wild for days. Finally, he found a place suitable for quiet cultivation within a thick, vast, remote mountain forest. Upon examining the area, Xie Lian was stunned at first, but soon his heart was filled with wild joy.

"Such luck... The feng shui here is excellent. I can't believe I've found a rare piece of blessed land!"

Xie Lian could hardly believe it—his luck had turned around so unexpectedly after so much misfortune. He checked and rechecked until he was absolutely sure—but this area was indeed a sacred land brimming with spiritual energy. If he could immerse himself in training and focus on cultivation for the next few months, then surely he could achieve twice the result with half the effort. He could make exponential progress!

Xie Lian finally saw a ray of hope, and his gloomy feelings from recent days suddenly cleared. His heart leapt with joy.

"Father, Mother, Feng Xin, wait for me. I'll be back very soon!"

He hiked the steep, perilous mountain path for many hours and finally entered the deepest recesses of the spiritual mountain just before sunset. As he moved through the dense forest, he could clearly sense that he was getting closer and closer to the source of the land's spiritual energy. His steps grew quicker and lighter. But just as he was picking out a location for secluded cultivation, he was interrupted by the clamor of footsteps behind him.

How could there be so many feet on such a secluded mountain? Xie Lian glanced over, but he couldn't have expected the sight that awaited him, and the smile on his face froze.

A number of people had arrived behind him, about thirty in total. They came in various shapes and sizes and all wore different styles of attire, but the one thing they had in common was that they were all heavenly officials. A few were officials of the lowest rank in the Upper Court, but most were officials from the Lower Court.

And among them were the junior officials who had stumbled upon Xie Lian's failed robbery!

When they saw Xie Lian, their faces subtly changed. They tugged at and elbowed each other, whispering amongst themselves under their breath.

And when Xie Lian saw them, his hands immediately started trembling.

Both parties stared at each other in dismay. It was some time before one of the heavenly officials cleared his throat.

"What a coincidence that we'd run into Your Royal Highness here."

"Indeed. Why has Your Royal Highness come here as well?"

Xie Lian gave a light nod, forcing himself to be calm and composed. He responded with neither haughtiness nor humility. "...I'm here to train."

Even though he was a different person now, Xie Lian still tried his best to speak with the same tone of voice he'd used before he was banished, refusing to allow himself to sound anxious or agitated.

The heavenly official smiled. "An even greater coincidence. We've come to train too."

"Yeah, yeah. Who knew that we'd run into each other here? Ho ho ho..."

As it turned out, Xie Lian wasn't the only one who'd spotted this blessed land—this group of heavenly officials had targeted it too.

Faced with this situation, Xie Lian hesitated. Would he have to cultivate alongside all these heavenly officials? Honestly, he despised the idea. He had come here to close himself off from the world and cultivate quietly—there'd no doubt be disturbances; he couldn't achieve solitude around this many people. Some people liked to cultivate in groups so they could take care of one another, but Xie Lian had always cultivated quietly on his own.

Furthermore, ever since the robbery incident, he became anxious whenever he saw heavenly officials he'd once known. Other people's eyes felt as piercing as needles, and the stares tormented him. He was perpetually gripped by the delusional feeling that they were all secretly watching and judging him. He wouldn't be able to focus on cultivation in such a state.

When it came to laying claim to blessed lands, there was a "first come, first served" rule. If Xie Lian was strong enough, he could simply state that he was there first and request they find somewhere else to train. However, the junior officials who had witnessed the robbery incident were right there, so he couldn't act too forcefully. Besides, it'd seem overbearing if he chased away so many heavenly officials to keep this blessed land all for himself. Even if Xie Lian didn't want to train with other heavenly officials nearby, he had no choice. He would never be able to find another cultivation place with such plentiful spiritual energy, at least not quickly. Xie Lian could only nod.

"Yeah, what a coincidence. I'll head in first. Please do as you will, everyone."

He began to hurry off to find the quietest cave to hide, yet a heavenly official behind him spoke up as he turned to go.

"Hold on."

Xie Lian paused and turned his head back, puzzled. "What is it?"

Some of the thirty-or-so heavenly officials exchanged looks, and some exchanged whispers. A moment later, one stepped forward with a smile.

"Your Highness took over many blessed lands in the past. Why don't you let us have this one?"

Xie Lian was stunned for a long while before he understood. They were going to force him to leave entirely!

How baffling...what *bullies*!

A rush of blood ran to his head. *I was here first, but I didn't ask you to go,* Xie Lian thought angrily. *Why are you all ganging up and trying to force me to leave?*

But he didn't dare act out. After a moment of silence, he slowly gripped the strap of his satchel tighter.

"What do you mean by this?" Xie Lian demanded, his voice hard.

One of the heavenly officials began to explain. "Well...didn't we just say...? Your Highness has claimed many blessed lands in the past—"

Xie Lian cut him off. "What does then have to do with now? Are you saying that since I've trained in spiritual lands before, I'm barred from doing it going forward?"

The heavenly official was stumped into silence, looking embarrassed.

Xie Lian tried to remain calm. "Also, I don't quite understand. It's not like the rest of you can't cultivate because I'm here. Isn't it common to share spiritual land when cultivating? Why can't we all just keep to ourselves? Why must you ask me to leave?"

Just then, he heard someone grumble, "Stop playing dumb... There are already more than thirty of us. What progress can we make if you're cultivating here too...?"

The man was instantly hushed by the rest of his group, but Xie Lian immediately understood. So *that* was it!

A blessed land's spiritual energy was limited. If someone took half when cultivating, then anyone who came afterward would have to share the other half. If someone took eighty percent of it, then only the remaining twenty could be parceled out. And a person with a greater ability to absorb spiritual energy would leave even less for others to use.

The heavenly officials were afraid that Xie Lian would absorb most of the spiritual energy if he was there to cultivate. Anything that remained would have to be shared among the thirty of them— barely a sliver for each!

Realizing this, the boiling blood in Xie Lian's head began to roil even more aggressively. He clenched his fists and stated coldly, "...I will cultivate here."

Another heavenly official spoke up. "Your Highness, we're only calling you 'Your Highness' out of respect. You're nothing more than mortal right now. Why must you fight with us over this spiritual land?"

"Since I'm a mortal and you're all heavenly officials, then what are you afraid of if I'm here to train?" Xie Lian said. "If I don't leave, are you going to chase me away by force?"

Of course they couldn't do any such thing—heavenly officials were not allowed to attack a mortal who hadn't committed any major sins lest they be punished. These heavenly officials couldn't do anything to him.

However, Xie Lian had forgotten one thing.

As he stubbornly faced those thirty-some heavenly officials, a voice broke in to say, "It seems Your Highness has grown more of a backbone after being banished to the Mortal Realm. Not only will you rob mortals, you'll even offend heavenly officials! Ha ha ha ha!"

It felt like Xie Lian had suddenly plunged into an icy cellar. He whipped his head up and saw that the one who had spoken was an unremarkable lower-ranking official...but not one who'd been among the group that had caught him red-handed during the robbery incident!

As Xie Lian had suspected, they had already gossiped about it! It hadn't all been in Xie Lian's head; everyone really had been staring at him with judgment in their gazes. Everyone knew. All of these heavenly officials—they all knew!

In an instant, Xie Lian felt like all of his bones had been pulled out. The fire burning in his veins was extinguished and his eyes turned red. He stiffly looked at the junior officials who had seen him that night.

"You said you wouldn't tell anyone..." he rasped.

Perhaps his burning stare pierced them too deeply, but the junior officials pinned under his gaze quickly waved their hands.

"We didn't tell any outsiders!"

His eyes burning red, Xie Lian demanded, "Then how did *they* know?!"

None of the thirty-some heavenly officials looked surprised when they heard his question. If so many of these heavenly officials already knew, how much of the Upper Court had been told?

His question stumped the officials for a moment, but they quickly argued back. "Well, it's not like they're outsiders! We're all close friends here, with no secrets between us—so this doesn't count as telling! But we won't say anything to anyone besides the officials here—"

Xie Lian didn't wait for him to finish before he cried out sharply. "Lies! What a bunch of lies! *I don't believe you!*"

The junior officials were starting to feel a little embarrassed at being cut off so pointedly, and they shrank back into the crowd.

Just then, one of the heavenly officials spoke up, his voice booming. "What does it matter if you believe them or not?! You're already lucky that no one has exposed all the *fine* deeds Your Highness has done here in the Mortal Realm, and you still ask them to keep a secret for you? Why are we obliged to keep your secrets? What a joke!"

It was like a bucket of ice-cold water had been thrown in Xie Lian's face, followed by a blade piercing his heart. "No! I..."

Another heavenly official piped up. "You wouldn't fear mere talk if you hadn't done anything immoral. You're the one who's gone corrupt, and you blame others for not keeping their word? Keeping such unjust affairs under wraps would be the real crime!"

"*No!*" Xie Lian cried. "I..."

He wanted to say that he had his reasons, that he hadn't wanted to do it. But deep down, he also knew that his reasons weren't important. All that mattered was that he did indeed try to rob someone!

A stain like this was like a brand of shame on his face, and it made him feel infinitely small before these heavenly officials, too afraid to even raise his voice to defend himself. Seeing that his will was fading, one of the martial gods stepped forward.

"Your Highness, now do you understand why we don't want you here to cultivate with us?"

Xie Lian lowered his head and tightened his fists.

The martial heavenly official continued, "We are not walking the same path, and travelers of different paths shall not meet. You should leave."

The way he said that so presumptuously, understanding suddenly dawned on Xie Lian. At the end of the day, they were throwing around all these insults and accusations solely to make him give up this spiritual land!

His fists clenched so hard that his knuckles cracked, and a lump weighed heavy in his throat for a while before Xie Lian said darkly, "...I'm not leaving. I will stay here and train."

Right now, his anger toward the thirty-some heavenly officials had surpassed his embarrassment. Now that things had gone this far, what did he have left to lose? He might as well go all out. Instead of running away with his tail between his legs, he'd rather stand his ground, thick-skinned and immune to their barbs, and keep them from getting their way.

Xie Lian's head snapped up. "I will train here," he repeated. "This mountain does not belong to any of you, so none of you have any right to ask me to leave!"

Now that he'd hardened his attitude, the thirty-some heavenly officials' faces darkened. Xie Lian heard them muttering amongst themselves.

"Why does he even bother?"

"I've never seen anyone so shameless..."

They could gripe all they wanted, but Xie Lian would stay where he was. Even if his heart was bleeding profusely from being stabbed by spears of lips and swords of tongues, he would stubbornly refuse to move an inch.

The martial heavenly official said, "It seems Your Highness is bent on having his own way and making everyone else unhappy in the process."

"Kick me out if you've got what it takes! Even if you want to, none of you have the skill!" Xie Lian said coldly.

At that, many of the heavenly officials' faces dropped and they pulled out their weapons!

Of course they would—Xie Lian's words had been a grave provocation to any martial god, and many of those present were just that. There was no way they could pretend they hadn't heard.

Xie Lian was quickly surrounded, but he wasn't scared at all. He had no blade in his hand except the branch he had been using as a walking stick.

One of the martial gods said severely, "Your Highness, if you apologize immediately, we will pretend you didn't offend us."

"If I've made anyone unhappy, I'm not sorry," Xie Lian replied. He pointed forward with the branch in his grip. "Because none of you are fit to be gods!"

A wave of outrage broke out around Xie Lian.

Someone snorted. "*We're* not fit? And someone who robs mortals is worthy?!"

Xie Lian couldn't hold back anymore, and he didn't want to either. He swept the branch through the air and charged at them, yelling, "*You bullies!*"

The martial gods readied their weapons to welcome his attack, and the other heavenly officials standing in the back cried out to Xie Lian, "It's not like we forced you to rob people! Why are you blaming us?!"

But they were too happy too soon. They'd assumed that Xie Lian would be easy to take down, considering he had no spiritual powers or weapons. Yet unexpectedly, even though Xie Lian wielded only an ordinary branch, it was no different from a vicious blade in his hands. His strikes were incredibly strong and forced his opponents back. Only a few moments had passed, and many of the martial gods' swords were nearly sent flying. They were even scared of being sliced by the sharp winds the branch's swings stirred up. Every single one of Xie Lian's opponents fled to hide at the back of the group.

These esteemed heavenly officials couldn't even defeat a banished mortal—what an embarrassment!

Just then, one of the heavenly officials watching the fight from a distance shrieked.

"What's this?!"

His cry alarmed the other heavenly officials. "What's going on?!"

The screaming heavenly official seemed to be in excruciating pain; he was doubled over and covering his face. "A...a ball of ghost fire just hit me in the eye... Did *he* do this somehow?!"

This was the official who had pointed at him and declared him a thief. Xie Lian snorted. "Ghost fire? If you want to steal this spiritual land, at least be frank about it. There's no need to slander me any further!"

His fury flared again, and his attacks grew more brutal. Every single spear and blade wielded by that circle of martial gods was knocked away by Xie Lian's entirely normal branch, and the weapons clattered as they scattered across the ground.

At that moment, someone yelled, "We caught it! We caught it! Look!"

Xie Lian paused and steadied himself. The heavenly officials were in a tizzy. One of them was gripping something in their hand and raised it high for all to see.

"There really is a ghost fire! He's playing dirty! We've got proof!"

Xie Lian looked closely, and sure enough, it was a little ball of haunting, blazing ghost fire.

"I don't even know what's going on! How dare you accuse me of playing dirty just because you caught some ghost fire!" Xie Lian cried out angrily. "It's not like ghost fires are rare! Do you see my name written on it?!"

The heavenly official who had shrieked was clutching his eye. "Why would a normal ghost fire attack my eyes? If it isn't under your control, why would it act like this?"

"And I say it's some wandering spirit from the mountain that was frightened by *you* lot and came crashing in here by accident in a daze! Your 'proof' is nonsense!" Xie Lian rebuked.

The martial god who had first attacked grabbed the ghost fire. "Who cares whose control it's under? Just disperse a harmful thing like this!" he said as he gripped it harder, looking like he planned to snuff out the spirit's fire.

Seeing this, Xie Lian blurted, "Let it go!"

He couldn't bear to have wandering spirits be dragged into their quarrel. He rushed to fight the martial god and retrieve the ghost fire. Since Xie Lian intended to rescue the spirit, he had to hold back a bit, and the two were soon at a standstill.

Suddenly, a few of the heavenly officials called out from behind them. "You're here?! Come quick! Come see for yourself what's going on!"

It sounded like someone had arrived.

"You're finally here!" another heavenly official cried.

"We've been waiting for you! Come give us a hand!"

Xie Lian was startled. *Has someone powerful arrived?* Then he thought, *Well, who cares who it is. If they're going to give me trouble, I'll just go another round! I'm not afraid of anyone!*

He was brimming with resentment and ready for a huge brawl. But when the crowd parted and the fashionably late arrival stepped forward, Xie Lian was absolutely stunned.

The newcomer was Mu Qing!

Mu Qing obviously wasn't expecting to see Xie Lian like this either. The moment they came face-to-face, they were both dumbfounded. Xie Lian's eyes went wide, and he completely forgot about the martial gods he had been fighting.

"Why are you here? Aren't you..." he muttered. But after only a few words, he noticed something and fell silent—he understood what had happened.

Right now, Mu Qing wasn't wearing his old, worn black robes from when he'd been with them on the run. Rather, he was wearing a uniform befitting a martial heavenly official of the Lower Court.

Feng Xin and Mu Qing had once been Xie Lian's left and right hands. Their abilities were highly praised and caught the eyes of many. When Xie Lian was banished, some heavenly officials had thought it a shame that Feng Xin and Mu Qing were banished with him. Some even had approached them in secret to ask whether they were willing to transfer their loyalties and serve another palace. It was feasible that a heavenly official had pulled Mu Qing up to the Lower Court as a gesture of recognition and had him work in their service.

That had to be it. And he was clearly doing well for himself if he was tagging along with this group of heavenly officials to search for blessed lands in which to cultivate.

Xie Lian was still in a mortal body, but Mu Qing had already returned to the Lower Court. It was strangely ironic.

With great effort, Mu Qing finally composed himself and asked in confusion, "What's going on here?"

The heavenly officials all fought to tell their tales. Xie Lian stood at a distance, his body rigid. He noticed that they weren't telling Mu Qing about his robbery. What did that mean?

It meant Mu Qing had already heard about the incident. Mu Qing knew he'd tried to rob someone!

Drop after drop of cold sweat rolled down the side of Xie Lian's face, and he backed up a few steps involuntarily.

The martial god who had been facing him earlier huffed in anger. "He wants to take this spiritual land all for himself and chase us out. Mu Qing, hurry and help us!"

Help? He wanted Mu Qing's help in the fight against Xie Lian?

Xie Lian was tingling with rage, shocked to the core. He finally snapped back to himself and stammered furiously, "Y-you... All of you are lying about what happened! So shameless! It wasn't like that at all! I clearly wasn't doing all that!"

Mu Qing was still just watching from the side, and it was making Xie Lian anxious with rage. He charged forward with his branch again. The martial gods were having trouble defending against his attacks and could only retreat in defeat.

"Mu Qing! Why are you just standing there?!" they yelled again.

The other heavenly officials joined in on the hollering, but Mu Qing still looked hesitant, like he didn't know whether he should attack. Xie Lian heard them urge Mu Qing to confront him directly, and wild fury blazed inside of him.

"Mu Qing isn't like you. He's my friend—he would never help you!"

He raged and raged and struck even harder. Another row of weapons was sent flying. The rest of the heavenly officials saw that he was growing bolder the longer he fought—that things weren't going the way they should have.

"Mu Qing!" they cried urgently. "Are you just going to watch him make a mess of things like this?!"

Mu Qing's expression changed erratically. He took a step forward, fingers twitching.

"Don't just stand there, give us a hand!" a heavenly official near him called.

It just had to be that moment when someone commented sarcastically, "It's understandable that Mu Qing doesn't want to move—he was His Highness's personal attendant back in the day, after all. Even if His Highness robs mortals and steals our spiritual land, he can't help but be affected by the sentiments of their past relationship. It's enough that he hasn't teamed up with His Highness. How can we possibly expect more than that?"

On the surface, the words sounded like they were giving Mu Qing an excuse to stay out of things, but the comment was insidious. Veins crawled across Mu Qing's forehead.

The air was growing delicate, and Xie Lian could tell this was about to go wrong. "Mu Qing..."

All he said was Mu Qing's name, but a moment later Xie Lian's hands felt light, then he heard a slashing sound.

Xie Lian blinked and looked down to find that his only "weapon," the tree branch, had been sliced in half. When he looked up again, Mu Qing was holding a long saber—and the sharp tip was pointed directly at Xie Lian.

"Please leave," said Mu Qing, weapon in hand.

Xie Lian stared at Mu Qing in silence for a long time, gripping the broken branch. Finally, he said, "I...didn't want to rob anyone. And I wasn't trying to take over this spiritual land either. I got here first."

Mu Qing didn't comment. Instead, he repeated blankly, "Please leave."

Xie Lian gazed at him. After a moment of hesitation, he asked tentatively, "...You know I'm not lying, right?"

He was a little hopeful when he posed the question but also a little scared. A voice in his head was telling him, *"Stop asking! Just turn around and walk away!"* Still, he couldn't help himself.

Before Mu Qing could respond, Xie Lian slumped forward and fell heavily to the ground.

The muddy mountain path was riddled with holes and ditches, covered in rocks and fallen leaves. Xie Lian lay sprawled facedown on the ground in a state of disbelief, his eyes bulging.

One of the heavenly officials had shoved him while he was standing there at a loss and made him take that hideous fall in front of so many eyes.

It was too humiliating. There were voices all around Xie Lian, high and low, filling the air and invading Xie Lian's ears. He stared with eyes that couldn't be wider at the blackened ground in front of his nose, then he slowly raised his head. Mu Qing was standing not too far away from him—standing among those heavenly officials, his head turned away, not looking at Xie Lian. Just like the rest of them, he had no intention of lending Xie Lian a hand to help him up.

And thus, Xie Lian understood. No one would lend him a hand to help him up.

He lay there prone for a long time before crawling up on his own.

The heavenly officials thought he was about to kick off another bout and were exceedingly wary, but Xie Lian wasn't looking for a fight anymore. He fumbled around, head bowed, and once he found the little satchel the queen had packed for him, he picked it up silently and secured it to his back. Then, he turned around and headed down the mountain step by step.

As he went, his steps grew faster and faster. It wasn't long before it turned into a mad dash.

Xie Lian held his breath and ran all the way down the mountain without resting for a moment. He didn't know how far he'd gone, and he didn't mind his footing, causing him to trip and fall once more. The breath he'd been holding was finally released, accompanied by a mouthful of angry blood.

Flustered, he didn't even think to get back up, just sat on the ground panting. Once his breathing slowly returned to normal, he still didn't think to stand up; he remained there in a befuddled daze.

Suddenly, a hand was extended to him. Xie Lian blinked slowly at it, and his eyes followed the arm up.

It was Mu Qing again. He was standing next to Xie Lian with his hand outstretched, looking a little ashen.

A long moment later, he asked stiffly, "Are you all right?"

Xie Lian stared at him with empty eyes and didn't speak.

Mu Qing averted his gaze; perhaps the chilling stare was making him uncomfortable. Nonetheless, he kept his hand outstretched. "Come on."

But he had reached out too late.

Xie Lian didn't take his hand, and he didn't get up either. He just kept staring at him with unblinking eyes.

The two remained at a standstill for a long time, and Mu Qing looked more and more upset. Just as he was about to pull his hand back, Xie Lian grabbed a handful of mud and flung it at Mu Qing. It hit him with a loud *splat*!

Mu Qing had never expected him to do something like that, and he didn't know whether to call it rude or juvenile. Filthy mud splattered on his chest and spots scattered onto his bewildered face. Anger rolled up a moment later, but he forced it down.

"I didn't have a choice," he said in a low voice.

He truly didn't. He had been getting along so well with all those heavenly officials, and they might have thought he was on Xie Lian's side if he just stood idly by and watched his colleagues get pulverized. And *that* would have made his life so much more difficult.

It was as if Xie Lian had forgotten how to speak and could do nothing but hurl mud at him. Mu Qing blocked a couple of shots but couldn't keep up with his pace.

"Have you gone crazy?! Didn't I just tell you that I didn't have a choice?" he cried furiously. "Didn't you rob someone because you didn't have a choice?!"

Scram! Get out of here! Leave! Those were the only words echoing in Xie Lian's mind, but he couldn't utter a single sound, could only crazily grab at anything nearby he could throw. He didn't care who he hurled things at either. Finally, Mu Qing couldn't take it anymore. With a gloomy expression, he left with a sweep of his sleeves. Xie Lian panted harshly for a bit and fell back down, spacing out once more.

He sat in that position until nightfall.

Once the skies turned dark, a crowd of phosphorescent flames approached and floated around him, dancing hauntingly about. But it was like Xie Lian didn't see them—he didn't bother mustering the strength to look. As if the phosphorescent flames were annoyed that they hadn't been noticed, more and more gathered around Xie Lian. He still ignored them.

That is, until a humanoid figure emerged from the assembly of flames.

The arrival of this man was always accompanied by a feeling of immense foreboding. When he sensed that ominous feeling, Xie Lian slowly lifted his head.

A white-clothed man was standing about ten paces away amidst the countless floating phosphorescent flames. Half of the mask on his face smiled eerily.

"How are you, Your Highness?" he greeted pleasantly.

N THE DARK NIGHT, Xie Lian's pupils instantly shrank to tiny dots. His voice quivered.

"It's you...?!"

White No-Face!

The hairs rose on Xie Lian's neck, and he leapt to his feet, groping for his sword—but there was nothing there, and only then did he remember that he'd pawned all of them. Even the branch he'd used as a weapon earlier had been broken. He was facing this creature without spiritual power or weapons!

Years ago, when Xianle fell, White No-Face had quietly disappeared. Xie Lian had never bothered to search for him back then, and he never considered searching for him now—he only prayed that he would remain missing and never reappear. Who could have expected that the creature would find him so suddenly?!

The white-clothed figure approached languidly. Cold terror filled Xie Lian. He couldn't help but back away a couple of steps, but then he immediately shook himself out of it. He couldn't back away—fleeing was futile anyway!

"What do you want?!" he cried sharply.

White No-Face didn't answer, just continued to approach with his hands clasped behind his back. Xie Lian was shaking from his fingers to his toes; even the white puffs of air from his lips seemed to tremble.

He forced himself to recall the jeering, the indifference, and the mocking laughter of the thirty-some heavenly officials, and the sight of Mu Qing turning his face away. With those images in his mind, he forgot his fear and shouted as he struck out with a hand chop.

However, before his strike landed, he was hit by a wave of excruciating pain. The creature had predicted Xie Lian's move and was a step faster, flashing behind Xie Lian to kick him in the back of the knee!

He was too fast!

Xie Lian dropped heavily to his knees, and, for the first time, a terrifying thought entered his mind—this creature was moving faster than he could even think!

The very next moment, Xie Lian felt something even more horrifying—a freezing hand, its fingers stretched wide, was gripping the top of his head!

He started screaming. The creature easily pulled Xie Lian's entire body up by the head. With strength like that, Xie Lian had no doubt his fingers could easily crush his skull should he curl them inward, turning his head into a pulp of bloody flesh mashed between bone. He also had no doubt that White No-Face planned to do exactly that!

Xie Lian drew sharp, erratic breaths, thinking he was dead for sure, and squeezed his eyes shut. Yet unexpectedly, the creature seemed like he wasn't planning on exerting any more force, and instead he withdrew his murderous intent with a soft sigh. For a long time after that soft sound, the creature stayed perfectly still. Surrounded by the dead silence, Xie Lian reopened his eyes little by little.

Ghost fires filled the air, dancing in wild joy. Each ball of flame was a spirit of the deceased cackling in uproarious laughter as they watched the show. However, most of the ghost fires did not dare to approach them—they appeared to have been cowed by something. But one ball of ghost fire, blazing abnormally brightly, was hanging above the two of them, using its flames to crash against the creature behind him again and again. It was impossible to tell exactly what it was trying to do, but for all the effect it was having, it might as well have been an insect fighting a tree.

And then, Xie Lian abruptly froze.

White No-Face was hugging him.

As Xie Lian tilted and fell to his knees in a slump, he had been captured by a pair of cold, powerful arms that pulled him into a lifeless embrace. At some point, White No-Face had sat down on the ground with him.

"So sad, so sad," he murmured. "Your Highness, look. Look at what they've done to you."

He whispered softly as he stroked Xie Lian's head, his hands gentle and full of pity. It was like he was petting a wounded puppy or his own gravely ill child on the brink of death. The smiling half of the crying-smiling mask was hidden in the darkness; the moonlight revealed only the half that was crying, looking like genuine tears of grief shed for Xie Lian.

Xie Lian remained stiff and curled in on himself, moving no further. The man in white behind him raised his fingers to wipe the filthy mud from Xie Lian's face. He sensed a peculiar kind of loving compassion in the man's touch. Like the embrace of a close friend or a dear family member, it miraculously returned a bit of warmth to Xie Lian's shivering body.

He never expected that this sinister creature would be the one to finally offer him compassion.

Choked sobs escaped from the depths of Xie Lian's throat, and he trembled harder and harder. The ball of ghost fire flew near his heart but didn't press close—it was like it wanted to warm him but wasn't confident that it could help chase away the cold.

White No-Face helped wipe Xie Lian clean of mud. "Come to my side," he beckoned.

Xie Lian's voice trembled. "I... I..."

Instead of finishing his sentence, his hand flashed out and went straight for White No-Face's mask! His attack was successful and smacked the mask high into the air. Xie Lian leapt to his feet and flipped meters away, his earlier terror now completely absent.

"Who would ever go to your side, you...monster!" he raged in a dark voice.

The ghastly, pale cry-smiling mask fell to the ground, and all the ghost fires in the air seemed shocked. They abruptly lost all semblance of order, dancing in a frenzy without pause, shrieking without sound. White No-Face, on the other hand, covered his face and started chuckling softly.

The laugh made Xie Lian's hair stand on end. "What are you laughing about?"

White No-Face humphed softly. "You *will* come to my side one day," he stated with certainty.

Xie Lian didn't understand what he meant and said in disbelief, "What even *is* your side? You destroyed Xianle, but you still want me to go to you? Are you crazy? I think you're insane!"

Xie Lian had never learned to cuss; even in extreme rage only those mild denouncements burst out of him. But if he had, he would've used the world's most vicious, most vengeful words to curse that creature. White No-Face laughed out loud, and he held his head high as he covered his unmasked face with his hand.

"You will come. No one in this world will ever truly understand you, and no one will stay by your side forever—except me."

Xie Lian was frightened, but he still tried to argue. "Get out of here! Enough with your self-righteous nonsense! That isn't true just because you say so!"

One ball of ghost fire flew to his side and moved up and down like it was nodding in agreement. However, Xie Lian was surrounded by wicked wisps just like it, so Xie Lian didn't notice that particular one.

"Oh? Is there someone?" White No-Face asked amiably. "Maybe there were people like that in your past, but do you really think they'll be with you much longer?"

"What do you mean...? What are you hinting at?" Xie Lian demanded.

White No-Face didn't answer. He only sneered and turned around like he was about to drift away.

"I will wait for you here, Your Highness," he said softly.

As if Xie Lian would let him go so easily. "Wait! Don't go! What did you do to them? Did you do something to my parents and Feng Xin?!"

He chased after the white-clothed man, reaching out to grab at him. Yet unexpectedly, the man snatched a ball of ghost fire with a light sweep of his sleeve. The motion wasn't intended as an attack, but Xie Lian sensed a horrifying force coming at him and he was thrown high into the air, landing hard by slamming against a tree. With a loud *crack*, the giant, thick-trunked tree split and fell from the force of the collision.

In the past, Xie Lian wouldn't have even batted an eye at crashing into and shattering ten trees. But he was mortal right now, and the impact made him feel like all the bones in his body were crumbling. He fell heavily to the ground and lost consciousness.

The final moment before his eyes closed, Xie Lian saw the white-clothed figure's hand. A ball of ghost fire blazed in his palm.

White No-Face chuckled. "Spirit, tell me, what is your name? How very interesting..."

When Xie Lian regained consciousness, everything was gone.

His chest and mouth were steeped in the thick, astringent tang of blood. His head spun for a good while before he suddenly jolted and attempted to crawl to his feet.

"...Father! Mother! Feng Xin!" he muttered.

He had remembered everything that had happened before he passed out and didn't dare to waste a single second. He ran frantically for dozens of kilometers, until he finally made it back to their hideout in the deep of the night, twenty-some days after he'd left with a satchel on his back.

Xie Lian was torn with panic and anxiety the entire way, scared that White No-Face had already murdered his friend and family. He slammed the door open the moment he arrived at the dilapidated cottage.

"Father! Mother! Feng Xin!" he blurted before even catching his breath.

Thank goodness—the house didn't look as wretched as he had dreaded. There was nothing out of place either. It still looked exactly the same as when he had left.

Xie Lian had been frantically running for a long distance with a battered body; his throat was so dry that he thought it might start smoking. He relaxed a little, then swallowed and continued deeper into the house.

"Feng Xin! Where are you guys—"

He pushed a door open, and his voice died in his throat.

Feng Xin was inside, and when he saw Xie Lian had returned, he exclaimed in amazement, "Your Highness! Why are you back?"

However, Xie Lian wasn't looking at him. He was staring intently at the one facing Feng Xin.

A black-clad man stood there. It was Mu Qing.

Mu Qing turned his head and saw Xie Lian. He pressed his lips together, looking grim. Feng Xin went around him and came over to greet Xie Lian.

"Didn't you go train? How was it? I thought you'd be gone for several months at least. Did you come back so soon because you made good progress?"

Xie Lian stared at Mu Qing. "Where are Father and Mother?"

"Sleeping in their room. They've already gone to bed," Feng Xin said. "Why are your clothes so dirty? What's with the cuts on your face? Who'd you fight?"

Xie Lian didn't answer. Only when he heard his parents were fine did he completely relax, and he turned to Mu Qing. "Why are you here?"

Mu Qing didn't speak, so Feng Xin replied on his behalf. "He came to deliver some stuff."

"What stuff?" Xie Lian questioned.

Mu Qing raised his hand slightly and pointed to the side, where there were several large, clean sacks that probably contained rice or grain.

Seeing Xie Lian so quiet, Mu Qing said softly, "I heard you need medicine. I'll think of a way to get some later."

"Sounds good," Feng Xin said. "I'll give my thanks, then. We do need all that stuff right now. Heavenly officials can't give mortals private gifts, so you be careful too." Then he shuffled over to Xie Lian's side and whispered, "I'm pretty surprised that he actually came back to help. I'm the one who judged him wrong. In any case—"

"Don't need it." Xie Lian interrupted.

Mu Qing's expression turned ashen for a moment, and he clenched his fists.

Feng Xin was puzzled. "What don't we need?"

"I don't need your help." Xie Lian said each word slowly and clearly. "I also...don't want any of your stuff. Please leave."

When he heard the words "please leave," Mu Qing's face got even more glum.

Now Feng Xin noticed that something was wrong. "Just what is going on?"

Mu Qing bowed his head. "I'm sorry."

They'd known Mu Qing for so many years, but this was the first time they ever heard him say those words—it was also his first genuine apology. But there was no more room in Xie Lian's mind for surprise.

"Please leave!"

With that, he lost his temper and started throwing the sacks at Mu Qing. White rice spilled across the ground and made a mess of Mu Qing. Nonetheless, the black-clad man only raised an arm to block and held back from making any further move. Startled, Feng Xin held Xie Lian down.

"Your Highness! What's going on? What did he do?! Didn't you leave to cultivate?! What happened out there?!"

As he was held down, Xie Lian said with red eyes, "Why don't you ask him? I did go to train...but why don't you ask him why I've returned?!"

Their argument was too noisy, and the queen was startled awake in her room. She emerged after pulling on an outer robe. "My son, you've returned? What happened to you—"

"Nothing!" Feng Xin quickly assured her. "Your Majesty, please go back inside!" He forcefully pushed her back into her room and closed the door, then he demanded, "What did you do? Mu Qing, what did you do?! Your Highness, did the cuts on your face come from him?!"

Xie Lian's breathing was growing increasingly frantic and erratic, and he couldn't utter a single word.

"It wasn't me!" Mu Qing exclaimed. "I didn't hit His Highness— I only asked him to leave. Other than that, I didn't say anything harsh, and I didn't move against him! They were determined to take over that spiritual land, and it would've kept escalating if you didn't leave!"

"You—!"

With just those few words, Feng Xin got the gist of what had transpired. His eyes widened, and he pointed at Mu Qing, unable to speak. A moment later, he bent down and grabbed a sack, then flung it at Mu Qing.

"Get out!" he roared. "Get out, get out, get out!"

Mu Qing was once again hit in the face by the sacks of rice he had brought and backed two steps away. All three of them were panting harshly.

"I was wondering why you suddenly had a change of heart!" Feng Xin cried. "I can't fucking believe this, holy shit... Don't let me see you ever again!"

"Yes! I was wrong, I admit it, and I apologize!" Mu Qing exclaimed with a cracked voice. "But I wanted to solve our current problems before considering anything else! Your parents and my mother, the three of us, who knows how long we would have had to struggle in this quagmire! But I thought that if I went back first, maybe we'd still have a chance—"

"All fucking bullshit—enough with your bullshit!" Feng Xin cussed. "No one wants to hear your excuses! Get out, get out, get out, get out, get out, get out, get out!"

Mu Qing tried again. "If you put yourself in my shoes—"

Feng Xin cut him off. "I told you I've had enough of your bullshit! I'm not listening! I just know that even in your shoes, I wouldn't have done what you did. No need to put myself in your shoes because you're nothing more than a traitor!"

Mu Qing looked angry now, and he took a step forward. "When His Highness was in a tight spot, wasn't he forced to commit robbery? So why can't you accept hardship as an excuse when it comes to me?"

Feng Xin sputtered. "Huh? Robbery? Who committed robbery? His Highness robbed someone? What crap are you fucking saying?"

Xie Lian stopped breathing.

Watching Feng Xin's rage gradually turn to shock, Mu Qing finally realized something wasn't right, and he hesitantly turned to Xie Lian. "You...you didn't...?"

It had never occurred to him that Xie Lian hadn't told Feng Xin about what happened!

"*Aaaaaaaaaah!*"

Xie Lian went mad and grabbed a random object to chase Mu Qing away. Mu Qing realized that he seriously screwed up and didn't dare to speak even after Xie Lian hit him multiple times. Yet when he looked back, the thing Xie Lian was using to chase him out the door was a broom. His face instantly darkened.

"Do you have to taunt me like this?!"

"Get out of here!" Xie Lian cried brokenly.

Sharp gales blew from the force of Xie Lian's punch. Mu Qing dodged the brunt of the attack, but only barely, and he still received a thin, bloody cut on his cheek. He touched the wound, then looked at the blood on his hand with an unreadable expression on his face.

"...Fine. I'm leaving."

Xie Lian was doubled over, racked with shivers from head to toe. Mu Qing took a few steps forward and placed the rice sacks back down on the ground.

"I'm really leaving."

Xie Lian's head shot up. When Mu Qing saw the look in Xie Lian's eyes, he swallowed and didn't linger any longer, leaving with a sweep of his sleeves.

Only then did the thoroughly stunned Feng Xin come running outside. "Your Highness! He's bullshitting, right? What robbery?"

Xie Lian covered his forehead. "...Don't ask anymore. Please, Feng Xin, I beg you, please don't ask anymore."

"No, of course I don't believe it," Feng Xin said. "I just want to know what really happened—"

Xie Lian screamed and covered his ears, fleeing back inside the cottage and locking himself in his room.

Feng Xin was genuinely convinced that he would never do such a thing, but that was precisely why this was the worst-case scenario!

Xie Lian wanted to just run away, to escape to a place where no one knew him. But when he remembered what White No-Face had said, he didn't dare go too far. He could only shut himself inside his room. No matter how Feng Xin and the queen called for him, he refused to emerge.

It took two days for Xie Lian to feel calmer, and next time Feng Xin knocked, he silently opened the door.

Feng Xin stood there, holding a plate. "Her Majesty made you this earlier today and wanted me to bring it to you."

The things on the plate were green and purple. It was a terrifying sight.

"Your Highness, if you're scared for your life, I can eat it for you," Feng Xin continued. "I won't tell Her Majesty, ha ha..."

Xie Lian could tell that Feng Xin still really wanted to prod and ask about the robbery, but he was also scared that Xie Lian might lock himself up again. He had forced his curiosity down and pretended not to care, like the incident had never happened and there was nothing to question to begin with. However, he wasn't good at joking, and his failed attempt at comedy only made things even more awkward.

The taste of his mother's cooking was honestly terrifying to the extreme. The more times she entered the kitchen, and the more effort she put in, the more she progressed down the wrong path. Xie Lian had never cooked in the past either, but the meals he made now didn't taste too bad. The only explanation was natural talent. Nevertheless, Xie Lian took the plate and sat at the table dutifully to eat it. He couldn't taste anything he ate anymore, either way.

There was one silver lining. He was sure the king had overheard their argument a few nights prior, and Xie Lian had thought he was done for. But based on how things had gone over the past few days, it looked like the king and queen still weren't aware of the robbery incident. Otherwise, considering the king's temperament, he would've bawled Xie Lian out already. He knew Feng Xin would never tell them about it, so Xie Lian could relax for now.

As he was thinking, Feng Xin abruptly rose to his feet, and Xie Lian snapped out of it. "What are you doing?"

Feng Xin grabbed his bow. "It's time for me to go busking."

Xie Lian stood up too. "I'll go with you."

After a moment of hesitation, Feng Xin said, "Nah. You just rest a bit more."

Although Feng Xin didn't ask any more questions, Xie Lian still felt miserable all over—now that Feng Xin had heard what he'd done, he kept feeling like something between them had changed and that they could never return to the way they had once been. Every word and look Feng Xin gave him seemed take on a different meaning, worthy of deeper interpretation.

Xie Lian shook his head and sighed. "I'll be honest with you. I don't have the mind to cultivate right now."

Feng Xin had more or less expected this, and he bowed his head, not knowing what to say.

"Since that's the case, instead of rotting inside the house, I might as well go busk too," Xie Lian continued. "That way I can earn us some money, so at least I'm not..."

At least he wouldn't be an invalid, he meant to say. Yet for some reason, he couldn't bring himself to speak the word. Perhaps it was because he already felt like an invalid, so he didn't dare say it so casually.

Feng Xin was still a little worried. "I'll be fine on my own too. Your Highness, you've only had one meal over the past two days, so why don't you rest for a while longer?"

The more he insisted, the more anxious Xie Lian was to prove himself, and he turned to look in the mirror.

"It's fine, I'll just clean myself up and—"

He'd planned to tidy himself up so he at least wouldn't look like a disheveled, crazy beggar. But when he looked in the mirror, a horrifying image was reflected back.

The "him" in the mirror didn't have a face. That was because his reflection was wearing a half-crying, half-smiling mask.

Xie Lian screamed, and Feng Xin jumped in surprise.

"What? What is it?!"

Xie Lian pointed at the mirror, his face pale. "*Him!* I... My... My..."

Feng Xin followed his pointing finger and looked at the mirror. A long moment later, he turned to look at Xie Lian again, bewildered. "What's with you?"

Xie Lian was terrified to the marrow. He gripped Feng Xin hard, only squeezing out a few words with great difficulty. "My...! My...! My face! Don't you see it? The thing on my face!"

Feng Xin stared at him and sighed. Xie Lian was still confused why he hadn't reacted when Feng Xin said, "Your Highness, have you finally noticed the cuts on your face?"

It was like Xie Lian had been plunged into an icy cellar.

Why? How could this be? Why would Feng Xin say that?

Did this mean that Feng Xin couldn't see the mask on his face in the mirror?!

"You don't see it? There's something on my face!" Xie Lian blurted.

Feng Xin was puzzled. "What thing? What do you mean? I don't see anything."

Xie Lian looked at the mirror again. "That's impossible! I..."

But when he looked again, the mask on his reflection's face had disappeared. Only his own panicked expression looked back at him.

There were bruises and crisscrossing cuts all over his face. He looked beside himself with fear and wretched to the extreme, like a laborer who had been beaten to a pulp by their landlord. Xie Lian was stunned in spite of himself and probed the side of his cheek as he wondered, *Is this...me?*

Just then, he heard Feng Xin speak. "Your Highness, are you...a bit overtired, perhaps? Or are you just exhausted from being angry at that stinkin' bastard? Listen to me, don't go out for the next few days. Just take it easy."

Xie Lian finally snapped out of it and saw that Feng Xin was about to leave, his bow slung on his back and a stool dangling from his hand.

"No!" Xie Lian exclaimed hastily. "I..."

Feng Xin pushed the door open and looked back. "Is there something else?"

Although the words almost made it to his lips, Xie Lian forcefully swallowed them, because a strange thought had appeared in his mind. Their life was already very difficult. If he told Feng Xin that White No-Face could be coming back to harass them, what would he do?

Feng Xin had also been traumatized by White No-Face. Would he distance himself from Xie Lian and leave like Mu Qing?

While Xie Lian's imagination ran wild, Feng Xin left. Xie Lian snapped back to reality at the sound of the door closing, but he could only shrink back to bed and wrap himself in blankets to take another nap.

Suddenly, he smelled something foul.

Xie Lian crawled upright. At first, he thought it was the queen cooking again, or that some rat had died in a corner, and he got up to check. He looked everywhere, but eventually he discovered that the source of the foul smell was actually himself.

Only then did Xie Lian remember that it had been over two weeks since he'd last washed up or changed clothes. Of course he smelled.

Xie Lian held his breath. A wave of self-hatred crashed through him. Just thinking about how his parents and Feng Xin surely must've noticed but hadn't bothered to tell him made him feel another wave of mortification. He sneakily opened the door and looked around; seeing there was no one outside, he found himself a set of fresh clothing and got to work heating some water for a bath.

After much struggle, he finally lowered himself into the bathtub. He sank beneath the water's surface and held his breath until he was drowning, only resurfacing when he felt like he was going to pass out. Then he scrubbed his face roughly a few times.

After he finished scrubbing himself down, Xie Lian reached out to grab for his clothes. He shook out the robes absentmindedly and was about to get out of the water and put them on when he suddenly noticed something wrong.

These weren't his clothes. This was White No-Face's ghastly white funeral garb, expansive sleeves and all!

In an instant, Xie Lian felt the hot water he was soaking in turn into an icy pond. His hair stood on end, and he cried out in dismay, "Who?! Who did this?!"

Who had swapped out his clothes in secret while he wasn't paying attention?!

He jumped out, still wet and dripping, and knocked the bathtub over with a loud splash. The entire cottage was flooded in an instant with bathwater, startling the king and queen in the next room. The queen supported the king as they walked out to see—only to find Xie Lian sprawled naked on the flooded floor. In her shock, the queen came rushing forward to hug him.

"My son, what happened to you?!"

Xie Lian was wet and dripping, his hair strewn around him. He looked up and hugged her back. "Mom, a ghost, there's a ghost, there's a ghost clinging to me! He follows me everywhere!"

He looked no different from someone who had lost his mind, and the queen couldn't take it anymore. She wept in anguish and held her son. The king also watched Xie Lian in shock. Although he was a man of only forty-some years of age, he now looked like he was over sixty. The frigid air of winter jolted Xie Lian, and he pointed.

"The clothes. Look at the clothes...!"

But when he looked at the clothes again, he didn't see the funeral garb at all. Those were just...his normal white cultivation robes?

Rage seized Xie Lian, and he slammed a fist against the wooden tub. "Just what do you want?!" he roared. "Are you toying with me?!"

The queen forced back her tears and hugged him again. "My son, don't be angry, just put on some clothes first, put them on, don't catch a cold..."

That day, Feng Xin came back very late. Exhaustion was written on his face, much more than usual.

Xie Lian had been waiting for him for a long time, and he said impatiently, "Feng Xin, I have something very important to tell you."

White No-Face was too strange and too powerful a creature; even if Xie Lian told Feng Xin about him, any warnings made ahead of time would probably be pointless. Nevertheless, after much thinking, Xie Lian still believed he shouldn't keep something like this a secret from Feng Xin. He decided to tell him the truth.

Unexpectedly, Feng Xin didn't ask him what it was and only said, "Oh good. I've got something I wanted to say to you too."

Xie Lian assumed the matter with White No-Face would be most critical, and important things were best talked of last, so he sat down at the table and asked, "You go first. What is it?"

Feng Xin hesitated for a moment but said, "Your Highness, you go first."

Xie Lian didn't care to decline politely anymore. "Feng Xin, you must be extremely careful. White No-Face has returned," he said in a hushed voice.

Feng Xin's expression abruptly changed. "White No-Face is back...? Why would you say that? You saw him?"

"Yes!" Xie Lian exclaimed. "I saw him!"

Feng Xin paled. "That's... That's not right. Why would he let you see him? Why are you still here in one piece?!"

Xie Lian buried his face in his hands. "...I don't know! Not only did he not kill me, he even..."

He had even hugged him and patted his head like a loving elder. He beckoned him to his side.

After listening to Xie Lian describe the strange encounters from the past few days, Feng Xin's shock gradually faded away and was replaced by confusion. "What exactly does he want?"

"It can't be anything good. He also seems to be following me everywhere," Xie Lian said. "In any case...you just have to be careful! Help me remind Father and Mother to be careful too, but don't frighten them."

"All right," Feng Xin said. "I won't leave for the next few days. The stuff that bastard gave us...should last for a while."

It was quite embarrassing to admit. When Mu Qing went away, he left behind everything he'd brought them. Although Xie Lian had lost control of himself, flung the provisions in Mu Qing's face, and declared that he didn't need his stuff nor his help, they'd still picked up everything in defeat once they calmed down.

Xie Lian sighed and nodded. Then he said, "Oh yes, what was it that you wanted to say to me?"

Now that the subject was raised, Feng Xin hesitated again. After a pause, he opened his mouth, hemming and hawing and scratching at his head as he stammered out, "Actually, it's... Your Highness, do you still have any money on you? Or something that can be pawned?"

Xie Lian was perplexed that he'd ask such a foolish question at a time like this. "Huh? Why do you ask?"

Feng Xin was sweating, but he replied boldly, "It's nothing... Just... If you happen to have some, can you...lend it to me?"

Xie Lian laughed bitterly. "Do you really think I have anything?"

Feng Xin sighed. "I didn't think so."

After giving it some thought, Xie Lian asked, "Didn't I give you that golden belt?"

"That's not enough," Feng Xin mumbled. "Far from it..."

Xie Lian was shocked. "Feng Xin? What exactly did you do? How could a golden belt not be enough to cover whatever you need? Did you beat someone up and need to pay them off? Tell me?"

Feng Xin came back to himself and quickly said, "Oh no! Don't take this to heart. I was only asking!"

Xie Lian pressed him over and over, but Feng Xin still swore everything was fine. Finally, Xie Lian said with worry, "Well, if there's anything, you must tell me. We can think of a solution together."

"Don't worry about me," Feng Xin said. "There's no way a solution will just fall from the sky. Your Highness, you just focus on solving your own problems!"

When he mentioned that topic, Xie Lian's heart sank again.

Just as he'd expected, the creature harassed him ceaselessly in the days that followed and wouldn't leave him alone.

Xie Lian constantly spotted a cry-smiling mask or a white silhouette in many unexpected places. Sometimes it'd be at the head of the bed in the deep of night, sometimes it'd be a reflection in the water, sometimes the door would swing open abruptly and it would be standing there, and sometimes it'd even be standing right behind Feng Xin.

White No-Face seemed to take pleasure in scaring him, and he purposely made certain that he could only be seen by Xie Lian. Whenever Xie Lian couldn't take it anymore and pointed at him screaming, he'd disappear as soon the others rushed to Xie Lian's side or looked over. Xie Lian spent his days in jumpy agitation, so bitter that he wished he could catch that creature and chop him into eight large chunks—but he couldn't even manage to step on his shadow. Inevitably, his days and nights flipped, and his heart and body were exhausted.

One night, deep in the darkest hours, he jolted awake and felt irrepressibly thirsty. Recalling that he hadn't drank anything the previous day, he crawled up to get some water. However, outside the room, he heard faint voices and weak candlelight. Startled, Xie Lian quickly hid behind the door, his heart thumping.

Who could it be? If it's Father, Mother, or Feng Xin, why would they sneak around like this?

But as it turned out, the ones sneaking around really were his father, mother, and Feng Xin.

Feng Xin's voice was extremely hushed. "His Highness is resting now, right?"

The queen also whispered her reply. "He's asleep."

"Finally," the king said. "Don't wake him too early tomorrow. Let him sleep some more."

Those words made Xie Lian's heart squeeze. Soon after, he heard the queen sigh. "If this keeps up, how will my son ever get better?"

Xie Lian could feel something amiss with those words, and Feng Xin replied in a quiet voice.

"He's only like this because he's exhausted. Too much has happened lately. Will Your Majesties also keep a close eye on him? Please let me know as soon as possible if there's anything not right with His Highness, but don't tell him you did. Also, avoid saying anything that might provoke him—"

Xie Lian stayed in his eavesdropping spot, his mind going blank as he listened. Waves of blood rushed to his brain.

What did this mean? What did they mean?

I'm not crazy! I didn't lie! I was telling the truth! he screamed internally.

Xie Lian slammed the door open, startling the trio inside the room. Feng Xin rose to his feet.

"Your Highness? Why aren't you asleep?!"

Xie Lian lashed out, shouting in his face, "You don't believe me?!"

Feng Xin was taken aback. "Of course I believe you! You—"

Xie Lian cut him off. "Then what did you mean just now? Are you saying that everything I saw was a hallucination? That I'm just delusional?"

The king and queen tried to intercept the argument, but Xie Lian stopped them. "Don't speak! You two don't understand anything!"

"No!" Feng Xin exclaimed. "I believe you, Your Highness, but it's also true that you've been exhausted lately!"

Xie Lian stared at him but didn't reply. There were chilling winds blowing somewhere inside of him.

He trusted that Feng Xin really did believe him. At least mostly… but not completely. After all, Xie Lian had spent his recent days in quite a disturbed state of mind—if any outsider saw him, they would no doubt declare him a madman. What right did Xie Lian have to demand anyone wholly believe him?

But it shouldn't have been like this. Feng Xin used to have absolute faith in him, without reservation! Even if he only doubted it twenty percent, that was still unbearable!

Xie Lian was filled with indignation and resentment, but he couldn't tell who it was aimed at—White No-Face, Feng Xin, everyone, or himself. Without a single word, he turned to leave. Feng Xin chased after him out the door.

"Your Highness, where are you going?"

Xie Lian said with forced calm, "Don't worry about it. Don't follow me. Go back."

"No, where are you going? I'll go with you!" Feng Xin said.

Having made up his mind, Xie Lian suddenly took off in a mad run. Feng Xin wasn't as fast as him and was soon left far behind— he could only shout after him. The king and queen both came outside and started shouting after him too, but Xie Lian pretended not to hear and ran faster and faster.

He had no choice but to go on the attack!

If White No-Face wanted to kill Xie Lian, or Feng Xin, or his parents, he could do it easily. Yet he wouldn't just kill and be done with it—instead, he was playing with Xie Lian like a toy, making a fool of him!

Xie Lian roared into the black night as he dashed. "Come the hell out! You gutter monster! Get the hell over here!"

White No-Face was coming for him specifically, so he believed that the creature would surely be following him. But even after Xie Lian cursed to hell and back with his insufficient vocabulary, none of the usual sneers drifted from unexpected shadowy corners, nor did anyone appear languidly behind his back to place their hand on his unsuspecting head.

Xie Lian ran madly for kilometers before he finally exhausted his strength. He doubled over, hands on his knees to support himself as he panted harshly. His chest and throat were flooded with a metallic taste.

A long while later, he abruptly straightened up and continued forward, muttering under his breath as he went. "So...you want to drag this out? Fine, we'll drag this out slowly!"

He walked alone for who-knew-how-long through the wild hills, old woods, and deep mountains. Fog gradually rolled in and thickened.

All around Xie Lian were old trees sunken in the darkness, flashing their claws. The trees leaned forward and bent at such extreme angles that it seemed like they were bowing, inviting him to step into a forbidden land of no return. Xie Lian could tell that whatever was ahead wasn't anything good but also that it was unavoidable. He needed to put an end to this, so he had to come here sooner or later. Thus, he continued forward with grim determination.

As he walked, something faint and shimmering emerged from within the white fog ahead. It looked like a glowing wall. Xie Lian had never seen anything like it, and he furrowed his brow slightly, coming to a stop. As for that "wall," it was slowly moving forward toward him!

Xie Lian tensed in alarm and snapped a branch off a nearby tree, gripping it at the ready. Only when the wall was less than two meters away did he realize in bewilderment that it wasn't a wall at all—it was countless ghost fires. There were so many that, from afar, it looked like a blazing wall or a giant net.

While the ghost fires were strange, they didn't show any murderous intent. They simply drifted toward him silently, blocking him from continuing onward. Xie Lian tried going around them, but the ghost fires immediately changed direction and continued to block him.

Xie Lian heard many voices, all talking at the same time:

"Don't go there."

"Don't go."

"There are bad things ahead."

"Turn around, don't continue onward!"

The voices were stoic and densely layered, washing over him like a tide and giving Xie Lian chills. He found himself surrounded. In the sea of ghost fire, Xie Lian noticed a ball of flame that was especially bright and especially silent.

A ghost fire didn't have eyes, but when Xie Lian looked at this one, he could almost sense its burning gaze staring back at him.

It seemed this particular ghost was the strongest of those present; all the other ghost fires were only following it.

"Move," Xie Lian said coldly.

The ghost fire didn't move.

"Why are you blocking my way?" Xie Lian demanded.

The ghost fire didn't answer. All the other, smaller ghost fires simply repeated, *"Don't go there!"* over and over again. Xie Lian didn't want to bother with all this, so he struck out with a hand. He didn't disperse their souls; the strike was only meant to break apart the formation of the ghost fires blocking him, like waving away a band of fireflies or a school of little goldfish.

Xie Lian quickly passed through them, dry branches and broken leaves crackling under his feet. Yet when he looked back, the ghost fires were swiftly catching up to him, poised to form another wall.

"Don't follow me," Xie Lian warned.

The brightest, hottest ghost fire was leading at the very front, and it did not heed his words. Xie Lian raised his hand like he was going to strike again.

"Keep following me and I might just disperse your souls!" he warned fiercely.

With a threat like that, many of the ghost fires were frightened, fluttering and shriveling away. However, the leading ghost fire only faltered for a moment in midair before it continued to trail him, no more than five paces behind. It seemed to be telling Xie Lian, *"It doesn't matter if you disperse me"*—or perhaps it knew that Xie Lian wouldn't really do it.

A sudden and inexplicable anger filled Xie Lian. In the past, what little minion would have dared continue to harass him if he shouted at them? They would've disappeared in a flash with their tail between their legs. Now, not only did people step all over him whenever they liked, even this tiny ball of ghost fire wouldn't obey him and took his threats as nothing.

Xie Lian's eyes reddened from anger. "Even a little ghost like you is like this... You're all like this... Everyone's like this!" he mumbled.

It was a little funny to be so enraged by something so small, yet Xie Lian was genuinely filled with furious indignation. Unexpectedly, after his grumbling, the ball of ghost fire seemed to understand his anger and anguish, and it stopped in midair, no longer trailing him. It slowly led the hundreds of little ghost fires away, and they disappeared into the night soon after.

Xie Lian exhaled, turned around, and continued onward.

After walking for seven or eight hundred paces more, he could faintly see the eaves of a building within the beguiling fog ahead. It appeared to be an old temple of the deep mountains. When Xie Lian approached and looked closer, his eyes widened slightly.

It was...a Temple of the Crown Prince.

This was a broken-down Temple of the Crown Prince, of course. It had already been pillaged and wrecked by mobs, and the establishment plaque had fallen to the ground, broken in half. Xie Lian paused in front of the temple's entrance for a moment, then he stepped over the sundered establishment plaque and went inside.

The divine statue within the great hall had long since vanished—perhaps it had been smashed, or burnt, or thrown into the sea. The altar was empty and desolate, and only the scorched base of the statue remained. On either side, the words, "Body in Abyss, Heart in Paradise," had been slashed some thirty times. Like a lovely woman whose face had been scarred by knives, it was no longer a beautiful sight, only chilling and hideous.

Xie Lian kept his composure and sat on the ground inside the great hall, waiting for White No-Face to appear. After an incense time, a figure really did emerge from the beguiling fog outside the temple.

However, it didn't look right—the figure had none of White No-Face's habitual ease, and its hurried steps were very unlike White No-Face's silent creeping. The one approaching mustn't be him, nor anyone Xie Lian knew.

But then who could it be?

Xie Lian was on high alert, but he only got a clear look when the person finally rushed into the Temple of the Crown Prince. Unfortunately, this person didn't match any of his guesses—no matter how Xie Lian studied him, he was only a human passerby, nothing suspicious or notable about him.

However, Xie Lian still didn't relax his guard. Who knew if this was one of White No-Face's disguises?

As could be expected from two people who had suddenly run into each other inside a broken-down temple out in the wild, Xie Lian was cautious of the man—and the man was similarly cautious of Xie Lian.

A moment passed, then the man finally ventured to ask, "Um... Daozhang? Do you know what this place is?"

Xie Lian knitted his brow slightly and looked up. "You don't know what this place is? Then how did you get here?"

"I got lost!" the man said. "I've walked around and around, but I just can't seem to get out of this forest!"

Xie Lian knew that this man hadn't gotten lost at all. If he really wasn't White No-Face in disguise, then he had most likely been lured in by something.

"Stop walking around. You won't be able to get out that way," Xie Lian said.

"Huh? What do you mean?"

But Xie Lian didn't respond further, just continued to meditate. If this man had been lured in by White No-Face, panicking would be pointless. There would be no leaving if he didn't want to let them go, so it'd be better for Xie Lian to wait quietly and see what he planned on doing.

The man was tired from running around, so he sat on one side of the room to rest, the two of them now at peace with each other. It wasn't long before another figure emerged from the fog and entered the temple—another confused traveler. Seeing that there were people inside, he quickly approached them.

"Hey, pal! Can I ask what this place is?"

The two travelers started chatting, and a premonition started growing in Xie Lian's mind.

It wasn't over. More would come.

Sure enough, dozens of people arrived at this Temple of the Crown Prince within the span of two hours, one after the other. There were all kinds: men, women, seniors, children, some by themselves, some in groups of three or four, some whole families, and most of them had come here after getting lost. The reasons for their getting lost were numerous and bizarre—some had even been strolling down a city street and had inexplicably found themselves lost in this forest. It was completely incredible. Xie Lian even noticed that one was the same street performer who had been so adamant about competing against him in boulder shattering. He didn't look very well; it seemed the competition had injured him badly. The two of them spotted each other but didn't say a word, only nodded in acknowledgment.

It was easy to see that these were all ordinary people, and they had all been intentionally brought into the deep mountains by White No-Face!

The alarm in Xie Lian's head was sounding louder and louder, but still, he didn't move. He dug out a cold steamed bun from his sleeve and bit into it forcefully, chewed forcefully, and then swallowed forcefully. He had to conserve all his energy to face the great battle that was likely coming.

Four hours later, this Temple of the Crown Prince was full to bursting with "lost" people. Xie Lian counted silently and determined there were about a hundred in total. Not a single one would be able to leave these woods.

With crowds came bustling noise, and everyone started chatting.

"Did you also randomly end up here? This reeks of evil!"

"Why don't we try to find a way out again?"

"Let's go, let's go. I refuse to believe that not a single one of us will be able to find a way!"

Xie Lian was sitting in the corner and looked up abruptly. "It won't matter how far you walk. There is no exit."

The crowd looked at him. "How come?"

"Because you were led here by a monster. You're his toys, so why would he let you go so easily?" Xie Lian said bitterly.

Silence descended upon the room.

Within the crowd, some thought he was an alarmist, some thought he was deliberately being cryptic, and some thought he shouldn't be underestimated.

One of them stood up and asked Xie Lian, "Who are you? What makes you say that?"

"I think he was the first one here. He was already sitting there when I came."

"Weird..."

"Yeah, and his face is covered too."

"Do you have any proof?" one asked.

"There is no proof. Believe it if you will," Xie Lian said evenly. "The monster certainly didn't lure you here to invite you all in for a meal. I don't think I need to tell you to be a little more careful."

After he spoke but before anyone could respond, the sound of frantic footsteps came from the far distance. Everyone instantly perked up.

"Another one's coming!"

There were some who wanted to go outside and check it out, but just as they crossed the temple threshold, they hastily slipped back inside. This was because the running noise was accompanied by waves of crazed screaming.

The screaming voice didn't sound human at all. Everyone's faces dropped, and they all backed further into the temple.

"What the heck! Who could that be? It's not some beast, is it?!"

As the figure within the beguiling fog swiftly approached the temple, Xie Lian narrowed his eyes. "No, it's a person!"

Except the person was running in their direction and howling deafeningly at the same time, his hands covering his face. Seeing that he would make it to the temple at any second, Xie Lian squeezed through the crowd and stood at the front to see what was happening.

It was as if the man had no eyes. He crashed straight into a tree at the entrance of the Temple of the Crown Prince. *Bang!* He bounced back a good three meters, then fell to the ground unconscious.

The crowd was shocked. Still crammed inside the temple, they all stretched their necks out to gawk. "What... What happened to that man?" they wondered apprehensively.

Some, like the street performer, were gutsier and declared that they were going to examine him.

"Don't go near him!" Xie Lian immediately called out.

Those people jumped at his severe tone. "Then what do we do? Just let him lie there?"

"*I* will go take a look," Xie Lian said.

"Then you be careful, okay?" the crowd said.

Xie Lian nodded and approached the tree slowly, then crouched next to the man. He was about to move the hand covering the man's face when he suddenly jumped and let out two shrieks.

Yes, two shrieks at once—two sounds happened at the same time. One came from his mouth and the other came from his face— another face on the man's face!

Human Face Disease!

Goosebumps instantly raised on Xie Lian's skin, and his pupils shrank. The crowd within the temple was frozen watching this horrifying scene. After the man sprang up, he dropped his hands and began to charge over to where the people were, but thankfully Xie Lian had quick reflexes and struck. The Human Face Disease victim was instantly sent flying dozens of meters away by his slap. Xie Lian then hastily backed away to shield the entrance of the temple while exclamations of panic and shock sounded from the crowd behind him.

"I thought that disease only appeared in the imperial capital! So many people died—but wasn't the plague extinguished?!"

"It's not real! It can't be real! Is that really a face on his face?!"

The horror only increased in the next moment when more wailing echoed from all around. Over ten wobbling figures were approaching the temple.

They didn't need to look closer to know they all had Human Face Disease!

"Everyone, run! Spread out! Don't let them come close!" someone yelled.

But Xie Lian shouted, "Don't spread out! Who knows how many more of them there are in the woods?! If there are others out there, it'll all be over!"

"Then what do we do?!"

"We can't stay here like sitting ducks!"

"Isn't that just waiting for death to come to me?!"

The branch Xie Lian had broken off en route was hanging at his waist, and he grasped it to wield like a sword. "Don't worry, they won't come here. *I* get to decide whether they can approach!"

This was his domain, the Temple of the Crown Prince!

"You..."

Not waiting for any further questions, Xie Lian leapt out. With a few swings of the branch, all the Human Face Disease victims fell to the ground in an instant. Committing word to action wasn't hard for Xie Lian at all, and sure enough, none of the disfigured wretches could get close. The crowd within the temple watched, punctuating the scene with harsh, gasping breaths, growing more and more shaken as the fight went on. When they saw that Xie Lian had triumphed, they all cheered, hollering thanks to the heavens.

At some point, ghost fires had come drifting on the night air from within the woods, and now they were dancing madly everywhere. Xie Lian couldn't tell if they were helping drive away the disfigured wretches, but in any case, he didn't think they were trying to obstruct him.

After making a sweep of the area, Xie Lian tried to sheathe his sword out of habit; only after his hand came up empty when grasping for his scabbard did he remember that he was wielding not a sword but a tree branch. He felt awkward for a moment.

Suddenly, he spotted a white-clad figure not far away, waving and beckoning him. Xie Lian's blood was still boiling from the fight, and he instantly gave chase.

"Don't even think about escaping!"

The band of ghost fires zoomed over and followed his charge like they were lighting his way. Naturally, White No-Face wasn't trying to escape. He strolled at an easy pace, his steps languid, but he always remained seven or eight paces ahead. Xie Lian pursued him for a few steps before he realized something and immediately turned back. Noticing that he wasn't chasing anymore, White No-Face stopped.

"Why aren't you following me?"

Xie Lian looked back. "You just want to lead me away so you can spread another wave of Human Face Disease. Why would I follow you and let you have your way?"

"No, you're mistaken. My objective isn't to 'lead you away.' My objective is *you*."

Although his expression was concealed by the cry-smiling mask, for some reason, Xie Lian could sense he was smiling.

Luring Xie Lian away truly made no sense. If White No-Face wanted to spread Human Face Disease again, he could've done so anywhere else in the world and Xie Lian wouldn't have been able to stop him. So why was he doing it in these deep mountains?

Xie Lian stopped. "Then what exactly do you want?!"

He had asked that same question countless times and was starting to lose his patience.

"I've already told you. I want you to come to my side," White No-Face replied.

Xie Lian wielded his tree branch and pointed it at him. While it was not threatening whatsoever—even a little funny—it was nonetheless the only weapon he had on hand. Thank goodness, a particularly bright ball of ghost fire landed on the tip of the branch and helped add some battle aura.

"Why do you want me on your side? To take your life?" Xie Lian demanded sharply.

White No-Face only chuckled softly. "Your Highness, you are a beautiful block of jade," he said warmly. "Allow me to guide and educate you."

Xie Lian could not immediately formulate a response. Feeling both incredulous and furious, he couldn't help but click his tongue. "You? Educate me? My master is the State Preceptor of Xianle. What the heck are *you*?! Where did you come from, you monster?!"

White No-Face extended a finger and waggled it.

"You're mistaken again. Your Highness, perhaps it would be better to say that I am the *only* one worthy to educate you. Your master? The State Preceptor of Xianle?" His voice turned strangely arrogant and condescending. "That *thing* isn't worth mentioning in my presence. On the contrary, you've been absorbing my lessons very well."

"What did you teach me?" Xie Lian spat angrily. "What the heck are you talking about? I don't understand at all!"

White No-Face snorted a laugh. "The first thing I taught you is that you are powerless in the face of many things in this world."

At his words, countless chaotic images and voices flashed through Xie Lian's mind. He gritted his teeth and lunged with his "sword," but White No-Face easily evaded.

"The second thing—"

He seized Xie Lian, making him lose his balance and almost trip. Xie Lian felt a hand stroke the top of his head.

"Do you want to save the common people? They don't need you to save them. They aren't worthy."

Xie Lian's movement faltered for a moment, but then he slapped that hand away before turning and stabbing again. White No-Face snapped the branch in his hand and dodged behind Xie Lian, quickly placing two ice-cold fingers on a fatal point on the back of his head!

Xie Lian was sure his brain was going to be pierced at any moment by those prodding fingers. He froze in place.

From behind him, White No-Face spoke again. "If you don't come to my side, then you will never win against me, and I will always defeat you."

Xie Lian panted and said darkly, "...Come at me anytime!" He paused for a moment, then kept speaking, saying each word slowly and clearly.

"I can't win, but that's only for now. You can defeat me countless times, but you can't kill me. And as long as you can't kill me, I will surely defeat you one day!"

When the ghost fire heard his words, it blazed even more ferociously, like it was going to brighten the entire night sky.

Behind him, White No-Face was silent for a moment. Then he said, "I can't kill you?"

Xie Lian held his breath and didn't speak. In truth, he didn't fully know what the undying body Jun Wu had granted him could handle. If White No-Face really did pierce his skull in a moment of fury, would he still live?

White No-Face continued, his tone even, "Indeed, I can't kill you. I *won't* kill you either. But don't be too confident, now—I hope you don't have any regrets about this later."

Regret? What would he regret?

Xie Lian hadn't yet figured it out when a hand chopped his neck violently. He instantly sank into darkness.

Within that darkness, there was light and warmth some distance ahead. Xie Lian moved toward the light and regained consciousness little by little.

He opened his eyes slowly. The first thing he saw was a ball of ghost fire floating above him. It seemed that the little ghost fire was the source of the light and warmth he had felt while unconscious.

Seeing that he was awake, the ghost fire immediately pressed close to Xie Lian, then quickly decided that getting too close wasn't acceptable and backed off a little. Xie Lian couldn't help but consider this ball of ghost fire exceptional—if he remembered correctly, it was the same one who had created a formation to block his path through the woods. He wanted to reach out and poke at it, yet when he tried, for some reason his hand didn't move at all.

Xie Lian was perplexed and instantly snapped out of his reverie. He dropped his head to look and quickly discovered why he couldn't move his hand. His arms and legs were bound.

He was firmly tied down on the altar atop the scorched base of the missing statue. There were many people squeezed around the altar, and hundreds of round, unblinking eyes were staring up at him.

WHY WERE THEY all staring at him like that?

Suddenly, Xie Lian heard a whisper from below.

"So similar..."

"He's not just similar...he's the exact same!"

"Is it really him?"

Someone bluntly asked, "Are you...that prince?"

Out of habit, Xie Lian blurted, "I'm not..."

Yet he trailed off when he realized that the white silk he used to cover his face had been untied. He was trussed to the altar by that same white silk, and his face was fully exposed to the crowd surrounding him.

Xie Lian's heart jumped to his throat, but he steeled himself and met the gazes of the crowd.

He didn't know if it was his mind playing tricks, but he felt those stares turn strange. But thankfully, perhaps due to the imminent danger, their eyes at least didn't bear the disgust or anger he had feared. And that imminent danger made itself known in the next second as a wave of inhuman howls rang out from outside the temple!

Xie Lian tried to twist his neck around and discovered that the howling was coming from the disfigured wretches he had already knocked down. They had somehow regained their footing, and there were more out there now. They had surrounded the Temple of the Crown Prince, and they screamed as they circled it hand in hand like they were performing some horrifying ritual, or perhaps it was purely the wild dancing of demons. The crowd inside the temple huddled together, cowering in absolute terror. A young child burst into tears and his parents took him into their arms, covering his eyes and ears. Every face in the room was stricken with fear.

"What do we do? What do we do?"

"Will they break in...?"

"Even if they don't, they're so close—will we be infected...? What will we do if we catch it?!"

Xie Lian fought against his bindings but couldn't loosen them in the slightest. It seemed that the white silk had been tampered with, likely injected with spiritual power.

With veins visible on his forehead from his ongoing struggle, Xie Lian roared, "White No-Face!"

There was no response. Instead, an icy-cold hand patted his head. Xie Lian froze, hair standing on end from the touch. And when he twisted his head back, what he saw had dread prickling from his head on down his spine.

No wonder the people below him were giving him strange stares. Not only was Xie Lian's face exposed, but White No-Face was seated in the darkness right behind him.

Confronted by such a strange-looking character dressed all in white, no one dared to breathe, let alone move carelessly. So White No-Face ignored them entirely as he helped Xie Lian sit upright under the watchful gaze of the crowd.

Xie Lian was pulled into a sitting position from where he'd been lying, and now he was sitting atop his own divine altar like a bound, living statue. Aside from his eyes and neck, he couldn't move at all.

Although his situation was beyond eerie, the howling Human Face Disease victims outside were more terrifying. The attention of the crowd below soon returned to the disfigured wretches outside.

"...From what I heard, anyone in the same district can infect you, and the disease spreads incredibly fast!" someone muttered. "We're so close, they're right there, we'll definitely, definitely—!"

Anguish, panic, and despair filled the temple at the thought that they would soon fall victim to the horrifying plague.

"Why don't a few of us go out there and knock some of them dead, and the rest of us escape?" someone suggested.

Setting aside the question of whether they would even be able to kill enough of those wretches, anyone that tried would surely become infected as well. It would mean sacrificing oneself to save others, so who would want to volunteer? No one.

Xie Lian would, if he could. However, he was being restrained by White No-Face. And although he could knock down seven or eight of the mad victims at a time, it would be hard to completely shut down a group of seventeen or eighteen. There was bound to be one who broke through and rushed into the Temple of the Crown Prince.

As for killing White No-Face? Xie Lian would be a fool to even consider trying.

However, the crowd needed someone to calm everyone down. Xie Lian gathered his composure and said calmly, "Everyone, please don't lose your heads! It won't spread that quickly. We still have time to think of a solution."

But a mere guarantee that it "won't spread that quickly" was hardly enough to reassure them. Surprisingly, the one who lifted the cloud of despair was none other than White No-Face.

"There is a way to prevent and cure Human Face Disease," he said, cutting in.

At his statement, the heads of the crowd shot up.

"It can be cured? How?!"

Xie Lian felt his heart stop.

"Why don't you ask His Highness? He knows the method," White No-Face mused leisurely.

In an instant, a hundred pairs of eyes were focused intensely on Xie Lian. The sharpness of their gazes made him instinctively recoil, but he was caught by White No-Face and shoved forward again.

Xie Lian could hear some hopeful voices in the crowd.

"Your Highness, do you really know?"

Before Xie Lian could answer, someone else shouted excitedly, "I heard from somebody that he does know!"

However, some were suspicious. "If he knew, then why did the capital still...? Unless he knew and deliberately didn't tell anybody?"

"Your Highness, please hurry up and tell us, yeah?"

Xie Lian immediately denied it. "I don't know!"

However, White No-Face insisted, "You lie."

Furious, Xie Lian wanted to rebuke him, but he was afraid it would instead drive White No-Face to leak more information.

He had a feeling that White No-Face would say it regardless, though, whether he denied it or not.

After struggling for a while, Xie Lian admitted in defeat, "There's... no way. It's useless!"

After a pause, the sea of people started to stir. "What do you mean, 'useless'? How can we know it's useless if you don't even tell us?"

A drop of cold sweat slid down his forehead. Xie Lian thought, *I really can't say it...*

He mustn't say it! If the truth ever came to light, it would all be over. Chaos would reign!

Within the crowd, someone was finally fed up and jumped to their feet. "We're already at death's door, so what's the point of keeping secrets? Unless you want us all to wait here like sitting ducks until we die?"

In a gentle voice, White No-Face offered, "Then let me tell you."

"Be quiet!" Xie Lian yelled angrily.

Naturally, his shout wasn't threatening in the least, and White No-Face ignored him. "Do you know which people in the capital were least likely to catch Human Face Disease?"

The crowd watched him in trepidation. Although afraid to get close, they couldn't help but ask, "Wh-which people?"

"Soldiers," White No-Face answered.

It was all over now.

"Why was it the soldiers?" White No-Face continued. "Because they all did one specific thing. It's something that isn't done by ordinary citizens, which is why those ordinary citizens caught Human Face Disease."

The crowd's eyes were growing wider and wider. Holding their breaths, they inquired, "And that thing was...?"

Xie Lian lunged headfirst in White No-Face's direction, but his effort was in vain. Laughing, White No-Face shoved him back in place.

"What was it, you ask?" He hummed. "Murder."

It was all over!

He'd actually said it. As he slumped on top of the altar, Xie Lian's heart felt cold as ice.

After the initial shock, some people repeated it in disbelief, "Murder...? You have to kill someone to become immune? You need to kill someone to be cured?"

"You're lying, right?!"

The terrible thing was—no, it wasn't a lie! It was the ultimate truth, and Xie Lian had verified it himself. One who was stained with blood, one who had ended another's life, was immune to Human Face Disease!

Nobody had expected this to be the secret to gaining immunity. Stunned, they discussed among themselves.

"How can this be?"

"I always thought it was odd, but it's true that I haven't ever heard of anyone in the army who got infected with Human Face Disease! So it's probably true!"

"It *is* true!"

"But doesn't that mean we have to kill someone to prevent infection?"

"Who do we kill?"

The person who posed the question immediately got lectured. "What do you mean, 'who do we kill'? Don't tell me you actually want to kill someone?"

The man didn't dare to say anything more. However, the hundred pairs of eyes that had been filled with nothing but simple terror now contained many other emotions; it was very subtle, very strange.

This was exactly what Xie Lian had feared. Once the cure for Human Face Disease was brought to light, one thing would inevitably happen:

Mass murder.

This was the sole reason that Xie Lian had kept the secret to himself after discovering the way to gain immunity. As long as one had killed another human being, they would be safe from the disease. Perhaps most people would be able to control themselves initially, but there was bound to be someone desperate enough to take the risk. The moment blood was spilled in the name of preventing the disease, it would soon be followed by a second killing, then a third... As more and more people followed suit, the whole world would be thrown into chaos. If that was the inevitable result, it was better for Xie Lian to firmly guard the knowledge and keep it only to himself.

Xie Lian smiled wryly. "Now you understand why I said the method is useless."

The crowd was silent. Xie Lian sighed. He forced himself to keep his chin up, then soothed them with a gentle tone.

"No matter what happens, please stay calm and don't act rashly or you'll play right into this creature's hands."

Among the crowd, there was a genteel-looking couple. With her child wrapped in her arms, the mother wept, "How did this happen?! Why is this happening?! Why does it have to be us, of all people? We've never done anything wrong!"

"Cry, cry, cry—what are you crying for?" a nearby person snapped at her. "All you know how to do is cry and cry! *No one* here has done anything wrong! You think you're the only unlucky ones?"

"What, you're not even going to let people cry?!" the husband retorted angrily.

"What's the use of crying so much that you annoy everyone around you? Shut your mouth!"

It was unbelievable that a fight could break out over such a petty thing. Everyone was clearly teetering on the edge of breakdown, and even a small touch could set them off.

Xie Lian was quick to pacify them. "Stop arguing! Stay calm! Only calm minds can bring solutions!"

However, the more he tried to calm the crowd, the more agitated they became.

"Stay calm? How can we be calm at a time like this? If you're so calm, why don't *you* think of something? Let's hear what you got!"

The request silenced Xie Lian. What kind of solution was there? None!

He dug through his mind desperately for an answer until his brain was on the verge of exploding. But he couldn't think of any way to resolve the situation in front of him!

Suddenly, he felt someone squeeze his cheeks. A hand had cupped his face and twisted it to face the audience below the altar. Xie Lian's eyes widened in confusion.

An icy cold voice spoke from behind him. "Who should you kill? You still don't know after seeing this face?"

"..."

At that question, not only did all movement cease below the altar, but even the ball of ghost fire hanging above him froze in place.

"Did you forget? He is a god," White No-Face reminded them amiably. "Which means—"

Before he could hear the rest, Xie Lian felt a chill wash over his chest. Stunned, he gazed down and saw the tip of a pitch-black sword pushing out of his abdomen.

The blade was long and slender, and was colored a deep, black jade. Its central ridge reflected the light in a crisp silver line. The blade was every bit as dangerous and frigid as the coldest winter night. It was, without a doubt, a rare and treasured sword—the exact kind that Xie Lian would have once obsessed over obtaining and then never let leave his grasp.

Xie Lian couldn't look away. The tip of the sword started to slowly inch back into his stomach until it disappeared once again.

"—His body is immortal," White No-Face finished.

Before anyone had the chance to react, White No-Face tossed the blade toward the crowd of onlookers. *Clang!* The tip pierced the ground, and the sword stood at a slant before all those pairs of eyes. Its thick, frigid aura quietly permeated the air.

A rush of blood gushed up Xie Lian's throat. The ball of ghost fire flew to him, pressing close as if trying to cover his wound.

Xie Lian choked on his bloody rage and gritted his teeth. "You... You!"

Lights danced in his vision. The ball of ghost fire shot straight at White No-Face as if suddenly furious. But White No-Face caught it effortlessly and held it captive within his palm.

"Watch," he ordered the ghost fire. In the next second, White No-Face yanked Xie Lian's head around so he was facing him. "And what *about* me? Aren't you the one who proclaimed that you wanted to save the common people?"

"But! But I... I..." Xie Lian stammered.

But he had never thought that *this* would be the only way he could save people!

Below the altar, there were already some who were scared to tears by the bloody scene, but the bolder ones were still watching.

"Will... Will he really not die?!"

"It's true... Look, there's barely any blood... He's still alive—still perfectly alive!"

Xie Lian was racked by another intense cough.

"So in other words, even if we kill him, he won't die?!"

"That's great!"

The one who cheered got scolded. "'Great'?! What's so great about this?!"

"Since he won't be able to die...don't we have a solution now?" the scolded person mumbled.

"But to stab someone, that's so..."

"He's a god! Even if he gets stabbed, he won't die! We're just ordinary people here. If we get infected with Human Face Disease, our fates are sealed!"

Watching the struggle unfold, White No-Face beckoned to Xie Lian. "The common people are here, waiting for you to save them. Please, go ahead."

Anger blazed in Xie Lian's eyes. "The only way to save the common people is to eradicate a twisted monster like you!"

White No-Face sneered. "What's the matter? Your Highness, didn't you boast to me so confidently of your inability to die? You couldn't possibly be scared now. Since you can't to die, you can sacrifice yourself and relieve others of their suffering. Isn't that a delightful thing?"

"Was this your plan all along?!" Xie Lian clicked his tongue. "Do you think that everyone in the world is as evil as you?!"

True to his words, the expressions of the people below weren't the ecstatic ones of those that had been rescued; instead, they were hesitant and split. There were conflicting opinions on the matter, and the crowd had yet to come to any sort of decision—and no one yet dared to pull out the black blade.

As if reading his mind, White No-Face laughed out loud. He shook his head disapprovingly and sighed. "Silly child. Foolish child."

Xie Lian twisted his head away and refused to let the creature pet him again. "Get lost!"

"You think they don't want to do it?" White No-Face asked. "Wrong. It's not that they don't want to do it, it's just that no one wants to go *first*."

"*Aaaaah!*"

A devastated cry erupted from under the altar; it had come from the genteel wife. "My child, my child!"

The infant in her arms wailed uncontrollably as lumpy, dark lesions began to rise from his chubby arm. The people around them immediately backed away, leaving them a wide berth.

"This is bad—the kid is infected!"

Anguished, the couple exchanged a look, then jumped to their feet. They walked to the altar, pulled the black sword from where it had been stabbed into the ground, and placed it between the child's hands. Grimacing, they lunged at Xie Lian.

"...!"

The black blade was extremely sharp, for the couple had already pulled out the sword before Xie Lian felt the excruciating pain explode from his abdomen. They dropped it to the ground with a loud clang and apologized over and over.

"Sorry... Our child is still young, there was really...no other way. Sorry, sorry, sorry..."

Their faces were pale as they apologized, and they kowtowed over and over in front of Xie Lian before disappearing into the crowd with their child.

The blood clogging Xie Lian's throat thickened, and he was about to cough it up when he heard White No-Face snicker beside him. He forced down the mouthful of blood and hissed, "What are you laughing at?! Do you think that you got what you wanted? You forced this whole situation!"

The ghost fire trapped in the creature's hand flickered even more fiercely.

Taking his time to do so, White No-Face explained, "Humans have to be forced before they'll reveal their true selves."

Among the hundred people here, there was now one who no longer had to fear Human Face Disease. As they saw the dark lesions slowly fade from the child's arm, the crowd swallowed heavily and remained silent.

After a long while, a young man finally stepped forward amidst the dead silence. Bracing himself, he walked toward the altar, then bowed several times with his hands clasped in front of him. "I'm sorry. I don't want to do this. I really don't, but I don't have a choice," he pleaded. "I just got married—my mother, my wife, they're both at home waiting for me..."

The man rambled on and on until he could no longer continue, then shut his eyes, raised the sword, and thrust it toward Xie Lian. Because his eyes were closed, his aim was off and the sword punctured Xie Lian in the side instead. When the man opened his eyes and realized he hadn't hit a fatal spot, he panicked, frantically pulled out the weapon with trembling hands, and stabbed Xie Lian again!

Xie Lian had gritted his teeth to prevent any sounds from escaping his throat, and he let out nothing more than a grunt at the two consecutive jabs. A stream of blood seeped from the corner of his mouth.

It was true that he wouldn't die. But that didn't mean he wouldn't be injured...or feel every bit of pain.

The sound of the weapon tangling on his flesh, the feeling of it scraping on his bones—it was so distressing and painful that Xie Lian almost went mad. When it came to this, he was no different from a mortal.

After the second person finished, he stepped down without offering Xie Lian a single kowtow. The expression on his face at the deed he had committed was a mixture of regret and the joy of survival—it was hard to say which feeling won out. Once he retreated into the crowd, silence returned.

It was another long time before a few more hesitant people began to look like they wanted to come forward with reasons of their own. Before they could rise to their feet, a man interrupted.

"I can't stand this anymore."

The crowd turned in the direction of the voice, and Xie Lian lifted his pale face too. The one who had spoken was the buff street performer.

"Are you seriously just going to do whatever that monster tells you to?" the street performer scolded the crowd. "From what I can see, he's just babbling nonsense. And even if it were true, just because this guy can't die doesn't mean this isn't murder!"

"Buddy, wake up—everyone here is about to die!" a bystander advised him.

"Aren't I here too? Won't I die too? But do you see me doing anything?" the street performer shot back.

That shut a few people up, but a second later, someone resorted to hurling accusations. "A guy like you probably doesn't have any elders or children in your family, right? 'Every man for himself' might be fine for you, but a lot of us here have families to look after. How can you compare yourself to us?"

The street performer pointed at the couple who had gone first so quickly. "It's true that I don't have a wife and son. But if I did, I would never let my son see me resorting to these methods even if it meant I died—let alone guide him into doing it himself! If a child grows up to be a bad apple, it's the parents who are to blame. If you were that eager to save him, why didn't you make your child take a stab at *you* instead?"

The wife covered her face and wept bitterly. "Don't curse my son! If you must curse, curse me instead!"

The husband was furious. "Are you listening to yourself? You want my son to kill his own father and mother? What reckless disregard for ethical principles!"

Although the street performer probably didn't understand what he meant, he retorted, "Murder is murder! At least it'd be courageous to sacrifice yourself for your son. Speaking of which, why don't any of you guys try going for the weird-looking guy in the mask?"

Upon hearing that, White No-Face burst out in laughter. The crowd was both terrified and furious. Their fear was directed at the monster, and their anger was directed at the street performer. They hushed their voices and chided him, "You...! Shut your mouth!"

What if they accidentally angered the monster?

But the street performer saw through them immediately. "Oh, so you don't have the balls to kill the big evil guy, so you chose someone else to stab instead?"

Unable to suffer such humiliation from a simple brute like him any longer, someone shouted, "This fella won't stop preaching at us! Here I thought he might have some bright ideas! But after taking a closer look at that deathly pale face of his, I'd say he probably only has a couple days left to live at most. That's why he talks so big. If you're so righteous, why don't you sacrifice yourself to help get us all out of this predicament?"

"I don't want to sacrifice myself, but neither does anyone else," the street performer countered. "Who does? Do you? How about you? But at least I won't stab anyone."

"But *he's* different," someone said.

"How so?" asked the street performer.

"He's a god! 'Save the common people'—he said that himself. Also...also, he can't die!"

The street performer was about to keep arguing, but Xie Lian couldn't hold back any longer. He coughed weakly and called out, "B-buddy! Hey, buddy!"

Because of the stab wounds he'd already sustained, his voice was quite faint. Still, the street performer turned to look.

Xie Lian's voice was filled with gratitude. "Thank you! But...just forget about it."

If the street performer kept arguing, he'd probably get beaten up. Xie Lian remembered that the man's grave internal injuries had been caused by their competition.

Guilty at heart, he repeated, "Thank you! Your injuries from shattering boulders on your chest—have they healed?"

"Huh? What are you saying? How could I have been hurt? Boulder shattering is my specialty!" the street performer exclaimed proudly.

The man refused to lose face even in a situation like this—it was practically the same as claiming to be completely fine while spitting out mouthfuls of blood. Xie Lian wanted to laugh.

Suddenly, a person pointed at the street performer and screamed. "It's spreading! It's spreading!"

Xie Lian was stunned, as was the street performer. Following the pointing finger, the street performer touched his face. As expected, he felt something uneven.

The people around him immediately moved away. Xie Lian opened his mouth, wanting to call the street performer over—but to do what? To get him to fatally stab him too?

The words were lost in his throat.

In the moment while Xie Lian hesitated, the street performer stroked his face several more times, then dashed out of the temple. Seeing the action unfold, Xie Lian called after him.

"Where are you going? Come back! If you don't treat it, it will spread!"

But the man only ran even faster and hollered over his shoulder, "I'm not coming back! If I said I won't do it, then I won't do it...!"

Soon, his figure disappeared. The disfigured wretches around the temple somehow knew that the man was one of them now and didn't block his path. Xie Lian continued to call out until he couldn't see the man's shadow anymore.

The people below the altar began to mutter amongst themselves.

"It's over, he's gone!"

"That idiot! It'll spread regardless of where he runs! It's already too late—he's already infected!"

"He...couldn't have gone down the mountain to kill others, right?"

The words that the street performer had said before he left held the people in the temple at bay. Time passed, and no one went forward to pick up the sword. The situation had stalled.

Xie Lian couldn't tell if he felt joy, worry, or fear, but most importantly, he didn't know what to do next. As he was fighting to clear his mind, someone stood up.

"Can I say something?"

It was a middle-aged man. Xie Lian looked up and thought the man seemed somewhat familiar, but he couldn't recall where their paths had crossed.

While Xie Lian was still trying to remember, the man announced, "To tell you the truth, he tried to rob me!"

Xie Lian was shocked into silence. It was that man!

The crowd was stunned.

"Rob?"

"Isn't he a crown prince? Isn't he a god? He robbed someone?"

"It's the absolute truth," the man confirmed.

"So? What are you trying to say?"

"Nothing... I just wanted to let everyone know that he tried to steal!" The man crouched again after he finished his statement.

The temple fell into a solemn silence again after the outburst. That single statement had planted a seed of darkness within their hearts.

Robbery...

Another scream came from below the altar. "My leg, my leg! It... feels strange!"

Again?! And to their surprise, it wasn't just one person this time. Another cried out, "Me too! My back! Someone please help check my back!"

No one dared to approach either of them, so they had to show their bodies from a distance. One rolled up their pant leg while the other took off his top. After getting a clear look at the state of their bodies, screams of terror erupted from the crowd.

The disease was so advanced that the lesions on their bodies had fully taken shape!

"How did it grow that fast?!"

"Did you guys forget? We've been stuck here for a long time!"

"But how did they not notice?!"

"It didn't grow in an obvious place and it's only a little itchy—how could I have known it had turned into this?!"

"It's over, it's over. We probably all have it growing on us already."

"Quick! Everyone do a checkup! Inspect your body!"

It was pure chaos inside the Temple of the Crown Prince. Screams rang out through the air as the inspection went on. And just as expected, quite a few of them already had lesions surfacing all over their bodies that they simply hadn't noticed. And now that they found them, they saw that the lesions had already formed all five facial features!

Like they had sensed the situation inside, the disfigured wretches outside the Temple of the Crown Prince danced even more wildly, hand in hand. A thick fog of dread had spread rapidly through the temple in all directions. Xie Lian's heart pounded nonstop like it was about to break through his chest.

From what he remembered, Human Face Disease took some time to spread.

Why was it manifesting so quickly tonight?

White No-Face. It had to be White No-Face!

Xie Lian whipped his head around to look at the cold-eyed spectator who had started all this. But before he could open his mouth, someone shot to their feet.

Panting heavily and eyes bloodshot, the person began to criticize Xie Lian. "You...you're a god, you're a crown prince, yet you dare to commit robbery?"

Xie Lian was dumbfounded, not understanding why the man had brought up that incident now of all times. "I—"

The man cut him off sharply. "We worshipped you, and what do you do? Rob people! What did you bring? A plague!"

He brought the plague? Shock was written across Xie Lian's face. "Me...? It wasn't me! I only—"

The crowd's patience had finally reached its breaking point.

With red-rimmed eyes, nearly a hundred people surrounded Xie Lian. The one that was closest grabbed the black sword from the ground. Xie Lian stopped breathing.

The man shakily grasped the black sword, mumbling, "You... You need to do penance for your sins, right? You need to atone, right?"

The dark blade coursed with chilling light. Xie Lian's fear soared to its peak.

There were so many people. If every single one of them stabbed him with that sword, what would be left of him by the end?

There was something that Xie Lian feared even more than the thought of being endlessly stabbed until nothing remained of him but an indistinguishable pile of flesh riddled with thousands of holes. He had a vague yet terrifying feeling that, should he allow them to do this, he might lose a part of himself that would never return.

Unwilling to consider this any further, Xie Lian couldn't help but cry out.

"Hel—"

Before the phrase *"Help me"* could leave his throat, the same icy black blade was thrust into his body once again. Xie Lian's eyes widened in horror.

The razor-sharp sword was stabbed in, then pulled out. The next person followed without wasting a second, and the next stab was shoved into practically the same spot. The sound locked in Xie Lian's throat finally broke free, and a long, painful scream tore through his entire body.

The anguished scream was so piercing that the people around him were gutted by the sound. Some closed their eyes and turned their faces away.

"...Don't let him scream. Let's speed things up and get the job done fast!"

Xie Lian felt someone muffle his mouth and restrain his hands and feet.

"Hold him down and don't let him fall," someone instructed. "Also, don't stab off the mark; it doesn't count if it's not fatal!"

"Line up one by one, no cutting the line! I told you guys not to cut—I was here first!"

"Which areas are fatal? How do I know if it counts?"

"Just aim for the heart, throat, or stomach!"

"If you're not sure you stabbed a fatal area, do it again!"

"No way! Where is everyone else supposed to stab if you get more than one turn?"

The initial hesitation and reluctance had turned into nonchalance. The more time that passed, the more fluid their movements became. The sword moved endlessly in and out.

Xie Lian's eyes were open as wide as they could be throughout. Fat tears rolled down his face. Deep down, a voice silently, viscerally screamed.

Help me.

Help me, help me, help me.

Help me, help me, help, help, help, help, help, help, help, help, help, help, help, help, help, help me!

It hurts, it hurts, it hurts, it hurts, it hurts, it hurts...it hurts, it hurts, it hurts, it hurts, it hurts, it hurts, it hurts, it hurts, it hurts, it hurts, IT HURTS, IT HURTS, IT HURTS, IT HURTS, IT HURTS, IT HURTS, IT HURTS, IT HURTS, IT HURTS, IT HURTS, IT HURTS, IT HURTS, IT HURTS, IT HURTS, IT HURTS!

Why can't I die?

WHY CAN'T I DIE?!

Xie Lian wanted to wail with the most devastating sound, but his throat couldn't gasp out a single word—it had probably already been sliced through. He wanted to thrash wildly from the pain. It was like suffering the sum agony of countless lifetimes, and he didn't know if he'd be able to feel any other pain again.

He couldn't see anything. The world was pitch-black save for the nearby ball of ghost fire, which burned furiously. The ghost fire was growing brighter and stronger, but it still couldn't escape the cage of White No-Face's hand.

Xie Lian's own heartbreaking screams couldn't be heard, but he could hear another heart-wrenching wail that seemed to come from the flame. Although it wasn't him, it felt like he was the one making that sound—its pain was the same as his own.

In the end, Xie Lian couldn't hang on to his sanity. His consciousness had completely shattered, and he was left to blankly gurgle from his throat.

Suddenly, an explosion shook the Temple of the Crown Prince, and a raging ocean of flames burst forth.

"Aaaaaaaaaaaaaaaah!"

A chorus of screams rang out. The searing fire set everything ablaze; none escaped. Ghost fire surged like blazing ocean waves. In an instant, the hundred living humans inside the Temple of the Crown Prince were reduced to a hundred sets of charcoal-black bones!

When the flame gradually subsided and coalesced once again, the tiny ball of ghost fire was no more—in its place, the figure of a young man was gradually taking shape.

The young man dropped to his knees in front of the scorched, black surface of the altar. Bent over deeply, he clutched his head in both hands. He bellowed in immense, devastating pain.

He didn't dare look at what had become of the person lying on the altar, for what lay there didn't resemble a human anymore.

Bones and skulls were strewn all over the interior of the Temple of the Crown Prince. White No-Face cackled uncontrollably as he turned and left the temple. The raging fire hadn't stopped at the temple's doors; even the frenzied, disfigured victims outside had been reduced to dried corpses and piles of waste. As if blind to the devastation, White No-Face tread across the ashen, charcoal remains.

The entire forest—no, the entire mountain trembled in agony and grief!

Countless black shadows flew upward into the night sky, souls of the local dead scrambling in terror to escape their resting place, but a strong gust of wind scattered them in all directions. A gigantic mass of black clouds slowly rotated above the Temple of the Crown Prince, rumbling restlessly. It resembled a colossal demonic eye.

This was the birth of a great evil—the signs of a wrath ghost taking form!

XIE LIAN COULDN'T tell if he was awake or asleep.

If he was awake, then he was reacting to nothing in the outside world and had no memory of anything. If he was asleep, his eyes had been open the whole time.

By the time he came back to himself, White No-Face had strapped the black sword to his waist like an elder giving a reward to a child.

"This is my gift to you." He patted the hilt. His voice was gentle and thick with deeper meaning. "It will certainly prove much sharper than any of the others you collected, even the ones from Jun Wu."

Xie Lian let him hang the sword as he willed, neither speaking nor retaliating. Retaliation would be pointless.

He put on a new set of robes in that state. Armed with a new sword, he dragged himself outside in what felt like a newly born body. He walked out of the Temple of the Crown Prince and toward the darkness.

White No-Face called after him. "Wait."

Xie Lian paused in his step. White No-Face soundlessly came to his side and placed a white silk band in his hands.

"You forgot this."

It was the silk band he had once used to cover his face...the one that had also been used to bind him.

Xie Lian wobbled down the mountain alone.

Day had already broken. The sun had come out, but Xie Lian didn't feel warm at all when it shined on him.

On his way down the mountain, he saw a little trickling stream, clear and lively. He approached the stream's banks. The water reflected his appearance. Xie Lian stared at his pale face.

The face was smooth and fair without a single cut to be seen. The neck was the same, which meant the chest and the abdomen and other places were all healed. He only looked for a while before he couldn't bear the sight any longer. Lowering his head, he cupped some stream water in his hands to wash his face and drink a few mouthfuls. He drank and drank...until he happened to notice something nearby.

Slowly, he looked up. Not far upstream, there was a corpse lying on the shore, slumped next to a giant boulder. Judging by the clothes, it was the corpse of the buff street performer.

The man hadn't descended the mountain—he'd died on the road. There was a particularly obvious bloodstain on the giant boulder— whether from pain or fear, it looked like he had smashed himself against it until he died. The corpse was already rotten and emitted a foul stench. Half of the body was soaking in the water of the stream. Although the body didn't move, the little deformed faces growing on its half-rotten face were still squirming.

Xie Lian knelt by the stream and puked his guts out for over an hour, heaving until blood came up.

After descending the mountain, he walked through the city for a long time, aimlessly wandering the main streets without a destination in mind. Suddenly, a hand gripped his shoulder and yanked him into an alley. Xie Lian looked around and saw an incoming fist before he even glimpsed the other's face.

"Where did you run off to for so long?!"

Behind the fist was Feng Xin's furious expression, but by the time Xie Lian saw, he'd already been knocked to the ground by the punch.

Feng Xin hadn't expected to knock him down so easily. Confused, he looked at his own fist, then at Xie Lian on the ground. Before he could think to help him up, Xie Lian had already crawled back up by himself. Feng Xin's face changed, but in the end, his temper was still flaring.

"You've got such an attitude! Dropping only a word before running away and disappearing for two months! Do you know how worried Their Majesties have been?!"

Xie Lian wiped away the splattered blood on his face from his nosebleed. "I'm sorry."

Seeing that he was making things worse by wiping, Feng Xin heaved a heavy sigh.

"Your Highness! Forget it with the apology, there's no need between us. But you... What happened to you? Why were you gone for so long? Can't you tell me?" He noticed the black sword hanging at Xie Lian's waist. "And where did you get that sword?"

Xie Lian wanted to tell him. But then he remembered the argument he'd had with Feng Xin before he left, and the doubtful expression on Feng Xin's face—and that brought to mind the experience he never wanted to think about again. So he just repeated, "I'm sorry."

The two returned to the hideout, and when the queen saw Xie Lian, she hugged him and wept. The king looked like he'd aged quite a bit again—before, it was a matter of finding white hair among the black, but now it was a search for black strands among all the white. However, he wasn't blowing his top for some reason, and he only spoke a few words before falling silent. The three of them were probably afraid that Xie Lian would run away for another two months if he was provoked again, so they were very careful with their words and gestures around him.

"Feng Xin."

After a meal so simple it was crude, Xie Lian untied the black sword on his waist and passed it over.

"Take this sword. Pawn it."

Feng Xin noticed that the hand holding the sword was shaking, but he couldn't guess what was causing it. "Why?"

"Didn't you ask for money before?" Xie Lian said.

A flash of hurt suddenly crossed Feng Xin's face, and he shook his head soon after. "I don't need it anymore."

Xie Lian didn't speak another word. He tossed the black sword to the side and stopped caring about it, then he flopped over and fell asleep.

When Xie Lian came back this time, he tried to act like nothing had happened in the hope that everything would return to normal as soon as possible—in the hope that he could return to the person he once was.

Soon, he and Feng Xin went out to perform in the street. Feng Xin was still worried at first and told him, "Forget it, just rest for a couple more days."

"I've already rested for almost two months," Xie Lian said. "If those street performers keep coming to cause trouble, it'll be easier to handle it with two people."

"They stopped coming a while ago," Feng Xin explained.

It wasn't because the buff street performer had died and there was no one to lead but because Feng Xin had been settled here for a while now. When he first arrived, everyone had regarded him as a novelty. But that novelty had worn away with the passage of time, and watching him was now no different from watching the other local buskers. Feng Xin had lost his competitive edge, and the other street performers stopped looking for trouble now that he wasn't a threat. Since everyone made about the same amount of money, it was fine.

But now, no matter how hard Feng Xin shot his arrows, no matter how expert his skill, the audience, and the reward they paid for his efforts, was less than half of what it once was—in fact, it was less than ten percent. After working for over half the day, Feng Xin was exhausted and sweating profusely as he sat down on the roadside.

"Let me go up," Xie Lian said.

"Nah, don't worry about it," Feng Xin replied.

However, Xie Lian didn't bother listening to him. The passersby became interested again at the sight of a new face.

"And what special skills do you have, lad?"

Xie Lian didn't respond. He picked up a branch and started to perform a swordplay routine. Though he wielded a mere branch, the technique was beautifully performed, and the sound of wind being cut carried the sharpness of the sword's intent. A few audience members did him the honor and cheered. Feng Xin looked on from one side, his expression complicated. He only watched for a bit before he turned his gaze away.

Xie Lian didn't feel shame at all, nor did he feel any burden. He just kept deliberately and gracefully swinging his branch.

Suddenly, someone in the crowd began to jeer. "It's so boring!

What a pathetic act! Who wants to watch you fucking poking around blindly with a tree branch?!"

Feng Xin immediately jumped to his feet and shouted, "You watch your language!"

Xie Lian faltered and looked over. There was a man in the crowd who was munching on a melon and spitting out the seeds—he was obviously there to watch a show.

"This ancestor's here to watch a street performance! I'll say whatever I wanna say. You're here to earn our reward, so what do you care what I say?" the man yelled back at Feng Xin. "Switch to a real sword! Use a real one and granddaddy will consider granting you some seeds!"

As soon as he started yelling, others in the audience followed suit. Feng Xin was furious and just about to strike out when a white shadow flashed past.

Xie Lian was already standing next to the heckler. He grabbed the man and threw him high into the air.

The strength he exhibited was incredible, and the heckler's melon rinds tumbled to the ground as he was thrown meters away. The crowd was left to gape in open-mouthed shock. The man landed with a heavy *thud*, bleeding from his orifices and screaming horribly.

However, Xie Lian wasn't done, and he went over to seize the man once again. His voice was flat and emotionless. "There are no real swords here, but I can really take your life. Do you want to see that act?"

The audience broke away and fled in terror. "Somebody! Help! Murder!"

Feng Xin was even more shocked. "Your Highness!"

Xie Lian ignored him and prepared to throw the heckler another several meters away and let him fall wherever. But Feng Xin hurried over and held Xie Lian down, even forgetting to hide his identity as he roared.

"Your Highness! Snap out of it! You're going to kill him!"

Xie Lian's eyes were burning with black flames. He smacked Feng Xin's hand away and pressed the man to the ground. The heckler passed out cold. Feng Xin bent down and was just about to check whether he was breathing when he heard someone yelling sharply at the end of the street.

"It's them! Over there!"

Oh no! The Yong'an soldiers had come!

Feng Xin bolted instantly, but Xie Lian still stood there staring at the Yong'an soldiers like he was contemplating starting a fight with them.

Feng Xin turned around and pulled him away. "What are you still standing there for? Run!"

The two of them ducked and hid under cover until they could make an escape and return to their little safehouse. The moment they passed through the door, Feng Xin started yelling right in front of the queen.

"Why would you do something like that?!"

Once, Feng Xin would have never dared to be so unruly before the two Majesties. But a lot had changed. They had all been ground down for so long.

Xie Lian turned to the queen. "Go to your room."

"My son, what—" the queen started.

"Go to your room!" Xie Lian shouted.

The queen didn't dare press further and retreated to her room. Xie Lian turned to Feng Xin.

"What did I do?"

"You were going to kill that man!" Feng Xin said angrily.

"He didn't die," Xie Lian countered. "And so what if he had?"

Feng Xin was dumbfounded. "What did you say? What do you mean, 'so what if he died'?"

"That filthy *peasant* was asking for it," Xie Lian said. "And since he asked for it, I gave it to him. Was I wrong?"

Stunned by Xie Lian's new vocabulary, it was a good moment before Feng Xin said, "He...was causing trouble, but you didn't need to kill him! Smack him around and let it go. He didn't deserve to die over some petty words!"

Xie Lian cut him off. "Of course he did. He dared to say it, so he had to pay the price."

"How could you say something like that?" Feng Xin asked, voice thick with disbelief.

"Like what?" Xie Lian asked.

"I've never heard you call someone a peasant like that before," Feng Xin said.

"What are you trying to say?" Xie Lian said. "It's not like I'm a god. Can't I be angry? Can't I hate?"

Feng Xin didn't know how to respond. A moment later, he arduously squeezed out a few words. "That's not what I meant. But still, you didn't need to—"

Xie Lian didn't want to listen anymore and stopped talking to him. He stomped into his own room and slammed the door.

The moment the door was shut, he screamed and threw himself onto the bed.

He was fooling himself! Utterly fooling himself!

No matter what, it was impossible to pretend nothing had happened! It was impossible for him to return to who he once was!

That evening, someone knocked on his door. Xie Lian assumed it was Feng Xin, so he ignored it. The queen's voice sounded from the other side a moment later.

"My son, it's your mother. Let Mother come in and take a look at you, all right?"

Xie Lian had just wanted to lie there without moving, but after staying there for one more moment, he still got up and opened the door. "What?" he asked tiredly.

The queen stood at the door holding a plate. "My son, you haven't eaten yet, have you?"

Xie Lian stared at her and endured the urge to speak for a long time before he finally, forcefully swallowed the words that were already rolling up his throat: *"Even though I haven't eaten, I don't want to eat anything you made."* He moved aside to allow his mother into his room, and the queen placed the plate on the table.

"Look."

Xie Lian looked, and he got so angry he wanted to laugh. "What is that?"

The queen spoke as if she were offering him treasure. "This is 'Lovebirds Upon a Branch Meatballs,' and this is 'Blooming Flowers and Full Moon Stew'—"

The "Lovebirds" looked like they were dead, and the "Full Moon" was full of craters. Xie Lian had to interrupt her. "Why did you name these things?"

"Don't dishes always have names?" the queen said.

"That's for imperial dining, in a palace," Xie Lian said. "Ordinary people don't give names to dishes."

Imperial dining. Palace. Ordinary people. The queen remained quiet for a while, then smiled.

"Well, no one ever said you have to dine imperially to give a dish a name. So just take this as a wish for good fortune. Come, try some? Mother spent a long time making this for you."

And then she passed a pair of chopsticks over. Xie Lian didn't smile, nor did he touch the chopsticks.

The queen sat there smiling for a while before her face gradually fell. "My son."

Xie Lian's tone was brusque. "What."

"Why are you fighting with Feng Xin again?" the queen asked.

Xie Lian didn't want to explain, and he didn't have the energy to do so regardless. "You two just stay in your room and relax. You don't need to worry about these things."

The queen hesitated for a moment. "Mother knows she probably shouldn't say this, but...that child Feng Xin was the one who looked after us during the many days that you were gone..."

"Mother, what are you trying to say?" Xie Lian demanded.

"My son, don't be angry. I'm not trying to blame you," the queen said quickly. "I'm really not—I know you're having a difficult time as well. I'm only saying that young Feng Xin has always followed us, followed you, and it isn't easy for him. I can sense that he's stayed with us until now not because he didn't want to leave, but because he still cares about your friendship..."

Xie Lian leapt to his feet. "Who has had it easy? Has it been easy for me?! Mother, can you please stop asking questions?! Can you please not involve yourself in things that you don't understand?!"

When she saw that he was running out the door, the queen started panicking and got up to chase after him. "My son, where are you going? I'll stop talking, Mother won't say anything else! Come back!"

"I know!" Xie Lian exclaimed sharply. "Everyone's having a hard time, but don't worry! I'll go right now to make things easier for everyone!"

The queen couldn't keep up with him, and it wasn't long before she was left behind.

Xie Lian returned later that night carrying a few sacks. When he opened the door, no one had gone to bed; they were all waiting for him, their expressions sullen.

Xie Lian shut the door with a backhanded push. "What's up?"

It seemed that the king had already lectured the queen, and the rims of her eyes were red. When she saw that Xie Lian had returned, she let out a long sigh of relief and forced a happy smile.

"My son, you've come back! I won't ask you any unnecessary questions from now on. Just don't leave us so suddenly, Mother will definitely listen to you if there's anything—"

Everyone was scared. Scared that if he turned around and left again, he'd go missing for another two months.

"You all think too much," Xie Lian said. "I wasn't going to leave. Just go and rest."

Feng Xin waited until the king and the queen had gone to their room. After a moment of silence, he began to speak. "Even if I asked where you went, you wouldn't tell me, right?"

Xie Lian didn't reply, just tossed the sacks to the ground. They made crisp clinking sounds as they landed.

"What's this?" Feng Xin asked.

Xie Lian opened the sacks and dumped them out. From within tumbled a large pile of shining gold and silver wares that nearly brightened the entire house.

Feng Xin instantly stood up. "You... Where did these things come from?!"

Xie Lian didn't bother to look up as he replied; he just sat on the ground and counted the haul. "There's no need to be like that. I paid a visit to a big household in the city. Relax, no one saw me."

Feng Xin's eyes were round and bulging. "You—" Remembering just then that the king and queen were in the next room, he lowered his voice. "You stole them?!"

"You don't need to look at me like that," Xie Lian said. "Everyone's having a hard time. This will make things easier."

"You still shouldn't have stolen them!" Feng Xin exclaimed. "We can just busk!"

"And how much do we earn from killing ourselves performing on the streets?" Xie Lian said.

Feng Xin staggered back a couple of steps. It was the first time Xie Lian saw him look like he was about to faint. He finally steadied himself and took a moment to make sure he hadn't heard wrong. Then he mumbled, "What made you this way?"

Xie Lian looked up. "What way?"

Feng Xin was furious. "I don't want to lecture you, but just look at yourself—at what you've become! I've already stopped asking about the robbery, so how did things get even worse?!"

Xie Lian snorted. "I knew it."

"Knew what?" Feng Xin asked.

Xie Lian rose to his feet. "I knew that robbery thing was still on your mind. You wanted to ask me, but you didn't have the heart. You've thought about it a thousand times, right? Don't obsess about it anymore. I'll tell you."

Step by step, he closed in on Feng Xin. "It's true. I robbed someone."

Feng Xin was forced back a step. "You..." Then he advanced a step and hissed in anger, "We've been passing our days in such hardship, and for what? If you were willing to do those things, then we could've done them already. Why suffer until today?! What are you doing, throwing away all your efforts?! Are you still the same Royal Highness I used to know?!"

"You're right. Why *have* we suffered until today?" Xie Lian said.

Feng Xin was taken aback, and Xie Lian continued, "What was I like in the past? I didn't talk back when I was cursed at, didn't fight back when I was beaten, and always overestimated myself. I was so determined to 'save the common people.' What kind of person does all that? A dumbass! Do you think being a dumbass is better? Do you think that's the kind of person I should be? Are you going to be very shocked if I'm not?"

Feng Xin was stunned. "Are you crazy? Why do you have to say it like that?"

"You're wrong. I'm not crazy," Xie Lian said. "I've just suddenly come to my senses. Now I know that the past me was the crazy one."

"Why are you being like this? When did you become this way?" Feng Xin mumbled. "I...I really don't know... I'm... Why did I follow you all this time—?"

"Then stop following," Xie Lian said.

Feng Xin couldn't wrap his head around that. "What?"

"I said, don't follow me anymore," Xie Lian repeated.

Then he slammed the door.

Four hours later, there was finally some rustling outside the room and low voices speaking.

It seemed Feng Xin was bidding farewell to Xie Lian's mother and father. Feng Xin's voice was extremely low, the queen's voice was choked with sobs, and the king didn't say much, but there was a lot of coughing. The door opened a moment later, then closed. Feng Xin's voice vanished, and the sound of his footsteps grew more and more distant.

Feng Xin had left.

Xie Lian was still shut in his room, emotionless and expressionless. A moment later, he closed his eyes.

He'd finally left.

Ever since Mu Qing left them, Xie Lian had been terrified of this possibility—that one day, Feng Xin would leave too. But he'd become so scared of it that he could no longer endure the torment. Rather than dragging it out, slowly grinding away all the kindness and friendship like sharpening a knife until nothing remained—until they loathed the sight of each other—it was better to make it explode now.

Before Feng Xin left, Xie Lian had been afraid. Now that Feng Xin was gone, he wasn't scared anymore.

But even though he no longer felt fear, he felt a deeper agony.

Xie Lian had initially held a one-in-a-million bit of hope at the bottom of his heart. He'd hoped that Feng Xin would still stay even if Xie Lian admitted he had done things he shouldn't have, even if he became the worst version of himself. After all, the two had never left each other's sides since he turned fourteen and Feng Xin was selected to be his personal attendant. They were master and servant, but more than that, they were friends. And Feng Xin had no one to care for aside from the crown prince either—or at most, him, and the king and queen.

But Feng Xin had really left.

Xie Lian had already guessed it would end like this, and he could understand it completely. He just couldn't bear it for the moment.

Just then, the queen's voice came from outside his silent room. "My son, I'm so sorry."

Xie Lian couldn't immediately think of a response. He crawled out of his bed and opened the door, then went out. "It's got nothing to do with you," he said tiredly.

The king and queen were both sitting at the old, creaky table. "Father and Mother dragged you down and made you do bad things for our sake. We even made you and Feng Xin argue," the queen said.

Xie Lian forced a smile. "What bad things? Aren't tales and legends full of stories about stealing from the rich to help the poor? Since Feng Xin's gone, he's gone. This is good, actually—with him gone, things will be more relaxed. Relaxed on both sides. You two just focus on healing. Tomorrow, we can buy the best medicine."

However, the king glared at him. "I won't use that money."

The queen tugged at him covertly.

"Then what do you want?" Xie Lian demanded.

The king coughed a few more times. "You... Go chase after Feng Xin and bring him back. I don't want this money."

Although the queen was still tugging at him, she agreed. "Yes, why don't you chase after Feng Xin? He's your most loyal servant and your best friend—"

"The loyal servant is no more," Xie Lian said. "We have money, so just use it. Don't ask about anything else. I already told you, you don't understand these things."

After a long silence, the queen said, "I'm so sorry, my son. Mom and Dad can see that you've been struggling very hard on your own. But we're only mortals, so we can't help you at all—you have to take care of us on top of everything else."

Xie Lian was out of energy to say more, so he placated them with empty words of comfort before sending them back to their room. To try to clear his mind, Xie Lian unwrapped his white silk band and stripped off all his clothes, then took a quick bath before passing out in bed.

He slept so deeply that when he woke the next day, he wondered blearily, *How come Feng Xin didn't wake me?*

It took some time before he remembered that Feng Xin had left.

Xie Lian flipped over and sat up, falling into a daze. But there was something else—even if Feng Xin had left, what about his parents? Why hadn't his father and mother come to rouse him either?

Normally, he would've heard the king coughing by now. That sound had never ceased, so why was it so quiet today?

Xie Lian suddenly felt uneasy. He put on his clothes and got out of bed, then reached for his silk band—but it was missing. He pushed open the door to the room next to his.

"Mother, have you seen my—"

The moment he opened the door, his pupils instantly shrank to two minuscule dots.

He had found his white silk band.

The silk band was hanging from the beam. Two unmoving figures dangled from it. Their bodies had long since gone stiff.

They were the bodies of his father and mother.

Xie Lian wondered if perhaps he was still dreaming. He staggered, reaching out to support himself on the wall. But he was swaying so badly that he couldn't catch himself and slipped down along the wall instead.

He sat on the ground, hands covering his face. He couldn't breathe—he choked on air. He cried and laughed, laughed and cried.

"I...I...I...I..."

He rambled incoherently to no one, then he added, "It wasn't... no. I, wait...you can't, I..."

In the end, he couldn't even form a complete sentence. He turned around and screamed, smashing his head against the wall over and over.

He should've known. His father was such a conservative, traditional king, and his mother couldn't bear the sight of her loved ones suffering, let alone suffering for her sake. They were both nobility, raised in prestige. It was already a miracle that they'd hung on for this long.

Xie Lian smacked his head against the wall hundreds of times. "Feng Xin, my father and mother are gone," he mumbled.

No one was listening.

Only then did he realize he needed to get his parents' corpses down. After he lowered them, Xie Lian acted like he had nothing left to do and walked around the house. He saw that there were a few plates of horrid-looking food on the table, long gone cold. They were the dishes that Xie Lian had made the queen take away the night before without eating a single bite. Now, he pulled them over absentmindedly and ate everything, not daring to leave behind a single leaf, afraid to miss a single grain of rice. After he ate, he heaved and began to vomit.

Suddenly, Xie Lian grabbed the white silk band and threw it over the beam, then put his own neck through its knotted loop.

Waves of suffocation assaulted him, yet his mind remained clear. Even when his eyes filled with blood, even when his collarbones cracked, he still remained conscious. As he hung there, the white silk band abruptly loosened on its own. Xie Lian fell heavily to the ground, and in the midst of his dizziness, he saw that the silk band had actually started moving by itself with no breeze to aid it. It was coiling like a venomous snake.

It had conceived its own spirit!

It had been dyed with Xie Lian's blood, had hung two royals to death—if Xie Lian could die, then it would have been three. Saturated with such deep resentment and evil, it would be stranger if it *didn't* turn into a spirit.

The little spirit had only just arrived in the world and didn't understand at all that it had been born from such despair. It happily drifted over to the one who had given it a soul like it was hoping for

a gesture of affection. However, Xie Lian had no eyes for it, and he clutched his head and roared.

"Somebody! *Somebody come kill me!*"

He could only pray that someone would come right that second to take his life and help him break free from this endless pain and torture!

Just then, in the far distance, he heard the roaring sounds of gongs and drums. Xie Lian panted harshly, his eyes bloodshot. *Who? What is that?* he wondered.

Something drove him to his feet, and he stumbled outside to look. He walked for a long time before he finally realized that it was the sounds of celebration—they were commemorating the imperial palace's construction in the newly established royal capital of the newly established kingdom of Yong'an.

The entire nation had joined in jubilation! All the former citizens of Xianle were now cheering for Yong'an. On the main street, everyone's faces bore bright smiles; it was such a familiar sight. Xie Lian remembered now. This was how the people of Xianle's imperial capital had cheered during the Shangyuan Heavenly Ceremonial Procession.

Xie Lian staggered back to the cottage and sat listlessly on the floor.

Why did he have to witness the laughter and cheers of the Yong'an people when the corpses of the king and queen of Xianle lay at his feet?

Xie Lian buried his face in his hands, crying and laughing. *Ha ha ha ha...nngh...sob...*

A moment later, he giggled. "Don't think it'll be that easy for you."

Memories flashed in his mind of a voice telling him, *"Human Face Disease is resentment... This is how you create Human Face Disease..."*

A savage light glinted in his eyes, and his voice softened. "I won't let *any* of you off so easily."

The expression on his face was like he was both crying and laughing, like joy and sadness mixed together. Using the wall as support, he slowly rose to his feet.

"Yong'an, Forever Peace?[5] Dream on. Keep dreaming forever! I... curse all of you. *I curse all of you!* I want all of you to die—all of you, to the last! Ha ha, ha ha, ha ha ha, *ha ha ha ha ha ha!*"

Xie Lian laughed and laughed and rushed forth like a whirlwind. When he passed the mirror, he suddenly paused and whipped his head around.

His reflection had already changed completely.

He wasn't wearing his white cultivator robes, which were threadbare from the wash. Instead, he was wearing snow-white funeral robes with expansive sleeves. His face was no longer his own, but a half-crying, half-smiling mask!

Xie Lian would have once screamed in horror at the sight of himself like this. However, the Xie Lian of today wasn't scared at all. He laughed maniacally and ignored the change. He stumbled to the door, crashing through it before breaking into a dash.

The former imperial capital of Xianle was now nothing more than a field of ruined wreckage.

There were still some who lived near the wreckage—residents who had been lucky enough to survive and refugees who had nowhere else to go. Ever since the plague of Human Face Disease had erupted and the imperial city had fallen, the once-glamorous capital

---

5   *The name "Yong'an" means "Forever Peace."*

was subject to frequent sinister, chilling winds. Today they seemed especially cold. The few disheveled beggars who had remained were fleeing, watching the skies as they ran. They sensed that something ominous was approaching and knew better than to linger in the streets.

The battlefield sprawled in front of the broken imperial city gates. Not many dared visit it. Now there was only an old cultivator scurrying around trying to catch some lost, wandering souls. He stuffed them into his sack once they were caught, ready to take them and tie them into lanterns. As he darted around, the old cultivator unexpectedly discovered that a strange, white-clothed figure had appeared at the edge of the battlefield.

Truly strange, truly peculiar. The man was wearing white funeral robes with expansive sleeves, and he had a band of white silk tied to one arm. The white silk band floated in the wind like it was alive. On the man's face was a ghastly white mask, half of it crying, half of it smiling.

The old cultivator shuddered violently, and before he knew why he was fleeing, his legs had already carried him away from the battlefield. He stopped before the fright had left him completely and looked back.

The white-clothed man didn't speak a single word as he strolled across the battlefield. Chilling wind whipped around him, and with every step, he trampled the bones of those who had died in the war.

Countless souls of the dead were struggling and wailing on this soil; even the air was black from resentment.

"Do you hate?" the white-clothed man asked coldly.

The dead souls wailed and cried. The white-clothed man took another few steps.

"The people you swore to protect, the people for whom you swore to die—they have now become the people of a new kingdom. Do you hate?"

The wails of the dead souls now had shrieking mixed in.

"They've forgotten those who died on the battlefield, forgotten your sacrifices. They are cheering for the ones who stole your lives away," the white-clothed man said slowly. "Do you hate?"

Amidst the shrieking there came howling and snarling.

The white-clothed man called out sharply, "What's the use in screaming? Answer me: *do you hate?!*"

The battlefield's air began to echo with innumerable voices of resentment and agony.

"I hate..."

"I hate..."

"Kill...I want to kill them!"

The white-clothed man opened his arms toward them and extended both hands. "Come to my side." He then made this vow, saying the words slowly and clearly: "I promise the people of Yong'an shall never know peace!"

The shrieking, the howling, the snarling—it shook the ground and crashed the heavens. The souls of the dead had answered him; fallen Xianle soldiers mingled with those who had died from Human Face Disease. And in that sky choked by black mist, they took shape!

The old cultivator witnessed the whole thing from afar in terror. "This... This is...!"

In an instant, only three words appeared in his mind.

White-Clothed Calamity!

Suddenly, the white-clothed man heard a young man's voice.

"Your Highness..."

He looked back, only to find that a black-clad young man was already standing there. And then, the young man bowed his head and bent one knee to the ground.

BASED ON HIS VOICE and physique, he was determined to be a "young man."

He was dressed in neat and orderly warrior gear, his physique tall and slender. Like new, fresh bamboo, he had an aura of the innocence of youth. Robes as black as ink, hair as black as ink, tied high. From his waist hung a saber, long and slim. He raised his head slowly, and upon his face there was a snow-white mask painted with a crescent-eyed smile.

Ball after ball of black mist took shape amidst all the hissing and wailing, which were all sucked cleanly into the array within the white-clothed man's qiankun sleeve. It was like he took an entire river into a small jade bottle. As for the young man, he remained steady and still within the chaotic black whirlwind.

"Who were you calling?" the white-clothed man asked.

The black-clad young man was still down on one knee. The pose was one of servile submission but also of swearing an oath. "I was calling you, Your Royal Highness."

"I'm not Your Royal Highness," the white-clothed man said coldly.

"You are," the black-clad young man replied. "I would never forget your voice or your form."

The white-clothed man's voice was now laced with anger. "I told you, I'm not him."

The white-clothed man was naturally Xie Lian, who had donned the funeral garb and put on the cry-smiling mask. No one could recognize him with his face hidden behind the mask, and he didn't want to be recognized. And yet, on this battlefield, a wandering black-clad warrior had identified him straightaway.

Suddenly, the white silk band wrapped inside Xie Lian's expansive sleeve lunged like a viper at the black-clad young man. Although it looked like soft white cloth at first glance, it was savage when it attacked and its evil qi burst forth. But just as the black-clad young man was about to be wrapped and bound, he reached out and firmly caught the white silk band.

One end of the white silk band was wrapped around Xie Lian's wrist, and the other was caught around the wrist of this black-clad young man. The silk band was gradually pulling itself taut. It was trying to break away, but the black-clad young man had a tight hold on it, like he was squeezing a venomous snake at its fatal point. Chilling qi flowed endlessly from his hand.

There was no doubt that this was a soul of the dead. And it was an extremely powerful one!

Xie Lian could tell that the strength passing through the white band was not to be underestimated. "What is your name?"

He remained silent for a moment, then the black-clad young man replied, "I do not have a name."

Xie Lian didn't push further. "No name would make you 'Wuming.'"[6]

"You may call me whatever you desire," Wuming said.

"Are you a soul of this battlefield's dead?"

"I am."

---

6   [無名] *"Wuming" means "Nameless."*

Only then did Xie Lian slacken his attack. The white silk band instantly leapt back to Xie Lian, swaying at Wuming to show off its might from afar, like it was lashing a venomous tongue.

If he was a soul who had died in battle, no wonder he had heeded Xie Lian's call. This black-clad warrior must have also been filled with resentment toward the people of Yong'an. In other words, he could be used because their objective was the same.

Thus, Xie Lian said, "Then follow me." He extended his hand to Wuming. "I will give you what you want."

Wuming's face was also hidden behind a mask, so his expression couldn't be seen. They were indeed the same.

After a moment of silence, he grasped Xie Lian's extended hand with conviction, bowed his head deeply, and pressed his cold forehead to the back of Xie Lian's fingers.

A long moment later, he vowed sincerely, "I swear to die following Your Highness."

Xie Lian, however, pulled back his hand and tucked his arms into his sleeves. He turned around and said coolly, "You're already dead. Come."

Wuming rose to his feet, and when Xie Lian looked back, he discovered that the young man was much bigger than he had expected. He was probably only around sixteen or seventeen years old but was enormously tall already. He was even a bit taller than Xie Lian. That was unimportant, though, and Xie Lian only took a glance before turning back around and continuing onward.

Xie Lian took the lead, and the nameless black-clad warrior followed right behind as expected.

"Your Highness, where do you want to go?"

Xie Lian gazed into the distance. "The Palace of Yong'an."

The Palace of Yong'an sat in a large city to the west. It was once a flourishing city in its own right, but it had been overshadowed by the imperial city of Xianle in the east. Now that Xianle had fallen, the new king had moved the capital here. It wouldn't be long before it overtook the old imperial city, basking in its newfound glory.

Xie Lian arrived at the new imperial city deep in the night. Beneath the moonlight, he was like a white cat soundlessly flying across the ridges of the densely packed rooftops, and Wuming was like a black spirit fox following closely behind. Soon, the two shadows landed before a large gate.

Xie Lian sensed something amiss. There was faintly ominous air surrounding the gate, and he paused. He was about to reach out to check it when Wuming stepped in front of him.

The black-clad man extended an open palm and said quietly, "Break!"

A line of firelight leaked from around the edges of the door as if something had been burnt away. Only after that did Wuming reach out and push the gate open.

"Your Highness."

Xie Lian crossed the threshold and looked at the ground. Just as he expected, there were some burnt shreds scattered there. Xie Lian picked a bit of it up to inspect, and he smelled the scent of herbs and talisman paper. He stole a glance at Wuming.

This ghost was indeed formidable.

These were the burnt remnants of charms, which obviously indicated there was someone on the other side of the door who had woven a defense spell—a strong one. If ordinary little minions tried to intrude or break the array, their innards would have burnt to ashes. Yet it only took this black-clad warrior an instant to destroy it completely.

Perhaps because it was newly erected, the Palace of Yong'an wasn't extraordinarily magnificent—it was even a little shabby. It couldn't be compared to the Palace of Xianle. But that wasn't the strange part—the truly strange thing about this building was the massive number of evil-warding traps and defense arrays set up throughout the palace. Still, every time Xie Lian noticed something blocking the way ahead, Wuming would immediately step forward and break through the obstacle to clear the path for him. In the end, his journey was entirely unimpeded.

An hour later, two tall, slender shadows kept watch from the roof ridge of the Palace of Yong'an's large great hall.

They both wore masks. The white-clothed man's expansive sleeves fluttered, and the white silk band wrapped around his arm danced madly in the wind. The black-clad man was sleek and agile and wore a long saber at his waist. He kept guard at the white-clothed man's side, gazing in the same direction he did. This scene under the moonlight was somehow at once dangerous, uncanny, and beautifully harmonious.

The newly crowned King of Yong'an was inside this great hall. Xie Lian snorted.

"He set up so many obstacles in his palace to ward off evil. It seems he's quite scared that something will come knocking, huh."

"Your Highness, I will open the path," Wuming said.

However, Xie Lian stopped him. "No need. I'll do it myself."

Then he leapt down like a white blossom blown off the tip of a branch by a breeze and landed soundlessly before the palace hall.

Just as he was about to push open the gates, he heard a baby's wailing from within.

Lang Ying didn't have any consorts, and his son had died a long time ago. Where had this baby come from?

Xie Lian didn't care, though. Never mind a baby, he wouldn't be afraid if an army of millions was hidden inside. He raised his leg and kicked open the palace door!

Strangely, there was only one person within the great hall. There was not a single other soul present, and certainly no baby. When the lone person saw who had arrived, he raised his head.

"You've come? I've been searching for you."

The one within the palace was Lang Ying.

Although he was now an esteemed king, he wasn't dressed in lavish robes, and he sat woodenly upon the throne. Xie Lian was puzzled for a moment at his reaction, but then he realized that he was wearing a mask and funeral garb. Lang Ying had taken him for White No-Face.

There were arrays set up within the palace hall as well, and when Xie Lian crossed the threshold, he could sense something blocking him from approaching further. However, it only took putting a little more force into his steps for him to easily walk forward into the hall. The sound of something shattering rang out.

Night and the chill of winter came pouring in from outside the palace hall, filling Xie Lian's sleeves with wild winds. "Why were you searching for me?" he asked gloomily.

When he heard Xie Lian's voice, Lang Ying's expression changed slightly. "It's you?"

Xie Lian approached slowly, his snow-white boots advancing across the icy stone floors step by step. "It is I."

Lang Ying, a brutish commoner, had led an army and destroyed Xianle. With the kingly aura surrounding his body, ordinary evil couldn't come close to him. However, Xie Lian had brought with him millions of souls of the battlefield's dead!

He refused to believe that Lang Ying would be able to defend himself against so many ghosts that bore him such powerful resentment. The vengeful spirits were agitated and impatient, ready to break free and seize the fresh, new flesh of their enemy as a host. It was impossible for anyone not to have heard their roiling, but Lang Ying didn't look particularly alarmed.

"You've come to kill me?"

Xie Lian didn't answer. In the blink of an eye, he appeared right in front of Lang Ying and grabbed him by the hair, yanking him down and pressing him to the ground.

Success!

Under the cry-smiling mask, Xie Lian's lips unconsciously curled upward.

He knew it! He knew it! He could now defeat Lang Ying!

His heavenly official status had once restricted Xie Lian and made him powerless before this man with a king's fortune. But now, Xie Lian was stripped of such bondage, had thrown away his godly state—and he could finally defeat Lang Ying. Xie Lian's heart was pounding, and he was just about to move on to the next step when his face dropped abruptly.

"What's that sound?"

Waaaaah, waaaaaaah! He heard a tiny baby's cry again—but there was clearly no baby within the great hall.

He listened again. This wasn't right—the crying was coming from Lang Ying, who was currently subdued under his hand! Or more accurately, it was coming from somewhere on Lang Ying's body. Xie Lian ripped off Lang Ying's robe, and his eyes widened. He jumped to his feet.

"What is this?!"

Lang Ying slowly rolled over and sat up. "Don't be scared."

His words weren't directed at Xie Lian but to the thing attached to his body.

There were two distinct faces growing on Lang Ying's chest like protruding tumors. Each one was about the same size as a normal human's face. The larger face was elegant and beautiful, and easily identifiable as a woman. The smaller face was slightly scrunched up like a baby's. The halting cries had been coming from the "baby's" mouth.

Human Face Disease!

Xie Lian was dumbfounded. "How did you get infected with Human Face Disease?!"

"This isn't Human Face Disease," Lang Ying said.

"How is it not? What is it, then?" Xie Lian exclaimed.

"This is my wife and my son," Lang Ying explained. "They're not a disease."

His voice was soft as he raised his hands to gently caress the two faces on his body, truly looking like a husband and father soothing his wife and child. However, the two faces couldn't even open their eyes; they could only open their mouths to cry and sob. They had the shape of humans, but they were not human at all.

A moment later, Lang Ying looked up. "Where's White No-Face? He said my wife would return if I did this, but it's been so long now. How come she still can't talk? What's going on? Tell him to come find me, quick!"

Hearing this, Xie Lian understood. "You let White No-Face plant the vengeful spirits of your wife and son on your body?"

So that was it. All the spells and arrays in the palace weren't to impede intruders from outside but to prevent the escape of the things hiding within! Lang Ying, who had already become king, was using his own flesh and blood to secretly raise these two vengeful spirits!

Xie Lian had come to seek vengeance, yet who could've guessed that he wouldn't need to do anything? Lang Ying had already infected himself with Human Face Disease. These two faces must've been on his body for a long time now; they had grown tiny, deformed arms and legs that drooped heavily off him in a disturbing display. Moreover, they had already sucked their host dry—Lang Ying's ribs were abnormally visible, his gut was shrunken in, and his skin was wax yellow. He looked wan and sallow, like he didn't have much longer to live. He was no longer the same brave, fierce warrior he'd been on the battlefield.

It seemed he hadn't been living well despite winning the war and becoming a king. But Xie Lian didn't feel gratified at all, and he seized Lang Ying.

"What kind of joke is this?!" he exclaimed angrily.

He didn't even get the chance to take his enemy's life—his enemy was about to die on his own! What the hell! What should he do now?

Something tumbled off Lang Ying as Xie Lian grabbed him. It shimmered and glinted red as it bounced and bounced and rolled away. Lang Ying clutched Xie Lian's hands; even such a simple gesture seemed quite difficult for him.

"Pearl... That pearl," he panted.

Xie Lian looked over. Rolling on the floor was the red coral pearl he had once given Lang Ying.

"I've always wanted to say this to you: thank you for the pearl," Lang Ying said.

Hearing this surprised Xie Lian; he never expected Lang Ying to say that so suddenly. Something within his heart was about to be unburied, but he forced it down.

"You...!"

"Things would've been better if you'd given it to me sooner, though," Lang Ying said softly. "Too bad..."

Before he finished, the body in Xie Lian's grip slackened. Lang Ying died just like that, his eyes still wide open.

Xie Lian hadn't had the chance to react before Wuming said, "Your Highness, he's dead."

"...Dead?" Xie Lian wondered.

He looked down, and Lang Ying's eyes were already going dull. He really had died.

"How is he just...dead?" Xie Lian mumbled.

He hadn't done anything to Lang Ying yet. How could he be dead?

And now that he thought about it, Lang Ying had died fairly fulfilled and happy. His revenge against Xianle was complete, and with his family so close at hand, he was prepared to immediately reunite with them in the underworld. He had suffered enough torment in the world of the living, so death was likely a form of release, an end to it.

But Xie Lian was left with nothing to avenge himself upon! His chest was filled with grievance and indignation, and in the end, they coalesced into a single emotion: hate. How despicable! How absolutely despicable!

Lang Ying had stopped moving, but the two faces on his chest seemed to know that their host was dead and suddenly started to cry. *Waaaaaaah, waaaaaaah.* The noise was piercing, worse than the sound of nails scratching on gold and silver plates. Xie Lian was already going mad from fury. He pulled out the black sword, ready to strike and shut them up, when Wuming swiftly drew his saber. *Sching!* The saber's light flashed past him, and Lang Ying's corpse was instantly chopped to pieces. Tens of pieces, hundreds of pieces... Flesh and blood splattered everywhere.

Xie Lian hadn't even moved before he was overtaken. "Who told you to do that?" he questioned coldly.

"There was no need to dirty Your Highness's hands," Wuming replied.

Just then, urgent footsteps sounded outside the door. "Uncle!" a young boy's voice called.

Who? Xie Lian turned around and saw that the doors of the palace hall were wide open. A boy, ten-or-so years old, was standing there and gazing at the scene in front of him. His face had been full of smiles at first, but they turned to shock when he entered and saw the gore covering the floor.

Xie Lian was unmoved. "Who are you?"

"I..." the boy started, then his gaze fell upon the chunks of dead body all around the room. *"Uncle...!"*

More people began calling to him from outside. "Your Royal Highness, don't run off! The king said you can't run around in the palace! Please don't make things difficult for me in the middle of the night..."

"Royal Highness"?

Lang Ying's son was dead, and this boy had called him "uncle." So he must be the one Lang Ying had named Crown Prince of Yong'an!

The reality of the situation seemed to have dawned on the young crown prince, and he cried out in terror. "Ghosts! There are ghosts! Somebody—"

He hadn't screamed more than a few words before Wuming struck him in the neck. The Crown Prince of Yong'an lost consciousness and fell into the blood pooling on the floor. However, his screams had already reached those outside, and a commotion began to rise.

"What? Did you hear that?"

"Guards! *Guards!*"

Xie Lian's eyes flicked, and Wuming inclined his head, indicating he would take care of it. He flashed away. In an instant, all the noise outside was choked off. Exiting the great hall, Xie Lian saw many guards strewn about on the ground. Wuming stood at the center of the fallen crowd, his thin, delicate saber dripping with blood. He had finished them all with a single strike.

More noise came from far in the distance, and a new batch of guards arrived amidst shouts of *"Protect the king!"* and *"Protect His Highness!"*

Xie Lian coldly turned around and ignored them completely. Sure enough, less than a second later those voices vanished completely, cut down like a harvest faced with a scythe. Soon after, Wuming silently caught up to him.

Xie Lian inclined his head. "Burn the palace."

Wuming bowed his head. "Yes, sir."

Roaring flames blazed to the sky. Two tall, slender figures stood before the raging fire. Their shadows on the ground writhed and contorted ceaselessly, pulling and twisting, changing shape.

The attendants within the Palace of Yong'an were jolted awake by the havoc, and the air was choked by the cries and curses of those putting out the fires and those making their escape. It was very much the same scene as when the Palace of Xianle had been set ablaze.

"Your Highness, what do you want to do next?" the black-clad warrior asked.

"To Lang-Er Bay," the white-clothed man said in a chilly voice.

Before the Kingdom of Xianle fell, Xie Lian had visited Lang-Er Bay countless times. Every time he went, it was to create rain to save the people; his body and heart were always exhausted, his steps leaden. This time, he was visiting for a completely different reason, and his body was light.

Having survived the drought and gained the support of the new king, Lang-Er Bay had been revived, lively and bustling. Streets and alleys were busy and joyful, the people cheerful and happy—it was a complete reversal from the misery of years ago. Only one place was still as miserable as before, and that was the Temple of the Crown Prince of Xianle.

No one would come to a broken-down Temple of the Crown Prince, so Xie Lian chose it as his place to rest. Right now, he was meditating within the hall.

The vengeful spirits should've quickly found a host in Lang Ying, the target of Xie Lian's revenge. Yet because he was already dead, they still struggled in agony, wailing and screeching relentlessly at Xie Lian.

Frowning, Xie Lian waved them away with his eyes closed. "Just wait, don't be impatient. I will allow all of you to find release!"

Just then, a voice called out, "Your Highness."

Xie Lian opened his eyes. He saw Wuming before him, one knee on the ground.

XIE LIAN'S MIND was still deeply mired in the screaming of the vengeful spirits, and he couldn't quite regain himself for the moment. Shaken, his face was drenched with cold sweat underneath the mask.

"...Don't address me by that title," he responded, still distracted.

Every time someone addressed him like that, it was as if they were trying to remind him of something. It made him particularly irritated, and each instance jolted his heart.

However, Wuming said, "Your Highness will forever be Your Highness."

Xie Lian looked over. He couldn't see Wuming's face, of course, just the smiling mask. And when Wuming gazed at him, he also could only see a ghastly white cry-smiling mask.

"If you keep calling me by that title, I'll disperse your soul," Xie Lian said coldly. "Don't think yourself to be so strong."

Wuming bowed his head and did not speak.

Xie Lian calmed himself. "Go search the area around Lang-Er Bay and find the best location to set up an array."

"Yes, sir," Wuming replied.

Xie Lian closed his eyes, paused, and then opened them again. He gazed at the black-clad warrior, frowning. "Why are you still here?"

"The location is settled," Wuming replied. "What about the time?"

"Time?"

"The souls of the dead cannot wait any longer. We must find a subject to curse soon, without delay."

They truly couldn't delay for long. After some silence, Xie Lian said, "Three days."

"Why three days?" Wuming asked.

For some reason, Xie Lian got easily agitated whenever he conversed with Wuming. "In three days, it will be the full moon. Unleashing the spirits at that time will increase the plague's power significantly. You ask too many questions, just go."

Wuming nodded and stood down without another word. Xie Lian closed his eyes again and covered his forehead with his hand, hoping to relieve this round of headaches.

Just then, he heard a cold, mocking chuckle from behind him.

That familiar, mocking laughter froze Xie Lian's blood solid. He whirled around, and sure enough, behind him sat a snow-white figure in a cry-smiling mask. His hands were tucked inside the expansive sleeves of his funeral garb, and he was watching Xie Lian from the altar.

White No-Face!

Xie Lian drew his sword and lunged. White No-Face caught the point of the blade between two fingers, sighing as he did.

"Just as I thought. This appearance suits you very well."

Wearing their masks, the two of them looked identical from head to toe. No one but the two men themselves could have differentiated one from the other as they clashed in a whirl of white.

White No-Face easily evaded all of Xie Lian's strikes, and as he did, he asked "Your Highness, you buried your parents in such deserted, foreign soil. Didn't you think that might wrong their memory?"

Xie Lian's heart sank. "You touched my mother and father's bodies?! Did you desecrate their corpses?!"

"No, just the opposite," White No-Face said. "I helped you give them a proper, solemn burial."

Xie Lian was taken aback.

"I helped you by carrying them to the Xianle Royal Mausoleum, and I even dressed them in a pair of rare, exquisite robes that will prevent them from rotting for thousands of years," White No-Face added. "The next time you visit them, you will still be able to see the same faces you knew from when they were alive."

He then told Xie Lian the location of the Royal Mausoleum and how to enter. This should have been something the king and state preceptor told Xie Lian, but before they were able, they had both either died or disappeared.

Xie Lian was stunned—and suspicious. "Why do you know how to enter the Royal Mausoleum?"

White No-Face smiled. "I know everything about Your Highness."

"You don't know shit!" Xie Lian hissed.

He still wasn't used to spitting such vulgar words from his lips. As if White No-Face had seen through him, he looked Xie Lian up and down and said gently, "Don't worry, it's all right. From now on, there will no longer be anything that can hold you back. There won't be anyone to hold unnecessary expectations of you, and there certainly won't be anyone who knows who you are. You are free to do anything you want."

His words planted a strange feeling in Xie Lian.

Why had this monster come here today?

To express his goodwill.

Although the very idea seemed absurd, Xie Lian's instincts told him that it was true. Providing his parents with a proper burial, trying to console him...it all came from this intent.

That must mean he was very, very happy—happier than any other time Xie Lian had met him. It was like he was exceptionally delighted to see Xie Lian like this, and it was making him unconsciously gentler and kinder. That kindness actually made Xie Lian feel a flash of gratitude, one so keen that it might have brought him to tears, but that was drowned out by overwhelming disgust.

"Don't be so happy so soon," Xie Lian said frostily. "I still won't allow a creature like you to remain in the world. Once I've wiped Yong'an from the map, I will come for you. You'd best prepare yourself!"

White No-Face opened his arms wide and shrugged. "I happily welcome you with open arms. Even if you come intending to kill me, I will still be here waiting for you. When you've truly become strong enough to defeat me, you will be able to take up my mantle. However—"

The smile under the mask seemed to fade.

"Will you actually destroy Yong'an?"

"What do you mean?" Xie Lian demanded.

"You could make your move right now. Why choose to move in three days? Are you hesitating now that things have finally come to a head? Could it be that, even with your kingdom destroyed and your family dead, you still don't have the courage to seek revenge? Will I witness another of Your Highness's failures?"

The word "failure" stabbed his ears. Xie Lian raised his sword and lunged, but he was sent to the ground by one kick from White No-Face—and the creature had somehow snatched away the black sword. His gentle tone was now condescending.

"Do you know how you're acting right now?"

Xie Lian grabbed the snow-white boot on his chest, but no matter how hard he pushed, it wouldn't move an inch. He remained firmly pinned down by that foot, trapped on the ground.

White No-Face leaned down slightly. "You're like a sulking child. You don't yet have the resolve."

"Who says I don't?!" Xie Lian cried angrily.

"Then what are you doing right now?" White No-Face questioned. "Where's your curse? Where are your *dead*? Your father and mother, your soldiers, your citizens—how truly pitiful that they had such a god thrust upon them! You couldn't protect them while they were alive, and you can't avenge them after their deaths! You useless trash!"

He put more of his weight onto the foot on Xie Lian's chest. Trickles of blood began to creep from the edges of Xie Lian's cry-smiling mask, choked from his lungs.

White No-Face lowered the hand that gripped the sword, and its black jade tip prodded against Xie Lian's throat. As it traced the cursed shackle there, the feeling awakened memories Xie Lian had pushed down.

"Would you like me to remind you what it feels like to be pierced by a hundred swords?"

Overwhelming fear made Xie Lian's breathing hitch. He was too terrified to move.

After successfully scaring him, White No-Face became amiable again. He withdrew his boot and helped Xie Lian, who was frozen in terror, to sit upright.

White No-Face grasped Xie Lian's chin and pushed it in a specific direction. "Come, look. This is what you look like right now."

He forced Xie Lian to view the desecrated divine statue upon the desecrated altar.

The flower and sword in the crown prince statue's hands were gone. It had been burnt by blazing fires, hacked by axes, and pelted by vegetables, lifted and smashed to the floor. Half of it was burnt black and there were limbs missing—it was a tragic sight to behold.

"Who do you have to thank for becoming like that?" White No-Face asked. "Do you think it's me?"

He was trying to forcefully indoctrinate Xie Lian once again. New ideas were being poured into his mind, filling him with more and more confusion, more and more doubt. He had even forgotten his anger.

"...What do you want? Why do you cling to me?" Xie Lian wondered, his tone distracted.

"I've told you," White No-Face replied. "I've come to guide and educate you. The third thing I will teach you is this: if you cannot save the common people, then destroy them. They will revere you only when you crush them underfoot!"

When White No-Face said those words, Xie Lian's head suddenly throbbed like it was going to explode. He clutched at it and screamed.

It was the vengeful spirits! There were so *many*, and they were shrieking and wailing inside his mind—Xie Lian's head hurt so much that he wanted to roll on the ground. White No-Face, on the other hand, started laughing.

"They cannot wait any longer," he cooed gently. "If you don't unleash the plague of Human Face Disease within three days, if you cannot give them a target to curse, then *you* will become their target. And do you know what will become of you then?"

Xie Lian could feel the freezing black sword being stuffed into his hand once again. A voice resounded in his ears.

"You no longer have the choice to turn back."

When the throbbing headache finally faded, Xie Lian dropped his hands and opened his eyes. Inside the broken-down Temple of the Crown Prince, he was alone. The white-clothed man who was his exact likeness had long since vanished.

He didn't know how much time had passed, but night had fallen. It was dim and shadowed inside the Temple of the Crown Prince. Xie Lian's heart stuttered when he realized something.

One day of three had already passed.

A tiny spot of white seemed to glow within the darkness of the hall. It was strange, and Xie Lian turned to look. But when he got a clear view of what that white spot was, his pupils shrank in shock—though his eyes could not be seen underneath his mask.

He snatched up the offending thing and demanded, "What... What is this flower doing here?"

It was a fresh, delicate, little white flower, and it had been placed on the left hand of the scorched, broken divine statue. The contrast between it and the blackened statue made it appear especially pure, like snow, but also especially bleak. It looked like this divine statue had suffered all its injuries to protect the little flower.

Xie Lian didn't know why this scene enraged him so keenly. "*Ghost!* Come out!" he bellowed.

Soon, the saber-wielding black-clad warrior appeared as expected. He hadn't yet spoken before Xie Lian demanded, "What's the meaning of this flower? Who did this? Did you do this?"

Wuming bowed his head slightly, and his gaze paused for a moment on the flower that seemed crushed to suffocation in Xie Lian's hand. Finally, he said quietly, "It wasn't me."

"Then who could've done it?!" Xie Lian exclaimed.

"Why is Your Highness so angry at seeing this flower?" Wuming asked.

Xie Lian's face darkened, and he threw the flower to the ground. "...Pranks like these disgust me."

Wuming, however, said, "Why would it be a prank? Perhaps Your Highness has believers here who still offer worship."

His words were like a slap to Xie Lian's face, and he turned to Wuming.

"Are you making fun of me?"

"No," Wuming replied.

"Then don't say such nonsense! Why would offerings still be here?!"

After a pause, Wuming said, "It's not impossible."

Xie Lian didn't know what to say. He couldn't take it anymore and snapped at Wuming, "That's enough. What are you trying to say? Weren't you a soldier of Xianle? I didn't rouse you from the battlefield to listen to you speak for Yong'an. You just need to heed my command!"

The flower on the ground pricked his heart and stabbed his eyes. All at once, he felt very wretched and unkempt. Xie Lian charged forward and stomped it under his boot, crushing it like he was venting his fury. Yet after he was done, he felt baffled by his own actions. Why did he throw such a huge fit over such a small flower?

Xie Lian rushed out of the Temple of the Crown Prince. Only once he felt the cool breeze did he gradually calm down. The black-clad warrior followed him outside.

"You've investigated the area. Have you found anything that seems unusual?" Xie Lian asked.

"No," Wuming replied.

"Are you sure?" Xie Lian asked. "In order to unleash the plague of Human Face Disease, there can't be anything amiss with the time, fortune, or location."

"I am certain," Wuming replied.

Xie Lian had nothing more to say, so he gazed at the sky.

After a moment of silence, Wuming asked, "Your Highness, have you decided on the method you will use to unleash the vengeful spirits' pestilence?"

"I'm still thinking," Xie Lian said.

He looked down at the black sword hanging from his waist. Millions of vengeful spirits were sealed within the sword, but it could only keep them contained for so long.

Suddenly, Wuming said, "Your Highness, I have a presumptuous request."

"Speak."

"I hoped that Your Highness might give me the sword and allow me to summon the plague."

Xie Lian turned his head. "Why?"

Wuming watched Xie Lian intently from behind his mask. "My beloved sustained terrible injuries in the war and suffered a fate worse than death. I could only watch helplessly as they suffered in torment and struggled in agony."

"And?" Xie Lian said.

"And so I hoped that I could be the one to wield the sword and avenge them."

That reason was very plausible, but Xie Lian found it hard to trust him, somehow. He narrowed his eyes.

"I find you rather odd." He circled Wuming and commented coolly, "Based on what I've seen, you don't seem like an avenger mired in resentment and hatred. Asking this of me...is it really so you can unleash the plague?"

Despite his doubts, he couldn't imagine why else Wuming would request to unleash it.

The nameless black-clad warrior bowed his head toward him. "Your Highness, I wish for the deaths of Yong'an's people more than anyone. And I wish for them to perish by my hand. If you don't believe me, I can go prove myself to you right now."

"How do you plan on doing that?" Xie Lian asked.

Wuming placed his hand on his saber and began to slowly back up, withdrawing from Xie Lian's presence and preparing to leave. By his third step back, Xie Lian suddenly realized what he planned to do: to prove to Xie Lian that he had a vengeful heart, he was going to go kill someone!

"Stop!" Xie Lian instantly called out.

Wuming stopped. Xie Lian sized him up critically, then declared with resolve, "No. I will unleash them myself."

The black-clad warrior bowed his head; thanks to his mask, it was hard to guess what expression he might be wearing. But Xie Lian didn't care about anyone's reaction, and he simply turned around.

"However...before that, there's something I need to do," he said softly.

He raised the cold, jade-like, black sword. He stared at the sharp blade in his hand, a peculiar glint flashing in his eyes.

Wuming noticed that something was off. "Your Highness, what are you planning?!"

But Wuming had no chance to stop him before Xie Lian turned the point of the blade on himself—and plunged the black sword into his own abdomen!

The next day, on the streets of Lang-Er Bay...

The weather had not been pleasant lately. It was perpetually cloudy and gloomy, with sudden wild gusts of wind and endless sinister rain.

For that matter, Yong'an had not been peaceful lately, not one part of it. Apparently the newly built palace had caught fire, and both the king and the crown prince were reported to be ill—

ill enough that they couldn't grant anyone an audience. Everything was chaos; there were ominous signs everywhere. The people were ill at ease and couldn't help but grumble. Only ignorant children continued to play and run around without a care in the world.

A blast of gloomy wind swept past, harsh enough to be blinding. Suddenly, a huge explosion echoed from a bustling fork in one of the city's thoroughfares.

A man had dropped from the sky!

The crowd on the main street was startled by the booming noise, and they all looked toward the sound. On the ground there was a human-shaped crater formed from the falling man's impact. Within the hole there was a person lying listlessly flat. His hair was strewn around him, and his body was covered in blood—so much that his white robes looked utterly horrifying.

Everyone on the street rushed to crowd around.

"Who is it?!"

"My heavens, where did he fall from? The sky?!"

"Is he dead?!"

"I...I don't think so! I think he's still moving!"

"I can't believe he could survive that! Wait, what's stuck through his chest? A sword?!"

Once the crowd was close enough, they could finally see the man's appearance clearly. Although he was disheveled, he was handsome; he had clean features and fair skin. His eyes were gazing unblinkingly toward the sky in a way that was very unlike the living—but he clearly wasn't dead since he was still breathing. The black sword that had pierced his stomach and penetrated his organs was rising up and down weakly with the movement of his chest.

Another person exclaimed in surprise, "Wait, isn't this...isn't this... *th-that* Royal Highness the Crown Prince?!"

Once he mentioned it, everyone else started to recognize him too.

"...It really is. It's the old crown prince, the Crown Prince of Xianle! I saw him once from a distance!

"Didn't they say the crown prince went missing?"

"I heard he ascended."

"Why is he like this...? What's with the sword? Did it really stab him all the way through? Scary..."

"Enough gawking! Let me through, will y'all let me through? I've got places to be!"

This street ended in a fork where the road split into two separate directions. Since the crossing was being blocked by a crowd of people, the carriages that came along couldn't get through, and drivers descended from their vehicles to check things out. It was causing quite the commotion.

Suddenly, someone shouted, "Wait! He seems...to be saying something?"

The crowd quieted down. Everyone held their breaths and listened intently, trying to pick up his voice. No one on the outer edges could hear anything, so a moment later they shouted, "What did he say? Did he tell you what happened?"

The ones in the front called back, "No!"

"Then what did he say?"

"He said, 'Save me.'"

Xie Lian lay flat on the ground. After those two words, not another sound escaped his lips. The people crowding around him reacted to the statement with varying emotions, expressions, and degrees of puzzlement.

A chubby man who seemed to be a chef said, "Save him? How do we save him?"

Someone took a guess. "He probably meant to ask for help pulling the sword out?"

The chef looked fairly gutsy and was ready to go and give it a shot—however, he was held back by several hands.

"Don't, don't, don't! Absolutely do not!"

The chef was confused. "Why not?"

"You mustn't! Haven't you heard? Didn't Xianle lose the war?" the bystanders explained. "Why did they lose the war? Because of Human Face Disease. And why did that plague descend? Because there was a God of Misfortune, and it was—"

"God of Misfortune?! Really?!"

The moment those words were said, any chance of someone recklessly stepping forward was dashed. In an instant, the area around that enormous human-shaped pit was entirely empty of people.

After all, no one knew exactly what had happened to the crown prince of the previous dynasty. Was he a God of Misfortune? Would they contract that horrifying disease if they came in contact with him? Or would they find themselves mired in bitterly bad luck? Besides, it seemed like he wasn't going to die for the time being even if they didn't pull the sword out—if he could fall from who-knew-where and crash so loudly from such a height without dying, then he was beyond human.

A moment later, someone said timidly, "Maybe we should report this to the authorities...?"

"Didn't they say this Royal Highness ascended and became a god? What's the use in reporting this to the authorities?"

"Then what should we do?"

The crowd squabbled amongst themselves but couldn't come to a decision. In the end, they sent someone to report the incident and promptly washed their hands of any further responsibility.

"You want to lie there? Well then, just lie there. Let's leave him be."

Thus, Xie Lian remained sprawled in the human-shaped pit, watching the curious heads peeking in above him gradually decrease in number until they completely disappeared. The blocked carriages detoured around him, and the children playing in the streets were dragged back inside by their parents. Every so often someone would pass by, but they kept their distance. Xie Lian was expressionless throughout, speaking not a single word more.

A water merchant finally couldn't bear the sight any longer. He whispered to his wife as she watched the stall, "Is it really all right to leave him like that? Why don't I give him a cup of water?"

The water merchant's wife hesitated for a moment and scanned their surroundings, then whispered back, "Let's not. If he really is a God of Misfortune, then who knows what could happen if you get too close?"

The water merchant was also hesitant and looked around. The other merchants were all staring at him from their stalls, their expressions nervous—it seemed that if he were to approach that pit, they had drawn their own lines and would stay far, far away from him in turn. In the end, he didn't dare step forward and abandoned the idea entirely.

Xie Lian remained like that from the thin mist of morning to the blazing midday sun, then to dusk, and on until deep into the night.

Many people saw him during that time, but those who approached were very few, and there certainly wasn't anyone who would help pull the black sword from his stomach.

In the deep of night, there was not a soul on the streets, but Xie Lian still lay there on the ground and watched the skies above. The stars twinkled in the dark sky, and his thoughts were meandering and mysterious. Suddenly, clear, crisp laughter sounded from above the pit.

"Ha ha ha... What are you doing?"

After receiving so many visits from the owner of that voice, Xie Lian no longer reacted as violently as he once had. When he didn't receive his customary angry, panicked "welcome," the voice's owner took the initiative and walked over himself. He stood by Xie Lian's head and bent down, and his voice seemed almost a little disappointed.

"What are you waiting for?"

That half-crying, half-smiling mask was upside down, and coincidentally also blocked Xie Lian's entire field of vision. They faced each other like that, with only centimeters between them.

"Get the hell out of here. You're blocking my view of the sky," Xie Lian said coldly.

White No-Face wasn't the least bit upset at being told to get the hell away. He straightened up with a laugh, and his reply sounded quite affable, like an elder tolerating a spoiled child. "What's so good about the sky?"

"It's prettier than you," Xie Lian snapped at him.

"Why the temper?" White No-Face asked. "It wasn't me who stabbed you this time, and it wasn't me who left you here. You did all this yourself. Even if you haven't gotten the results you were hoping for, you still can't blame me."

Xie Lian said nothing.

"You've wasted an entire day here," White No-Face continued. "What exactly are you trying to prove? Or are you trying to convince *yourself* of something?"

"It's none of your shitty business," Xie Lian said.

White No-Face chuckled sympathetically. "Silly child. Did you think someone would help you pull out that sword?"

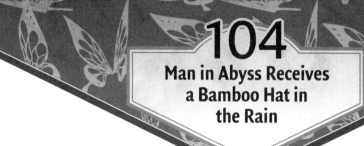

"**I** KNOW NO ONE WILL COME, but it's none of your shitty business," Xie Lian retorted with force.

"Then why did you poke a hole to lie down in?" White No-Face languidly asked. "Are you trying to get some attention? No one will cry over you."

"I'm doing this because I want to," Xie Lian countered. "It's none of your shitty business."

"If someone does come to help you, what will you do? And if no one comes, what will you do?"

Xie Lian didn't answer his questions but instead started cursing. "Why do you talk so much shit?! I'm gonna throw up! It's none of your shitty business, *none of your shitty business!*"

Even as his words became more vulgar and rude, his tone more frustrated, he still only knew so many curse words.

White No-Face laughed out loud in amusement. "Silly child." He sighed and turned around. "Just as well. Either way, there is only one day left. It's fine to let you foolishly struggle for a bit. Regardless, no one will come give you a cup of water or help you pull out the sword. Remember..."

White No-Face reminded him once more of the consequences.

"Tomorrow at sunset, if you still haven't unleashed the plague of Human Face Disease, the curse will fall upon you."

Xie Lian listened quietly and didn't move a muscle.

The third day, Xie Lian was still lying in that deep human-shaped pit in the middle of the road. His position hadn't even changed.

The crowd that day wasn't much different from the crowd from the day before. They all detoured around him at a distance and simply went about their day. Although the incident where a strange man fell from the sky had been reported to the authorities, when they heard that it might be a God of Misfortune, they didn't want to deal with it—he wasn't really causing any trouble, after all, just lying there like a dead man. The authorities brushed off the affair with a vague promise to keep an eye on it for a few days. That basically meant they weren't going to bother. Besides, maybe something would change on its own.

Several curious children came scurrying over and squatted by the edge of the pit to look at the strange man inside. They picked up a tree branch and began to surreptitiously poke at him, but Xie Lian was like a dead fish and didn't react. They were still fascinated and wanted to try to throw something at him to see if he'd respond to that—but they were discovered by their parents before they could follow through. The children were lectured harshly, then dragged home and grounded.

The water merchant from the day before still kept sneaking glances in his direction. Xie Lian hadn't had a single drop of water for a day and a night, and a layer of dry, withered dead skin had formed on his lips. Feeling sorry at the sight, the water merchant ladled out a bowl of water to deliver it, but his wife deliberately elbowed him and made him topple the bowl. He was forced to relent.

Perhaps the heavens wanted to join in on the fun, for after midday, drizzling rain began to fall.

The street vendors hurriedly packed up their stalls, and the pedestrians shouted at each other to hurry home. They all quickly left. The rain poured harder and harder, scouring Xie Lian's face until he looked even paler and soaking his entire body until he was utterly drenched.

A shadow silently appeared next to Xie Lian, its owner dressed in white. No one on the street seemed to have noticed this peculiar figure.

White No-Face looked condescendingly down at him. "The sun is about to set."

Xie Lian was silent.

"You aren't the God of Misfortune, but they would rather believe that you are, and they're unwilling to believe you aren't. Once upon a time, you defied the heavens and created rain for Yong'an. Yet now, they won't even give you a cup of water.

"Stabbing you a hundred times might have been done in desperation, but now, they're not even willing to do something as simple as pulling out a sword. They all consider it too much trouble.

"I've told you this time and again. No one will come help you," White No-Face finished, his voice soft with pity.

There was a voice deep down in Xie Lian screaming hysterically, *Admit it. What he said is true. There's no one, no one, no one! There isn't a single person who will help me!*

As if he had heard the desperate cry in Xie Lian's heart, White No-Face seemed to smile a bit. He reached out and gripped the hilt of the black sword.

"It's all right. They won't help you, but I will."

He exerted some force and pulled the black sword from Xie Lian's stomach, then tossed it down beside Xie Lian with a resounding *clang*.

Soon after, the shadow of white cloth in the rain laughed lightly and backed away, as if he had achieved all he wanted to do. Leaving Xie Lian to his own devices, he vanished.

Once the black sword was pulled out, Xie Lian's wound was left exposed to the harsh rain. The once-numbed pain had started to spread again. But that was the only thing he could feel in that moment.

Splash sploosh, splash sploosh. The sound of wild footsteps stomping through water drifted over, like some passerby was rushing through the rain nearby. But Xie Lian was no longer secretly hopeful.

He slowly sat up, yet the motion was still unexpected. He was interrupted by a loud yell, and a man fell heavily next to him.

The man had carried a large basket on his back and wore a bamboo hat to shield him against the rain. It was probably due to the downpour that he hadn't seen that there was someone in a pit on the road; he'd been running fast, and he'd only noticed when he'd gotten closer and Xie Lian suddenly appeared. He'd tried to stop short but had instead fallen quite badly. As he tumbled to the ground next to the human-shaped pit, he began to scream a barrage of curses on the spot.

"What the fuck?!"

His bamboo hat had flown off, and the basket on his back had toppled and spilled its cargo of white rice everywhere. The man sat back and screamed in frustration, slapping at the ground. The wet mud and rice splattered Xie Lian. Outraged, the man leapt to his feet in a flurry and pointed a finger squarely in Xie Lian's face.

"What the hell?! This ancestor worked his ass off to earn a bit of money to buy this rice, and now it's all gone just like that! How many lifetimes' worth of awful luck is this?! Pay me back! Don't sit there pretending to be dead, pay me back!"

Xie Lian didn't bother to spare him a single look, planning to simply ignore him. However, the man was unrelenting, and he grabbed Xie Lian by the collar.

"Are you asking for death?! Huh?! I'm talking to you!"

"Yes," Xie Lian replied coldly.

The man clicked his tongue. "Well, if you wanna fucking die, go scamper off somewhere and die quietly on your own! What are you doing blocking people's way in the middle of the road?! Can't even die in peace—what a nuisance!"

Xie Lian let himself be shaken wildly by his collar, stoic and expressionless and utterly numb.

Cuss. Cuss all you want. Nothing matters anymore, so curse me however you want.

Everything will disappear soon.

The sun was about to set.

The man gripped the wooden Xie Lian, pressing him for compensation, and when Xie Lian remained unresponsive, he bawled him out. That wasn't enough for the man, but after pushing and shoving him for a long time, he picked up his bamboo hat from the ground, put it on his head, and walked away grumbling. Xie Lian was thrown back into the pit with a dull thud.

Gradually, he began to hear a clamor louder than the sound of the rain.

It was the shrieking of millions of souls of the dead sealed within the black sword.

As the sun sank bit by bit in the west, they started hollering and wailing like mad inside Xie Lian's head—cheering and rejoicing for the arrival of freedom and revenge.

Xie Lian raised a hand and covered his face. As his other hand shakily reached out to grab the black sword on the ground, he noticed something strange.

The rain seemed to have stopped.

No.

The rain hadn't stopped. Something had been placed over his head to shield him from the downpour!

Xie Lian's eyes snapped open, and he looked up. He saw someone crouched in front of him, pressing the bamboo hat that had once been on his own head onto Xie Lian's.

...It was the man who had just been bawling him out!

Xie Lian glared at the man, and the man glared back at him.

"What are you looking at me like that for? What, it was just some cussin'. You really wanna go die over it?" He spat on the ground as he spoke. "Looking so miserable, like you're in mourning. It's unlucky, I tell ya!"

Xie Lian was speechless.

The man had been rough and aggressive earlier, but he must have felt a little guilty after thinking about what he'd done. He grumbled a bit more, but then he started to try and explain himself. "All right, all right, I was over the line earlier. But you still deserved that scolding. Who told you to act so nuts? And who's never been cussed at before?"

Xie Lian's eyes were round and bulging, and he found himself unable to speak.

The man grew impatient. "Fine, fine, fine, it's my bad luck today. You don't have to pay me back for the rice. But what are you still lying around here for? You're a grown man, not a child—are you waiting for your ma and pa to pick you up? Get up, get up, get up, get up."

As he urged him, he tugged at Xie Lian and finally pulled him to his feet. Then he heartily slapped Xie Lian twice on the back.

"Stand up. Hurry home, now!"

And just like that, Xie Lian was pulled from the human-shaped pit. The two slaps almost sent him tumbling to the ground, he was so dumbfounded.

By the time he snapped out of it, the man was already gone.

Only the bamboo hat on his head remained, reminding him that someone had stopped to pull him out. It hadn't been a hallucination.

He didn't know how long he had been standing there when White No-Face reappeared behind him.

This time, he didn't laugh. His voice wasn't so easy and carefree anymore; he instead sounded vaguely worried and displeased when he asked, "What are you doing?"

The rain was still pouring down, but Xie Lian was wearing a bamboo hat that someone had given him. While his body was drenched, at least his head and face were spared.

But his cheeks were still wet.

When Xie Lian didn't answer, White No-Face reminded him in a dark tone, "The sun is about to set. Take up your sword. You know what will happen if you don't."

Xie Lian didn't turn to look at him as he softly said, "Fuck you."

"What did you say?" White No-Face's voice carried a trace of frost.

Now, Xie Lian turned to him. "You didn't hear me? Then I'll say it again," he said calmly.

Suddenly, he struck out with a violent, thunderous kick that sent White No-Face flying dozens of meters away!

Xie Lian stomped his foot to the ground, and, with one hand clutching his wound, he pointed at White No-Face. In his most booming voice, he yelled with everything he had.

"I said *fuck you*! Who do you think you are to dare talk to me like that?! I am the crown prince!"

Tears were streaming down his face.

One person. Just one.

Really.

Just one person was enough!

While White No-Face was sent flying by his kick, he flipped in the air and landed easily.

"Are you mad?!" White No-Face shouted at him in absolute fury.

In all these years, this was the very first time Xie Lian had seen the creature react with such emotion—the sight gave him enormous pleasure. He grabbed the black sword from the ground and charged forward.

"I'm not mad, I've just come back around!"

The first kick had caught him by surprise, but the next attacks wouldn't be so easy. White No-Face dodged Xie Lian's blows as he flung icy accusations at him. "Have you...forgotten? How your parents left you, how your people treated you, how your worshippers betrayed you?! All because of that man—that puny, insignificant person—you've forgotten everything?!"

"I haven't forgotten! But—" Xie Lian swung the sword and bellowed with angry vigor, "It's none of your shitty business!"

White No-Face seized the tip of the sword and gripped it extremely firmly. Blood dripped from his fingers, and his knuckles cracked.

He was losing it a little. He muttered incredulously, "Useless trash...useless trash! You're absolutely useless trash! You've come so far, but you can still regret—you can actually turn back!"

Xie Lian pressed harder into his thwarted sword strike and replied through gritted teeth, "...You disgust me. I refuse to ever become something as disgusting as you!"

That seemed to stun some calm back into White No-Face, and he regained the tone of voice that made it sound like everything was under his control. "...Never mind. This is simply one final, minuscule struggle in the face of death. Or did you forget what I told you?"

Xie Lian exhaled harshly as White No-Face slowly and clearly reminded him, "You summoned the souls of the battlefield's dead. Now, it is too late. They will not be stopped!"

Amidst the heavy rain, the black sword in Xie Lian's hand emitted a sharp, ringing cry that stabbed painfully at his ears and head.

"What will you do?" White No-Face asked. "Is it worth it to take on the curse of the ages for these people?"

Ever since his kick connected, Xie Lian's blood was boiling in his veins and rushing to his head. All the sword-swinging and the words he spat came straight from his heart, with no thought of what he'd do or anything that came next. When he heard White No-Face's question, he didn't know how to answer it.

"You won't see what I plan to do. I'll get rid of you before that!"

White No-Face snorted. "How arrogant."

Just as he finished speaking, Xie Lian felt himself leave the ground, and his entire body was sent flying.

He instantly steadied his mind to find his center, but before he could find his balance, a white figure flashed above him and struck down with force. It was like Xie Lian had become a ball of iron thrown by a sling, and he crashed deep into the ground with a resounding *boom*.

Xie Lian had started out with a sliver of hope that if he gave it his all with a sudden burst of strength, he could come out victorious. But after this strike, he was painfully aware of the reality.

He couldn't win!

Too strong... The creature's strength absolutely overwhelmed him!

Xie Lian had never found an opponent *overwhelming* like this before. The very idea would flash through his mind on rare occasions, such as the few times he sparred with Jun Wu. But while Jun Wu was incredibly strong, his power was measured and controlled, deliberate and careful—the complete opposite of White No-Face. There was a maliciousness in White No-Face's strength that bordered on vicious, and his murderous intent brimmed with resentment.

It only took one strike for Xie Lian to understand. He would never be able to win against White No-Face. Perhaps only Jun Wu would be a match for the creature.

But the voice of Xie Lian as he was now would never reach Jun Wu!

A violent stomp, and White No-Face's snow-white boot crushed down on Xie Lian's chest. "Your arrogance and naive dreams caused everything, right from the start!" he snapped chillingly.

Xie Lian could feel his organs twist and retract from the stomp, the pain excruciating, but he held back a mouthful of blood. "No. It wasn't me!"

"Huh?" White No-Face queried in an unpleasant tone.

Xie Lian reached out and firmly clutched the boot on his chest. His eyes were clearer than ever before, shining bright. "*You* brought the plague. *You* caused everything!"

White No-Face humphed. "...Perhaps. If you must think of it that way." Then he seemed to smile. "But you need to understand something. If it wasn't for your arrogance in defying the heavens, I never would have appeared in this world. I was born by heaven's will."

The flames in Xie Lian's eyes weren't snuffed out by the heavy rain; in fact, they blazed all the stronger. "Enough with the arrogance! I don't need you to teach me anything—I can learn on my own. If a thing like you represents heaven's will, then heaven's will should be destroyed!"

Muffled thunder rolled in from the horizon; whirling winds blew.

White No-Face's voice dropped deep and soft. "I took the utmost care in teaching you, but you remain obtuse and stubborn. Crown Prince, I've lost my patience."

Xie Lian coughed a few times, and White No-Face continued, "However, it makes no difference. Either way, you already roused them, and there is only one step left to take. Allow me to help you with that."

"What are you doing?" Xie Lian cried in alarm.

White No-Face bent down and seized Xie Lian's hand, then stuffed the black sword into his palm, forcing him to grip it and raise it to the sky!

A blinding bolt of heavenly lightning struck the black blade and infused its heart with power—it gleamed eerie light. Dense, gloomy clouds began to stir, and soon, a sea of black had enveloped Yong'an's skies entirely. Countless faces, arms, and legs roiled within the storm, as if hell had moved to the heavens.

Right then, the last sliver of the sun sank below the horizon.

Xie Lian lay on the ground. His eyes reflected the roiling black clouds and the sky torn by flashing lightning and squalling thunder. White No-Face walked away, and the black sword dropped to the ground with a *clang*.

It was like millions of horses were shrieking and howling in the clouds—an apocalyptic parade. Throughout the streets and alleyways, the citizens were confused and alarmed by the cacophony and came outside to see what was happening.

"What's going on?"

"What's all that noise?"

"What the hell?! What's that in the sky?! Is that a human face?!"

"It's chaos! It's a bad omen—the world is ending!"

Xie Lian was covered in mud and grime, and he stumbled as he crawled off the ground. "Go home! Go back to your houses! Don't come out! Go home—run!" he yelled.

Human Face Disease was about to be unleashed once again!

Xie Lian frantically waved his hands while White No-Face stood to one side and chuckled softly. Xie Lian whipped his head around and glared at him in fury.

White No-Face tucked his hands into his sleeves and said with easy calm, "Why so angry? You can't turn back now, so why not just enjoy the sweetness of revenge? Your hands wrought this—you should appreciate your handiwork."

"...You really think I can't do anything about this?" Xie Lian said.

"If you have a plan, then please, go ahead," White No-Face replied.

Xie Lian drew in a deep breath, then he picked up the black sword on the ground and approached the crowd on the street.

Everyone recognized him as the crown prince of the previous dynasty who had been lying in the street for the past two days— a living ghost, an ungodly god, an inhuman human. They all backed away cautiously at his approach.

"All of you, stop where you are!" Xie Lian barked.

Although he was covered in mud and grime from head to toe, there was a strange aura about him. For some reason, everyone actually stopped.

"Do you see those things in the sky?" Xie Lian asked.

The crowd nodded unconsciously.

"Those are vengeful spirits that will trigger a plague of Human Face Disease," Xie Lian continued. "Very soon, it will erupt once again!"

The black sea of clouds was indeed terrifying, and the people watching didn't need much convincing to believe his words. Horror gripped the crowd.

"H-Human Face Disease?!"

"Why has it returned?!"

"Could it really be...?"

Some were at a complete loss, some turned around and hoped to flee, but most of them stood where they were, apprehensively waiting for Xie Lian to say more. But he had no more to say—he only gripped the sword and raised it to the crowd.

The crowd jumped back in fear the moment he raised that chilling weapon, but Xie Lian barked again, "Take this!"

The people could only gape, mute with fright.

"What...?" someone choked out.

Xie Lian held the sword like that, offering it to them under the pouring rain. "As long as you stab me with this sword, you won't be affected by the plague," he said grimly.

White No-Face's smile seemed to falter. A moment later, he asked with relative calm, "Crown Prince, have you gone mad?"

The people were bewildered as well.

"What... What are you saying?"

"Is he crazy?"

"Take the sword and stab him? Really? What is he planning?"

The crowd babbled and muttered, and White No-Face suddenly burst out laughing.

"Have you lost your mind? Or do you miss the taste of being pierced by a hundred swords—no, I'm afraid this time it will be ten thousand. Open your eyes and look properly at the sky!" His voice quickly lost all its mirth as he pointed up.

"The vengeful spirits have enveloped all of Yong'an! If you want to 'save the common people,' all of Yong'an will need to stab you— you will become nothing but a puddle of flesh within a day! This foolishness is no different from when you tried to defy the heavens and create rain! Do you really think you can save everyone?"

Xie Lian kept his back turned to him. "If a day isn't enough, let it take a month. If a month won't do, then two months, three months! If I can't save ten thousand, then I'll save a thousand. If I can't save a thousand, then I'll save a hundred, or ten, or even just one!"

"Why?!" White No-Face demanded in outrage.

Xie Lian raised the sword with both hands and roared to the skies, "I don't have a reason—just because I want to! Even if I explained it to you..." He cocked his head to glance at him. "...Useless trash like you wouldn't understand."

His condescension and disdain were too obvious and cut too deeply. White No-Face couldn't retain the calm in his voice as he said, "You. What did you call me?"

Xie Lian pointedly ignored him and turned calmly to the crowd. "Just one stab and everything will be all right. I won't die—you've all seen that for yourselves over the past two days. However, everyone is only allowed one turn with no messing about, and you all must listen to my instructions. If anyone tries to start anything, I'll smash your head. Trust me, I can smash a hundred of you with one hand."

White No-Face was incredulous. "The useless trash who brought ruin to his kingdom dares to call *me* useless trash?"

No one dared take the sword in Xie Lian's hand, but no one dared to flee either. As he was ignored, White No-Face sank deeper and deeper into anger.

"...Very well," he said coolly. "Then I will sit back and watch you be ruined by your obstinance. However, no matter how this ends, you've brought it upon yourself. I hope you don't fall apart and come crying to me in regret."

As the people shuffled around and waffled in confusion, the black clouds in the sky grew denser by the minute and pressed down heavier; they seemed ready to collapse. The shrieking cries of countless human faces were so loud, it was like they were right beside their ears.

Finally, one father was so scared he couldn't take it anymore. He dragged his child over and took the sword. "I... I'll give it a try with my Xiao-Bao, I guess..."

The others in the crowd were still hesitating, and they exclaimed in surprise, "You're actually going to do it?!"

The father seemed just as hesitant, but he braced himself and stammered, "But... But...I really don't think he'll die! I'm sorry, buddy, I'm really sorry! My Xiao-Bao..."

He raised a hand to cover the eyes of the small child in his arms and forced him to grip the black sword. White No-Face didn't interfere, just chuckled mockingly.

Xie Lian clenched his fists and waited for the pain to seize him. In his head, he told himself, *It's all right. I've already been hurt so many times, I'll get used to this soon enough.*

But just as the black sword was about to pierce his gut, someone unexpectedly knocked it aside.

The pain Xie Lian was expecting never came. Instead, he heard a loud, clear, *"You can't!"*

Xie Lian whipped his head around to look. The one who had knocked the black sword off course was the water merchant!

The water merchant had been in the crowd, but he stepped forward after his tolerance was exhausted. "Well, this is an ugly sight. Can't you see that huge bloody spot on his stomach? Are you really sure this won't kill him? And even if he doesn't die, he'll clearly still bleed!"

The father scrunched up his face miserably. "But...but..."

The water merchant's wife subtly elbowed him again, but the water merchant turned and admonished her with a hushed, "Stop poking me! If you have a problem, we'll talk later!" Then he turned back around. "Besides, for all we know, we could contract the disease from stabbing him. So let's not just stab blindly, huh?"

The father pointed to the sky. "But soon..."

Just then, the small child in his arms started crying, and the water merchant pointed at him. "Look, look! Your son is scared to tears because you're forcing him to stab someone!"

Sure enough, the small child started crying even louder and threw the black sword to the ground. He probably didn't understand what his father was thinking, but he was scared, nonetheless. This killed the father's plan completely, and he retreated into the crowd holding his son.

There were some among the crowd who had been ready to try, but they didn't feel as brave anymore when they saw how the first person who stepped up had been sent packing. They could only yell anonymously from the safety of the crowd, "Didn't you hear what he said? A plague of Human Face Disease is about to descend upon us! He's a God of Misfortune—he brought this on our heads!"

However, the water merchant countered, "Even if he's the God of Misfortune, you don't think he'd willingly ask to be stabbed, do you?"

His arguing had started to piss some people off.

"He said that he's willing, so what's the problem?! Do you want us all to die together?!"

"Just focus on selling your water. You shortchange people all the time, so what are you doing sticking your neck out now?"

The water merchant's wife had kept elbowing him through all this, but when she heard that accusation, her face went red and she exploded. "Fucking bullshit—who shortchanged you?! Come the hell out here and say that to my face!"

The accuser instantly shrank back. The water merchant also flushed, but soon after, he hardened up again.

"I say! Whether he's willing is his business, but whether we act on it is *our* business! We're talking about picking up a blade and stabbing someone! If I had given him water or something over the past few days, maybe I'd be more willing to try this, but...I didn't! And who among us did?! If I injured him now...I'd feel ashamed!"

Everyone fell silent at this because he'd really had hit the nail on the head. Over the past two days, not a single person had tried to help Xie Lian. The water merchant had at least *wanted* to help, but he still hadn't managed it. The rest of them hadn't even dared to spare a glance Xie Lian's way!

"Then what should we do? If we can't do this, why don't you come up with a better plan?!" someone grumbled.

The crowd was about to get rowdy again, and some even tried to push themselves to the front. Just then, another bellow echoed out.

"Who's making all this racket?! If anyone wants to get rough, this ancestor's got a knife!"

It was the chubby chef who had wanted to pull out the sword just after Xie Lian fell from the sky. He'd been provoked into action, and he roared at the crowd, "That fella's right! Yesterday, a bunch of people were so adamant about stopping me from going up to him—if not for them, I would've pulled out that sword! So why are the ones who stopped me the same ones making the most noise now? *Pathetic!* Think you're special? Well, you certainly don't see such shamelessly thick skins every day!"

The chef was a large man with a booming voice at the height of his anger. It seemed he had just emerged from his kitchen, so he still had a butcher knife in one hand. Instantly, the ones who had been complaining the loudest didn't dare make another sound. Some members of the crowd had been absent from the area for the past few days, and when they asked what had happened, they were all surprised.

"No way... None of you tried to help him?"

"Yeah, you all just left him lying there for two days? You didn't even help him sit up or anything?"

The more questions they asked, the more shame the others felt. "Don't act like you would've gone over to help! It's easy to say those pretty things after the fact," they countered. "Don't forget, none of us will escape when those hellish things descend!"

"Ha! I assure you, if I were there, I definitely would've pulled out the sword!"

"It's easy to run your mouth after the whole thing is over..."

"Wait! What are you all arguing about? Pulling out a sword isn't the problem right now!"

The argument was wild and unruly on both sides; it was a brawl waiting to happen. The rain slowly receded and stopped. However, the black clouds were only growing thicker; their pressure was so intense it was suffocating the hundreds of people below. Suddenly, startled screams exploded from within the crowd, and fingers pointed to the sky.

"It's coming!"

Xie Lian's head shot up. The human faces churning within the black clouds began to riot, and they plunged to earth like black shooting stars, dragging long tails behind them.

The plague of Human Face Disease was descending!

The crowd was terrified and lost all sense. Some bolted, some retreated inside houses to hide, and there were also a few who went to grab for the black sword that had been knocked to the ground earlier—but they came up empty, as at some point it had gone missing.

Xie Lian had been too shocked by the people's reactions to notice this until now. "Where's the sword? Who took it?!"

No one had the time to answer, for they were fleeing in all directions. But how could they possibly be faster than the falling vengeful spirits? The wails and screams of the living and the howls of the vengeful dead erupted from all directions!

Once the vengeful spirits had caught up to the living, they became like roiling, thick, black smoke, unrelenting and clingy as they burrowed into every pore and slowly melded into peoples' bodies. Xie Lian fought arduously to drive them out, but alas, there were too many and he couldn't manage it alone. He helplessly watched countless people wail and howl as the ghosts chased them down—the water merchant and his wife, the chubby chef, they all rolled on the ground, wrestling with the tangled, black smoke. The whole while, White No-Face stood close by, watching everything and jeering.

Gripped by anxiety and fury, Xie Lian steeled his mind and roared at the spot that was densest with vengeful spirits. "Hey—!"

He caught the creatures' attention easily—he was the mastermind behind their awakening, after all. Xie Lian opened his arms wide.

"Come to me!"

The vengeful spirits that had already tangled up living victims hesitated, undecided on whether they should go, but the vengeful spirits still in the air instantly changed course and hurtled straight for Xie Lian.

Success!

Xie Lian's heart was beating so fast it was going to seize and stop. He didn't know what would happen...or what would become of him. But fueled by the hot blood rushing to his head, he was going to give this everything he had. Even if he could only hope to prove his point while that vile monster watched him be beaten black and blue, he would still never back down; even if another hundred thousand souls of the dead were to come, he would still be invincible!

You want to see me feel sorry for myself and self-destruct?

Well, I won't!

I will never!

Wave upon wave of the black tide that drowned the heavens and earth surrounded Xie Lian, and a vengeful spirit wailed as it passed through his body. It felt like Xie Lian's heart had frozen in an instant, and he shuddered. Soon after, a second one came, then a third...

The creatures sliced through him like sharp blades as they penetrated his body. Each time, they took away a sliver of whatever warmth Xie Lian still had left. His face grew paler and paler. Nevertheless, he remained firm and did not back down.

He had only been touched by a few hundred, and he had only stood his ground for a short time. There would be many more to come—they were the black clouds that blanketed the sky!

Xie Lian closed his eyes, gathering his strength to endure the flaming fury of all the vengeful spirits. Yet unexpectedly, the next attack never came. Confused, he opened his eyes, and to his surprise, the black tide surrounding him had vanished...

It had transformed into a roiling black current—which was now flowing away from him!

Stunned, Xie Lian turned to look. At the end of the long street, there stood a black-clad warrior who gripped a long, black sword.

Wuming?

Xie Lian had ordered him to leave the area while he activated the plague of Human Face Disease. Why was he here now?

Xie Lian had no idea what Wuming was doing here, but he was only stunned for a moment before he charged toward him. "Wait! What are you doing?! Don't touch that! Give me back the sword!"

Wuming seemed to have heard his voice and looked up. Xie Lian couldn't see his real face; he only saw that mask with its drawn-on smile.

But Xie Lian had a strange feeling that beneath his mask, Wuming was really smiling.

The feeling was fleeting, however. The vast black torrent and the screaming tide gathered to form a tempest, and it swallowed Wuming whole in an instant.

And in that instant, Xie Lian heard a heart-wrenching, blood-curdling scream.

He thought he had heard that voice somewhere before... No, he *knew* he had heard that voice somewhere before!

Pain. It hurt like he was feeling the same agony. It hurt like a fate worse than death. It hurt so much that his mind and body were being torn apart. It hurt so much he thudded to his knees, hugging his head as he screamed along too.

"Aaaaaaaaaaaaaaaaaaah!"

The explosion of excruciating pain in his heart came suddenly and left equally fast, and after some unknown time had passed, silence slowly descended upon the area. Xie Lian gradually dropped the hands that hugged his head.

Dazed, he looked up and scanned around him. The ground was covered with people, most of them unconscious. But all the vengeful spirits entangling them had vanished.

The scene confused him. What happened to the plague of Human Face Disease? What happened to the vengeful spirits?

What happened to him?

There was no trace of the black torrent. The only thing that remained where the black-clad nameless ghost had once stood was the black sword, which had fallen to the ground. Beside the point of the fallen blade, there was a tiny white flower.

Xie Lian staggered to his feet and walked over, picking up the flower and the sword.

He felt his face, looked at his arms. Nothing on his body seemed different—there was nothing to indicate he'd taken on some powerful curse. As he stood there, mystified, he heard a voice behind him.

It said softly, "Ah."

Xie Lian turned around. White No-Face was standing behind him, his arms crossed and tucked into his expansive sleeves, which fluttered in the wind. Xie Lian hadn't yet processed what had happened, but he felt a vague sense of foreboding.

White No-Face glanced at him and started chuckling. The sense of foreboding was growing stronger, and Xie Lian knitted his brows.

"What are you laughing about?"

Instead of answering, White No-Face asked him, "You still don't understand what happened?"

"What?" Xie Lian asked.

"Do you know who that ghost was?" White No-Face asked.

"A... A soul of someone who died on the battlefield?" Xie Lian tried.

"Yes," White No-Face replied. "But he was also your very last believer in the world. And now, he's no more."

Believer...?

He still had a believer in this world?

It was a long moment before Xie Lian could squeeze out a few choked words. "What do you mean...no more?"

"His soul has been dispersed," White No-Face replied languidly.

Xie Lian had a hard time accepting this. "How did his soul just disperse?!"

"Because he was cursed on your behalf. The souls you summoned devoured him whole, leaving not a crumb behind," White No-Face said.

Xie Lian couldn't manage a reply.

The souls he summoned? Cursed on his behalf?!

"Oh yes, that's right. This wasn't the first time you've met him," White No-Face continued.

Xie Lian stared at him blankly. White No-Face seemed amused.

"That ghost had been following you for a while. At first, I thought he was simply deeply resentful, so I caught and interrogated him; his answers were quite interesting. The Zhongyuan Festival. A night of lanterns. A wandering ghost fire. Do you remember?"

"The Zhongyuan Festival? Night of lanterns? Wandering ghost fire?" Xie Lian mumbled.

"In life, he was a soldier under your command," White No-Face lazily hinted. "In death, his soul followed you. He died in battle for you, turned into a wrath ghost because you were pierced by a hundred swords. And now, his soul has been obliterated because you unleashed the plague of Human Face Disease."

Xie Lian seemed to vaguely recall something, but he hadn't even seen his believer's face, he didn't even know his name—what could he recall? How much could he really recall?

"Perhaps Your Highness has believers here who still offer worship."

Yes. There was a believer.

And he had been the one and only!

White No-Face was still speaking, going on and on about many things, but Xie Lian was lost in a daze and took none of it in.

Finally, White No-Face concluded, "A god like you is both sad and laughable. And he's even more sad and laughable to have believed in you."

"..."

When White No-Face had mocked him earlier, Xie Lian hadn't reacted. But when he heard this creature insult his believer so condescendingly, it was like Xie Lian was jolted awake by the stab of a sword. An uncontrollable rage roiled up from within him and he charged at White No-Face. The creature easily seized him.

"You can't win against me like this. How many times must I tell you before you see the truth?" White No-Face said coldly.

Xie Lian hadn't wanted to win against him in the first place, and it didn't matter if he couldn't. He simply wanted to beat the creature to a pulp.

"What do you know?! How dare you mock him!" he cried angrily.

That was his last believer in this world!

"Of course I dare to mock the follower of a failure," White No-Face replied. "You're a fool, and your believer is even more of a fool. Listen! If you wish to defeat me, then you must obey my teachings. Otherwise, you can never dream of winning against me!"

Xie Lian wanted to spit at him with everything he had, but even breathing was difficult. White No-Face opened his hand with a flourish, and another cry-smiling mask appeared in his palm.

"Now, let us start over!"

As he was about to press the mask onto Xie Lian's face, there came a sudden, loud rumbling.

Lightning flashed and thunder roared on the horizon, and a mysterious light shot from within the clouds. White No-Face stopped in alarm.

"What is this? A Heavenly Tribulation...?" After a pause, he dismissed that statement. "No, that's not it!"

That wasn't it.

It *was* a Heavenly Tribulation, but that wasn't all!

A man's deep voice resounded across the entire sky. "If he cannot win against you, what about me?"

Xie Lian's head shot up.

A martial god had appeared at the end of the long street. He was clad in white armor and brimmed with a propitious aura. A thin sheen of white spiritual light enveloped his body, and he walked toward them step by step with sword in hand, carving out a path of light in this gloomy, dark world.

Xie Lian's eyes grew wide.

Jun Wu!

After the rain had ceased and the skies had cleared, Xie Lian sat on the burnt earth, panting lightly.

Jun Wu sheathed his sword and walked over. "Xianle. Welcome back to the ranks."

He wore a tired expression, traces of blood still on his face from the wounds inflicted by White No-Face. Jun Wu was covered in injuries, large and small. They were serious, but White No-Face's wounds were far more so—his body had been ripped apart and his form had been dispersed, leaving behind only a shattered cry-smiling mask.

When he heard him say "back to the ranks," Xie Lian blinked. He touched his neck, and only then did he notice that the cursed shackle was gone.

Jun Wu smiled. "As expected. I was not mistaken. It took you even less time to return than I anticipated."

Xie Lian slowly regained himself. He flashed a small smile in return, but his was a bitter one.

After catching his breath, he spoke up. "My Lord, I want to beg something of you."

"Permitted," Jun Wu said.

"Are you not going to ask what it is first?" Xie Lian asked.

"Since you would be asking for a gift upon return to the Heavenly Court regardless, let today's incident serve as my gift to you for returning to the ranks."

The corners of Xie Lian's lips tugged, and he rose to his feet. He looked Jun Wu squarely in the eyes and said with the utmost respect, "Pray My Lord banish me to the Mortal Realm once more."

Hearing this, Jun Wu's smile faded. "Whyever for?"

"I've done wrong," Xie Lian explained the honest truth. "I was the one who unleashed the second plague of Human Face Disease. Even though the consequences weren't as severe as the first."

This time, the only casualty was a nameless ghost, and perhaps no one in the world had cared for him. In the end, the consequences of this second plague weren't nearly as severe.

"If you knew what was wrong, then you are already in the right," Jun Wu said slowly.

However, Xie Lian shook his head. "Just knowing is not enough. If I make a mistake, I should be the one punished. But I committed the wrong, and the one who took the punishment for me was…"

He trailed off, then raised his head once more.

"So as punishment, I pray My Lord will grant me a cursed shackle—no, two cursed shackles. One to seal away my spiritual powers, another to disperse all my luck and fortune."

Jun Wu frowned slightly. "Disperse all your luck and fortune? Will that not make you unlucky beyond belief—truly make you a God of Misfortune?"

Xie Lian had resented being called a God of Misfortune; he was repulsed by the very idea and considered it a great humiliation. However, he no longer cared about things like that.

"If I am to become a God of Misfortune, then so be it. As long as I know deep down that I'm not."

Once his fortune was dispersed, it would naturally flow to the less fortunate. It would be a form of atonement.

"It will be very embarrassing," Jun Wu reminded him.

"It doesn't matter," Xie Lian said. "And to be honest, it feels like...I'm almost used to it by now."

It wasn't something he'd wanted to get used to, but once he did, it really felt like nothing could harm him.

Jun Wu watched him. "Xianle, you have to understand that you will no longer be a god if you have no spiritual power."

Xie Lian sighed. "My Lord, I know that better than anyone." After a pause, he said in a tone that was a little frustrated and a little forlorn, "People say I'm a god, and so I have spiritual powers. But in truth, I'm...not the god they thought I was, and I might not be as invincible as they hoped.

"Would a real god be such a failure? I wanted to protect my people, but I let their corpses spread across the land; I wished to avenge them, but at the very last minute I abandoned the plot. White No-Face wasn't wrong about me being a failure.

"If I'm no longer a god, then so be it."

Jun Wu gazed at him intently, and after a long while, he said, "Xianle has grown up."

That should've been something Xie Lian heard from his elders.

Unfortunately, his father and mother had no more chances to say it.

A moment later, Jun Wu continued, "Since this is the path you have chosen, I will do as you ask. However, I will need a reason to banish you to the Mortal Realm."

He couldn't just casually banish a heavenly official like this was a child's game—otherwise, how would the world see the heavens?

But Xie Lian had an idea. "My Lord, I don't believe we've ever sparred with everything we've got."

Jun Wu instantly understood what he meant and smiled. "Xianle, I am injured."

"Me too," Xie Lian said. "So we're even."

Jun Wu nodded. "If that is the case, then I will not hold back."

Xie Lian smiled, his eyes brightening with excitement at the prospect. "I won't either."

His Highness the Crown Prince was banished again.

After his smashing and grandiose second Heavenly Tribulation, the Crown Prince of Xianle rampaged across the heavens with fierce belligerence. Before even one incense time had passed, he was knocked down below once more by the Heavenly Emperor. None of the heavenly officials could figure out what that man was thinking.

But Xie Lian couldn't figure out what the other heavenly officials were thinking either.

Were they really that curious what he was up to? Watching him day after day, disguising themselves as mortals to watch him, disguising themselves as *animals* to watch him—they had been stalking him for days! Was a grown man laying bricks really that interesting?

As he wondered about this, the foreman behind him began to shout.

"Newbie! You, yes you, I'm talking to you! Get back to work! Stop being lazy!"

Xie Lian hastily sat up with a loud, "Oh!"

And then, he picked up a ragged cattail fan and started fanning the flames in front of him. He was seated in front of a small stove stacked on several bricks, and upon the stove was a large pot of rice that bubbled as it cooked.

This was a construction site, where he was paid to haul earth and mud. However, the bricks had already been transported, so Xie Lian's task for the moment was cooking. He cooked and cooked, and as he worked, two carriages approached, hauling two very large divine statues for the two newly built temples nearby. Xie Lian absentmindedly tossed whatever was at hand into the pot, stealing glances at the statues as he did.

The two divine statues were carried into their respective temples. From within the hall of the temple on the left, he heard cheers.

"General Xuan Zhen is great! General Xuan Zhen is generous and kind!"

Xie Lian was speechless. Using "generous and kind" to praise Mu Qing; were those devotees serious?!

But they apparently had their reasons—after all, everyone knew that Mu Qing had ascended because he had cleared away the vengeful spirits that stubbornly tarried about the old capital of Xianle. Calling that "generous and kind" wasn't unreasonable. In any case, everyone in the old capital of Xianle was very grateful for him.

From within the hall of the temple to the right, he heard roars from another set of devotees who refused to be beaten by those of the left temple.

"General Ju Yang is great! General Ju Yang is brave and mighty!"

Xie Lian nodded. To this, he had no objections—although that praise might not hold true in the face of women.

The devotees on both sides were screaming with all their might, doing all they could to be louder than each other until Xie Lian's ears ached. He sighed and rubbed his forehead as he thought, *Why must they be like this?*

If they hated each other so much, wouldn't their problems be solved by *not* building temples right next to each other?

The answer to that was: of course not! This area was a bustling domain with excellent feng shui, and the devotees of those two heavenly officials would never abandon such tempting land solely for the sake of avoiding each other. They had to do all they could to steal each other's worshippers and disgust one another.

It didn't take long before the devotees from both sides progressed from yelling to fighting. Over by the stove, Xie Lian determined that the time was about right, so he started banging the pot cover with the spatula and calling out loudly, "Everyone, stop fighting! Come eat!"

It was the height of the brawl, so who would bother listening to him? Xie Lian shook his head and opened the pot cover, and the fragrance wafted ten miles around. Now he'd done it—the brawl instantly stopped, and everyone started howling.

"What the fuck...? What's that smell?!"

"Who's cooking shit?!"

"Not just shit—shit that smells like pot bottoms!"[7]

"What?! This is a hidden, treasured royal recipe—" Xie Lian began to argue back.

The foreman approached with his hand covering his nose, his face green, and he exclaimed as he jumped in anger, "Bullshit! What

---

7   *"Pot Bottom" is the layer of rice at the very bottom of a cooking pot that is usually burnt.*

hidden, treasured recipe? Who's royalty—*you*?! Get the hell outta here! That's disgusting!"

"All right, fine, I'll go," Xie Lian agreed. "But will you please give me my pay first—"

"You dare to even mention pay?!" the foreman exclaimed angrily. "Why don't you tell me this—ever since you came, how much have I lost in damages?! Huh?! When it rains, lightning strikes—aimed right for you! Houses have caught on fire three times—and collapsed three times too! You're like a God of Misfortune! And you dare ask me for pay?! Get outta here! Come back again and I'll beat you up!"

"Hey, that doesn't work," Xie Lian said. "You just said all those things were coming especially for me, so that means nothing happens to anyone else. I think you just want to get out of paying your bill—"

Before he could finish, the foreman and all the other laborers couldn't take the smell wafting out of the pot anymore. They all fled the area, leaving Xie Lian in the dust.

"Wait!" Xie Lian called out.

He glanced around and saw that all the brawlers had also been chased away by the stench. Xie Lian was speechless.

"If you weren't going to eat it, why make me cook such a large pot? Don't waste it just because you've got money," he mumbled to himself.

Shaking his head, Xie Lian contemplated for a moment, then ladled out two large bowls of rice. He offered one at the Temple of Ju Yang and the other at the Temple of Xuan Zhen. Feeling that he'd made the best use of everything, he clapped his hands together, completely satisfied.

He went back outside to pack up his stuff. He rolled up the straw mat on the ground very seriously and tied it to his sword before strapping both to his back. The white silk band wrapped around his wrist nuzzled him furtively, and Xie Lian patted it before righting the bamboo hat on his head.

"Fine. Don't pay. I'll go busking."

He still had his specialty trick, after all: shattering boulders on his chest!

As he walked, Xie Lian suddenly noticed a tiny red flower on the side of the road, which looked absolutely precious. He crouched to gently touch its petals, feeling quite cheerful.

"I hope we shall meet again," he said to it.

Even after he had disappeared into the distance, the tiny red flower still danced in the wind.

THE STORY CONTINUES IN
Heaven Official's Blessing
VOLUME 7

Heaven Official's Blessing

TIAN GUAN CI FU

Character
&
Name Guide

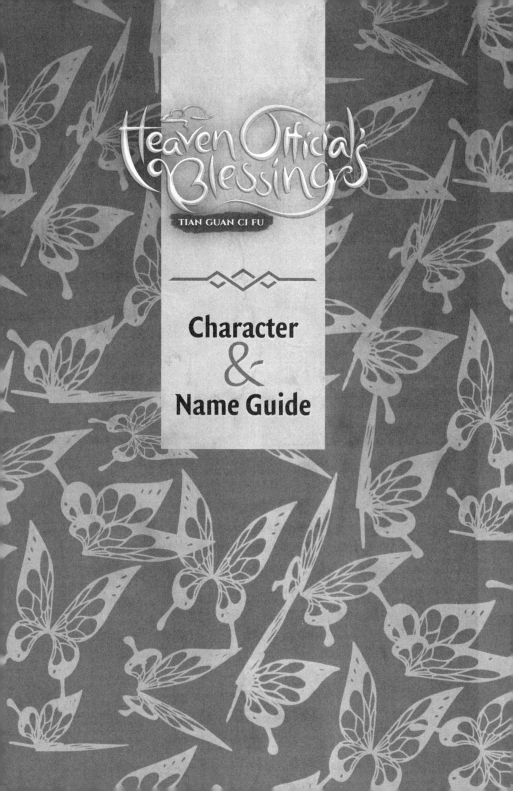

Characters

> The identity of certain characters may be a spoiler; use this guide with caution on your first read of the novel.
>
> Note on the given name translations: Chinese characters may have many different readings. Each reading here is just one out of several possible readings presented for your reference and should not be considered a definitive translation.

MAIN CHARACTERS

Xie Lian
谢怜   "THANK/WILT," "SYMPATHY/LOVE"

HEAVENLY TITLE: Xianle, "Heaven's Delight" (仙乐)

FOUR FAMOUS TALES TITLE: The Prince Who Pleased God

Once the crown prince of the Kingdom of Xianle and the darling of the heavens, now a very unlucky twice-fallen god who ekes out a meager living collecting scraps. As his bad luck tends to affect those around him for the worse, Xie Lian has spent his last eight hundred years wandering in solitude. Still, he's accepted his lonely lot in life, or at least seems to have a sense of humor about it. Even for the perpetually unlucky, there's always potential for a chance encounter that can turn eight hundred years of unhappiness around.

Xie Lian has seen and done many things over his very long life and originally ascended as a martial god. While it was his scrap-collecting that saw him ascend for the third time, Xie Lian's feats of physicality are hardly anything to scoff at...though he'd sooner use them as part of a busking performance than to win a fight.

His title Xianle is a multi-layered nickname. "Xianle" is Xie Lian's official heavenly title and also the name of his kingdom. "Xianle" itself can translate to "Heaven's Delight," which ties into Xie Lian's "Four Famous Tales" moniker, "The Prince Who Pleased God." Jun Wu referring to Xie Lian as "Xianle" sounds professional and businesslike on the surface (as Jun Wu generally refers to gods by their heavenly titles only), but it deliberately and not-so-subtly comes across as an affectionate term of endearment.

Hua Cheng
花城   "FLOWER," "CITY"

NICKNAME: San Lang, "third," "youth" (三郎)
FOUR CALAMITIES TITLE: Crimson Rain Sought Flower

The fearsome king of ghosts and terror of the heavens. Dressed in his signature red, he controls vicious swarms of silver butterflies and wields the cursed scimitar known as Eming. His power and wealth are unmatched in the Three Realms, and for this he has as many worshippers as he does enemies (with considerable crossover between categories). He rules over the dazzling and otherworldly Ghost City in the Ghost Realm and is known to drop in to spectate at its infamous Gambler's Den when he's in a good mood.

In spite of all this, when it comes to Xie Lian, the Ghost King shows a much kinder and more respectful side of himself. He does not hesitate for a moment to sleep on a single straw mat in Xie Lian's humble home, nor to get his hands dirty doing household chores at Puqi Shrine. That being said, it's impossible to deny that as he and Xie Lian grow closer, Hua Cheng seems to be growing more and more mischievous... From the very start, his secret identity as

San Lang seemed to be no secret at all to Xie Lian, but Xie Lian still calls him by this name at Hua Cheng's request.

Honghong-er
红红儿 "RED," "RED," FRIENDLY DIMINUTIVE

A young street urchin who Xie Lian saved from certain death long ago, when Xie Lian was a prince in Xianle. Honghong-er is tiny, emaciated, and hardly looks like the ten-year-old child that he is, nor does he act like it. He is constantly on guard and quick to attack, though he strangely seems to become tame—and quite bashful—when Xie Lian is around. He bears immense shame regarding his supposedly ugly appearance and refuses to remove the bandages he wears to cover half his face.

Honghong-er's life has been one of immense suffering and hardship, and he clings to every one of Xie Lian's fleeting acts of kindness toward him as if he has never experienced anything like it before.

The name "Honghong-er" is clearly a nickname—it can be roughly translated to "Little Red."

Wuming
無名 "NAMELESS"

A nameless ghost in an ever-smiling mask. He seems to have been following Xie Lian since the bygone days of Xianle, though Xie Lian was unaware of his fealty at the time. He is staggeringly powerful and absolutely loyal to Xie Lian's command.

Wuming has lingered as a ghost for the sake of the one he loves. He seeks to avenge the suffering his beloved endured at the hands of humanity and protect them from further harm—even though they likely don't even know his name. Whoever his beloved might be, they are truly fortunate to garner such devotion.

Young Soldier

A nameless young soldier in the Xianle army. He keeps half of his face hidden beneath bandages at all times and seems determined to stick by Xie Lian's side in battle to protect him, even if it takes him to the most dangerous parts of the battlefield. His remarkable skill with the sword caught Xie Lian's attention and made the god-prince remember him fondly even during the difficult times leading up to Xianle's fall.

HEAVENLY OFFICIALS & HEAVENLY ASSOCIATES

Feng Xin
风信   "WIND," "TRUST/FAITH"

HEAVENLY TITLE: Nan Yang, "Southern Sun" (南陽)

The Martial God of the Southeast. He has a short fuse and foul mouth (especially when it comes to his longstanding nemesis, Mu Qing) but is known to be a dutiful, hardworking god. He has a complicated history with Xie Lian: long ago, in their days in the Kingdom of Xianle, he used to serve as Xie Lian's bodyguard and was a close friend until circumstances drove them apart.

In order to follow Xie Lian in secret, Feng Xin created an undercover identity for himself: Nan Feng, a Middle Court official. This failed to fool Xie Lian from the start, not in the least due to Feng Xin's completely unchanged personality and questionable ability to create a believable pseudonym: "Nan" / 南 is the same character as in Feng Xin's heavenly title, and "Feng" / 风 is the same character as in Feng Xin's proper name.

Jun Wu
君吾 "LORD," "I"

HEAVENLY TITLE: Shenwu, "Divine Might" (神武)

The Emperor of Heaven and strongest of the gods. He is composed and serene, and it is through his power and wisdom that the heavens remain aloft—quite literally. Although the heavens are full of schemers and gossipmongers, Jun Wu stands apart from such petty squabbles and is willing to listen to even the lowliest creatures to hear their pleas for justice. Despite this reputation for fairness, he does have his biases. In further contrast to the rest of the rabble in Heaven, he shows great patience and affection towards Xie Lian to the point that many grumble about favoritism.

Ling Wen
灵文 "INGENIOUS LITERATUS"

HEAVENLY TITLE: Ling Wen

The top civil god and also the most overworked. Unlike the majority of gods, she is addressed by her colleagues and most others by her heavenly title. She is one of the rare female civil gods and worked tirelessly (and thanklessly) for many years to earn her position. Ling Wen is exceedingly competent at all things bureaucratic, and her work keeps Heaven's business running (mostly) smoothly. She is the creator and head admin of Heaven's communication array.

These days, her name Nangong Jie [南宫杰, "South" 南 / "Palace" 宫 / "Hero" 杰] is only used by her close friend Pei Ming—though he usually calls her the friendly nickname "Noble Jie." She is also close to Shi Wudu, who is known in the heavens for his self-serving personality. Their friend group is dubbed the "Three Tumors."

Mu Qing
慕情　　"YEARNING," "AFFECTION"

HEAVENLY TITLE: Xuan Zhen, "Enigmatic Truth" (玄真)

The Martial God of the Southwest. He has a short fuse and sharp tongue (especially when it comes to his longstanding nemesis, Feng Xin) and is known for being cold, spiteful, and petty. He has a complicated history with Xie Lian: long ago, in their days in the Kingdom of Xianle, he used to serve as Xie Lian's personal servant and was a close friend until circumstances drove them apart.

In order to follow Xie Lian in secret, Mu Qing created an undercover identity for himself: Fu Yao, a Middle Court official. This failed to fool Xie Lian from the start, not in the least due to Mu Qing's completely unchanged personality and self-aggrandizing naming tendencies: "Fu Yao" / 扶摇 is a figure of speech for someone who is skilled or ambitious.

Pei Ming
裴茗　　SURNAME PEI, "TENDER TEA LEAVES"

HEAVENLY TITLE: Ming Guang, "Bright Illumination" (明光)

FOUR FAMOUS TALES TITLE: The General Who Snapped His Sword

The Martial God of the North. General Pei is a powerful and popular god, and over the years he has gained a reputation as a womanizer. This reputation is deserved: Pei Ming's ex-lovers are innumerable and hail from all the Three Realms. He is close friends with Ling Wen and Shi Wudu, who are also known in the heavens for their self-serving personalities. This friend group is dubbed the "Three Tumors."

Pei Xiu is Pei Ming's indirect descendant, and Pei Ming took him under his wing to help advance his career in the heavens. He was very displeased when Pei Xiu ruined that career for Banyue's sake, but he seems to have accepted the situation and does not hold a grudge against Xie Lian for his involvement in uncovering the scandal.

Pei Xiu
裴宿   SURNAME PEI, "CONSTELLATION"

HEAVENLY TITLE: N/A

An exiled martial god and a distant (and indirect) descendant of Pei Ming. He's usually called "Little Pei" or "General Pei Junior" for this reason. He is often called in to clean up after his ancestor's messes, but regardless of the circumstances, he always maintains his composure with a polite yet detached air. His ascension to godhood occurred because he led the charge to slaughter the Kingdom of Banyue, and his exile from godhood occurred because of his morally dubious attempts to save his childhood friend Banyue from her fate of eternal punishment.

Quan Yizhen
权一真   "POWER/AUTHORITY," "ONE," "TRUTH/GENUINE"

HEAVENLY TITLE: Qi Ying, "Stupendous Hero" (奇英)

The (current) Martial God of the West. He previously shared this title with his shixiong, Yin Yu. After Yin Yu was banished from heaven, Quan Yizhen holds the title alone. He still yearns for his shixiong's companionship and is convinced that their falling-out was caused by a misunderstanding.

Quan Yizhen has a single-minded focus on martial arts and is considered a prodigy even among heaven's elite. He also has a reputation for beating up his own followers, though this somehow does not damage his popularity in the Mortal Realm. While his skill cannot be disparaged, he is widely disliked in the heavens for his lack of social etiquette. He cares not for the friendship or opinions of his fellow gods, though he has warmed up to Xie Lian.

Rain Master
雨师篁   "RAIN," "MASTER," "BAMBOO GROVE"

HEAVENLY TITLE: Rain Master

The elemental master of rain, proper name Yushi Huang. Ascended to the heavens shortly before Xie Lian's own first ascension. The Rain Master is a reclusive heavenly official who is known to reside on a secluded mountain farm named Yushi Country (雨师乡) with many subordinates working in the fields. One of these subordinates is an intelligent talking ox, who is also capable of transforming into a human form that's equally as beefy as his bovine build.

While the Rain Master prefers a quiet and modest life of agriculture, any nefarious creature that's foolish enough to target the domain's farm hands is in for a very rude awakening indeed...

Shi Qingxuan
师青玄   "MASTER," "VERDANT GREEN/BLUE," "MYSTERIOUS/BLACK"

HEAVENLY TITLE: Wind Master

FOUR FAMOUS TALES TITLE: The Young Lord Who Poured Wine

The elemental master of wind and younger sibling of the Water Master, Shi Wudu. Shi Qingxuan ascended as a male god, but over the years, he began to be worshipped as a female version of himself. Shi Qingxuan eagerly embraced this, and she leaps at any opportunity to go out on the town in her female form...and will try to drag anyone she's traveling with into the fun.

Shi Qingxuan is as flighty and pushy as the element they command, and as wealthy as they are generous with their money. They possess a strong sense of justice and will not be dissuaded by notions of propriety. They appear to be close friends with the Earth Master Ming Yi, despite the latter's insistence to the contrary.

GHOST REALM & GHOST REALM ASSOCIATES

Bai Jing
白锦　"WHITE BROCADE"

The human spirit fused with the Brocade Immortal. He was once a young man with immense talent in martial arts who was destined for godhood. However, his life was gruesomely cut short when the girl he was in love with manipulated him into dismembering himself.

Banyue
半月　"HALF-MOON"

Former state preceptor of the Kingdom of Banyue, now a wrath ghost. She is a scrawny young woman who nonetheless possesses the power to call upon and control deadly scorpion-snakes. Despite her gloomy disposition, she earnestly wishes to save others from suffering, even if it means that she has to suffer in their stead.

Cuocuo
错错　"MISTAKE" (A CHILDISH TERM, LIKE "OOPSIE")

A malice-level ghost resembling a monstrous-looking human fetus. It targets pregnant women and seeks to usurp the place of the children in their wombs—killing both mother and unborn child in the process.

He Xuan
贺玄   "CONGRATULATE," "BLACK," "MYSTERIOUS"

FOUR CALAMITIES TITLE: Ship-Sinking Black Water

One of the Four Calamities, Ship-Sinking Black Water. He is a mysterious and reclusive water ghost who rules the South Sea. Like Hua Cheng, he won the bloody gauntlet at Mount Tonglu and wields the power of a supreme ghost. He is consumed by ceaseless hunger and is driven by an equally consuming lust for revenge.

He Xuan disguised himself as the Earth Master Ming Yi for many centuries, and during this masquerade he cultivated a friendship with Shi Qingxuan. Although founded on falsehood, the feelings of friendship that "Ming-xiong" held for Shi Qingxuan seemed to be legitimate.

Kemo
刻磨   "MILLSTONE"

A former general of the Kingdom of Banyue, now a wrath-level ghost. He bears great resentment against the State Preceptor of Banyue, even after his own death, and great hatred for the long-dead kingdom that destroyed his own.

Lan Chang
蘭菖   "GLADIOLUS [FLOWER]"

A malice-level ghost. Formerly a prostitute in Ghost City and now on the run with her monstrous child, the fetus spirit Cuocuo. She is hardly as delicate as her floral name implies—when it comes to throwing insults around on the streets of Ghost City, she can give as good as she gets. In Chinese flower language, the gladiolus flower means "tryst" (for romantic rendezvous) and also "absence." She was formerly known as Jian Lan (剑兰), which is another term for the same flower.

Lang Ying (Ghost Child)
郎萤   "YOUTH," "FIREFLY"

A mysterious ghost child afflicted with Human Face Disease. He has known nothing but abuse for hundreds of years due to his horrifying appearance, save for the fleeting kindness and warmth of the human girl Xiao-Ying. The combination of this trauma and his almost total lack of human interaction has left him mostly mute and constantly on high alert. Xie Lian was the one to give him this name: Lang being the national surname of Yong'an, and Ying to commemorate the girl who once took care of him.

Qi Rong
戚容   "FACE OF SORROW" OR "RELATIVE," "TOLERATE/FACE"

FOUR CALAMITIES TITLE: Night-Touring Green Lantern

One of the Four Calamities, also called the "Green Ghost." Unlike the other three Calamities, he's actually only a wrath ghost, not a supreme. Gods and ghosts alike agree that he was only included in the group to bump up the number to an even four. (Also, he's just that big a pest.) He is infamous for his crude behavior and ostentatious attempts to copy the style of the more successful Calamities, as well as for his ravenous appetite for human flesh.

More recently, his crimes have expanded to include kidnapping and body-snatching. In an attempt to hide from heaven's detection, he possessed the body of a human man and in doing so acquired a young son named Guzi.

Qi Rong is Xie Lian's younger cousin on his mother's side, much to Xie Lian's everlasting dismay. Surprising no one, Qi Rong has been a source of stress and trouble ever since their mortal childhoods in Xianle. His royal title in Xianle was Prince Xiao Jing.

Rong Guang
容广 "APPEARANCE/TOLERATE," "VAST/NUMEROUS"

A former military officer of the fallen Kingdom of Xuli. He was once Pei Ming's right-hand man and close friend; they were close enough for General Pei to name his sword "Mingguang," a portmanteau of their names. However, he now seeks revenge against Pei Ming as a malice-level ghost fused with that same broken sword.

White No-Face
白无相 "WHITE NO-FACE"

FOUR CALAMITIES TITLE: White-Clothed Calamity
One of the Four Calamities, White No-Face is mysterious, cruel, and powerful enough to battle with the Heavenly Emperor himself—truly, a supreme among supremes. He destroyed the Kingdom of Xianle with the Human Face Disease pandemic. His peculiar fixation on Xie Lian is unnerving, as are his equally peculiar displays of affection.

Xuan Ji
宣姬 "DECLARE," "PROCLAIM" / "CONCUBINE [ARCHAIC]"

A former general of the Kingdom of Yushi, now a wrath-level ghost. Also known as the Ghost Bride. She is obsessed with Pei Ming, who rejected her affections after she tried to take their physical-only relationship to the next level. Her fury at being scorned led to the gruesome deaths of many happy brides-to-be and her eventual imprisonment under heavenly law.

Yin Yu
引玉   "ATTRACT," "JADE"

Yin Yu, also known as the Waning Moon Officer (下弦月使), is Hua Cheng's right-hand man, subordinate, and all-around errand runner. He has been described by some as having a very weak sense of presence and a forgettable appearance. He bears a cursed shackle on his wrist, which marks him as a banished heavenly official. Yin Yu is the former Martial God of the West, who was cast out of Heaven after an incident where he endangered the life of his shidi, Quan Yizhen. He has mixed feelings toward his shidi, and even more mixed feelings over said shidi's dogged insistence on rekindling their former friendship.

Yin Yu's name is taken from the idiom 抛砖引玉/ "pao zhuan yin yu," or "throwing out a brick to attract a jade." It describes the act of making a rudimentary suggestion that is intended to prompt others to come forward with better ideas.

MORTAL REALM & MORTAL REALM ASSOCIATES

Guzi
谷子   "MILLET"

A young human child that Qi Rong kidnapped as a byproduct of stealing the body of the boy's father. Because Qi Rong is possessing Guzi's father, the poor little boy seems blissfully unaware that he's in any danger at all, though that hardly prevents him from enduring plenty of suffering at Qi Rong's hands.

Lang Ying
郎英   "YOUTH," "HERO"

A Yong'an man that Xie Lian made the acquaintance of in the Xianle era. He is a troubled man who has lost much—some might say everything—to the drought and famine that struck his home region. After toppling the Kingdom of Xianle in a bloody civil war, he was named king of the new Kingdom of Yong'an.

Heaven's Eye
天眼开   "HEAVEN'S EYE"

A wealthy, pompous human cultivator who leads a team of cultivators with a similar member profile. Despite his personality flaws, his powers are the real deal. His third eye can see the unseen, and in the process inadvertently reveal exactly how you've been "borrowing spiritual energy" recently.

State Preceptors of Xianle

A quartet of cultivators who serve as Xianle's state preceptors. They are also the religious leaders and head instructors at the Royal Holy Temple, Xianle's premiere cultivation school and largest place of worship for several gods. They are highly skilled cultivators and specialize in the art of divination, though they are very easily distracted by the allure of a game of cards.

The Chief State Preceptor, Mei Nianqing (梅念卿 "plum blossom," "to lecture/to long for," archaic word for minister/high official), is the most talkative of the bunch and has a close relationship with his most cherished student (and biggest headache), Xie Lian. While the names of the three deputy state preceptors are unknown, Xie Lian clearly respects their skill and wisdom.

The plum blossom in Mei Nianqing's name is a symbol of

endurance in Chinese flower language, as it blooms in the depths of winter. The plum blossom is also one of the four flowers of the *junzi* (the ideal Confucian gentleman).

Xianle Royal Family

The king and queen of the Kingdom of Xianle, and Xie Lian's parents. Xie Lian's father is of the ruling Xie (谢 "to thank/to wilt") clan, and his mother is of the Min (悯 "to feel pity for/commiserate with") clan. Xie Lian is very close with his mother, who is a doting—if rather naive and sheltered—parent. Xie Lian has a more contentious relationship with his father and frequently squabbles with him.

When Xie Lian's given name (怜 / lian) and his mother's clan name (悯 / min) are written together, they form the word "compassion" (怜悯 / lianmin).

SENTIENT WEAPONS AND SPIRITUAL OBJECTS

Brocade Immortal
锦衣仙   "BROCADE," "IMMORTAL"

A semi-sentient brocade robe possessed by the ghost of a human man, Bai Jing. The name of this object is meant to be a play on the name of the spirit of the man who inhabits it. The Brocade Immortal is an immensely powerful and dangerous artifact—those who wear it can be controlled like puppets if they were given the robe by a person with nefarious intent, and even gods are not immune to its effect.

Eming

厄命   "TERRIBLE/WRETCHED," "FATE"

Hua Cheng's sentient scimitar. With a single blood-red eye that peers out from its silver hilt, it is a cursed blade that drinks the blood of its victims and is the bane of the heavens. It enjoys nothing more than receiving praise and hugs from Xie Lian, and its childish, forward personality is a great embarrassment to its ghostly master.

Fangxin

芳心   "AFFECTIONS OF A YOUNG WOMAN"

An ancient black sword with ties to Xie Lian. An antique, it easily tires when dealing with high-flying heavenly adventures. Xie Lian used the sword's name as an alias while serving as the State Preceptor of Yong'an.

Mingguang

明光

Pei Ming's famously broken sword named after a portmanteau of the sounds from Pei Ming and Rong Guang's names. Rong Guang fused with it to seek revenge.

Ruoye

若邪   "LIKE/AS IF," "EVIL" OR "SWORD"

Xie Lian's sentient strip of white silk. It is an earnest and energetic sort, if a bit nervous sometimes, and will go to great lengths to protect Xie Lian—quite literally, as it can stretch out to almost limitless dimensions.

Locations

HEAVENLY REALM

The Heavenly Capital is a divine city built upon the clouds. Amidst flowing streams and auspicious clouds, luxurious palaces dot the landscape, serving as the personal residences and offices of the gods. The Grand Avenue of Divine Might serves as the realm's main thoroughfare, and this road leads directly to the Palace of Divine Might—the Heavenly Emperor's residence where court is held.

The Heavenly Court consists of two sub-courts: the Upper Court and the Middle Court. The Upper Court consists entirely of ascended gods, while the Middle Court consists of officials who—while remarkable and skilled in their own right—have not yet ascended to godhood.

MORTAL REALM

The realm of living humans. Often receives visitors from the other two realms.

Kingdom of Xianle
仙乐   "HEAVEN'S DELIGHT" OR "HEAVENLY MUSIC"

A fallen kingdom, once glamorous and famed for its riches and its people's love for the finer things in life—such as art, music, gold, and the finest thing of all, their beloved crown prince, Xie Lian. Xianle's gilded exterior masked a declining kingdom plagued by corruption, and Xie Lian's meddling hastened its inevitable collapse in a most disastrous fashion.

Xianle's largest cultivation center, the Royal Holy Temple, sprawled across the peaks of the auspicious Mount Taicang. Its qi-rich landscape nurtures the blanketing forests of fruit trees and flame-red maples. The mountain hosted the kingdom's largest Palace of Xianle for worship of Xie Lian after his ascension, and the Xianle Imperial Mausoleum is located far underground.

Kingdom of Wuyong
乌庸   "CROW/BLACK," "MEDIOCRE/ORDINARY/TO HIRE"

An ancient kingdom that was destroyed over two thousand years ago in a volcanic apocalypse and wiped from the annals of history. Mount Tonglu looms at the center of this once-prosperous realm, forever brewing chaos and destruction within its fiery womb. Wuyong is sealed within an evil domain that only opens when Mount Tonglu issues its call to slaughter. Its landscape and remaining wildlife have been distorted by the enormously evil power that periodically spews from the depths of the mountain. However, one just might be able to piece together the remaining fragments of its shattered civilization and learn the truth about what took place during its last days...

Kingdom of Yong'an
永安   "ETERNAL PEACE"

A fallen but once-prosperous kingdom. Yong'an began its existence as an impoverished city located within the Kingdom of Xianle. It later became a powder keg of social unrest which kicked off a lengthy and bloody civil war that eventually resulted in Xianle's end.

The Kingdom of Yong'an rose out of the ashes of the Kingdom of Xianle after the latter's collapse, but it very soon fell to the very same corruption and excess that doomed Xianle.

Puqi Village
菩荠村 "WATER CHESTNUT"

A tiny village in the countryside, named for the water chestnuts *(puqi)* that grow in abundance nearby. While small and unsophisticated, its villagers are friendly and welcoming to weary travelers who wish to stay a while. The humble Puqi Shrine—under reconstruction and welcoming donations—can be found here, as well as its resident god, Xie Lian.

GHOST REALM

The Ghost Realm is the home of almost all dead humans, and far less organized and bureaucratic than the Heavenly Realm. Ghosts may leave or be trapped away from the Ghost Realm under some circumstances, which causes major problems for ordinary humans and gods alike.

Black Water Demon Lair

The domain of the reclusive Supreme Ghost King who rules the South Sea, Ship-Sinking Black Water. If one is unfortunate enough to wander into his territory, it will quickly become their final resting place. Should they avoid being eaten alive by the colossal skeletal fish that serve as threshold guardians, the sea itself will devour them instead. Nothing can float upon the waters of the Black Water Demon Lair—all intruders are forfeit to the abyss.

It is said that Ship-Sinking Black Water dwells on Black Water Island, located at the heart of his realm. His residence on the island is called the Nether Water Manor. In stark contrast to Hua Cheng's lively Ghost City, Black Water Island is a silent, gloomy place with few residents other than the master himself.

Ghost City
鬼市   "GHOST CITY"

The largest city in the Ghost Realm, founded and ruled by Hua Cheng. It is a dazzling den of vice, sin, and all things wicked, which makes it the number-one spot for visitors from all three realms to shop for nefarious goods and cavort under the glow of the blood-red lanterns.

Hua Cheng is rarely present in the city and does not often make public appearances. On the occasion he is in the mood to do so, he is met with considerable adoration; clearly, Ghost City's citizens love their Chengzhu and respect him immensely. His residence within the city is the secluded Paradise Manor, which has never seen guests—at least until Xie Lian came to call, of course.

The city is also home to the beautiful, secluded Thousand Lights Temple, which Hua Cheng dedicated to Xie Lian for reasons the man seems reluctant to elaborate on. It serves double-duty as a place of worship and private school of calligraphy, though Xie Lian doesn't seem to be making much progress on teaching Hua Cheng to write legibly.

OTHER/UNKNOWN

Mount Tonglu
铜炉山 "COPPER KILN MOUNTAIN"

Mount Tonglu is a volcano within the domain of the fallen Kingdom of Wuyong, and the location of the Kiln, where new ghost kings are born. Every few hundred years, tens of thousands of ghosts descend upon the city for a massive battle royale. Only two ghosts have ever survived the slaughter and made it out—one of those two was Hua Cheng.

Name Guide

NAMES, HONORIFICS, & TITLES

Diminutives, Nicknames, and Name Tags

-ER: A word for "son" or "child." Added to a name, it expresses affection. Similar to calling someone "Little" or "Sonny."

A-: Friendly diminutive. Always a prefix. Usually for monosyllabic names, or one syllable out of a two-syllable name.

XIAO-: A diminutive meaning "little." Always a prefix.

Doubling a syllable of a person's name can be a nickname, and has childish or cutesy connotations.

FAMILY

DIDI: Younger brother or a younger male friend. Casual.

GE: Familiar way to refer to an older brother or older male friend, used by someone substantially younger or of lower status. Can be used alone or with the person's name.

GEGE: Familiar way to refer to an older brother or an older male friend, used by someone substantially younger or of lower status. Has a cutesier feel than "ge."

JIEJIE: Familiar way to refer to an older sister or an older female friend, used by someone substantially younger or of lower status. Has a cutesier feel than "jie," and rarely used by older males.

MEIMEI: Younger sister or an unrelated younger female friend. Casual.

XIONG: Older brother. Generally used as an honorific. Formal, but also used informally between male friends of equal status.

YIFU: Maternal uncle (husband of maternal aunt), respectful address.

YIMU: Maternal aunt, respectful address.

Cultivation, Martial Arts, and Immortals

-JUN: A suffix meaning "lord."

-ZUN: A suffix meaning "esteemed, venerable." More respectful than "-jun."

DAOZHANG: A polite address for Daoist cultivators, equivalent to "Mr. Cultivator." Can be used alone as a title or attached to someone's family name—for example, one could refer to Xie Lian as "Daozhang" or "Xie Daozhang."

SHIDI: Younger martial brother. For junior male members of one's own sect.

SHIFU: Teacher/master. For one's master in one's own sect. Gender neutral. Mostly interchangeable with Shizun.

SHIXIONG: Older martial brother. For senior male members of one's own sect.

YUANJUN: Title for high-class female Daoist deity. Can be used alone as a title or as a suffix.

ZHENJUN: Title for average male Daoist deity. Can be used alone as a title or as a suffix.

Other

CHENGZHU: A title for the master/ruler of an independent city-state.

GONGZI: Young master of an affluent household.

Pronunciation Guide

Mandarin Chinese is the official state language of China. It is a tonal language, so correct pronunciation is vital to being understood! As many readers may not be familiar with the use and sound of tonal marks, below is a very simplified guide on the pronunciation of select character names and terms from MXTX's series to help get you started.

More resources are available at **sevenseasdanmei.com**

Series Names

SCUM VILLAIN'S SELF-SAVING SYSTEM (RÉN ZHĀ FǍN PÀI ZÌ JIÙ XÌ TǑNG):
ren jaa faan pie zzh zioh she tone

GRANDMASTER OF DEMONIC CULTIVATION (MÓ DÀO ZǓ SHĪ):
mwuh dow zoo shrr

HEAVEN OFFICIAL'S BLESSING (TIĀN GUĀN CÌ FÚ):
tee-yan gwen tsz fuu

Character Names

SHĚN QĪNGQIŪ: Shhen Ching-cheeoh
LUÒ BĪNGHÉ: Loo-uh Bing-huhh
WÈI WÚXIÀN: Way Woo-shee-ahn
LÁN WÀNGJĪ: Lahn Wong-gee
XIÈ LIÁN: Shee-yay Lee-yan
HUĀ CHÉNG: Hoo-wah Cch-yung

XIĂO-: shee-ow

-ER: ahrr

A-: ah

GŌNGZǏ: gong-zzh

DÀOZHĂNG: dow-jon

-JŪN: june

DÌDÌ: dee-dee

GĒGĒ: guh-guh

JIĚJIĚ: gee-ay-gee-ay

MÈIMEI: may-may

-XIÓNG: shong

Terms

DĀNMĚI: dann-may

WǓXIÁ: woo-sheeah

XIĀNXIÁ: sheeyan-sheeah

QÌ: chee

General Consonants & Vowels

X: similar to English sh (**sh**eep)

Q: similar to English ch (**ch**arm)

C: similar to English ts (pan**ts**)

IU: yoh

UO: wuh

ZHI: jrr

CHI: chrr

SHI: shrr

RI: rrr

ZI: zzz

CI: tsz

SI: ssz

U: When u follows a y, j, q, or x, the sound is actually ü, pronounced like eee with your lips rounded like ooo. This applies for yu, yuan, jun, etc.

Heaven Official's Blessing
TIAN GUAN CI FU

Glossary

Glossary

While not required reading, this glossary is intended to offer further context to the many concepts and terms utilized throughout this novel and provide a starting point for learning more about the rich Chinese culture from which these stories were written.

China is home to dozens of cultures, and its history spans thousands of years. The provided definitions are not strictly universal across all these cultural groups, and this simplified overview is meant for new readers unfamiliar with the concepts. This glossary should not be considered a definitive source, especially for more complex ideas.

GENRES

Danmei

Danmei (耽美 / "indulgence in beauty") is a Chinese fiction genre focused on romanticized tales of love and attraction between men. It is analogous to the BL (boys' love) genre in Japanese media. The majority of well-known danmei writers are women writing for women, although all genders produce and enjoy the genre.

Wuxia

Wuxia (武侠 / "martial heroes") is one of the oldest Chinese literary genres and consists of tales of noble heroes fighting evil and injustice. It often follows martial artists, monks, or rogues, who live apart from the ruling government, which is often seen as useless or corrupt. These societal outcasts—both voluntary and not—settle disputes among themselves, adhering to their own moral codes over the governing law.

Characters in wuxia focus primarily on human concerns, such as political strife between factions and advancing their own personal sense of justice. True wuxia is low on magical or supernatural elements. To Western moviegoers, a well-known example is *Crouching Tiger, Hidden Dragon*.

Xianxia

Xianxia (仙侠 / "immortal heroes") is a genre related to wuxia that places more emphasis on the supernatural. Its characters often strive to become stronger, with the end goal of extending their life span or achieving immortality.

Xianxia heavily features Daoist themes, while cultivation and the pursuit of immortality are both genre requirements. If these are not the story's central focus, it is not xianxia. *The Scum Villain's Self-Saving System*, *Grandmaster of Demonic Cultivation*, and *Heaven Official's Blessing* are all considered part of both the danmei and xianxia genres.

Webnovels

Webnovels are novels serialized by chapter online, and the websites that host them are considered spaces for indie and amateur writers. Many novels, dramas, comics, and animated shows produced in China are based on popular webnovels.

Heaven Official's Blessing was first serialized on the website *JJWXC*.

TERMINOLOGY

ARRAY: Area-of-effect magic circles. Anyone within the array falls under the effect of the array's associated spell(s).

ASCENSION: In typical xianxia tales, gods are conceived naturally and born divine. Immortals cannot attain godhood but can achieve great longevity. In *Heaven Official's Blessing*, however, both gods and immortals were born mortal and either cultivated deeply or committed great deeds and attained godhood after transcending the Heavenly Tribulation. Their bodies shed the troubles of a mortal form and are removed from the corporeal world.

AUSPICIOUS CLOUDS: A sign of good fortune and the divine, auspicious clouds are also often seen as methods of transport for gods and immortals in myth. The idea springs from the obvious association with clouds and the sky/heavens, and also because yun (云 / "cloud") and yun (运 / "luck") sound similar.

BOWING: Bowing is a social custom in many Asian nations. There are several varieties of bow in Chinese culture, which are distinguished by how low the bow goes as well as any associated hand gestures. A deeper bow indicates more respect, and those with high social status will always expect a deeper bow from those with low status. The kowtow (see associated glossary entry) is the most respectful level of bow. "Standing down in a bow" means holding a bowing position while leaving someone's presence.

BUDAOWENG: A budaoweng (不倒翁 / "wobbly old man") is an oblong doll, weighted so that it rolls back into an upright position whenever it is knocked down.

CHINESE CALENDAR: The Chinese calendar uses the *Tian Gan Di Zhi* (Heavenly Stems, Earthly Branches) system, rather than numbers, to mark the years. There are ten heavenly stems (original meanings lost) and twelve earthly branches (associated with the zodiac), each represented by a written character. Each stem and branch is associated with either yin or yang, and one of the elemental properties: wood, earth, fire, metal, and water. The stems and branches are combined in cyclical patterns to create a calendar where every unit of time is associated with certain attributes.

This is what a character is asking for when inquiring for the date/time of birth (生辰八字 / "eight characters of birth date/ time"). Analyzing the stem/branch characters and their elemental associations was considered essential information in divination, fortune-telling, matchmaking, and even business deals.

Colors:

WHITE: Death, mourning, purity. Used in funerals for both the deceased and mourners.

BLACK: Represents the Heavens and the Dao.

RED: Happiness, good luck. Used for weddings.

YELLOW/GOLD: Wealth and prosperity, and often reserved for the emperor.

BLUE/GREEN (CYAN): Health, prosperity, and harmony.

PURPLE: Divinity and immortality, often associated with nobility.

CONFUCIANISM: Confucianism is a philosophy based on the teachings of Confucius. Its influence on all aspects of Chinese culture is incalculable. Confucius placed heavy importance on respect for one's elders and family, a concept broadly known as *xiao* (孝 / "filial piety"). The family structure is used in other contexts to urge similar behaviors, such as respect of a student towards a teacher, or people of a country towards their ruler.

COUGHING/SPITTING BLOOD: A way to show a character is ill, injured, or upset. Despite the very physical nature of the response, it does not necessarily mean that a character has been wounded; their body could simply be reacting to a very strong emotion. (See also Seven Apertures/Qiqiao.)

CULTIVATORS/CULTIVATION: Cultivators are practitioners of spirituality and martial arts who seek to gain understanding of the will of the universe while attaining personal strength and extending their life span. Cultivation is a long process marked by "stages." There are traditionally nine stages, but this is often simplified in fiction. Some common stages are noted below, though exact definitions of each stage may depend on the setting.

- ◇ Qi Condensation/Qi Refining (凝气/练气)
- ◇ Foundation Establishment (筑基)
- ◇ Core Formation/Golden Core (结丹/金丹)
- ◇ Nascent Soul (元婴)
- ◇ Deity Transformation (化神)
- ◇ Great Ascension (大乘)
- ◇ Heavenly Tribulation (渡劫)

CULTIVATION MANUAL: Cultivation manuals and sutras are common plot devices in xianxia/wuxia novels. They provide detailed instructions on a secret or advanced training technique and are sought out by those who wish to advance their cultivation levels.

CURRENCY: The currency system during most dynasties was based on the exchange of silver and gold coinage. Weight was also used to measure denominations of money. An example is something being marked with a price of "one liang of silver."

DAOISM: Daoism is the philosophy of the *dao* (道), known as "the way." Following the dao involves coming into harmony with the natural order of the universe, which makes someone a "true human," safe from external harm and who can affect the world without intentional action. Cultivation is a concept based on Daoist beliefs.

DEMONS: A race of immensely powerful and innately supernatural beings. They are almost always aligned with evil.

DISCIPLES: Cultivation sect members are known as disciples. Disciples live on sect grounds and have a strict hierarchy based on skill and seniority. They are divided into Core, Inner, and Outer rankings, with Core being the highest. Higher-ranked disciples get better lodging and other resources.

When formally joining a sect as a disciple or a student, the sect becomes like the disciple's new family: teachers are parents and peers are siblings. Because of this, a betrayal or abandonment of one's sect is considered a deep transgression of Confucian values of filial piety. This is also the origin of many of the honorifics and titles used for martial arts.

DRAGON: Great chimeric beasts who wield power over the weather. Chinese dragons differ from their Western counterparts as they are often benevolent, bestowing blessings and granting luck. They are associated with the heavens, the Emperor, and yang energy.

EIGHT TRIGRAMS MAP: Also known as the bagua or pakua, an eight trigrams map is a Daoist diagram containing eight symbols that represent the fundamentals of reality, including the five elements. They often feature a symbol for yin and yang in the center as a representation of perfect balance between opposing forces.

ENTRANCE COUPLETS: Written poetry verses that are posted outside the door of a building. The two lines of poetry on the sides of the door express the meaning/theme of the establishment, or are a wish for good luck. The horizontal verse on the top summarizes or is the subject of the couplets.

FACE: *Mianzi* (面子), generally translated as "face," is an important concept in Chinese society. It is a metaphor for a person's reputation and can be extended to further descriptive metaphors. For example, "having face" refers to having a good reputation, and "losing face" refers to having one's reputation hurt. Meanwhile, "giving face" means deferring to someone else to help improve their reputation, while "not wanting face" implies that a person is acting so poorly/shamelessly that they clearly don't care about their reputation at all. "Thin face" refers to someone easily embarrassed or prone to offense at perceived slights. Conversely, "thick face" refers to someone not easily embarrassed and immune to insults.

FENG SHUI: Literally translates to wind-water. Refers to the natural laws believed to govern the flow of qi in the arrangement of the natural environment and man-made structures. Favorable feng shui and good qi flow have various beneficial effects to everyday life and the practice of cultivation, while the opposite is true for unfavorable feng shui and bad qi flow.

THE FIVE ELEMENTS: Also known as the *wuxing* (五行 / "Five Phases"). Rather than Western concepts of elemental magic, Chinese phases are more commonly used to describe the interactions and relationships between things. The phases can both beget and overcome each other.

◇ Wood (木 / mu)
◇ Fire (火 / huo)
◇ Earth (土 / tu)
◇ Metal (金 / jin)
◇ Water (水 / shui)

Flowers:

LOTUS: Associated with Buddhism. It rises untainted from the muddy waters it grows in, and thus symbolizes ultimate purity of the heart and mind.

PINE (TREE): A symbol of evergreen sentiment / everlasting affection.

PLUM (BLOSSOMING TREE): A symbol of endurance, as it blooms in the depths of winter. The plum blossom is also one of the four flowers of the ideal Confucian gentleman.

WILLOW (TREE): A symbol of lasting affection and friendship. Also is a symbol of farewell and can mean "urging someone to stay." "Meeting under the willows" can connote a rendezvous.

FUNERALS: Daoist or Buddhist funerals generally last for forty-nine days. It is a common belief that souls of the dead return home on the night of the sixth day after their death. There are different rituals depending on the region regarding what is done when the spirit returns, but generally they are all intended to guide the spirit safely back to the family home without getting lost; these rituals are generally referred to by the umbrella term "Calling the Spirit on the Seventh Day."

During the funeral ceremony, mourners can present the deceased with offerings of food, incense, and joss paper. If deceased ancestors have no patrilineal descendants to give them offerings, they may starve in the afterlife and become hungry ghosts. Wiping out a whole family is punishment for more than just the living.

After the funeral, the coffin is nailed shut and sealed with paper talismans to protect the body from evil spirits. The deceased is transported in a procession to their final resting place, often accompanied by loud music to scare off evil spirits. Cemeteries are usually on hillsides; the higher a grave is located, the better the feng shui. The traditional mourning color is white.

GHOST: Ghosts (鬼) are the restless spirits of deceased sentient creatures. Ghosts produce yin energy and crave yang energy. They come in a variety of types: they can be malevolent or helpful, can retain their former personalities or be fully mindless, and can actively try to interact with the living world to achieve a goal or be little more than a remnant shadow of their former lives.

Water ghosts are a notable subset of ghosts. They are drowned humans that haunt the place of their death and seek to drag unsuspecting victims underwater to possess their bodies, steal their identities, and take their places in the world of the living. The victim then becomes a water ghost themselves and repeats the process by hunting new victims. This process is known as 替身 / *tishen* (lit. "substitution"). In *Heaven Official's Blessing*, there is a clear story parallel between the behavior of water ghosts and the birth and actions of Ship-Sinking Black Water.

GUQIN: A seven-stringed zither, played by plucking with the fingers. Sometimes called a qin. It is fairly large and is meant to be laid flat on a surface or on one's lap while playing.

GU SORCERY: The concept of gu (蛊 / "poison") is common in wuxia and xianxia stories. In more realistic settings, it may refer to crafting poisons that are extracted from venomous insects and creatures. Things like snakes, toads, and bugs are generally associated with the idea of gu, but it can also apply to monsters, demons, and ghosts. The effects of gu poison are bewitchment and manipulation. "Swayed by gu" has become a common phrase meaning "lost your mind/been led astray" in modern Chinese vocabulary.

HAND GESTURES: The baoquan (抱拳 / "hold fist") is a martial arts salute where one places their closed right fist against their open left palm. The gongshou (拱手 / "arch hand") is a more generic salute not specific to martial artists, where one drapes their open left palm over their closed right fist. The orientation of both of these salutes is reversed for women. During funerals, the closed hand in both salutes switches, where men will use their left fist and women their right.

HAND SEALS: Refers to various hand and finger gestures used by cultivators to cast spells, or used while meditating. A cultivator may be able to control their sword remotely with a hand seal.

HEAVENLY CAVES AND BLESSED LANDS: Refers to a collection of sacred sites in Daoism. There are said to be ten large caves, thirty-six small caves, and seventy-two blessed lands in existence. They are places with excellent feng shui and are therefore flourishing with life and rich in spiritual energy/qi. These sites are ideal training spots for cultivators who seek to achieve immortality or heavenly ascension.

HEAVENLY REALM: An imperial court of enlightened beings. Some hold administrative roles, while others watch over and protect a specific aspect of the celestial and mortal realm, such as love, marriage, a piece of land, etc. There are also carefree immortals who simply wander the world and help mortals as they go, or become hermits deep in the mountains.

HEAVENLY TRIBULATION: Before a Daoist cultivator can ascend to the heavens, they must go through a trial known as a Heavenly Tribulation. In stories where the heavens are depicted with a more traditional nine-level structure, even gods themselves must endure and overcome tribulations if they want to level up. The nature of these trials vary, but the most common version involves navigating a powerful lightning storm. To fail means losing one's attained divine stage and cultivation.

HUALIAN: Shortened name for the relationship between Hua Cheng and Xie Lian.

IMMORTALS AND IMMORTALITY: Immortals have transcended mortality through cultivation. They possess long lives, are immune to illness and aging, and have various magical powers. An immortal can progress to godhood if they pass a Heavenly Tribulation. The exact life span of immortals differs from story to story, and in some they only live for three or four hundred years.

IMMORTAL-BINDING ROPES: Ropes, nets, and other restraints enchanted to withstand the power of an immortal or god. They can only be cut by high-powered spiritual items or weapons and usually limit the abilities of those trapped by them.

INCENSE TIME: A common way to tell time in ancient China, referring to how long it takes for a single incense stick to burn. Standardized incense sticks were manufactured and calibrated for specific time measurements: a half hour, an hour, a day, etc. These were available to people of all social classes.

In *Heaven Official's Blessing*, the incense sticks being referenced are the small sticks one offers when praying at a shrine, so "one incense time" is roughly thirty minutes.

INEDIA: A common ability that allows an immortal to survive without mortal food or sleep by sustaining themselves on purer forms of energy based on Daoist fasting. Depending on the setting, immortals who have achieved inedia may be unable to tolerate mortal food, or they may be able to choose to eat when desired.

JADE: Jade is a culturally and spiritually important mineral in China. Its durability, beauty, and the ease with which it can be utilized for crafting both decorative and functional pieces alike have made it widely beloved since ancient times. The word might cause Westerners to think of green jade (the mineral jadeite), but Chinese texts are often referring to white jade (the mineral nephrite). This is the color referenced when a person's skin is described as "the color of jade." Other colors of jade will usually be specified in the text.

JADE EMPEROR: In Daoist cosmology, the Jade Emperor (玉皇大帝) is the emperor of heaven, the chief of the heavenly court, and one of the highest ranked gods in the heavenly realm, lower only to the three primordial emanations. When one says "Oh god/lord" or "My heavens," it is usually referring to the Jade Emperor. In *Heaven Official's Blessing*, Jun Wu's role replaces that of the Jade Emperor.

JOSS PAPER: Also referred to as ghost paper, joss paper is a form of paper crafting used to make offerings to the deceased. The paper can be folded into various shapes and is burned as an offering, allowing the deceased person to utilize the gift the paper represents in the realm of the dead. Common gifts include paper money, houses, clothing, toiletries, and dolls to act as the deceased's servants.

KOWTOW: The *kowtow* (叩头 / "knock head") is an act of prostration where one kneels and bows low enough that their forehead touches the ground. A show of deep respect and reverence that can also be used to beg, plead, or show sincerity.

MERIDIANS: The means by which qi travels through the body, like a magical bloodstream. Medical and combat techniques that focus on redirecting, manipulating, or halting qi circulation focus on targeting the meridians at specific points on the body, known as acupoints. Techniques that can manipulate or block qi prevent a cultivator from using magical techniques until the qi block is lifted.

MID-AUTUMN FESTIVAL: Zhongqiu Jie (中秋節), or the Mid-Autumn Festival, falls on the fifteenth day of the eighth month of the Lunar Calendar. It typically falls around September-October on the Western Calendar. This festival is heavily associated with reunions, both family and otherwise. Mooncakes—also known as reunion cakes, as they are meant to be shared—are a popular food item associated with this festival. Much like the Shangyuan Festival, the Mid-Autumn Festival involves the lighting of lanterns to worship the heavens. It is also commonly associated with courtship and matchmaking.

Numbers

TWO: Two (二 / "er") is considered a good number and is referenced in the common idiom "good things come in pairs." It is common practice to repeat characters in pairs for added effect.

THREE: Three (三 / "san") sounds like *sheng* (生 / "living") and also like *san* (散 / "separation").

FOUR: Four (四 / "si") sounds like *si* (死 / "death"). A very unlucky number.

SEVEN: Seven (七 / "qi") sounds like *qi* (齊 / "together"), making it a good number for love-related things. However, it also sounds like *qi* (欺 / "deception").

EIGHT: Eight (八 / "ba") sounds like *fa* (發 / "prosperity"), causing it to be considered a very lucky number.

NINE: Nine (九 / "jiu") is associated with matters surrounding the Emperor and Heaven, and is as such considered an auspicious number.

MXTX's work has subtle numerical theming around its love interests. In *Grandmaster of Demonic Cultivation*, her second book, Lan Wangji is frequently called Lan-er-gege ("second brother Lan") as a nickname by Wei Wuxian. In her third book, *Heaven Official's Blessing*, Hua Cheng is the third son of his family and gives the name San Lang ("third youth") when Xie Lian asks what to call him.

PHOENIX: *Fenghuang* (凤凰 / "phoenix"), a legendary chimeric bird said to only appear in times of peace and to flee when a ruler is corrupt. They are heavily associated with femininity, the Empress, and happy marriages.

PILLS AND ELIXIRS: Magic medicines that can heal wounds, improve cultivation, extend life, etc. In Chinese culture, these things are usually delivered in pill form. These pills are created in special kilns.

PLAGUES AND DISEASE: In ancient China, plagues and pandemics were considered to be the work of demons or other evil creatures, and were thought to be karmic punishment from the heavens for humanity's evil deeds. It was thought that the gods would protect the righteous and innocent from catching the disease, and mass repentance was the only way to "cure" or banish a plague for good. When the gods determined the punishment served to be sufficient, they would descend and drive out the plague-causing demons.

This outlook is why Human Face Disease is considered in-universe to be a mark against the Kingdom of Xianle's morality and a mark against Xie Lian as both a leader and a god—the plague only affecting Xianle is "proof" that they angered the heavens, and Xie Lian being unable to cure it by his own power is "proof" that he does not have heaven's blessing and is not a true god.

PRIMORDIAL SPIRIT: The essence of one's existence beyond the physical. The body perishes, the soul enters the karmic wheel, but the spirit that makes one unique is eternal.

RELIGIOUS ICONOGRAPHY AND CAVES: It is not uncommon to find religious iconography in cave networks, as caves have long been used as places of secluded meditation for followers of Daoist or Buddhist faiths. The Bezeklik Thousand Buddha Caves and the Tianlongshan Grottoes are extreme examples of this practice, containing hundreds of religious murals and over a thousand divine statues.

STEP-LITTER: (步輦) a "litter" is a type of wheelless vehicle. Palanquins and sedan chairs are in the same category of human-powered transport, but they often have boxed cabins. A step-litter is an open-air platform with a seat/throne atop it, often with a canopy of hanging silk curtains for privacy. Step-litters are usually reserved for those with high status.

QI: *Qi* (气) is the energy in all living things. There is both righteous qi and evil or poisonous qi.

Cultivators strive to cultivate qi by absorbing it from the natural world and refining it within themselves to improve their cultivation base. A cultivation base refers to the amount of qi a cultivator possesses or is able to possess. In xianxia, natural locations such as caves, mountains, or other secluded places with lush wildlife are often rich in qi, and practicing there can allow a cultivator to make rapid progress in their cultivation.

Cultivators and other qi manipulators can utilize their life force in a variety of ways, including imbuing objects with it to transform them into lethal weapons or sending out blasts of energy to do powerful damage. Cultivators also refine their senses beyond normal human levels. For instance, they may cast out their spiritual sense to gain total awareness of everything in a region around them or to feel for potential danger.

QI CIRCULATION: The metabolic cycle of qi in the body, where it flows from the dantian to the meridians and back. This cycle purifies and refines qi, and good circulation is essential to cultivation. In xianxia, qi can be transferred from one person to another through physical contact and can heal someone who is wounded if the donor is trained in the art.

QIANKUN: *Qiankun* can be translated to "universe." Qiankun pouches (乾坤袋) or Qiankun sleeves (乾坤袖) are containers that are bigger on the inside, used to easily carry cargo a person normally couldn't manage. Qiankun items are common in fantasy settings.

RED STRING OF FATE: Refers to the myth in many East Asian cultures that an invisible red string connects two individuals who are fated to be lovers. The string is tied at each lover's finger (usually the middle finger or pinky finger).

SECT: A cultivation sect is an organization of individuals united by their dedication to the practice of a particular method of cultivation or martial arts. A sect may have a signature style. Sects are led by a single leader, who is supported by senior sect members. They are not necessarily related by blood.

SEVEN APERTURES/QIQIAO: (七窍) The seven facial apertures: the two eyes, two nostrils, mouth, and two ears. The essential qi of vital organs are said to connect to the seven apertures, and illness in the vital organs may cause symptoms there. People who are ill or seriously injured may be "bleeding from the seven apertures."

SHANGYUAN: Shangyuan Jie (上元節), or the Lantern Festival, marks the fifteenth and last day of the Lunar New Year (usually around February on the Solar Calendar). It is a day for worshipping and celebrating the celestial heavens by hanging lanterns, solving riddles, and performing Dragon Dances. Glutinous rice ball treats known as yuanxiao and tangyuan are highlights of this festival, so much so that the festival's alternate name is Yuanxiao Jie (元宵節).

SHRINES: Shrines are sites at which an individual can pray or make offerings to a god, spirit, or ancestor. They contain an object of worship to focus on such as a statue, a painting or mural, a relic, or a memorial tablet in the case of an ancestral shrine. The term also refers to small roadside shrines or personal shrines to deceased family members or loved ones kept on a mantle. Offerings like incense, food, and money can be left at a shrine as a show of respect.

SPIRIT BANNER: A banner or flag intended to guide spirits. Can be hung from a building or tree to mark a location or carried around on a staff.

STATE PRECEPTOR: State preceptors, or guoshi, are high-ranking government officials who also have significant religious duties. They serve as religious heads of state under the emperor and act as the tutors, chaplains, and confidants of the emperor and his direct heirs.

SWORDS: A cultivator's sword is an important part of their cultivation practice. In many instances, swords are spiritually bound to their owner and may have been bestowed on them by their master or a family member, or obtained through a ritual. Cultivators in fiction are able to use their swords as transportation by standing atop the flat of the blade and riding it as it flies through the air. Skilled cultivators can summon their swords to fly into their hand, command the sword to fight on its own, or release energy attacks from the edge of the blade.

SWORD GLARE: Jianguang (剑光 / "sword light"), an energy attack released from a sword's edge.

SWORN BROTHERS/SISTERS/FAMILIES: In China, sworn brotherhood describes a binding social pact made by two or more unrelated individuals. Such a pact can be entered into for social, political, and/or personal reasons. It was most common among men but was not unheard of among women or between people of different genders.

The participants treat members of each other's families as their own and assist them in the ways an extended family would: providing mutual support and aid, support in political alliances, etc. Sworn siblings will refer to themselves as brother or sister, but this is not to be confused with familial relations like blood siblings or adoption. It is sometimes used in Chinese media, particularly danmei, to imply romantic relationships that could otherwise be prone to censorship.

TALISMANS: Strips of paper with spells written on them, often with cinnabar ink or blood. They can serve as seals or be used as one-time spells.

THE THREE REALMS: Traditionally, the universe is divided into Three Realms: the **Heavenly Realm**, the **Mortal Realm**, and the **Ghost Realm**. The Heavenly Realm refers to the Heavens and

Celestial Court, where gods reside and rule, the Mortal Realm refers to the human world, and the Ghost Realm refers to the realm of the dead.

VINEGAR: To say someone is drinking vinegar or tasting vinegar means they're having jealous or bitter feelings. Generally used for a love interest growing jealous while watching the main character receive the attention of a rival suitor.

WEDDING TRADITIONS: Red is an important part of traditional Chinese weddings, as the color of prosperity, happiness, and good luck. It remains the standard color for bridal and bridegroom robes and wedding decorations even today. During the ceremony, the couple each cut off a lock of their own hair, then intertwine and tie the two locks together to symbolize their commitment.

WHISK: A whisk held by a cultivator is not a baking tool but a Daoist symbol and martial arts weapon. Usually made of horsehair bound to a wooden stick, the whisk is based off a tool used to brush away flies without killing them and is symbolically meant for wandering Daoist monks to brush away thoughts that would lure them back to secular life. Wudang Daoist Monks created a fighting style based on wielding it as a weapon.

YAO: Animals, plants, or objects that have gained spiritual consciousness due to prolonged absorption of qi. Especially high-level or long-lived yao are able to take on a human form. This concept is comparable to Japanese yokai, which is a loanword from the Chinese yao. Yao are not evil by nature but often come into conflict with humans for various reasons, one being that the cores they develop can be harvested by human cultivators to increase their own abilities.

YIN ENERGY AND YANG ENERGY: Yin and yang is a concept in Chinese philosophy that describes the complementary interdependence of opposite/contrary forces. It can be applied to all forms of change and differences. Yang represents the sun, masculinity, and the living, while yin represents the shadows, femininity, and the dead, including spirits and ghosts. In fiction, imbalances between yin and yang energy can do serious harm to the body or act as the driving force for malevolent spirits seeking to replenish themselves of whichever they lack.

ZHANMADAO: A large, two-handed bladed weapon that was designed to counter cavalry units.

ZHONGYUAN: Zhongyuan Jie (中元節), or the Ghost Festival / Hungry Ghost Festival, falls on the fifteenth day of the seventh month of the Lunar Calendar (this usually falls around August/September on the Solar Calendar). The festival celebrates the underworld, and offerings are made to the dead to appease their spirits and help them move on.

FROM BESTSELLING AUTHOR

MO XIANG TONG XIU

Grandmaster of Demonic Cultivation

MO DAO ZU SHI

Wei Wuxian was once one of the most outstanding men of his generation, a talented and clever young cultivator who harnessed martial arts, knowledge, and spirituality into powerful abilities. But when the horrors of war led him to seek a new power through demonic cultivation, the world's respect for his skills turned to fear, and his eventual death was celebrated throughout the land.

Years later, he awakens in the body of an aggrieved young man who sacrifices his soul so that Wei Wuxian can exact revenge on his behalf. Though granted a second life, Wei Wuxian is not free from his first, nor the mysteries that appear before him now. Yet this time, he'll face it all with the righteous and esteemed Lan Wangji at his side, another powerful cultivator whose unwavering dedication and shared memories of their past will help shine a light on the dark truths that surround them.

Available in print and digital from Seven Seas Entertainment

耽美 Danmei
Seven Seas Entertainment
sevenseasdanmei.com